DISTANCE

Ewan Morrison is the author of the novel *Swung* and a collection
of stories, *The Last Book You Read*. He lives in Glasgow.

By the same author

The Last Book You Read
Swung

EWAN MORRISON

DISTANCE

JONATHAN CAPE
LONDON

Published by Jonathan Cape 2008

2 4 6 8 10 9 7 5 3 1

Copyright © Ewan Morrison 2008

Ewan Morrison has asserted his right under the Copyright, Designs
and Patents Act 1988 to be identified as the author of this work

First published in Great Britain in 2008 by
Jonathan Cape
Random House, 20 Vauxhall Bridge Road,
London SW1V 2SA

www.rbooks.co.uk

Addresses for companies within The Random House Group Limited
can be found at:
www.randomhouse.co.uk/offices.htm

The Random House Group Limited Reg. No. 954009

A CIP catalogue record for this book is available from the British Library

ISBN 9780224082372

The Random House Group Limited supports The Forest Stewardship
Council (FSC), the leading international forest certification organisation.
All our titles that are printed on Greenpeace-approved FSC-certified paper
carry the FSC logo. Our paper procurement policy can be found at
www.rbooks.co.uk/environment

Mixed Sources
Product group from well-managed
forests and other controlled sources
www.fsc.org Cert no. TT-COC-2139
© 1996 Forest Stewardship Council
FSC

Typeset in Janson by Palimpsest Book Production Limited,
Grangemouth, Stirlingshire

Printed and bound in Great Britain by
CPI Mackays, Chatham ME5 8TD

To 'You'

CONTENTS

I love you. That is all I know. But all I know, too, is that I am writing into space: the kind of dreadful, unknown space I am just going to enter. I am going to Iowa, Illinois, Idaho, Indindiana, but these, though mis-spelt, are on the map. You are not.

Dylan Thomas, Letter to his wife Caitlin

Perhaps the greatest gift we can give another human being is detachment. Attachment, even that which imagines it as self-less, always lays some burden on the other person. How to learn to love in such a light, airy way that there is no burden?

May Sarton, *Journal of a Solitude*

1
DEPARTURES

Gate

She didn't want to make a scene, she'd said. Which was funny, her being in the movie business after all. That and the whole leaving-on-a-jet-plane end-of-holiday-romance thing. Because she hated cliché, had theories on how people walked round quoting lines from movies without even realising it. So he told himself that for her sake he wouldn't make a scene. But the problem was they were, for real, approaching the international departures gate at Newark and he was, for real, desperately in love with her and really did live nine thousand miles away and might never see her again and they were, in many ways, about to take part in potentially the most powerful airport farewell ever imagined.

As soon as he saw the departures sign the hollow ache opened inside him. He gripped her hand and sensed she'd felt it too. Her eyes confirmed this. He leaned to kiss her but was slightly too short to do it properly. His fault. He'd asked her to put on her heels for their finale. And now had to go up on his tiptoes, and the whole height-difference thing was making her self-conscious. Ideally he would have liked to have been more masterful and masculine and left her with a potent memory of their last moments together. Just as this morning he would have greatly preferred to have satisfied her sexually, but he'd come too quickly and spent all of their post-coital moments and dressing and breakfasting apologising. She'd told him it was OK, fine, he was making too much of it, all she'd wanted was a hug. So now, this anonymous waiting space. A passing family had distracted her and she pulled away from his lips. He stood there in front of the flight announcement screen in terminal 3, holding her hand, silently waiting for the panic to pass. Say something. Be Bogart. 'If that plane leaves the ground and you're not on it ... you'll regret it ... maybe not today ... maybe not tomorrow, but soon, and for the rest of your life.' But it was him leaving and he recalled that Woody Allen had done exactly the same thing, repeating Bogart's lines. That's me through and through, thought Tom – aiming for Bogart and ending up Woody Allen. The short funny guy. So at least be that – make her laugh. She'd said he made her laugh like no man ever had.

'God, I am so fucked now,' he said. 'I had it all planned . . . the shit job in the shit city. The bachelor pad, the ex-wife . . .'

'The girlfriend.'

'. . . exactly, the soon-to-be ex-girlfriend, the alimony, the estranged son, the shit diet, drinking alone, no pension, no real friends . . .'

'I know, my love.'

'But it was perfect. That was going to be it till the end, I was even looking forward to it – then I bloody well had to meet you.'

His attempt at humour wasn't working, just like his dick this morning.

'I'm sorry, You.' She said.

You and You. His second name was Eustace and it sounded like useless but it started with 'you'. He was her You. And she was his too. Although it didn't rhyme with her name. They'd made up this singular love name for each other on that second night after they'd made love for the second time. You and You. Flight 215 Icelandair to Edinburgh via London with BMI was boarding at Gate 53. There were only three gates in Edinburgh.

'What are we going to do, You?'

'Shh, I'm coming to see you in two months, I promised. It's going to be OK.'

'Yeah. No. I know, but – I mean now.'

'We got twenty minutes. We could . . . shop,' she smiled. 'It's the answer to everything.'

No woman like her in the world. The way she could take him by the hand and lead him away from doubt. The way she could turn shopping into some clever anti-shopping experiment. He had to be clever like her. He couldn't spend their last minutes doing exactly what he felt like doing, which was clinging and telling her over and over how hard he'd fallen for her. My love, my You. And they'd already agreed they weren't going to cry. Not like she had when he'd kissed the tears and cum from her face on that third night. Or on the fifth, when he'd told her how he'd thought all of his love had been spent, wasted over the years, how it scared him now to realise he still had more within him. Eye to eye whispering their new names. You. You.

She led him by the hand past the alcohol stores and the perfumeries. 'Souvenirs.' She turned with a wry smile.

And there it was, just like everything they'd done in the last week. They talked about something and somehow magically it appeared before them. The gift shop. Stetsons and discounted American flags. Fluffy grizzly bears and cougars and buffalo and American eagles and rattlesnakes and a sign saying they produced authentic noises if you squeezed their bellies. Yes, buy her a big fat fucking toxic snake to hold between her legs every night after he'd gone. Be her joker. This was the one thing she knew about him that he'd never willingly revealed to anyone before. How he could swing from maniacal humour to oppressive aggressive sentimentality, then back again, turning it all into a play of words. She knew how to turn him around, after only seven days. But he worried that when he boarded that plane she would be left still trying to work out the source of the anger that fuelled his wit.

They picked up a few toys from the big row of shelves at the back. Hers an American eagle – his a rattlesnake. Jesus, he'd completely forgotten to buy a present for his son. Sean was too old for toys now. He'd get something at Heathrow, a CD or some of those software magazines Sean was so into – if he was awake enough to find his credit card; if it still worked. God, he'd abused the thing in this last week with Meg. Pretending to be the hotshot. There would be a price to pay. There always was. He had to stop being such a mean Scotsman, had only seventeen minutes left with this woman he'd known for a only week whom he'd already promised to grow old with.

'Hey, let's make them look like they're fucking,' he said, tickling her face with his snake. She was being so brave. So he put his snake between her eagle's legs and she stuck two very fluffy grizzly bears into 69 position and stood back and giggled, then gripped his hand tight as if remembering that night when they'd done the same. Then he pretended they were being watched by the shop assistant and whispered to her to be more discreet while he got two buffalo to do it doggy-style. They had Velcro hoofs and he stuck one on the arse of the other; they'd probably be like that for those two months he and Meg would be apart. He put on a deep Texan-hick accent and said, 'Gee – two for the price of one! They come together?' And she laughed so hard they just had to get out of there.

She led him away, round the whole circle, past the food arcade. Moroccan, Thai, Chinese, generic American. Food was out of the question. They stopped by the departure display again. Now Boarding. He gripped her hand. She squeezed back.

'Shh, I know, I know.'

His guts twisting as he thought of that thing she'd said, three days ago, when he'd freaked out about having to return to Scotland. When he'd first talked openly about his son. Night of tears and rage. She'd told him it wasn't her first time dating a man with a kid or doing the long-distance love affair either. There had been a guy from Los Angeles, another from London, way back. That she, of course, had doubts – maybe she'd been deluding herself – that all she could attempt was impossible relationships. And it had almost broken him – because they *were* impossible. His son and this distance and their pasts. But he was damned if he was going to have a glimpse of happiness only to have it snatched away. If they were impossible then so be it, it was all he had left to live for. This he'd yelled at her on that drunken fifth night.

'I'd say we've got fifteen minutes.' Her brave smile. To just kiss her, like before. But she'd taste it in his mouth. The acid anger at everything. She'd promised to come to his country at the end of August. She had work to do, she wasn't free till then, she'd always wanted to see the Edinburgh Festival. Focus on that, don't make a scene.

'Meg, I need to be alone with you just for a few minutes.'

'I know, my You, but we can't.'

Play the joker.

'The prayer room, they've got one in every airport.' He twisted her hand to bring her closer, whispering, dirty, in her ear, like she liked.

'There's never anyone there. We go in, you stand with your

back to me, you bend over a table, I go down on my knees, lift your skirt, pull off your panties and lick your pussy. Your taste on my face for the whole trip. Come on, it'll only take a minute. I saw the sign by the escalator.'

She pulled away as if tickled.

'You,' she said. 'So You.'

He worried about the You. There is Me and there is You – a distance that could never be crossed. She was three feet away, staring at the departures sign. He couldn't bear this, standing there, her back to him. Five feet away. Her Victorian shoes, her long slender legs and taut worked-out thighs. Her school-girl ponytail. Her tiny waist, her irreverent Vivienne West-wood dress with the tartan trimming that she'd put on specially because he was going back to Scotland. My God. He couldn't just stand there as if taking a last photograph. My You.

And now she was fussing in that high-pitched rapid-fire organisational voice that was the one thing, the only thing, he didn't like about her. Talking about bag sizes. Because there were restrictions now because of the terrorist threat and did he have any aerosols? Then saying something about the layout of the departure gate. How last time she did this – those semi-opaque doors. You turned that corner and they moved behind you and you were gone. No wide shot, no long waiting watching as the loved one slowly became part of the human throng then vanished. No hoped-for turns and waves goodbye. When you went through those doors you were gone. His name had been Michael. The guy from London. Ten, fifteen years back. She'd broken it off. Three nights of no contact and she'd dumped him. Tom fell silent. Stage fright of an actor trying to upstage the original star in a sequel.

'Sorry,' she said. 'I didn't mean . . . I was just . . . the doors.'

He felt angry with her now, for having said that, for having tried to unsay it. For giving his ever-present jealousy the name of a real person. He watched the glass slide behind the last entrants. Only minutes left. Music from the perfume shop, the food court. His palm sweaty in hers. Staring at the other couples kissing. Trying not to think of her, right here, years before, kissing this man, this Michael, goodbye.

'God, I hate . . . I mean . . . How the fuck do we do this?'

'I know,' she said. 'I know.'

Five minutes till the gate closed. There was bag check, X-ray machine and passport check. My love, my love. Staring at the other kissing couples. The retirement-age American with his petite Thai girlie. The obese Midwest girl with her anorexic British boyfriend. This image before him. The holiday romance. That you had given up on people to such a degree that the only intensity you could feel was with someone who was inevitably leaving. To give her the goodbye kiss. Better than her long-lost lover did. That would guarantee her return to him.

'If we kiss with eyes closed then maybe it won't seem so cheesy,' she said.

Hesitation. The desperate awkwardness in her eyes. He lifted his finger to her mouth, that delicate tiny scar on her top lip that he loved; she raised her shoulder to her cheek, that way she did, even when asleep, like last night when he'd spent hours just watching her.

The loudspeaker. Final call. Gate closing. He closed his eyes and pulled her mouth to his. Deep, searching, urgent, wet. Tongues circling. Her gripping his head, pulling him in. His hand on her breast squeezing through the fabric where the nipple stiffened. No care for who was watching. Her breath in his ear. Him, hard against her, her pelvis grinding, closer. Her teeth on his neck.

'Last call for Flight I-215.'

He pulled away slightly. She bit harder. High school hickey. Badges in blood. Him submitting, laughing as her teeth held him tight. Never mind that he was going to have to see his son in the next few days. And Sean's question – how was New York? Answered by a love bite. Bring it on. He weakened as she sucked. He was weak. He'd warned her of this.

'Final call for Flight I-215.'

She stopped. He was about to make a joke about how adolescent it was but there were tears in her eyes.

'You. I'm sorry,' she said. 'I promised I wouldn't.'

'Is it big?' He smiled, playing the joker.

'The biggest.' Her finger tracing his neck. 'It's blue and red like an orchid.'

'When I get back I'll get the outline tattooed.'

'Would passenger Eustace please make his way to Gate 53 where Flight I-215 is now closing the gate?'

Something had to be done. This idea, image, came to him. It was in his pocket, on his key ring with his house keys. It all made sense. God only knew why had he kept it all these years. His fingers on it in his pocket.

'You,' she said. 'You have to go.'

'Shh, got something for you.'

He pulled out his key ring and there it was. Worn and thinned through years of fidelity, through that year after the divorce when he took it off every time he tried to pick up a girl in a bar. He fumbled with the key ring. Hoping he hadn't destroyed the moment with a slapstick routine.

'No!' She'd seen what it was.

'Wait.'

Free from his key ring, he held it in his palm, showing her – his wedding ring. He took her finger. The correct one. Held it firm.

'Jesus, no, I can't.'

'You can – just say, "I do."'

Her finger was thinner, it didn't quite fit. It was on. No one to witness, just passing tourists and it was well past time.

'But, I mean, it's your ex-wife's . . . maybe it'll be bad luck,' she said, lifting her hand to her face, watching the ring fall down past her knuckle. 'I mean, what does this mean?'

'Just say – "I do."'

But even as he said it he knew she was right in her doubt. It was a divorce ring now. A vow betrayed. I will love you till I walk away. And now he had to do just that.

'Wait,' she said. Staring at the gate, hands to the back of her head. 'Wait.' Her face said she'd found whatever she was looking for. She pulled it from her hair, put the thing in her mouth and twisted it, then held it just right. It was purple, seemed elastic. She lifted his hand and forced it on to his wedding finger – her hairband. Suddenly the tears she'd been holding in burst out.

'You fucking Scottish fuck,' she said. 'I hate you with all my heart, I fucking do . . . I do.'

'I do too,' he said.

'You have to go now,' she said, wiping her eyes, 'Don't forget . . .' but it didn't sound like the end of a sentence. '. . . to call me when you get home, OK.

'Go!' she said. 'I'm not going to be the one who turns away. Go! Or do I have to push you?'

Her eyes. Not tears but more. Anger – at everything, at airports, at nine thousand miles.

'I can't – Push me. Push me away.'

Her hand on his chest like the way she did on those nights when she slept, just testing, to see if there was a human presence beside her. She pushed. He stumbled, steadied himself. She'd already turned her back to him. He watched her go. Saw her hands reach to her face and her pace quicken. Her ribs spasm. She did not turn to look back.

Just like she said. Just four steps forward and the opaque glass door closes behind you and you are gone even though you are still there. This was International World, and their future. So many bag checks and searchings. He beeped as he went through the metal detector and swore at himself for not having taken his house keys from his pocket. He stood, arms in the air, submissive to the process, as the man's mechanical hands ran over his shoulders, waist, hips, outer and inner legs. The hairband on his wedding finger and this stranger touching his body. He closed his eyes and tried to picture her walking away. Her ponytail holding its form then slowly unravelling with each step.

Tunnel

Auto-rewind. Like a videotape once it reached its end. Meg was driving back along the New Jersey Turnpike towards the Holland Tunnel, feeling, with each mile, that home was becoming ever more distant. A plane roared overhead. No, it wouldn't be his. He'd still be on the runway. One every fifty-five seconds at Newark. There'd be twenty or more, none of them his, passing overhead before the tunnel. She had to stop this. This sense as she moved closer to home of a counter-force pulling her back to him.

The signs ahead for the tunnel turn-off. Manhattan shimmering in the heat haze. The tower blocks wavering, incoherent. The traffic slowed as the tunnel took her in and she was staring at the reflections of brake lights, random red patterns on the white shining walls. No sense that she was driving, that she was in control. Feeling as if pulled back, without will, to those minutes, an hour before, with him beside her going in the opposite direction. He had fallen silent as the tunnel surrounded them and now she felt his silence hanging heavy in the recycled, air-conditioned air.

On exiting, the sharp slap in the face that is Manhattan, always. The eyes adjusting to the light, the height of the buildings. Canal Street. And she was back with him again, hand in hand, heading towards the Lower East Side. All the stories she'd told him. The Village and the Aids protests of the eighties. The street where they shot *Taxi Driver*, where they shot *Midnight Cowboy*, where they shot *Manhattan*, where Andy Warhol was shot. Him asking to see all the places that had led her to come here in the first place. That sense she'd had even as she told him, that she was trying to remind herself why she was still here. So many places that were stories without substance now. The buildings changed, gone.

She drove her usual route, south through the Financial

District towards the Brooklyn Bridge. Not feeling the sense of escape she'd had once a week every week for the past eight years as she headed home to Fire Island. Escaping from her career. The constant fight over words and meaning that was her daily work. The struggle to repair flawed film scripts that were based on other people's flawed ambitions, no longer hers. Heading home to be alone.

The turn-off to the bridge, where he had stopped on that second night in tears and told her he was trying so hard not to fall in love with her. On the fifth when he had climbed the railings threatening to jump.

The suspension wires were a familiar rhythm in her head. The predictable patterns of taxis pushing out without signalling. Get into the right-hand lane. Merge. The view ahead of Brooklyn Heights – where they'd gone to the party, when she'd introduced him to her friends and the madness had started.

Get home. Beware of the traffic, stop drifting. She was over the bridge and on the other side. Manhattan like a memory, like it had to be, like she had learned to make it be. This ritual she went through every time, to not look into the rear-view mirror to where the towers should have been. That last day with him when he had wanted to see Ground Zero.

Just forty more miles till the ferry. The I 95, the I 495. The air outside was humid, the smog of car fumes hanging in the air along the Brooklyn tailbacks, but still she had to open the window. To let his air go, to stop thinking about him. To just get back to the ocean and her little wooden shack and all that she had tried to build for herself, from old things, found things, things washed up on the beach. Walking the sands in an hour she would stare out at the sea and get back to her routine. Put Tom in some kind of perspective.

But no, the waves, the ocean he was flying over, were his now, and he was there again with her in the car on their third day. The day she'd decided to take him home, so she might know for sure. Him smiling in the seat beside her, eyes roaming her body. 'What?' she kept asking. Him silent, stroking her thigh. 'Stop it. I'm driving.' 'I like watching you in control,' he'd said, taking her free hand and placing it on his crotch.

Her feeling the hardening through his jeans as she kept her eyes on the road.

She opened the window. Click click click. Damn, it was the front wheel, passenger's side. Something about the brake blocks, she'd been meaning to get it fixed. It wasn't dangerous, the garage guy said, just annoying. Click click click. She'd have to do what she always did. Roll the window up and put on a CD to drown it out. She waited for a safe gap in the traffic and leaned over, finger finding the button.

The CD, the song. Their album. *Treasure*. The Cocteau Twins. She'd burned three copies, one for him, one for his son, one for the car. He'd asked her to turn it off earlier. Just before the tunnel. It was all too much, he'd said. She always listened to music when she drove home. But now her CD was theirs, and he was gone and the songs that calmed her before would from now on sing of loss.

The traffic had almost ground to a halt and she found her eyes scanning the buildings. She'd driven this very same route for years, thinking only of home. But he'd sat there beside her on that third morning and said 'Fucking hell' every mile or so. 'Jesus, Christ.' He'd been excited, ranting about the mess it all was. Pointing things out to her. The high-rise housing schemes sitting beside the nineteenth-century palaces of Park Slope, the mock-colonial town houses next to ruined warehouses with one good wall turned into advertising space. A Bauhaus modernist tower, a shanty-town shack, a parking lot, a solitary row of brownstones – all in one street. 'Terrifying – like there's no structure to it at all,' he'd said, 'like everyone can just do what they want.' 'This is America,' she'd said, 'this is cultural differ-ence.' 'Indifference, more like,' he'd said. Her looking then, seeing. The road rising higher on the concrete stilts, the rooftops a mass and mess of styles, aerials, satellite dishes, water tanks, ads. She'd felt ashamed then for never really looking at it before. 'No structure,' he'd said and she needed structure, a plot, Act One – Two – Three – The End. She needed Fire Island and her view of the ocean. She needed to stop his ghost voice from the passenger seat, asking her to wake up and see how she really lived.

Click click click.

Home and work. When she got back there would be the cheque waiting for her in the mailbox for the sci-fi love affair that the producer pitched to her as *Aliens* meets *Cast Away*. There would be the conference call about the new project and the hundred pages of notes by her laptop on that astounding piece of crap that was pitched as *Fatal Attraction* meets *Doctor Zhivago*. 'If you hate your work so much,' Tom said, 'why do you do it?'

The turn-off to the 495 was just a mile away and the right lane was moving faster. She checked the rear view then signalled and merged. Westbury, Jerusalem, Lindenhurst. Another twenty-five. Park the car at Bay Shore. Catch the ferry just in time if she was lucky or a coffee at Jack's shack, a stroll by the pier, stare across the water to Fire Island. She would stand on the top deck, looking forward, not back, and slowly sink into the rhythm of waves, feeling the cleansing salt air on her face. She would wait for the others to leave the ferry first and go last and say her usual hello to Jonas, the pier master, and ask him how his old dog Nebuchadnezzar was doing. She would set foot on her island and feel the relief of that first sand step and walk past the wooden shacks where the summer renters stayed and Sal's family store to the bike stand where she always left her rusty trusty old Raleigh Invincible, then cycle down the sand-strewn road, so glad to be in a place where cars and everything they stood for were forbidden.

Click click click. It was back. The window was up. It made no sense. And she was making speed now, heading through the suburbs of Lindenhurst. The passing Hasidim and their hats. The wheel clicked only when she was going slow – this noise made no sense. Focus on the now, on the traffic, on the turn-off.

Finally. The parking lot for the ferry. There it was, just thirty feet away from the pier, turning its full circle before the crossing. Heading away. She checked the time on her cell. Did her mental ferry timetable. It would be twenty minutes at least, it was never exact, that was part of the process, the decompression from Manhattan time, the wait for the ferry taught you humility.

Sitting alone in the car, no music to listen to because it was his music now. No silence to sit in because it was his silence. The morning of the third day. Just like this, when they'd missed the ferry, them sitting in the car, his hand on her thigh, hers on his. 'There's no one else around,' he'd said. His fingers through her hair then, pulling her face to his and this sense that he was perverse. His lips on her neck. With his free hand he'd undone his fly, whispering. 'See what you do to me. There's no one around.' His fingers gripping her hair, tight, her saying, 'Oh my God, my God.' So turned on by this violation of everything. Her leaning down, taking him in her mouth. His finger under her skirt, finding her wetness. Both inside each other.

Meg had to get out. Even her car was his now. But on the tarmac, no other cars around, there was still no escape. The fog was coming in fast, the water vanishing into white. Fire Island, a line sketched on the horizon, nothing more. Telling herself not to panic. Calm down. Rationalise. OK, she'd gone a bit crazy with him. Probably because she knew he was only here for one week. Because she was nearing forty and he was the last gasp of madness before accepting the quiet life and she would never see him again. And each day together was one day less. That was what pushed her to go further than she had ever been before. People did that, they went crazy before the end of things. She had been sucking him and he'd been whispering to her that the parking lot was filling up. 'All these people you probably know, just feet from us.'

The white was growing, the water vanishing beneath the fog. Fire Island, a line sketched on the horizon, nothing more.

The ferry horn shook her back. The prow pushing through the fog. It docked and the drive-on gangway descended. She waited and watched as a few holiday sharers in T-shirts and cut-off jeans climbed on before her. A young gay couple, pretty boys, twenty-ish. One Latino, squat and muscular; the other tall Germanic, long blond hair, a trace of eyeliner. Their hands in each other's hip pockets.

Jed, the ferry attendant, was waving her to get on. She got her resident's year pass ready and walked slowly on to the ferry. The fog was coming in fast.

Even on the ferry crossing, day three, their kissing had not stopped. Fumbling like teenagers. And all the neighbours around her and she hadn't even cared. Fire Island. Even the name, now, was taking on different meanings. Fire of passion. Burn it all. This place of carefully constructed quiet which last week she had destroyed with her voice, screaming with joy.

Damn this man, this Tom, who had opened her up to things long buried. This man who'd whispered that he wanted to grow old with her, this man from this old country, whose face was lined and scored with Old World pain. This man whose cynicism could break in an instant into innocent laughter. She closed her eyes, trying to make him disappear. His long Scottish nose, his weak Scottish chin, his sunken chest, his world-weary shoulders. His hard grey Scottish eyes. The pupils dilating, opening for her as she opened for him. Those eyes that promised a lifetime, that made her cry as she came. That made her promise she would visit him so soon. It was stupid. This idea that they could live together. He had a son in Scotland.

The ferry was moving, she could feel it in her feet, but there was nothing to see that could give a sense of speed, direction. Not the gradual growing of the line of the dunes, no sight of the villages of Atlantique and Ocean Bay Park. Of the light-house. She gripped the railing and stared out into the white where Fire Island should have been. Shivering in the heat. Paranoid silence of sounds smothered by fog.

The only person on the top deck was Old Pete. He was alone now, sixty-five or more. She'd been told in the local shop that his lover of twenty years had just died. He was staring out at the waves. Oblivious to her or anyone.

'This place is like a dream,' Tom had said. 'I want to grow old with you here.'

She went to the railings and held the cold metal. From the white came the sound again. Click click click. She was not in her car now. It made no sense. Tick tick tick. She looked round and down then finally found the source of the noise. Her hands on the railing. Tick tock tick tock, like a clock. The fingers twitching nervously. The sound of his wedding ring against the railings.

Flight

Tom felt it in his gut. The plane falling. He woke with a jolt, searched the window for a fuselage on fire. The horribly chirpy loudspeaker announced they'd soon be landing in Reykjavik. Three-and-a-half-hour stopover. No flames and somehow a glow like a semi-sunset over this thing called Iceland. That was just not credible as any place on Planet Earth. Glacial, volcanic, lunar, scored by millennia of seismic struggle. Somehow, people lived here.

Pins and needles. Her hairband cutting off the circulation on his wedding finger. Deep-vein thrombosis. There would have to be an amputation. It was perfect. He'd send her his finger as a souvenir. They'd swap by FedEx. Microsurgery – walk about with each other's fingers. He pulled the hairband off. There was one of her short brown hairs caught in it. He held it to his nose to try to find her scent. Rubbed it against his lips then carefully slipped it into his shirt pocket.

Disembarking. His mobile was still on New York time, it said three and it must have been p.m., but the sky outside could have been dusk or dawn or just overcast. He'd been herded out of the plane into the waiting area and was wandering back and forward, to the gate, away from the gate, round duty-free, lost in the lost hours. Why did it do that, the plane? Go north almost to the Pole and then descend – some kind of short cut? Or just because it was the cheapest flight available. Sub-economy with Icelandair. Small plane, not a 777. Refu-elling. He was in no mood for laughter now but it was funny. This plane that transported fish round the world, that smelt of fish, on which they served you three kinds of fish as your dinner and breakfast – no doubt defrosted and cooked by the fuselage.

At the gate an air hostess had stuck a sticker on him that

read HEATHROW, PLEASE FIND ME. People passing, like him, lost in transit, caught between countries. He recalled some anecdote about a man in Charles de Gaulle, an illegal immigrant, Moroccan, who'd been denied entry to France and had no money to fly back home. Some legal loophole. This guy had lived in the departures lounge for two years on the charity of passing tourists.

Tom's neck stiff; he rubbed it then felt the hickey. When they kissed they were nowhere. To live with Meg, forever in departures.

Wandering half awake in near awe. He bought a bottle of duty-free vodka because trying to work out the currency was engaging for a good ten minutes – a gift for Morna it would be, when he broke the news to her. He bought a second because there was a 50 per cent off deal on two. He contemplated buying Sean a present, a CD, but Meg had already burned one as a gift for his son, and the exchange rate was surreal.

The pacing again, taking in the impossible differences of the place. New York too had shaken him. Of course he'd visited on holiday before, had dreamed of moving there, but the two weeks, one of work and one with Meg, had changed his perspective for ever. This old phrase of his that all the world was the same now – globalisation – no longer made any sense. New York had seemed like the twenty-fifth century and the eighteenth all at once. Space-age cars, fifties refrigerators, and at the same time the extreme polite formality of talk, like you were all new immigrants. Iceland. The view of the car park through the windows, some statue in sheet steel of an egg erupting into shards of ice, reaching for the sky. What century was this? What fucking planet? There was a McDonald's in the mall but even that looked different. His eyes scanned the passing females as if to find some innate primal grounding. Fragments of her. Long legs like her. Dark hair like her. Curly like her. Slender-faced like her. He stopped pacing and took a seat on a bench. It wasn't desire he was feeling now for the passing females. He was witnessing how different they were from her. With bigger breasts, with blonde bobs. The one in the smoking lounge with the tarty leopard-skin top and leather pants. The six-foot

German in heels that must have taken her to six three. Their difference from each other, from her. He had to stop there by duty-free and just snatch a moment to take in this feeling. Her memory now a filter through which he was seeing all women, that made them all seem beautiful. And that old pressing need he'd felt so strongly on the outgoing flight, to chat, to seduce, a stranger, even if only for a minute before they took their different flights. It had gone too. He was not thinking about tits and ass and trying to memorise them for a wank later in the plane toilet. No, he was staring at a Latina woman on her mobile phone sitting on a mock-marble bench beside a plastic yucca and wondering whether she came from South America or Spain or Italy, why she seemed so anxious on her phone – if she was going through a traumatic separation, if her flight had been postponed, and there he was, her lover, waiting for her at arrivals in Barcelona or Rome. Feeling for her with her head in her hands as she pressed the mobile to her ear. And the intercom and the adverts, all in this incomprehensible language like a transmission beamed in from some other planet. He hated adverts because he used to direct them. He hated corporate videos because he still did. But there he was standing in front of a monitor. A picture of a beach and then some food, then a hotel in some country, not here. Adverts and more adverts. But the voice was just sounds, abstract and musical. The language incomprehensible. Yes, he could live here with Meg and it would be a way to finally escape from this world that screamed its banality in his ears every day. They would walk hand in hand across this lunar terrain and understand nothing and only ever learn enough of the language to be able to eat, to find somewhere to sleep.

And Sean, yes, he and Meg would walk hand in hand through this primal landscape, Sean between them, swinging from their arms. Sean's stutter wouldn't matter any more. It would be a language all of its own and they would stutter with him. Singing the nonsense language of nowhere land, wandering its wilderness, together.

A hand on his shoulder. He turned. A small oriental woman in airport uniform, somehow Japanese.

'You London?'

He laughed. 'Am I London?'

And he thought of those lines from *Hiroshima Mon Amour*, that old classic French movie he and Meg knew line for line. Two lovers and the man was from Hiroshima and the woman from Nevers in France. Strange, the names the French had for their towns: Nevers and Angers. In the final sequence, on their last night, they called each other by the name of their cities. 'You are "Nevers",' the Japanese man whispered, over and over as he stroked her cheek, knowing he would never see her again.

Island

Cycling home was part of her routine, but he had thrown everything out of whack and she couldn't summon the energy. Neither could she face the short cut along the beach because they'd walked it together on the fourth day and his shadow would be following her across the sand. The old paths then. Walking the two miles would be her penance. Her mind was at war. On one side was her career and the script by her laptop and the phone meeting with film agent Josh in four hours' time, the other was flashbacks to all the screaming transgressions she'd committed with Tom – night three and she'd made love blindfolded. Night four and she'd begged to do the same again. The walk, the sand, so hot. The script on her desk was a studio love story that had had five writers fired already. Full of clichés. This sense that everything was connected. That fucking Tom had been some way of expressing how much she hated her life.

Days three, four and five all merged together as the sand burned her feet. 'Glass is melted sand,' he'd said. 'We're walking on glass.' The way he said things like that, so casually. That he just threw away.

She was walking past the tiny wooden shacks. The aged wood, the mailboxes, the paint dried and cracking. A mile till home. She should not be thinking these things. Feeling these thoughts.

On the morning of the fifth day, he'd browsed the script and said again that she should stop whoring herself to Hollywood – she should write for herself. He'd gone down on her. Her grasping his head, gasping, 'I'm your whore, I'm your whore.'

That was the last night of the blindfold.

The key that never quite fitted and had to be pushed up

before turning. The sun-beaten door that swung open by itself, that ached on its hinges, then seemed to sigh as she entered. That he said he would fix with a screwdriver but never got round to. The sand following her feet inside on to the bare pine beams as it always did. Through the door and everything was as it should be. The photo of her and friends, 1996, at her sister's wedding, that he'd accidentally knocked from her photo-wall – back in its old place among the fifty or more of all her friends and past lovers. The old futon that he'd moved so they could make love on the floor – sitting back where it belonged in the dents in the wooden beams. Her thousand books that had been in alphabetical order till he'd browsed them, that she'd asked him to put back as they should be. The tree stump she'd found on the beach that she used as a seat. The moth-eaten Persian throw rug. The old Victorian dollhouse, with the inhabitants made of pipe cleaners that he'd told her were something to do with her family and would take him years to psychoanalyse. The door and window frame half stripped of paint. All these things, he'd said, that showed how contradictory she was. That she lived with so much mess but each part of it had to be in its exact place. Kind of eccentric, he'd said, like an old maid. Her handmade chunky teacup for the every-morning cup of tea, three inches from the laptop as it always was. The neat script pages and notes with corrections. Her laptop exactly where it should be on the big old wooden table she'd sat at from nine to five for the last eight years. All as if he'd never been there.

Everything the same and yet nothing was. She was in the middle of her own living room, three feet from the door, keys still in hand, standing still in a place she'd always only passed through to go to the bedroom, bathroom, kitchen, desk, laptop. Standing as if she'd just walked into someone else's home by accident. He had gone. Everything was back to normal. Normal, that was what she was sensing. Her normal. But there was something missing in her normal now.

Damn him. He was still there, or his absence was now a thing in itself. There was something of his, here, somewhere. She sensed it, something he'd left behind. The wine glasses on the table from two nights before? His empty, hers still half full. No, not that, it was – my God – his smell. My love, my You. It was no good, it was too late. He had ruined everything.

Her feminist head was shouting – it was appalling that it took a man to bring you to yourself. Her philosophy head screaming that we are each alone. Her pragmatic head telling her that she just had to get back to her routine.

Eleven forty. Well past time for her beach walk. Without routine there is only chaos and fear. No more than six glasses of wine per week. Wake at six thirty, put on the aerobics video, work out till seven fifteen. Breakfast of organic fruit and muesli. Walk along the beach, the mile and then back. Three hours at the laptop correcting the mistakes in other people's scripts. The lunch of organic vegetables, the tablet of echinacea, the three of omega 3, 6 and 9. Work till five, tone down the critique. Spellcheck then send. The night alone with the pre-defrosted meal that was the leftovers from something last week. Eight p.m. and one glass of Chardonnay and the world-cinema DVD. The quantity of wine left in the bottle that would be checked tomorrow, to see if she'd drunk more than she should have. The orthopaedic mattress and the pillow between her knees, to correct posture, not to make up for the absence of another body. The earplugs and eye mask to drown out distractions. Go to Manhattan once a week. Date men once a month but don't see any of them more than twice. Never take them home to Fire Island.

She couldn't take that first step. The kitchen was his now, was where he'd cooked that Scottish fishcake thing on night three and she never ate fish but had loved it. The bathroom was him coming up behind her as she did her exfoliation, rubbing his erection between her buttocks, their faces laughing together in the mirror. The bedroom. No possibility of going there.

It was only twelve but she was so, so tired. The chaos coming at her. Tom, the tomcat that had sprayed his scent in her home. He'd kept her up till 3 a.m., night after night, had her drink another bottle of wine, had her debating movies till their argument was forgotten in a haze of alcohol, making love till daylight came. This man who had moved and terrified her with his volatility.

The sickness was maybe a migraine starting. To just close her eyes. Her feet walking across that space that was supposed to be hers. Something of him there in the bedroom. The tangled bed sheets. She forced herself to lie down. A bump in the pillow. Her hand underneath finding the familiar texture of his jeans. The ones he'd torn, that she'd felt his bare ass through on the beach. That he'd ripped even more to do his silly bum dance. His jeans here, why? He needed two pillows, he'd said. She had only two, both for herself, that became one for him and one for her even though they only ever shared the same one, their faces so close in sleep. He must have put the jeans under there to pad up the pillow. His smell, there in her hands. On that fourth day he'd wiped the cum from her belly with the jeans. She closed her eyes and breathed him in. The sunlight, his semen. When was the last time she had held a man's clothes to her face? She couldn't rest. Stop it, Megan. Stop.

You are pathetic, she told herself. She had a teleconference with her agent and Forward Features in just over an hour. She had a career, a life to go back to. A life without him. He was gone. It was for the best.

I-Map

Tom took the handset and hit the buttons for the flight map. Time at origin, time at destination, remaining flight time 2 hours 12 minutes. Altitude. Speed 571 mph. The globe came up on-screen with a superimposed ellipse of night and day. They were on the edge of the darkness, flying headlong into accelerated night. The black in the graphic obliterated the land beneath. The tiny twenty-pixel blob that was called Britain. To just sleep, to forgo the early fish breakfast. To wake as the wheels hit the ground. Tom ran the words over in his head: home. I am going home. Hours still to go. Turbulence safety announcements in English, French, Icelandic. A body next to him. Male, forty, American as the obligatory politenesses had revealed. Why did it nauseate him now? The petty negotiations over ownership of an armrest. The smell of this body you would never see again.

His little complimentary travel pack with headphones, eye mask and toothbrush at his feet. Meg and her improvised blindfold. This kink that had started so innocently, these feelings more tender than anything before. How he had taken off her blindfold when they were spent and it was wet with her tears and she made him look into her eyes, deep, minute after minute until the tears came to him. Her voice whispering over and over. You. You. No. He could not put on the eye mask.

The in-flight entertainment unit had only one feature film left. It seemed to be nearing its end. The noise was of screaming and burning. He took the headphones off and watched in silence. An American woman tied to a wall in a blazing mansion. Succumbing to the flames while two men fought hand to hand to the death. An old woman and boy of about seven watching them, screaming.

The air hostess was proffering drinks. God, yes. But no.

There would be no G&T, no V&T, no double Whyte & Mackay's, no gazing at her cleavage as she bent over to serve. He and Meg had promised they wouldn't drink or fuck to fill each other's absence. It had been a mistake to buy the duty-free vodka. He hadn't told her about his drink problem, had somehow kept the lid on it when he was with her. He feared the return to the drink when he got home, only worse. Drinking to fill her absence. How to endure these two months apart? He'd have to be strong. No sinking into self-pity. Drinking, fucking any other woman that might approximate just one tiny aspect of her. He was nauseous, dehydrated. It would be a long night.

'Just water please.'

The American beside him smiled and toasted him with his 'Scatch'. Tom smiled back, turned to the window. The rain on the glass – some clichéd metaphor for tears. There would be no tears. The red light flashing on the wing. The sign. Do. Do not. Do not walk. Do not walk on this area.

I-Map said they were over the ocean. Nothing but blackness below. He closed his eyes and struggled to picture Meg. Tracing an imaginary finger down the gentle incline from her breasts to ribs to waist. Her laughing face again. The tiny scar on her lip.

The darkness below was scaring him. To fall from thirty thousand feet of air into two thousand of water. Nothing between her and him, no land masses, no countries. Ocean, uncharted, alien, ever-shifting. Depth, death. Your name, which is mine, names this space where no man can live. Lakes on the moon. Sea of forgetfulness. Sea of longing. Sea of eternity. Meg. My love. Sea of You.

She would visit in forty-nine, fifty days. The whole time thing had to be worked out. Gaps, her six hours behind. She had a fear of people disappearing. He was to call her when he arrived to tell her he'd arrived safely. No matter what time, she'd said.

Two hours till arrival, and that was only London, then three and a half more to kill and then there would be the connecting shuttle to Edinburgh. And the voices round him would change.

No more the twang and drawl of her New York accent, no more the ironic inflection that turned words into games. In Edinburgh he would not be the exotic wit at the party. No one would ask him to repeat what he had just said and tell him how wonderful his accent was. There would be no Meg to stare at his face after he'd said something simple which she'd heard for the first time.

'Dreich?'

'Yeah, dreich, but you say it more like you were going to spit. Chhh.'

'Ch, like loch.'

'Yeah, exactly. It means, grey, wet, it's a mood also. We say it's dreich today. Or he's a bit dreich. The Scots are very dreich.'

'Right, right. Like when I was a kid and I'd be doing a painting and there'd be red and blue and yellow and I'd get so excited I'd mix them all up together and it always, it just turned to this sad grey-brown mess. Is that dreich?'

He could have wept. 'Yes,' he'd said. 'That's Scotland, that's "dreich".'

Then the face before him was not Meg but Sean. All those moments of joy over the years, teaching Sean new words, only for Sean to develop in the last year this chronic stutter. Waiting and watching his son gasping for that next impossible word. That was home for him now. Legacy from father to son. He had gifted his son a stutter. If it wasn't for Sean, he would not be sitting on this plane now. If it wasn't for Sean, he would never go home.

Script

The phone woke her. She was up and on her feet and without thinking pulling Tom's jeans on. It couldn't be Tom, he'd maybe be at Heathrow by now but not home. It must be the teleconference with Josh. When Josh called he talked like an actor playing the part of 'agent' in a satire on the film industry. She always thought of everything he said in script format. She couldn't face him today. The answerphone clicked on.

> [JOSH]
> Hey, Sweetie, how's you? We're here for our
> conference call. I got Thierry on the line here,
> we're ready when you are?

She looked at the pile of paper beside her laptop. *Fatal Attraction* meets *Doctor Zhivago*. Thierry Hubert. Scriptwriter. Title of script. *Fatal Love*.

> [JOSH]
> Meg, you there? Call us right back. I'll try your
> cell.

But what could she say? The stupid script. Days ago Tom had walked round in only a T-shirt, his flaccid dick peeking out, picked up a random page from the script, scratching his hairy ass and putting on a funny American voice, and they'd been in hysterics about how crap it all was. Quite literally *Doctor Zhivago* but without the Russian Civil War, the snowy wastelands of Siberia and a tragic love separated by the forces of history.

She quickly turned off her cell so Josh couldn't call. Rummaged around for the page she'd scrawled down that night

when Tom had paced about ranting, wine in hand, spouting
forth his own improvised script review after she'd told him the
plot. Here it was. Hysterical.

> This script attempts to be an old-fashioned epic romance but
> is set in the era of casual sex. There is no drama in it. The
> characters fuck on their first date. They go shopping. She gets
> bored of him. He has to work out and buy some dance classes
> to win her back. He does the dance classes, he wins her back.
> There is no great dilemma of choice. Nothing fatal. No lack of
> freedom with which to test the will. Too much choice is their
> only crisis. This is not romance . . . it's shopping.

She needed to go for her walk. Josh could wait. This need
that Tom had seeded in her. To fuck, to fuck up everything.
She slipped on her sneakers and filled up her water bottle at
the kitchen sink then headed out the back door. Over the dune,
past Old Pete's shack, to the beach. She'd walk the long way
today past Dunewood then east to the lighthouse. Miles. Her
feet on the sand. Feel the sand.

Reaching the crest of the dune, the view seemed wrong. The
water too distant.

How could she go back and face her agent and that stupid
script? Tom's constant questions about why she did this for a
living. OK – how had it started? She'd explained it to him – her
useless PhD on avant-garde feminist film theory, her desire to
write films, failure after failure, the little jobs as critic then as
script reader, then a dare to herself, ten years ago, to see if she
could master the impossible laughable language of Hollywood,
then somehow she'd got good at it and it was no longer so funny,
and now she was what she did. As Tom said – 'Doctor, Doctor,
this script is sick!' She was a script doctor.

Every story is the same, she'd told him. 'To follow a sympa-
thetic protagonist over insurmountable obstacles to achieve the
realisation of their compelling desire.'

'Right, right – Jesus descends, the orchestra swells, the credits
roll,' he said. 'But why do it? Every time you go near your
laptop I see the energy drain from you. You have so much to

say. Why spend your life critiquing other people's stupid stories? Why not write about something you love?'

'I wouldn't know where to start.'

'My love. The things you say to me. No one has ever written anything so beautiful.'

'I couldn't write what we say! No way.'

'We must be a good story, a fucking great story.'

'C'mon. No one would believe it! I write the first draft, then I get fired and they bring in some hack, then another, then a script doctor just like me. They'd turn it into a musical or a comedy.'

'I want to see what you write just for yourself . . . If I had your half your talent, I'd write poetry, a song, a fucking opera, I dunno, even a shopping list.'

The waves on the beach, the empty sky. She had once believed that writing meant something. Had walked this beach hand in hand with Tom last week and felt almost ashamed of the joy he brought her. The sun and the wind and the sand. And they were happy together without obstacles and they were, the pair of them, as unsympathetic as any two characters could be, and every time she'd tried to write of love in the past they'd said it was no good, love couldn't be written about, only conflict. Joy was inexpressible. A stupid dream. Him and the idea of writing for herself. Jesus descends, the orchestra swells, the credits roll.

It was crazy, she was going crazy. Two hours ago she'd decided that Tom had to go the way of the fog. But now the fog had lifted and she was staring out at the lighthouse and the gulls. The sun overhead, the shadows of birds, perfect silhouettes circling her in the sand. A memory of how once she had tried to capture passing moments. She had taught herself to let them pass, that they were just that, shadows. Memory of Tom, three days ago, lying together on this same beach, his head on her breast, his eyes to the sky, the sand. 'Look, fuck! The bird shadows – Jesus, didn't you see that?' It angered her now that Tom had been sent to her like this, a reminder that she had once known beauty.

And Josh and *Fatal Love*. Her feet fought their way through the hot heavy sand, a kind of plan forming in her mind. To have a break from this soul-numbing torture. She didn't need the money now. She could do it. She had saved enough to live off

for four, maybe five months. Minus the costs of the flight to
Tom and living expenses. And the problem with *Fatal Love* and
every other bloody modern love story she'd doctored was that
there was no love in her work and no love on the page and she
did know again, now, what love might be. Her feet found the
crest of the dune where the sand was firmer. She tried to force
herself to recall all the things she'd once believed – writing was
not of the self but some gift. Ten years ago, fifteen, the words
flowing from her. Page after page. Ten lovers and as many
attempts at writing. The producers said her work was too intellectual. Her great project, abandoned. *The Stages of Love*. Seven
hundred pages. Each rewrite an act of love in itself. Trying and
failing year after year to get back to those moments of spontaneity. She could only ever lose herself to writing when she was
in love. All these things that others told her were so naive, that
made her hate them all, that made her at moments scream to
herself that, yes, she was naive and God save the rest of them.

Running back through the scorching sand, stumbling. At the
door, she knew it was crazy, but she couldn't stop. Rummaging
through the boxes in the closet, the old files. *The Stages of Love*.
Ten years of writing for other people, selling herself for their
goals. She had to find *The Stages of Love*. The phone kept on
ringing. The answer machine filling up.

[JOSH]
Meg, don't keep me waiting, baby. I got
Forward Features here and the scriptwriter
calling long distance. They'll only wait so long.

She pulled the phone line from the wall and tore into the boxes
and dust and old coats and galoshes and gloves and sand. Beneath
the CD files, the paperwork, at the back, somewhere in there. The
old box of floppy disks that she'd never been able to throw out.
There, the box in her hands. Over a hundred floppies. All these
titles she couldn't even recall having written. Treatment4.doc.
International7.doc. Rewrite7hav2.doc. One that looked like it might
be the one – Stages23.doc, another stagescompiled.doc. And the
journals, all the diaries that'd been worked up into script pages,

into fragments of stories, of a novel. She was running round plugging the portable floppy drive into the ISDN. Hoping the old files would still be readable; they were PC – she was Mac now. The folder opened up. Ninety-five files. Dates – 1992 to 2002. File sizes – 358–672mb. The titles made no sense. She clicked on the biggest one. *Macintosh does not recognize the program that created this file. Some of your initial formatting may be lost in transfer. Click OK.* The line spacing was gone, no tabulation, no full stops. It was one huge sentence seven hundred pages long. It read:

> The Stages of Love by Megan Foster Hunt June 21, 1996 Chapter One Stage One The Surprise May stepped outside and drew her first breath from the morning and the air seemed new to her like she'd never tasted it before on her tongue in her lungs He was sleeping and she . . .

Meg closed her eyes and the next word, the next line was there in her head. She steadied herself on the edge of her work table as the tears came. Yes, she was back. Awake at last. And she was a character called May and May was twenty-five and May was with a man called Michael from a foreign country and May was in love in a way that touched her so deeply that she had to write about it. She had never had the guts to read the thing from beginning to end. The lover changed his name every thirty pages or so, but it was always the same female protagonist. May was Megan and May was in love and Megan had spent fifteen years running from May and this unfinished story. Somehow she would find the courage to read it again. These seven hundred pages. These many years. The seventeen journals. These many loves. This one new love called Tom who had made her face what she had feared for so long. What she had once wanted to be.

Change

POSH AND BECKS SPLIT AGAIN. I LOST 38 POUNDS IN TWO WEEKS. NOKIA PULLS OUT. 800 REDUNDANCIES. Tom had to escape from the headlines because they made his nausea worse. Three-hour delay at Heathrow. Trying to sleep over three seats but being moved on as mothers and children arrived with needing, pleading faces. Pacing around. Finding a seat jammed between two of the Great British obese. Pacing again. Going back to his seat to find it occupied by a peroxide blonde from Birmingham chatting on her mobile about Posh and Becks.

So then it was no seat and the earplugs from the travel bag and two hours to kill. Walking the shops of Heathrow, half deaf, half in a dream. For a while it was better not having to hear the inane chat of the British, but then it got worse. The mute sight of them. Two weeks in New York and every face and race so different. Here there were types. Four white girls in miniskirts passed by with wheelie bags and he knew without hearing that they were Glasgow office temps heading for Marbella. A couple, middle-aged, dressed in clothes ten years out of date, colours washed grey, sitting not speaking to each other, and he saw their home in Leith and their five kids and their picture of Jesus on the wall beside their ceramic dogs. Jesus. White, white, everyone was white. The blacks were shadows, not like in New York where Meg had introduced him to her agent. This black man from Bed-Stuy who called you nigger if he liked you, who made half a million a year.

Domestic flight, and the guy next to him white and proud. Number-two haircut and attitude and shoulders that invaded Tom's space.

'Fuckin' London, eh? Snobby cunts, no like Edinbra, down tae earth, know whit a mean?'

Tom nodding his way through the diatribe and the in-the-

event-of-emergency-landing procedures, waiting for the opportunity to put the earplugs back in.

'Best place in the fucking world. Where you fae then?'

In New York, where you come from was a question asked
openly, not an accusation. Tom took a beat.

'New York,' he said in his best De Niro.

'Fuckin' Yank then, eh? Fuckin' Iraq, eh?'

The wheels left the ground and Tom closed his eyes,
wondering how long he'd have to wait till he could put on the
eye mask without offending or provoking further violence.

Down to earth. Landing. And he had done the whole trip
with eyes closed. Customs and arrivals a memory before it even
happened. The earplugs somehow accidentally still in his ears
on the bus home from the airport. So many stops. Princes
Street. Down Leith Walk. Single mothers and screaming children. OAPs hunchbacked with shopping bags. Downturned
mouths scored into grey skin like knife marks through clay. The
conversations he couldn't hear, but knew already – 'the fuckin'
price o' bus tickets – the bloody weather – the fuckin' NHS –
Debbie's in trouble way the polis again – the fuckin' bastards'.
Down to earth. Yes, they prided themselves on being down to
earth.

You flew across the globe through day and night, through
infinite skies and expansive thought, then slowly you circled your
city and it pulled you down till your feet were on the ground,
then it was your street, then the walk, then through the tene-
ment door, the keys in your hand. Gravity sucking you slowly
downwards. The curvature of the planet flattening. The weight
increasing as the dimensions shrank. The gravity of where you
came from, pulling you in, squashing you, till you fitted this
tiny hole that was for a key that opened the door to your home.

Tom was inside. A beat, a breath. Bags down and staring at
the seventies yellow-and-silver wallpaper, the swirly chocolate-
coloured worn-out carpets that belonged to the last owner. The
generic Ikea furniture. Some smell was wrong. Pungent, florid.
Maybe empty wine bottles fermenting by themselves, a pizza
box gone fungal. A smell of something living or dying.

He walked cautiously into the kitchen. A cinematic flash of

some local junkie dead on the floor by a broken window, of his girlfriend Morna's wrists slashed on the floor. He looked up.

A potted plant – rosemary – on his table and a note. Recycled paper, hand-drawn calligraphy.

Give me water twice a week and I'll be just fine. Morna xxx.

Of course, Morna had his keys, she'd come to water his plants. He plucked a rosemary leaf and crushed it beneath his fingers, bringing it to his nose to inhale. Meg's home – Rosemary Cottage. Morna my girlfriend.

Deathly silence. He laughed as he remembered he still had his earplugs in. Kept them in, what the hell, didn't want to hear the sounds of his street or the radio or TV or his own footsteps in the empty space. He went through to the living room and sat on the grey fake-leather second-hand sofa and stared at the facing wall. No pictures. No ornaments or posters or photos of family members. No design plan or nice little throw rugs or colour-coordinated curtains. The place looked like he'd just moved in. Anonymous. Unloved. Looked like what it was – a place for a divorced man to eat and drink himself to sleep. He checked his watch. It must have still been on New York time. Four thirty with her now – a.m. He'd call her at seven thirty, as agreed. Prepare some jokes for her about his flight. Then call his ex to say he was too tired to pick up his son from school as arranged and could he see Sean tomorrow. Then call Morna – tell her he couldn't see her again, ever, not in the way that they had been seeing each other. He thought about changing his watch to Edinburgh time but stopped short. He took one of his earplugs out. A sound of shouting from the street.

'Johnnie, Johnnie, for fucksake! Johnnie!'

The duty-free vodka in his bag. Just a shot to calm him. No, it would have to be chilled first – fridge. Damn thing smelt of fungus. No mixers inside. Nothing but mustard and mayo and a black wet thing in a bag that must once have been a lettuce. He slammed the door shut and put the earplug back in. Walking back through to the sofa, collapsing on to it. The wallpaper and the white light of the overcast sky hurt his eyes. He went into his pocket and pulled out the free in-flight eye mask, as

Meg had done accidentally on that third night, as they had done on their last night, deliberately.

'I feel you so much more when I can't see you,' she'd said.

He sat there in this flat he'd never made his own, with the decor that so many passing occupants had not changed in decades. Single mothers and alkies and students with their wild parties. Ignoring the stains on the carpet from wine or sick, the pen marks on the kitchen wall that marked the growth of some child or other. Jimmy four, Jimmy four and a half. He would call Meg in two hours. Just over seven weeks till she came to stay but he couldn't picture her here. Couldn't even see himself here. Couldn't see their future.

The voddie waiting. So stupid to have bought it. Their week of love had been fuelled by alcohol. He'd snuck a shot here and there in between their chats. Finished off the last of it before bed each night. Had hidden it from her as he had his ex-wife. The word 'alcoholism' had always seemed too prescriptive and common for him. He had at least thirty reasons why his drinking was not common or garden. Meg found him funny when he was drunk but never seemed to twig that that was what was making him so funny.

Two bottles in the fridge. The eye mask in his hand. A choice. The image of her laughing face gave him strength. No, he couldn't go back. After just one drink the descent would start. Meg or drink? If he lost her now then the drinking would never stop. It would kill him this time. Hands shaking, he lifted the eye mask to his eyes and was in darkness.

2
HOME

Call

'Meg, my love.'
  'Hello, You.'
  'Sorry, I couldn't wait any longer. My mobile says it's your seven. Couldn't work out if it was a.m. or p.m. I nodded off on the sofa. Dunno if I slept two hours or fourteen. I guess I'm just a little disorientated.'
  'It's morning silly.'
  'Right, six hours behind not ahead. My God, listen to your voice. My You.'
  'And you, you sound so . . .'
  'It's like you're here with me, there's no . . . The marvels of modern technology, eh . . . I thought there'd be a delay or something, you know, an echo.'
  'Listen to us. Our first long-distance call.'
  'Hey, but you know, [laughter] it's our first phone call too – full stop.'
  'Really?'
  'Yeah, we usually just texted or . . . or were in the same room or . . .'
  [Laughter.]
  'My You. So, you got home OK?'
  'Sure, sure. I was all set for strangling a suicide bomber – fact is getting home safely is kind of a disappointment.'
  [Laughter.]
  'There was this hold-up at fucking Heathrow – I think my unwashed underwear must have aroused the sniffer dogs.'
  'You make me laugh, my You.'
  'So you just woke up?'
  'No, no. Was up an hour ago. I was . . . no, I want to hear all about you. How's Edinburgh? Your flat?'
  'My flat. Nothing flat about it at all.'

'Tell me.'

'Well, I'm sitting here at the cocktail bar with my Macintosh airport terminal just scrolling through my share prices on the interactive video projector – there's my favourite Warhol on the wall and Bauhaus replica chair set over there by the bay windows that look out over the Japanese Zen garden.'

[Laughter.]

'Seriously, babe, Zen – to be honest, that would be the word for this aesthetic. Stripped down, just the bare essentials. In fact, the place looks like it's been burgled, must have left the door open before I left. God, you have no idea. It's like I've been away for a decade. There's dust, maybe it was always here. I dunno, it's like Tutankhamen's tomb here. I keep waiting for the sands of time to flood in and suffocate me. Maybe I should buy a vacuum cleaner.'

'Tom, why do you make me laugh so much?'

'Laughter is the last refuge of the disillusioned.'

'Who was that? Oscar Wilde?'

'Nah, just made it up. I know, I know, I could have been a contender. But Meg. I want to hear you. Your sexy American voice.'

'Well . . . what do I say?'

'Hey, another thing is, I've come back with a goddamn American accent. Weird, huh? I was going through customs and the guy said, "How long are you planning on staying in the country?" I almost told him, "You can take dis country and stick it up ya ass." I think I must have been copying you. Like your accent must have entered me, like your finger in my ass. Which reminds me, I should get my prostate checked. It's free here, by the way. The NHS. You can go, like, three times a week, till they wise up.'

[Laughter. Silence.]

'Meg, what's up, babe?'

'You, you make me laugh. I can't laugh by myself. I had these things to tell but you make me laugh.'

'I'm sorry, I guess I'm kind of laughable. You know, people often laugh after they witness death, the insane laugh, I'm kind of on that level. You have no idea how much I hate this place,

I shouldn't be telling you that. You're not going to want to come here. Really, Edinburgh is one huge toilet bowl of history and I feel like shit.'

'Stop it. I can't think when I'm laughing . . .'

'Meg. My love. I called to hear your sweet voice and here I am, rabbiting on. What did you have to tell me? Sounds ominous.'

'It's a surprise.'

'OK, here we go. You've decided this won't work. It's over, right? Come on, hit me with it.'

'Stop it. Just give me a minute.'

'I'm counting the seconds here. Four, five, six. You know time is money. Not that I want to pressure you but this is sixty-eight pence a minute.'

'OK. Here goes – I threw in my job.'

'Really?'

'Emailed my agent. I'm going to, like you said, I'm going to do some writing just for me. [Silence.] My You. Aren't you happy for me?'

'Yeah, great. Fantastic. God! That's so good. Incredible.'

'I wouldn't have done it if it hadn't been for you.'

'Wow! Well. I always wanted to be a muse.'

'You do amuse me, my muse.'

[Silence.]

'Meg. What are you doing now? Have you gone for your walk yet?'

'We're not very clear on this yet, are we? [Laughter.] Wait. I'll get a pen.'

'Meg? Hello? Hello?'

'I'm back.'

'God, thought you'd hung up or something.'

'Just getting a pen, going to work this out once and for all.'

'Work out what?'

'Shh, just give me a minute.'

'What are you doing?'

'Shh, just wait.'

'I'm waiting, I'm waiting. God, I wonder how much this is costing, we really should be talking. What you doing? Writing a novel? We're losing time here, baby. Don't get all Proust on me here. Jeez.'

'OK, I'm done, you want to hear it.'

'Hit me.'

'OK, I'm six hours behind so when you get up at eight it's 2 a.m. with me. When you have lunch at one I wake up.'

'So this is what, a list?'

'A call schedule.'

'Right, right. I'm never going to remember this.'

'I go for my walk at 8 a.m., which is plus six for you, which is . . .'

'Me and maths, you say math in your country, me and math – you tell me.'

[Laughter.]

'It's 2 p.m. for you.'

'God, listen to us.'

[Laughter.]

'So then, you get home at around six thirty so that's twelve thirty with me, which is a good time to call. In fact, any time between then and whenever you go to bed is fine, so we've got a window of about four hours.'

'You're going to have to email me this. So can I call you tonight?'

[Laughter.]

'Whose night. Yours or mine?'

'Well, mine. No, yours. Oh Meg, I miss you.'

'But I go to bed at ten, so that would be 4 a.m. with you.'

'Fine, I'll set my alarm clock. Got jet lag anyway. Or I could call you at eight when I get up.'

'You're impossible. That's 2 a.m. my time.'

[Laughter.]

'I know, I know. OK, so run this past me again.'

'OK, so your late afternoon till your night is fine. Anything else and I'll be asleep.'

'Christ! We have to get – what d'you call them? – calling cards. I know, I'm a mean Scotsman. I don't want to spend all my money on phone calls when I could save and buy an air ticket. International calling cards, I think they're called.'

'I'm on to it already.'

'Listen to you – "already". I love that. Or do that Internet thing. I read there was some way we could do this online for free. Like cybersex. We have to buy PC webcams.'

'I have a Mac already.'

'But you know what I mean . . .'

[Laughter.]

'I don't think I could do cybersex.'

'Jesus, me neither. God, I wish I could just see you. I could do with a hug, Meg. Already.'

'I know, my love.'

'How we going to do this though? I mean, what . . . phone sex?'

[Laughter.]

'Well, you're always saying how sex is such an important part of –'

'Tom – have you done it before?'

'No, of course not. Well, actually just the once.'

'You're such a slut boy.'

'You want me to tell you?'

'Yes!'

'Total disaster. We kept interrupting each other just when it was getting somewhere. I guess you have to take it in turns . . . talking and wanking. Get one done then do the other.'

'Like the way people talk now.'

[Laughter.]

'Meg, my love, I just want you here.'

'We're going to drive ourselves crazy if we start in on that.'

'"Start in on that." My God, I love the way you talk. I'm sorry, my love.'

'My You. I guess it's just going to have to be phone sex.'

'We'll have to practise. Do some online research.'

[Laughter.]

'My lovely man. I have to go now. I'm going to try to write now. For you, my love. I'm going to write a story just for you.'

'Not yet, I mean, I . . . Can't we just . . . ?'

[Silence.]

'I have to do my walk and then some writing.'

'You and your rules. I have to learn how to do that. I should walk. Self-respect. I have to learn how to do that.'

[Silence.]

'Meg. I love you.'

'I love you too, my You.'

'I know, I know . . . OK. I'll let you go then. Goodnight. I mean, good morning. Can't we talk for a bit more?'

'My love, I have to work. Have a pleasant British evening . . . Oh, wait. Did you give Sean my present?'

'Tomorrow. I'll see him tomorrow.'

'Send him my love, will you? Oh, and a picture . . . can you email me a picture of him? I'm sure he looks just like you.'

'I will. Well, I'll try. You know me and technology.'

'I know.'

'Night-night, Meg.'

'It's my morning, my love, how many times do I have to –'

'Morning-morning then.'

'Morning-morning.'

Journal

DAY ONE. Five hours since Tom called. The curlew is back again, passing overhead shrieking in the air. Her nest must be near here. The beach walkers probably startle her and set her on her circling. The air is humid again, eighty-five on the barometer and CNN say we're in for a heatwave. The wind is strong and the house in the shade of the beech tree, so there's a cool breeze here at my desk. I'm worried for the lettuce and spinach, though. I must have neglected them when Tom was here. They're turning brown. Might be too late to save them. It's amazing I can get anything to grow in the garden at all. This constant battle against the beach.

Why am I writing about all this?

Forced some food down and I'm feeling down – spent most of the day reading *The Stages of Love*. To be honest, it depressed me. The characters' names keep changing. Michael – Tobe – Jez. No wonder no one could make sense of it. A total mess. Pages of dialogue and then story analysis, bits of film script. Three hundred pages of notes on rewrites. Makes me dizzy and sick inside. I can't write. I should get out for some air. Get some groceries.

Tried to fire myself up with energy this morning cc-ing everyone. Saying I'd be taking a break to work on my own thing and would be out of the country soon and only in occasional contact. Feel like a fool now. Tom tells me to write like I speak but then it's all about the garden and the beach and the weather. I'd rather write like he speaks. To capture just one little moment of our time together, I would happily throw these seven hundred turgid pages away. I should start from scratch.

The apartment in Soho brings me 65K. I have another 35 due. He's right. It is my time now. Time for me to write. My chance. Either I become a writer or a landlord. Try to write about Tom.

THINGS WE TALKED ABOUT
Repetitive strain injury
Vegetarianism
Domesticity
Same-sex experiments
Relationships/marriage
Living in the country
How good it feels to be almost forty
Anal sex
Facial exfoliants
International terrorism
PC versus Macintosh
Courtney Love versus Kurt Cobain
Marx versus Nietzsche
Aerobics
People we've lied to/cheated on
George W. Bush
That 60% of all our thoughts are the same thought
Comparative toe and finger sizes
How people won't understand us
Past lovers' performance/endowment
Global warming

THINGS WE AVOIDED TALKING ABOUT
Edinburgh
Money
His smoking/drinking/aggressive outbursts
How we do this
Iraq
His son, Sean
His ex-wife
Morna, his girlfriend
His career
Our future

THINGS HE SAID
I want to grow old with you.
We're like the same person. Two heads on one body.
Shh. He was always saying Shh (but not in a patronising way).
NB: his funny accents.

New File: Day One
Our first moment. June 29. Between 10.30 and 11 p.m.
SET THE SCENE. Party. Marriott. 43rd and 5th. Tribeca
Film Festival. Two hundred people. Actors, agents, producers,
directors, liggers. I was a guest. He was a ligger.
QUESTIONS. How did it start? Was it love at first sight?
No. Check library – psychology – philosophy – romantic fiction
– How to Write Screenplays that Sell. Genre. To fall in love
at first sight requires – make a list – at least one of the following
conditions:
1. *To be lonely, hunting. Receptive to change at that exact point
in your life.* NO. I'd certainly not gone out that night with the
intention of hunting for a man.
2. *To be immediately struck by someone's unique appearance.* NO.
I'm not sure, even now, if I find him physically attractive. Not
my type. (God, I hate that.) Seriously though. To be struck by a
thunderbolt (as Stendhal would have said). No one has thunderbolts these days (only Ally McBeal and even then it was semi-
ironic. The script played on her vulnerability. Her skinniness.
Having thunderbolts is a sign of weakness. The romanticisation
of the anorexic. Skinny girls have thunderbolts. The fat girl,
the secretary in the series, just fucks). STOP ANALYSING.
3. *To be the two most drunk people at the party.* NO. But almost.
4. *To be the only 'outsiders' at the party.* (The two people who
think it's fancy dress and turn up dressed as vegetables at a
tuxedo do.) NO but in a way YES. OK. I had maybe felt that
way that night. Like a vegetable.
DESCRIBE. All night surrounded by people who talked
about themselves, their futures, their last audition, their next.
Movies – the ones they loved and the ones they were in and
the ones they would be in soon and the celebrity friends they
had and the ones they knew and the ones they wanted to meet.

I'd prepared myself for this. And no one knew who I was and I certainly wasn't going to tell them. No one likes a script doctor.

EXPLAIN. Typical film project – between six to ten scriptwriters over three to four years with rewrites on the whim of every casting director and executive producer that comes on board – systematic humiliation – until they literally lose the plot – fired – the script a mess of failed attempts but budget in place – finally, casting almost ready to go, the script doctor is brought in to make sure the thing has a pulse.

NOTE. I've always chosen to go uncredited on feature films. (Five I've done now.) I never turn up at premiere parties, because everyone denies that my job exists at all.

EXPLAIN. Typical job. Line-by-line script deletions. Fifteen-page script analysis/critique of structure. One-line pitch for final rewrite. Ten pages of recommended changes. Occasional report at the end that reads: unfixable, premise flawed. $16K a consultation. $39K additional for rewrite.

BACK TO PARTY. NIGHT ONE. God knows why I even went. It wasn't like the producer was going to introduce me to all of the writers he'd fired and I'd taken to pieces. It wasn't like I wanted to meet actors. Note: Actors act even when they're trying to be real. (Geoff: once made the mistake of dating this actor. He was crying at end of our date and I said, 'You're getting all Douglas Sirk on me.' He called me up a year later to thank me for the line because he'd checked out who Douglas Sirk was and he'd just used it on this 'total babe'.)

NOTE. Why I chose to be a script doctor. It suits my temperament. My shrink says I should have been a shrink. I think it goes beyond that. I can't be in a situation and not analyse. I hear people speak and know what books they've read. I look at couples and see what their problems are. Structure. I see it in everything. It was maybe semiotics. Yale. My shrink says it's indicative of a lack of trust in relationships. Fear of relinquishing control. But I see through her too. She's had three broken marriages. She wants me to attempt a serious relation-ship. To open up and cry. I see her structure. She wants me to be like her.

GET BACK TO SCENE. Film premiere. The script had been a challenge. Mixed genre. Futuristic and still a love story. I'd made it clear in my notes (much to the consternation of the lead actress) that sci-fi was essentially a male-protagonist-led genre and that the love story would have to be relegated to love interest or it would damage the forward thrust of the narrative. Words like that make me laugh. Thrust. (So much of the movie business is still the story of men trying to prove their worth. The lives of producers, directors, actors – actually the same as their scripts. Even their emotions are genre-specific.)

THE DRESS. Or maybe it had been that I'd bought that Westwood dress for self-esteem and it needed to be worn. But as soon as I got there and got a glass of bubbly and slipped unnoticed past all the film stars who didn't know how much I'd affected their roles I felt . . . How did I feel? Disappointed. (Not in them.) There was a certain comfort in watching them air-kissing and running off with 'We must stay in touch' and 'Here's my agent's card.' Disappointed with myself. I'd thought that, for once, I could do this and not judge and somehow engage. The bubbly was Veuve. (My one extravagance.) I thought it would have helped. It was an act, me and the dress and the make-up, but I remember thinking that if I had just another glass I might actually attempt speaking to someone. Remember: There was actually a group of beautiful people within earshot who were discussing Kate's weight, Winslet or Blanchett? And the silicone enhancement of some woman . . . Then this higher-level name-dropping thing happening in the group to my left. This talk of 'Steven'. Steven said this and did that and 'Oh Steven is so wonderful'. I couldn't help getting caught up in it, wondering who Steven was. (Note: Being too inexperienced to know that that was part of the ploy. The withholding of the second name which must have meant that the person talking was on first-name terms with Steven so that someone would ask. Note: Remember for next time.)

'Seagal?'

'Ohmigod, no!' then the whispering of a name so obviously calculated to make others lean in closer. That might have been Spielberg.

How did I feel? Overdressed. Oversober. Awkward. Geek in designer clothing (I couldn't walk in the heels). YES. Someone dressed as a vegetable at a fancy-dress function. YES.

LOVE AT FIRST SIGHT. How did you notice him? Situations in which people fall in love. Write them out. The first thing I noticed about him was – the image of him at the party was – on the edge of everything and everyone. The corner-of-the-eye guy. The gatecrasher. Just that and worse. Something between office worker and technician. Foreign, possibly refugee from something. Something about his suit jacket that was trying too hard for his budget and his shoes which had given up the pretence. Not only out of place at the film party but out of place with himself. Short too. Same height as me, maybe smaller (because of the heels, and I prefer tall men). Skin – white, pasty. Haircut – the kind that guys who weren't balding but were forty liked to have. Showing off their growth but no style to it. Just abundance. Which said he worked in IT or some kind of job that didn't require meeting people much.

THE GIRLS. There had been two girls with him. He'd had them laughing. One was the third AD on the film. (Must find out what a third AD does. Something to do with walkie-talkies and trash bags.)

I am not a snob. I don't care who is who. I'd been very good, not judging, standing on the fringes and that was where he had been too.

THE MOMENT. A general shift in the masses then, toward the centre of the room, when some film star or other had arrived. Girls in Prada and Gucci suddenly pushing past me. Elbows and sorry's and excuse me's. (Readjusting their push-up bras. A girl in Lagerfeld stuffing something in.) Suddenly alone with my empty glass. How did I feel? I remember feeling guilty for still being in judgment mode. Note: It had been a sci-fi movie. Thought: They were being sucked into the black hole. I told myself I was a comet. I wouldn't come to one of these things for a few years. I was looking away, in the opposite direction from the throng of thongs toward the door.

That was when . . . I met his eye.

DESCRIBE. Twenty feet of empty floorboards between us.

He had been abandoned by the wannabes. This sense of awkward empty space between us. The thought of the sound my stupid new heels might make if I went to leave.

GENRE. Two characters in a movie from the seventies. Maybe that was what it was – Enigmatic Outsider.

But no enigma. He was not lit from behind. He did not slowly look up broody and masculine and catch my eye across the crowded room. Empty space between us. Something had to be said. What was the first thing he said?

5. *Humiliation provokes passion.* Ref: Stendhal, Kierkegaard, *Diary of a Seducer.* NOTE: Would still make such a great movie. Two hundred years ago. Note: Out of copyright.

FIRST IMPRESSIONS. Not a cad or ruthless seducer. Not nineteenth century. But still a man out-of-date. No one should speak to him. Any encounter would lead to humiliation. (Note: The ego must be broken, woken from its sleep by a challenge. Act One. Ref: *Doctor Zhivago*, two on either side of ideological divide.)

FIRST THING HE SAID? Twenty feet away and he'd raised his empty glass to me.

6. *Cliché. To meet a man by chance with a similar intellect.*

It goes like this. The first time they meet, she is walking through the university/office/govt office with her big file of notes – he bumps into her. The pages fly. They collect the pages together, he says sorry but they find themselves holding the same last page. Fingers touching. He picks up a page and says, Nietzsche, huh. Then he smiles and she knows.

But he had not bumped into me or spilled my drink or trodden on my foot.

NO. He was standing twenty feet away. No contact.

The first thing he said?

7. *Defiance of social mores. Romeo and Juliet.* He is a Capulet. The families will never allow it. Ridiculous now. In this era without inhibition or prohibition, of consumerism and casual sex. HE SAID THIS AT SOME POINT. To just have a lover say 'NO'. To forbid or have something that was forbidden. Note: He set down his glass and he said something. WHAT?

I was thinking of calling it a night. Another predictable failure.

He had laughed as he looked over at me. Is there such a thing as knowing laughter? He had moved toward me.

'Look, let's get the fucking hell out of here.'

Americans don't talk like that, don't say 'fucking', don't admit to a moment of desperation. WAS THAT WHY?

'Really? Sorry, so what are you doing here?' (I'd said something like that.)

'Just here for the free booze. I'm how you say eet een thees cultura. Io sono, je suis un ligger. I'm a ligger,' and extended his hand, 'Tom.'

'Drink?' he asked. 'I know, I know, I shouldn't be here, but I get the sense you don't want to be here either. Am I right?'

New File. Microsoft Word: Notes

Too many digressions. To much analysis/parenthesis. I can't write romance. How did I end up in his hotel room? I am not a writer. Am a writer of questions/lists. *Are you sure you want to delete this file?* Yes/No.

NO. SAVE AS. TOM 1. RETURN.

New File. Microsoft Word.

SAVE AS. SHOPPING LIST TOMORROW.

  Miso
  Toilet roll
  Tofu
  Mineral water
  Valerian
  International calling card

Sean / Morna

Tom couldn't face it. Any of it. The sleep, the waking, the bedroom, the view from the window. Morning two and he'd been restless all night craving that one drink or two that would make the muscles relax, the mind stop, the sleep come quicker, dreading that time which was the only certain thing, three fifteen, the time he had to pick up his son from school. Waking only to reply to texts – one from Meg, two from Morna, one from work. He called in sick. Finally – up, panicked, parched, rough-shaven, shivering as he put on the clothes left on the floor, he got himself to the car, the schoolyard.

Trying to focus away the jet-lag nausea – staring at the playground mural from the seventies. Multicultural kids playing against a rainbow background. Falling to pieces, covered in graffiti it was. This same playground twice a week, every week, for the last three years, but this seemed like the first time he'd ever really taken it in. He reached for his watch like it would tell him something for certain. Nine, it said. Plus six. Minus six was Meg time. Something fundamental had stopped him from changing it back to UK time. The guilt of having left Sean for two weeks had got him there maybe fifteen minutes before the bell would ring.

Multicoloured faces against a rainbow.

There were no kids yet, only mothers filing in. Tom would have to work out his first thing to say to Sean. The simplest questions were often the hardest.

'Hey, kiddo. How ya doin?'

'Fi . . . fuh . . . Fii . . . fuh . . . fih . . . fuh . . .'

'Fine.' The word he knew would be 'fine'. Minutes of Sean struggling to say it as the other kids tore round the playground with their swear words and screaming sentences. And you must never pre-empt a child with a stutter and tell him what the word he is desperate to say is. You must wait, no matter how painful it is, to let your child speak for himself. That was what she had said. Not Sean's mother, not Meg, but Morna. And what was troubling him now was Morna. The mother of Ian, Sean's only real friend in primary six.

'She's just this friend I have. No, it's nothing serious. I have other girls too,' he'd said to Meg. At the time he'd thought it made him seem more cosmopolitan, to have girls-plural. It had diluted the truth. His only lie. The only one to Meg. Those texts from Morna this morning. Each beep waking him. Each gently asking was he OK? Implying one of their hook-ups. He'd sent only one reply.

Jetlagd. Fukd. Can't speak. Few days. OK.

He'd hesitated then deliberately left off the usual single X on the end that acknowledged what had built between them over the last year. That signified, in their own quiet way, that they had become lovers. And no reply from her. None of her smiley faces made of colons and brackets.

Lovers.

No, he didn't like that word. He took his usual seat on one of the concrete hippos. And he didn't like the words 'Fuck buddies'. No, they were 'good friends'. Their sons were 'best friends'. They met up, usually, on a Thursday when Morna's mother was babysitting Ian and Sean was at the ex's. Round at Morna's they'd get through a bottle of voddie and have one of her special spliffs, then go to bed and she'd massage his back with rosemary oil then stay on her knees, as he rolled from under her and rolled on the condom she'd laid out. She never came. They were all about backs. No eyes together as he came. Not like with Meg. It's OK, she said. I like it like this. And she was maybe right. It would have felt wrong to have looked into Morna's eyes. Their kids didn't know their parents met once a week to fuck.

Sitting on his hippo waiting. Sad hippos. He was trying not to think of all the concrete animals and tower blocks. The tragic history of socialist town planning in Scotland. He always met Morna at the hippos.

How could he end it with her? Couldn't face it. Their relationship was not geared for endings or even beginnings. It had
started by accident. Something maybe more mature than love.
No mention of futures, no time for arguments or recrimina-
tions. The quiet silences instead, of two people who knew they
had been beaten by the world, who in the wreckage of their
marriages didn't cling, but simply held each other gently and
asked no more. Morna had never sworn him to fidelity. Never
questioned him over the occasional bit of make-up or pair of
stockings left lying round his flat. Had silently forgiven in
advance his drunken Saturday-night flings. Why was it that
Tom now felt he'd betrayed Morna to a greater degree than
when he'd cheated on his ex-wife? It wasn't like a divorce. It
was ending a friendship, and that seemed worse. Made him
sick. It had to be done. No time for subtlety. He was with Meg
now.

Twelve minutes till the bell. Seven or so mothers, talking in
their quiet conspiratorial voices. A hundred feet across the
concrete play area and past the security-locked fence and he
could pick out the tired features of Julie, son called Tim,
primary six, daughter only two in a Maclaren buggy. Julie of
the jogging pants and grey flannel sweatshirt with a logo that
read ATHLETIC. Tom doubted she had ever exercised in her
life. She seemed to wear these things as a badge of pride, to
demonstrate to the world the sad decline of the flesh. So typically Scottish. The same with the two other mothers she was
talking to. Their mouths moving and their eyes shooting round
to see if anyone could hear and he knew the things they were
saying. About dieting and exhaustion, and Maclaren buggies
and school bullies and men who leave and some kid that was
such a bad influence. About better schools and grades and the
weather and how little control any of them had over any of
these things. All of this so foreign to Meg's American positivity. Miss Megan Hunt.

Minutes and he'd have to face Morna. Tell her straight up.
Sean and Ian would be running around and he'd have that
minute with her alone while she sat on the next hippo. 'Look,'
he would say and without saying anything more, she would see.

Because Morna was Morna and she'd decided that nothing was worth the fight and finding a secret way to accept failure was all that could be done.

No, he would not tell Morna about Meg, he'd postpone and postpone their Thursday nights, cancelling with different excuses till she got the message.

But she was no fool, she would see it in his face in a second. He had to tell her that no matter how much he'd wanted to live quietly with her there was still this passion and it might well destroy him but he had to see it through . . . Did she understand? What was he doing – trying to think of ways to ask her permission to leave her?

The schoolyard filling up now. The men whose names he could never remember. The ex-BBC cameraman in khakis, standing alone by the railings. This stilted conversation months ago about the halcyon days of the BBC. Tom had said he was doing corporates now, the guy said he was a full-time child-minder.

Eight minutes till the bell rang and he felt like walking away. How could Meg and all her optimism have brought him to hate all of this? Nothing is real, she'd said. It's all stories.

He would arrange to meet Morna tomorrow to talk. They'd sit in a café, not a pub, and he would confess. A second, it would take. Morna had no claim on him, she hated all that. Morna was different. The other mothers didn't talk to her, but talked about her. Morna grew up in a housing scheme but had dragged herself up. Morna used to be a singer in a grunge band. Morna chose to throw her bass-playing drunk of a man out and bring up the child he gave her alone. Morna looked like a hippie but was dark, goth-like, not just her jet-black waist-length hair that she said was dyed to hide the grey, but her past. Morna had been hospitalised on three occasions for self-harm. Morna's world view was dark. Morna was training to be a music therapist, to work with children with severe learning difficulties. Morna had a greater understanding of Sean's stutter than his ex-wife and had practical tips on coping. Melancholic Morna who somehow had hope. Morna of the charity-shop clothes that she carried off with style. Whose son

was his son's only friend. Who had told him that singing might
cure Sean's stutter. Morna. Only three weeks ago he'd said
those same words he'd said to Meg a week ago. 'I want to grow
old with you.'

Mothers passing by the fence. The sight of her then. Black
shadow cutting through the bleached blondes. Three hundred
yards away. His phone beeped.

*My You. Just woke. Couldn't sleep w/out you. Missing your soft
kisses and your hardness. When can I call? Meg x x x*

My God. He should reply. Morna had made it to the school
gates, was looking around for him. Had spotted him. A hundred
yards away and trying to text Meg.

Am picking up kid now. Can't talk 4 hrs.

Delete.

Am @ school – Sean – would love u 2 meet him 1 day

Not '1 day'. Delete.

when u come to visit

No – 'visit' sounded too temporary.

when u come 2 stay with me.

Why did he feel Meg was watching him now? Morna was
fifty feet away and waving. He had to end it with Morna. Had
to send a text to Meg. He was typing then stopping, panicking
over what to type next.

'Hey, jet-lag guy.'

Morna's eyes smiling through her hair. Melancholy Morna.
Suddenly remembering the hickey on his neck, he pulled up
his collar to hide it.

'How wisit? Thought yee might never come back!' Her local
accent. She was leaning towards him, the shoulder squeeze.
They never kissed in front of the kids.

'How's yir back anyways, after the flight?'

'Fine, fine, yeah. How are you?'

His tone of voice had maybe set it off. Her gaze on his face.
He snapped the phone shut. She could read minds; he hoped
she would, then it would be done.

'Must uv been great, eh. Ye gotae the place I telt yee? CBGB.
The Ramones. Eh?'

'Yeah. No. I don't think so.'

The Ramones. This was how you lived in Edinburgh, through your CDs from cooler places and times. She had given him a list of streets to check out in New York – the Chelsea Hotel on 23rd, Leonard Cohen and that song about Janis Joplin he wrote there. They were all tourist spots now, Meg had explained. He'd lost Morna's list. Sean would be here in a minute.

'Goat sum bubbly. Welcome-home thingy. Ye gid for wir usual the moro?'

'Yeah, yeah. No. I mean . . . Look,' he said. Like he'd planned, but she was looking at him and he had his eyes hidden trying to find the next word. He no longer wanted to grow old with her.

'Look,' he said again. 'We need to –'

The school bell. The eyes of all the parents turning. Saved by the bell. A hundred parents holding their breath as if every day your child would not appear. She turned to look for Ian.

A second and they exploded from the front doors. Laughter and shrieks, school bags falling and gym shoes running. Two hundred spreading out virus-like. Sean knew he always sat on the hippo at the back and would find him. Morna's back to him, three feet away, this distance that was their secret. As the kids ran past and there was no sight of Sean or Ian, he felt this incredible need to reach out and hold her hand. You fool. Tell her with touch. You owe that to her at least.

'Sorry,' he said.

'Sorry for whit?'

'Look, tomorrow and the bubbly, I have these things I have to –'

'S'OK, s'cool,' she said without turning.

Her son in her arms then and the chat-chat of everything. 'Where's Sean?' he could have asked. But he sat and watched Morna lift her boy in her arms, kissing his head, trying to calm his excitement so she could understand all the new words bursting from him with the hope of finding meaning in her face. Mother and child.

'Bye then,' Morna said, 'Gies a wee call soon,' and she was

stepping away with Ian and she had never before said 'soon'.

A flash of what the aftermath would be without her. Ian was Sean's only friend. Handing over their kids at each other's doors a kind of torture she'd avoid. If he ended it with Morna he would be depriving his child of contact with other kids, and of Morna's music therapy, the cure for Sean's stutter.

'Morna! Wait. I . . . uh . . . need . . . t . . . to, ju . . . just . . .' and now Tom was the one stuttering, calling after her. The mind racing with many things to say and all of them impossible.

'Die . . . dying to have some time with you. Bubbly. Maybe day after tomorrow.'

She didn't turn round, her son bouncing beside her, her hand in his.

'Fabby. See you then,' she called back.

He was a coward. A stuttering coward. Meg's glance on him from across the globe. His first promise to her broken – end it with Morna. Not broken but postponed, and that was weaker.

Tom scanned past the passing children to locate Sean's familiar anorak on the fringes of a group of ten-year-olds, in their usual corner that was not playground because playing was for little kids and Sean wanted to be a grown-up. The kids were not arty like Ian, were more working class. This bothered Tom also. Sean had recently started trying to fit in with the masses. Sean no longer ran round the playground anxiously searching for his father as he had done in that year when Tom had moved out.

The little gang had their pocket computer games out and were in a huddle. Each seemed alone in his own pixelated world. Jumping over obstacles, blasting bad guys to pieces. Game Boy it was called. Sean had his own now, after a complicated discussion with the ex over the price to be paid for their child fitting in with global consumerism and the boys down the street. Sean had his Game Boy but was not in the central core. His mother would have seen it as Sean's unique and wonderful difference from others. But from where Tom was standing all he saw was a kid, alone, two feet away from this gang who thought he was a freak.

Minutes of this to endure before Sean came to him, eyes down, his embarrassed 'Hi' not a 'feared word' but one Sean could do because, as the child psychologist said, it was easier to say words that were habitual greetings and required little conscious reflection and which started on an outward breath.

Tom knew these things to be true because Tom, aged eight, had started stuttering, three months after his father had left.

Sean was now trying to show some shell-suited kid the score he'd got on his Game Boy. Touching the kid's arm, but the boy shrugged him off. Sean was trying to say something. A hundred feet away and Tom could feel his son's stutter in his own spine. The eyes rolling upwards to reach for breath. Then some kid, some fucking little Nike-trainered bastard, said something, and the other kids were laughing. Sean wasn't, they were laughing at Sean. Tom was on his feet, he was going to go down there right now. To grab the little proletarian piece of shit and teach him a few fucking things. But Sean had walked away, like his mother had taught him to do. Walking up towards the hippos. Tom tried to prepare himself.

'Hi.'

Sean had said Hi.

'Hey, kiddo. Howzit goin?'

Sean usually liked it when he did an American accent. Because Sean liked gangsta rap. Sean stared at his feet. A hug was out of the question. A pat on the head also. All Tom wanted was to hold his son and kiss his head and tell him everything would be OK and that these stupid fucking neds could burn in hell for all he cared, and their fucking dead-already parents too. Just you and me, my beautiful boy. But all Tom could say was 'Home' and 'Walk'. And he had to stop doing that. Truncating his sentences to accommodate Sean's stutter. Tom ruffled Sean's hair in a way he thought was acceptably laddish. Sean started towards the car park. Tom opened the car door for Sean and Sean had his Game Boy out again. This would be the way it was. The only sounds coming from Sean on the drive would be the squeaks and shrieks from the game. The ex would have a lot to say about that too. This was Tom's role in the upbringing of Sean now, silently defying and trying to undo all of the 'appropriate methodologies' and 'education plans' his ex had imposed.

Sean stood behind him as he unlocked his flat door. Tom could have fallen to his knees and told Sean of that one day last week when he'd called long distance from Fire Island – and had almost wept at hearing his son's voice.

Sean dragged his feet through Tom's flat, silently heading towards the PC.

'Missed you in New York, big fella.'

'Shooo. Shoe . . . sure . . . Y . . . yuhh . . . yooos, you suh, see, see . . .'

Tom was stuck there at the door. 'Sure, you see . . .' The way Sean could speak slightly better without eye contact. The way his son saw his flat as only a PC screen. The way his son could speak more easily when he was logged on to Windows.

Tom moved to Sean's side. Sean was struggling to speak again. Proximity, pressure, judgement, anticipation.

'See uh . . . see a . . . uh . . . ut . . . du . . . guh . . .'

To interrupt him with your guess. To see his self-blaming face when you guessed and still got it wrong.

'Uh gug, gro-ow, zeee.'

Let him finish all by himself. Don't pity, encourage.

'A gug a ground . . . zeee, zzzz, zuh . . . zeer . . . oh, zero?'

'Jesus. Ground Zero. Yeah. God!'

He was nervously filling the silence with anything, he must not do that.

'Just looks like a regular subterranean car park now. Naw, there was this . . . this photo on the railings . . . I mean from a distance, like how it was before. You know, the skyline, you look at the picture and see this thing that's not there. So yeah, basically, you're looking at nothing. I mean some clouds.'

'Cooo . . . coo . . . cool,' Sean said as AOL said WELCOME with that sexy female American voice. The shrug of Sean's shoulders told Tom that it was cool to say no more.

'So you wanna play computer games, that's cool. Got pizza for supper. OK?'

A nod and then Sean was typing at a speed which still amazed Tom. Online and cruising effortlessly the world of words.

So there was pizza to unwrap and put in the oven. He'd promised Meg he'd call or email later, tell her of his day. He wouldn't be able to till after Sean had had his supper and his mother came to pick him up. Tom had tried to play down Sean's stutter to Meg. He was not sure why.

As Tom turned on the gas he felt his eyes move by habit to the fridge. The Smirnoff inside. To just have one to help him get through this. Meg, my love. The frozen pizza in the oven and eight minutes till it was called food and he felt again that Meg was watching him. She won't see. Sean won't see. So easy – the one big shot hidden in a glass of vitamin-C-enriched apple juice.

Drink and you lose her.

Tom closed the oven door on the oven-ready pizza and set the timer and then was standing there in the doorway watching his son's back as he typed. Sean was eyes and fingers leaping through screens. A genius on the PC. He spent all of his time here on something called Second Life. An interactive world with two million inhabitants. It was supposed to be for over-eighteens but Tom didn't mind. The inhabitants came from Paris, Boston, Hong Kong, everywhere in fact. Tom had picked up a few facts over the last year. A virtual world, but still there was a currency. US dollars. There was some guy, the Internet said, who'd made a million trading in virtual property. People actually did this – took out second mortgages to buy pixelated homes. Sean was good at it, traded game cards and software, had a hundred dollars in a virtual account. Tom was sure Sean stuttered less when he was in Second Life.

An idea, something to do to keep himself from that sweet cold vodka, the hope that a surprise gesture might break the silence – Meg's present for Sean. He went through to the bedroom and his travel bag, still unpacked. Unzipped it. The CD, gift-wrapped in not entirely appropriate pink paper. She wouldn't tell him what the CD was. It was to be her surprise for him and his son.

'Hey, big guy. A present for you.'

'Cuh . . . cool, Cool!' Sean shouted back through. Yes, he definitely stuttered less when he shouted.

Tom was there with it in his hand, and Sean was turning back to him. Smiling now and eye contact.

'Well, you going to open it?'

Just a flash then as Sean tore the paper off – of one Xmas morning past or one birthday or many. Tom waiting for Sean to turn and look at him eye to eye. 'Actually, it's not from me, strictly speaking, I mean, but from my . . . my girlfriend, for you, she lives in Manhattan. You know, like Mum has a boyfriend, well, I've got a –'

'Uh . . . huh . . . so . . . so . . . wha . . . who?'

Tom looked down. It was the Cocteau Twins. Jesus Christ.

'S'c . . . coo . . . s'cool.'

Sean shrugged and smiled. 'Ta. Dah.'

But Tom was in shock as Sean set the CD down on the worktop and got back to the PC screen. Not at how quickly his son had resumed what he was doing before, but at the CD. What had Meg been thinking? The Cocteau Twins for a ten-year-old? Jesus, this was their secret music, not Sean's. Their song. The pizza smelt like it was ready or burning. Tom walked to the kitchen. Meg had meant well, but the gift was inappropriate. The entire album was experimental vocal noise, avant-garde, for serious adults, not kids, no words, nonsense words.

What the hell would he tell Meg on the phone after Sean was gone? That now he was back home he knew he could never leave his son to be with her. That she would have to move to Edinburgh. That within a month she'd find that everything he said was not music to her ears but banalities. Was it just an accident that she'd picked this album, or her way of telling him, already, that she knew? He was thinking of the vodka again. Damn it and there was that track on the album where the singer experimented with stuttered sounds. A-me . . . a-me . . . a-bah . . . a ba. Damn the Cocteau Twins.

The pizza out of the oven. Slightly charred. He got the plates. An hour to go till Sean's mother came to pick him up. And in that time the silence would grow between him and his son. Tom checked his watch to find out how long it would be till he could be alone again, mulling over what the hell Meg had meant by the gift. An hour with no drink to calm him.

Call

'**D**id Sean like his present?'
    [Silence.]
    'Yeah . . . yeah . . . He loves it, it's fine.'
    'My You, you sound . . . Are you OK . . . Tom?'
    'I'm fine. Tell me things, anything. Like what you had for breakfast, like what you're wearing. Where are you exactly?'
    'I'm in the bathroom on the extension.'
    'That makes me sad.'
    'I miss you in my bathroom.'
    'Are you brushing your teeth?'
    'Uh?'
    'Meg, you brushing your teeth? Hello. What's that noise. Hello?'
    'Hi, I'm back.'
    'What were you doing?'
    'Flossing.'
    'Fuck, you were flossing.'
    'Just had lunch. I floss. It's so American. I hate that about myself. Sorry.'
    'Sweetheart. I want you to floss with me.'
    'I know, my love. You sure you're OK?'
    'I'm OK, it's hard being here, I just want to . . . Tell me about your day. Your writing, how's it going?'
    'I'm sick of it already.'
    'I love that.'
    'What?'
    'The way you say "already" – so New York already.'
    'My You.'
    [Silence.]
    'What do we say, Tom? I feel like a teenager on a first date.'
    'I dunno already.'

[Laughter.]

'Your funny accents, they're better than mine. You sound like a gangster from Queens already.'

'*Hey, what can I do?*'

'You see. You make me laugh.'

[Silence.]

'Have you booked your flight yet?'

'I'm looking – online. Seven weeks' time. Yes, I'm coming.'

'I want to make you come.'

[Laughter.]

'I want you to make me come.'

[Silence.]

'You're here right now. In my bed. I'm in my bed, Meg.'

'I want to be in your bed.'

'Look at you. Look at you. Your soft skin. You know what I'm doing?'

'Tell me.'

'I'm running my hand from your pelvis, to your waist, so beautiful, the slope.'

'Tell me.'

'Shh, now just listen to my hand.'

'You're touching me.'

'My hands are following your curves, like you're leading me there – you're warm, you're wet.'

'I want you to touch me there.'

'You're touching yourself, aren't you? You're lifting your fingers to my mouth. I'm tasting you as I kiss your fingers.'

'I am, yes, tell me what to do.'

'I'm in bed, in my bed. Say bed to me.'

'Bed.'

'Aw, baby, I want to be in your bed. Go to your bed.'

'OK.'

'What was that noise?'

[Silence.]

I was just – It was the extension. We're in my bed now.'

'A beep?'

'I got a text.'

'Mystery caller – this late. Sorry, early.'

'My agent. Josh. You met him. It's done now, but he's still, you know, they don't want to let me go. Aw, You, where were we?

'I'm touching you. I'm hard. You want to hear how hard I am. Hear that? I'm slapping it against my gut. Here, I'll put the phone down there . . . you hear that?'

'My God!'

'You like that? I'm thinking of your face, touching myself. [Pause.] Hey, can you email me all the photos? The ones I took on your phone. I'd like to look at your face now in my bed. Sorry. So . . . is your pussy wet?'

'So wet, you're making me wet. Tell me what you're doing to me.'

'You're in my bedroom, you're leaning out the window. Your pretty Westwood dress on, nothing else, hiked up over your ass. You're looking out the window at all the other windows out there, there's maybe fifty.'

'Fifty?'

'Tenements. Whole streets, just one building and lots of flats. Like brownstones. Like Brooklyn. You're leaning out the window, sticking your bare ass out at me, I come up behind and pull the curtains round myself so no one can see me.'

'Aw. There's other people?'

'Lots, in their windows, you're looking into their flats and they can see your face but they can't see me. I'm behind the curtains, rubbing my hard cock against your sweet puss.'

'Are we really, for real, having phone sex?'

'Guess so, phone foreplay anyway. I have my dick in my hand. How about you? You touching yourself?'

'Might be. [Laughter.] I've never done this before. Phone sex, Jesus.'

'I know, I know, but you should see my dick, seriously, I've grown an inch since the airport. It must have been the hormones in the in-flight salmon à la king.'

[Laughter.]

'You are my king, my Scottish king.'

'Meg, my You, shh, listen. My sweet wet love. I'm whispering now, can you hear me?'

'Aha.'

'I'm holding your hips. You have to be quiet. So quiet. You can't make a sound cos they'll hear you out in the street, and you have to keep your eyes open, so anyone who looks up'll just think you're looking out my window, and you can't move your hips, got to stand firm so no one can see the thrusts, and I'm going inside you really slow, watching my cock – in and out – your lips stretching, sucking in my dick.'

'God, I'm so wet, so wet.'

'You're so wet and I'm slowly taking my cock out and slapping it against your ass and pulling your cheeks apart, taking all that juice and smearing it over my dick.'

'Aw aw, that's good. You going to . . .'

'I'm going to fuck your tight little ass.'

'Aw, I'm gonna, if you do . . . I swear I'm gonna . . .'

'That's right. I'm putting your cock in my tight little – [Laughter.] Shit!'

'What?'

'I said . . . got mixed up . . . Jesus fucking Christ . . . I said your cock!'

'Don't stop.'

[Laughter.]

'I'm sorry, babe. I just got a bit lost there for a second. Got us both mixed up.'

'It's OK.'

'Kind of lost it now. Just seeing you with a cock! [Laughter.] Shit. Don't know why it's so funny. Sorry, I was jerking off, and staring at my vacuum cleaner and I said "My ass".'

'It's OK.'

'Hell hath no fury like a woman scorned, huh?'

'No, it's fine.'

'What's that noise?'

'I was just uh . . . getting out of bed, it was my cell again. Another text.'

'I'm sorry, baby, I wanted to make you come.'

'Make me laugh again. Tell me something else in Scottish.'

'It's a braw bricht moonlicht nicht the nicht.'

'You already taught me that one.'

'OK. OK – Ahava stoater o' a boner.'

'What? [Laughter.] What the hell was that?'

'An impressive erection.'

[Laughter.]

'A boner, right, right. I love your boner.'

'I said you when I meant me.'

'I wish we could swap. You be me and me you.'

'We could meet halfway.'

'A little island in the middle of the ocean.'

'Yeah, made of driftwood and sardine cans – we could grow bananas and condom trees, live off whatever washes ashore.'

[Laughter.]

'My Meg. So how's your writing?'

[Silence.]

'I can't. I just wish I'd taped everything you said when you were here. Our talks. If I could just . . . I dunno. You're the one with the talent. Hey, how's work?'

'Going back tomorrow.'

'You should direct films again. Seriously, you have so much talent.'

[Silence.]

'I really don't want to talk about work. OK?'

'OK, but I was just saying –'

'Aw, babe, I'm so sorry I didn't make you come. You want me to try again? I could get hard, we could try again.'

'No. It's OK. Hey, d'you tell Morna yet?'

[Silence.]

'How'd she take the news?'

'Yeah, I told her. Well, I texted.'

'You texted?'

[Silence.]

'What is it, Meg?'

'Well, don't you think – I mean, you were with her so long. Wouldn't it have been better face to face. I mean, dumping her by text.'

'She knows, there's no need for –'

'But a year, I mean. [Silence.] I just think you should tell her face to face. Will you do that? Not that I'm pushing you.'

'OK, I'll do that.'

'If you ever did that to me . . .'

'Meg, are we having our first fight? [Silence.] I'm sorry I didn't make you come.'

'By text, Jesus!'

'We're not fighting.'

'You send me a text, you go silent on me – I'll draw up the worst ten scenarios . . .'

'You are my one, my You. It's done, she knows.'

[Silence.]

'OK, I'm sorry, I'm just hormonal. I guess. I think I'm getting my period. That's good news, I suppose.'

'Great news.'

'Cos we weren't exactly safe. Last thing we need is . . .'

[Silence.]

'Meg, you OK?'

'I need to go work now, still got a few things to clear up on this stupid script. Gotta go.'

'I love you.'

'Me too, sorry. Bye, my You, love you too.'

Journal

July 13

A week now since he left and we've been on the phone every day. Sometimes twice. Sometimes he sends texts in the middle of the night. I've turned off my ringer so he won't wake me. Sent him instructions about the hours and my schedule. Will he ever get it right? Makes me laugh. I've taken to copying them down.

> *How u r perfect to me. How have I found u? Been working my butt off 2 try to keep strong 4 the battle ahead. WE shall overcome and rule this world of crap with fists of iron. Pologies – 4 mixed metaphors!! X*

> *Meg. Couldn't sleep. Erection issues! Want to kiss those lips, pry them open with my tongue and hide inside. Send photos. Goodnight, sweet princess. Your ugly toad. X*

> *Send me those pics. I get like this – moody – needy. Time for my pyjama party of one. You are a TOTAL babe dude. Dude-ess??? Dunno. Happy writing! Nitey nitey xxx*

One thirty and I've just attempted lunch. An Arugula salad with lettuce from the garden, saved from what's left. Couldn't face it though. Stood there staring at it like a fool. The thought of it in my mouth making me ill. I know this from before. I could call it love sickness, but I know it's more. The simplest things are a task now. I start one thing then it seems pointless and I stop short. It's almost as if my body's telling me that I'm not built to be alone. So many years I've been postponing exactly this confrontation with myself. It is the old fear again. Reread an old journal. Summer 1992. Michael. London.

Five days he's been gone now. Five days and three hours forty-five minutes. I know I'm being ridiculous. I know when he's coming back. Thursday at five. Tried to write for a bit today but kept thinking of him. Every sentence I tried seemed false. I know I'm being weak. I fill up all my time with him because I'm afraid of being alone. It is so much easier to soak him into my every pore, minute by minute, day by day. So much easier than to have one second alone staring at the empty page. I'm so confused. When he's here I get these moments when I want to scream at him – to have some space from him, time to write in my journal, to try to write my stories – but when he's away I am a blank. I am starting to resent him and I hate that. I will have to hide this journal from him too. I need him to stay away so I can find some semblance of self but when he is gone I am nothing. I am so weak.

Have to write for four hours today at least. Things with Tom are different from before, from others. Reread last file. 'Love at first sight'. Michael was classic swept-off-feet. Tom the opposite. Try to learn from it. Ten points already written.

New File: Day One. Version 2

NOTE. I got it wrong before. The first thing he said. I think it was after the bubbly not before.

RECAP. Film party. No words at first. He'd indicated the bar and his empty glass and mine. I'd nodded yes and said bubbly please and he had made his way through the back of the crowd to the bar but it was three-deep and the waitresses were ignoring him. He looked back and smiled. There was a crate of Veuve beneath the table. No one was watching. He reached down and pulled out a bottle. His face said naughty. His face said, you and me, go now. He was making a show of secretly hiding it inside his bad jacket. Something about him said he'd done this before. (He's from Europe. They drink too much.) Then he said his line about getting the fuck out of there.

Possible reasons why I went with him:

8. *Spontaneity. A man surprises you with something out of the blue.* YES. At that party full of so much predictable pretension. A surprise to be in the company of a petty thief.

And I'd let him lead me away. Was my hand in his? Not sure. Left with him – not from any real desire or curiosity but perhaps just because he was hiding the bottle under his jacket and if he didn't leave then he would get caught and since I was beside him then by association I too would be guilty. (Stupid American sense of ethics.) And he was doing such a terrible job of hiding it – eyes looking around the room, lowered voice, like a joke, playing some street bum or Bogart or Bukowski. Note: The next thing he said was something with a fake American accent: 'Let's quit dis joint and really make it.'

9. *Curiosity about difference.* YES, his weird play-accent was different, but in the past men with funny voices have always signified danger. NB Michael.

We left the party, walked the deserted boards of the five-star ballroom to the doors. The next thing he said: 'Got something to show you.' I recall he apologized – such a clichéd thing to say. Yes, at some point in the corridor, my hand was in his.

10. *Women fall for men that make them laugh.* YES. He had done that. But it's another cliché – like only someone else could make you come (that way they do so rarely) – NB Reich. Fromm – the dissolution of self in laughter and orgasm.

OK, maybe I hadn't laughed in a while. (It's not something you do alone.) A sense of being naughty. Running away with a stolen bottle. Were we running? Was I even laughing at that point? No. He was just fascinating – diverting is a better word, but slightly derogatory. The corridor. Generic paper borders – fake textured wallpaper. Possibly blues and violets(?). Not my first time there in the Marriott or in the Marriott with a man. He was bouncing along in front of me, joking with his phoney American accent. I recall wondering what his real accent was. Wondering if he was, as they say in Scotland, 'taking the piss'.

'So what's a dame like you doin' in a joint like dis?'

Three things I've never found attractive in men: 1. Walking ahead of a woman. 2. Talking in accents that they can't do properly. 3. Manic chat to fill the silences.

He had stopped at a corner. Lost (all the corridors are the same). I'd decided to give him another thirty seconds.

Elevator.

'Floor four . . . we need five.' That was when I heard his Scottish accent. Thought at first it might be Irish. Memory of him squeezing my hand. And of two questions then I'd been meaning to ask: 1. Where are you taking me? 2. Why are you holding my hand? Maybe 3. Where are you from anyway? 4. Actually, do you do this often – abduct total strangers from parties you're not supposed to be at?

I recall his eyes, tired-looking, but something childlike, playful. His goatee beard. Always a signifier of either trying to look arty or hiding a weak chin. Or both.

He'd pushed the button. Waiting for the elevator. Assessing him. Curious. I figured if he tried to force a move on me I could handle myself. Being the same height. Him being slightly overweight. My self-defence classes.

11. *Women fall for men who are exotic.* Yes, the Scottish thing was a challenge having had – list them: A six-foot-five German, a muscular Greek, a skinny French indie geek, a Californian surf guy with tats, corporate gym junkies – plural.

Waiting for the elevator. Watching him. He seemed to lose confidence.

'Sorry,' he'd said. He'd let go of my hand. He said:

'You probably thought I was taking you to my room. Nope. You asked what I'm doing here. Easier just to show you. Floor five. You OK with that?'

If that is right then I must have asked him who he was, etc. No memory of having done so.

12. *Women are drawn to men who are passionate, who sweep them off their feet.* It wasn't sweeping or passionate. More like a manic kind of dragging, but I recall not feeling alarmed. No memory of the elevator. Other movie scenes – people awkward in elevators – standing apart looking at each other as the numbers went up – throwing themselves at each other, tearing at clothes. No memory. There may have been talk. Definitely not holding hands. We hit floor five.

'Nothing glamorous,' he said. 'I'm not a film director or anything like that.'

An affinity with that. It didn't seem like an admission of failure. His smile as he told me all that he wasn't.

Empty corridors. Mostly conference suites, and I let him take my hand again. He stopped at a double door, the lights were off inside. (Another thought/fear. Not convinced by the flow from one to the other then back.) Describe. Floor five Marriott. Sign on door. A4 page. Blu-tack. CALEDONIAN ENTERPRISE CONVENTION. He threw open the doors dramatically. Big empty space, banners in darkness. I'd asked him something then, not wanting to enter a darkened room.

'So are you a cultural representative or a –'

'AV technician,' he said, 'cameraman, director, editor, grunt, switch flicker and "creative". Really something, isn't it?'

The room empty, black. He was laughing. Not the evil cackle of a bad guy. He stepped inside. His footsteps echoing round the empty hall.

He must have felt an explanation due, from my stance just on the very edge of the doorway. My eyes adjusting. A passing flash that there were others in there, men, waiting to abuse me. My usual paranoia.

Can't remember. The words that follow are just the gist of his.

'As you can see no one's here cos the event clashed with three other more glamorous ones, the Tribeca Film Festival, some fashion thing and a bigger thing run by the Finnish government with an all-night free bar, so all the representatives of Scottish industry and government have headed over there.'

His laughter I do recall with clarity. Refreshingly different. So un-American. Not laughing at others but at himself. I said something vague, to ask for explanation, typical unfinished question like:

'Wait, sorry, you're saying that –'

'Forty Scottish VIPs flown over at great expense to sell Scotland to the world and all they did was talk to people that they sat across desks from back home in Edinburgh. No one showed up. No Americans. They courted America's biggest tycoon last year. Big news story: he was going to invest a billion in Scotland, build the greatest outdoor leisure complex in the world, but some tiny local council fucked him about. Scotland's a joke now. Massive capital flight. I'm amazed we had the audacity to even show our faces here after that. It was like

turning up in party costumes – for a funeral. I wasn't the first
to leave.'

Funny, was he for real?

'Are you sure we should be here?' I'd asked. I'd stepped in
then, curiosity maybe, a sense that he was harmless. The double
doors shut behind me but it was OK. Three huge video-projector
screens empty on the far wall. Some kind of scaffolding holding
up banners. Thirty tables with partitions, covered in posters
and publicity brochures. Video projectors on stands.

It was hard not to laugh when he explained.

'They flew me all the way over here to make sure the plugs
fitted the DVD players. Things like that. There was a rumour
that they were different in the US which turned out to be true.
Here.' He passed me the bubbly. 'Been here a week already,
got seven days more. Supposed to be writing an assessment of
the convention. As you can see, it's off to a great start.'

I'd told him it seemed like a very bad sad joke. So hard to
believe even now.

'Yeah, I know, the Scots are good at tragic irony.'

OK, OK. 13. *Women fall for men with a dry wit.* The cleverness in their choice of words that conceals and at the same time
reveals the power of their contempt for the world.

He went behind a table, flicked a switch. He took the bubbly
from me, cleared a space on a table full of publicity brochures
with pictures of lochs and castles, pushed them to the side,
patted the table beside him for me to sit. I stood and watched
him as the bubbly spilled everywhere and he took the first slug.
He passed it to me. That had been the sequence of events.

The strangest thing was he'd been speaking to me like he
already knew me. Even stranger was that I felt the same. His
self-deprecating demeanour felt already comfortable, like a night
stoned with grad-school friends. This sense that he needed
someone to do this with – a total stranger. Maybe I'd looked
distant at the party, and he'd sensed somehow that we both had
this in common.

Funny, 'we' and 'both', to use such words now. I trusted him,
somehow, to show me his work that he so denigrated. To laugh
with him.

God. Remembering it now. My love, did I fall for you then?

His fingers on the remote control. The three screens burst into light and sound. Synthesisers, bagpipes, lochs and castles.

'Look upon his works ye mighty and despair.' He shouted over the noise, motioning at the screens. Passed me back the Veuve. He rested against me as we stared at the screens. Glaring light – rivers and ancient bridges and Edwardian and Victorian buildings and empty moorlands and Stone Age dwellings. A seagull flying overhead.

'Wait for it.' He held his finger in the air. The music rose to a crescendo, peaked, then hit a plateau.

'"Scotland,"' he said, perfectly in time with the voice-over. Lip-syncing.

'"Land of History, rich with the past . . ."'

'Wait, wait,' he said. 'The next line is a revelation.'

And I still wasn't sure if he was being ironic.

'"Scotland, land of opportunity, focused forever on the future."'

I could have laughed – so corny. But he got there first.

'Stole that line from a corporate promo for antivirus software.'

And I was thinking – is he really smart? Or really dumb? Is he proud of this? Trying not to laugh. God, it was so kitsch. I had to ask.

'Wait, so you . . . you wrote this?'

And he said yup – devised, directed, shot and edited it all for about seven thousand sterling and came over to here to check the plug sockets. He wanted to use The Smiths on the soundtrack but they cost too much and he wasn't clever or subversive enough, yet, to manage to squeeze that past the sponsors. The track he'd wanted was 'The Joke Isn't Funny Any More'. That was why it was the usual – synthesisers and bagpipes.

14. *Women fall for men who love The Smiths.*

I was laughing. Couldn't help it. I am such a geek and love the Smiths and I've never been able to share that with anyone before. Well, not since I was twenty or so. Did he even find me attractive? Didn't he know that this whole designer-label dressing-up thing wasn't me at all? That I spend most of my life in T-shirt and slippers?

15. *Women fall for men who can laugh at themselves.* We get taught this in high school – to never laugh at those more unfortunate than ourselves. His smile told me it was OK to laugh. There was no anger in that laugh. He carried his failure with grace. I recall being touched by that. So un-masculine, so un-American. I passed back the bubbly. Watching him then.

'We're all like this in Scotland,' he said. 'Shit, that's the one thing we missed in the presentation.'

'What?'

'A sense of humour. Yeah, yeah exactly, but I guess that's kind of funny too. Very Scottish to have forgotten that.'

Laughing out loud together. The music rose to another crescendo as rather inappropriate footage came on of signs saying Enterprise Park with shots of empty warehouses. He hit the remote and the sound level fell. A conversation then.

'So, you've directed other things?'

'I have . . . I used to, but like I say . . .'

'No, but what, I mean, they were what? Features, documentaries?'

'Yeah, well, shorts mostly, all very low budget. Won an award for one. They said it was Godardesque. Cannes, it came to nothing.'

16. *A woman is drawn to a man who is shorn of ambition.* Who has failed and his acceptance of his failure sets him apart from all of the other men who drag you after them as they chase success. A man who has failed and knows he has failed has quiet dignity. He can be trusted.

'Really, so what was it called . . . your short?'

I asked him something like that. He told me Shhh. There was someone coming.

Security man at the door. And I felt like some dumb teenager on a first date hiding from the grown-ups. He said something to the guy. Just checking the equipment, something like that.

17. *A woman falls for a man who brings back the sense of rebelliousness that she thought she'd lost.* Possibly. It was his hand in mine again, no resistance then, because I had to know. Him

pulling me out through the doors. Me, then, hiding the bubbly. I recall giggling. He stopped beside the elevator. Pushed the down button.

'Well, it's been charming,' he said. 'Thanks for witnessing my contribution to the collapse of Western civilisation . . . Sorry, I don't think I caught your name.'

The elevator door opened. He had said, in passing, that his room was on the same floor. He was motioning for me to get in. So it was goodbye.

18. *A woman is drawn to a man at exactly the point that the encounter announces itself as over.*

'Why don't you come back to the party?' I asked.

'I think not. I could do with another drink, but it's not my scene.'

'We could go to the bar downstairs.'

'Twenty dollars a shot, no thanks. I like to drink, a lot. I can get comatose for twenty bucks if I pick the right places.'

19. *A woman is touched by a man's pain.* His honesty in letting you see his weakness. I was inside the elevator. He outside. The doors closing: film-like moment of departure. Light sensors, my foot in the doorway. The doors opening again. That thing I said. It was me not him. (So unlike me.)

'OK, I'll come to your room on one condition.'

Maybe not that – he freaked.

'Sorry, did I even invite you?'

And I felt a little like I was another one of the clichés. The desperate woman who fucks strangers. Scenarios running through my head when he said, basically, that he was too drunk to even attempt to try and fuck me.

20. *Women are drawn to men who say, 'I'm not going to fuck you.'* Who admit to failure in advance. The next thing he said had me laughing, it was maybe how sincere he seemed. Absurdist British humour. 1970s. Monty Python (?)

'It's going to be an hour of cunnilingus at best. I know, I know, I'm sorry. I mean till I fall asleep, and by the way, I also snore. You may find me snoring between your legs before the deal is done.'

21. *Women are drawn to men who promise an hour of cunnilingus.*

'What was your one condition?' he asked, my still foot in the elevator door.

'My what?'

'You said you'd come to my room on one condition, but then you said you weren't going to fuck me.'

The elevator door trying to close then shooting back open again.

'No, *you* said, "I'm not going to fuck you".'

'It's fine, me, you, it's all the same. No one will be fucking anyone. That cool?'

'No, I didn't say that.'

'So you might?'

'Might what?'

I was standing there and we were arguing about who was me and who was you, and who was not going to fuck the other. For real.

'I have no idea who said what. Sorry, I'm a very drunk Scottish man and your country terrifies me.'

22. *American women fall for European men because they know so much more about America than we do.* They seem to hate it but are at the same time drawn to it. (NB So many friends going off on their midlife-crisis trip to find a European man. I've done the European man thing before.)

'You know, the thing is, just before you go,' he said, 'your eyes are very dark and deep and full of questions.'

23. *A woman falls for a man because it is the stupidest thing she can do.* Because on that night she needs to be gloriously wilfully dumb and escape the structures of control that make her who she is. A woman falls for a European man because America is shallow and Europe has depth. And no matter how powerful America is it always asks Europe to justify it to itself.

'Bye.' The door started sliding shut again.

24. *A woman says Yes because he says Bye.*

I put my hand in the closing doors and they opened again. I said:

'You're very funny.'

'And you are very, very, very . . .'

His lips moving as he repeated those words. Very what?

25. *A woman falls for a man because he has started to tell her
something about herself but will not finish the sentence.* And she
hopes that in or after coitus he will finish that sentence.

'Very what?' I asked again.

26. *A woman needs to be held for a night.* No matter who he
is and she knows at the same time that he has no hold on her.
That she will never see him again. Perhaps that's why she agrees.
Note: This is all wrong. Feminist nonsense. Women like cuddles,
men penetration. Such a cliché. Be honest.

New File: Notes

Sad. It makes me sad on reading over. Twenty-six points and
personal rules and none of them adds up to anything true. The
narrative breaks down. Too many voices telling me to deny
what happened. And it was nothing. Nothing really. Feel stupid
now. Flashes of stilted silences – us both talking at the same
time. Fumbled touches and undressings and more bubbly. We'd
both been so awkward and joking about how awkward we were.
He said maybe I should go. I cannot recall either a decision or
an impulse. He had trouble sustaining an erection. He blamed
the bubbly and his smoking and the stress of this and that.
Joking that his cock would awake with a vengeance at 6 a.m.,
but that all he needed now was a hug. These words foreign to
me. Cock so vulgar, hug so effeminate.

Not sure if I was fully awake. We'd been lying like spoons.
A sense that he was inside me. Slow gentle movement. My usual
panic over condoms and he muttered, yes, of course, shh. So
gentle, sleepy. It went on for hours, it seemed, kisses, many
sleepy kisses. No finality, no need to push it to its end. A plateau.
Waking, sleeping, waking to feel him still inside me.

I woke around five. He'd fallen asleep on top of me. He'd
been snoring. I recall looking at his body. His flabby gut, his
socks, still on, his greying temples. Trying to work out how he
fitted with this half-memory of our hours of lovemaking. Trying
to equate it with what I knew of dating and hotels – something
functional, transactional, to be got over quickly so I could be
alone again. The TV was still on, on mute. He'd played with
the remote for a bit before he slept and complained that in

America too much choice gave us no choice at all. Some repeat of Larry Clark or something. My leg was cramping under his shoulder. His head was in my lap, he was snoring. I was lying half upright, half awake. It was maybe the TV or the film party but I was thinking about American men – how they are brash, and well groomed and worked-out and forever positive in conversation and outlook. And here was this snoring vulgar overweight cynic who had made such gentle love to me for hours as if we were married already. Not concerned with showing off – with performance. (How strange that these negative qualities somehow seemed strong to me.) Maybe I'm imposing interpretations, post-fact, maybe it wasn't that moment, but I got a sense, still have it, that there was something about his life that was lacking in mine. I got up because of the cramp in my leg, and remember thinking that I could just put my shoes on and go. The view of the hotel room. The view from the window, the wide-shot skyline that no longer impresses me. The bed and him lying there so small, hugging the duvet, still only half undressed. I felt, and this seems strange now, that if I left there would be something about myself that I'd walked away from. That I needed to be more awake next time we made love. Next time – I told myself, the first time in so long I had said those words. Next time. I took off his socks and climbed back into his bed.

I-Com

'Hi ho, hi ho, it's off to work we go!' A week dry, of drifting into work for an hour or two, postponing the inevitable nine-to-five with his many excuses. Meg's hickey now just a shadow. The week nearly up and now the necessity of attending the 'Team Meeting' in the 'Creative Suite'. Somehow, he was feeling chirpy. He'd managed to resist the temptation waiting for him in the bottle. He'd kept Meg laughing all week on the phone. And maybe that was the way to survive this. To laugh at everything. Yup, 'Fabby dooby.' 'Sure thingy.' This laughable office space like any other in Leith Enterprise Zone. The high ceilings with 'modern variations' on the theme of Victoriana. The walls decorated at great expense with scumbling in pinks and greys which must have been meant to resemble marble. The predictably oppressive-looking corporate veneered teakstyle table which was actually too big for the room and made it difficult to get in and out of the pompously plush leather seats that made fart noises when you sat on them. The iMac video projector and screen, the touch-pad remote that controlled the blinds and the air conditioner also, which no one could operate and did actually have a panic button, which had had to be disabled after too many accidental pressings. That and the passion-fruit-flavoured bottled authentic Scottish sparkling mineral water and the team of jargon-junkies dressed for their creative meeting. A film set, thought Tom, and the characters in this comedy are:

McGregor: his boss and CEO of I-Com Communications, a company of fewer than five employees which nonetheless needed to have a CEO. Who insisted everyone call him Terry. Buzzwords were Londoner, secret drinker, business-card fetishist, third-time divorcee, late forties, cheap aftershave, nineties Armani, failed in the big city and moved on to pick the smallest pond he could find to be a big fish in.

Stephanie: McGregor's secretary, personal assistant and production manager for all of I-Com's output. Buzzwords: McGregor's mistress, vengeful bitch, petty bourgeois, self-help addict, corporate-speak devotee, 'fur coat and nae knickers'. She was in fact someone who had aspired all of her life to work in corporate communications and hated anyone, namely Tom, who had any ambitions beyond the event horizon of her world view from halfway up the corporate ladder.

And the meek little woman called Debbie who did the accounts and planned the video shoots, the schedules, who in fact did most of the logistical work, who had a furry gonk by her PC and a picture of her two kids. Divorcee also. Pendulous breasts and a chocolate habit. Tom had never been able to meet her eye. Or her his. He sensed that she harboured some secret, albeit typical office-type attraction towards him. McGregor had joked that, one day, he'd found her on an online dating website.

Yes, yes, all the usual, but now they were waiting for the client.

Laughable, really, that this was what corporate communications had become. A decade ago and there were three vast companies that did all the stuff in Scotland, all the banks and quangos. Forty staff each and two floors of editing machines. High-end graphics, all done in-house. But then the innovations in technology came. I-movie. You could shoot hand-held and edit on your own Mac and the corporate clones would be none the wiser. TV had been the same. News programme shot and edited by kids straight out of college. About '94, the corporate video business, the safest haven for the failed film-maker, home of the comfortably mediocre, had collapsed. Everything was outsourced now – research, post-production, graphics – with the poor suckers who had bought all that hardware, all those editing suites, undercutting each other and even themselves just to get the next contract. This was how I-Com made its profits. Only four key staff members. The big three in-house companies had gone down with over two hundred redundancies. I-Com was one of the few hi-tech survivors. Was, in fact, with this proposed new contract, potentially number one.

The Client: the name had been mentioned but had been infinitely forgettable during the handshakes and the squeezing into the leather seats, and the guy had actually been intimidated enough by the decor to have made a joke about the fart noises that leather seats could make. Tom would have to wait for someone else to say his name again. Stephanie. She always said people's names at the start of sentences, having no doubt read about such strategies in one of her many How-to-Get-Ahead-in-Business manuals. Buzzwords for client: monosyllabic, working-class male elevated well above station, amateur jargon user, humourless, fifty, football supporter, ashamed of his local accent, trying to hide it with this painfully forced BBC voice, cracker of vulgar jokes.

'So, in short, to recap,' McGregor announced, 'Caledonian Enterprise Week in New York was a great success. Wasn't it, team?' He always said Team when he meant Tom, asking Tom to back up his unfounded hype.

'Very . . . powerful, great visibility,' said Stephanie, and already she'd started taking shorthand notes of everything she was saying. Oh boy, this was a blast.

'Not the attendance we would have wanted, but it's clear our message was clear. Selling Scotland to the world. Very powerful.'

Truth: no one had turned up in New York. The world wasn't buying. Thankfully, the company had four contracts from quasi-autonomous non-governmental organisations that would keep him in employment over the next year. The New Caring Face of the NHS, Easterhouse Enterprise Zone . . . I-Com made corporate videos but there were no corporations left in Scotland. Four hi-tech multinationals had pulled out in the last six months. The tycoon debacle had ensured a decade or more of capital flight. All that was left was the manufacturing of shortbread, whisky and tartan bunnets. Or little start-up initiatives for the junkies in the schemes who needed a hundred quid to get clean and have the government subsidise the learning of how to type up their CVs.

Tom had to resist the giggles. This whole scene could be survived if he thought of it as Mel Brooks. Or some film adaptation of Kafka's *The Trial* perhaps. And . . . action!

[MCGREGOR]
So, moving on. The proposal in front of us.
'Edinburgh, City of . . .'

McGregor swilled the word round his mouth like a good
malt, like he'd probably done more than a few times at lunch
already today with the real thing.

[MCGREGOR]
Let's 'brainstorm'. What does our 'Creative'
think?

And that meant Tom. A brainstorm in a teacup, he thought,
and then the other sardonic thought that would be hilarious with
Meg on the phone later, but not here. That it was incredible,
unpardonable, that the Scottish Executive had already embarked
on a million-pound worldwide campaign to promote Edinburgh
without having first come up with a slogan. Of course, this wasn't
really promotion. Everything was done in reverse in Scotland.
You jetted lots of bureaucrats and local celebrities round the world
to meet the biggest tycoons and then, after you had let them
down with false promises, you made a DVD, to prove to the
taxpayer that their hard-earned pennies had not been wasted. You
came up with an advertising concept after the £40,000 worth of
sushi dinners and taxis and five-star hotel-room fumblings with
PAs in New York, Sydney and Berlin. Tom tried to recap, he
hoped that his silence had not been too long. He was allowed to
do that, being the 'Creative'. He knew how to look like he was
thinking.

[STEPHANIE]
I thought, Edinburgh, City of . . . Culture

The client nodded.

[TOM]
Naw, Glasgow 1990.

[STEPHANIE]
City of Discovery.

[TOM]
Dundee, I'm afraid. Still.

[STEPHANIE]
City of Festivals.

[TOM]
London, Liverpool and Bath 2004.

The look Stephanie gave him. Eyes on his neck, no doubt judging the last traces of Meg's hickey. OK, he couldn't just shoot down everything. Think fast.

[TOM]
Look, Edinburgh is the capital city right? We want to attract capital. A play on words. Edinburgh, Capital City – City of Capital.

The client nodded, hummed, drank some passion-fruit-flavoured water.

[MCGREGOR]
Capital of Capital.

Right, thought Tom – all in capital letters.

[STEPHANIE]
European Capital of Capital.

Of course Stephanie had to add something, but Edinburgh was not the capital of Europe. OK, his one good idea was already wasted. It would be the thesaurus again. City of opportunity, nope – already five avenues of opportunity in the UK. That last one he'd passed by a month ago, the concrete wasteland between Nitshill and Darnley. Edinburgh, City of

Love, of Passion. Of Passion-Fruit-flavoured water. A sudden flash of Meg, prostrate before him, ass in the air. McGregor's voice brought him back.

[MCGREGOR]
I love the European bit. European City of . . .

But of course they were just adding another word at the start of this impossible sentence, and it wasn't helping. City of millionaires on every street. City of eternal hope and promise. Like you just completed the sentence and reality would follow.

[STEPHANIE]
And of course we can't rule out the possibility
of advance sponsorship.

[CLIENT]
Ideally. Really, aye.

[TOM]
Sorry, you mean, like what? Like City of Coca-
Cola, City of Nike?

McGregor shook his head and the client laughed and Tom was off.

[TOM]
This city was brought to you by the makers
of . . .

[CLIENT]
Aye, that's a good one, eh. If only, eh.

Stephanie's eyebrowless brows frowning at him. Why did she do that, pluck her eyebrows then draw them on again? Perhaps they had originally met in the middle. McGregor was frowning at him too. OK, he'd gone too far. But the client was still laughing.

[CLIENT]
City of Irn-Bru, of Bell's Whisky, eh?

[TOM]
Of Tennent's lager and a Grouse chaser. Two
sponsors!

And the guy was in hysterics and maybe he wasn't so bad,
Tom thought. Working-class guy, no doubt knew what a pile
of impossible shite this all was, knew how to have a laugh at it
all while the government paid for the consultation. Still.
McGregor cleared his throat.

[MCGREGOR]
So we agree. The fundamental concept is sound.
'City of . . .'

And he drew his hands through the air like he was projecting
a banner across the sky.

[MCGREGOR]
Billboards, TV adverts, messages on the
motorway. Street signs.

[STEPHANIE]
On the Internet.

[CLIENT]
Aye, aye.

Tom just sat there and observed it all. Of course, this was
the purpose of the meeting. To get the poor mug to sign up
for this huge campaign without, as yet, a slogan. This consultation had already cost the taxpayer five thousand pounds and
McGregor would stretch it out for another ten or fifteen. These
people, my God, you had to hand it to them. And so there were
leave-it-with-us's and handshakes and more jokes about the plush
leather seats that made fart noises when you stood up and then

Tom was there at the door shaking hands again and worrying that he'd fucked up. But then as the guy walked away McGregor was thanking him for making the client feel comfortable and coming down to his level and how it had been a great meeting.

Edinburgh, City of . . .

Back at his desk trying to ditch the godlike overview on who he was. The catch-22. He needed his job so he could make enough money to visit Meg. So he could survive without her, so he could entertain her when she was here. But his gut told him, the gut he'd had to force food into to stay off the drink, his fat gut, that he'd through exercise turn into a six-pack before Meg arrived – It was telling him he was trapped here. *Catch-22* had been an extremely witty, satirical novel, but wit and satire scared Tom now, even though they constituted about 99 per cent of who he was. He'd have to force himself to live without them.

Stop it. Looking up from his monitor at everything in the office – the posters for past campaigns. Cumbernauld Business Centre and that not quite catchy sing-songy rhyming slogan – 'What's it called? Cumbernauld.' The plastic plant on McGregor's PC monitor that had little arms and a guitar and sunglasses, and gyrated its stem in time with the beat every time McGregor tried out a new corporate music CD. The swift glances that Stephanie shot McGregor every hour or so that were evidence of the affair they were having. McGregor's fake-gold framed photo of his third wife and kids. Tragic. Yes, he had started sighing.

If only his job was some automatic, mindless labour that could be done without any engagement at all. But no, Satan had designed this career precisely so as to rub Tom's face in it. Edinburgh, City of . . . Telling the lie to himself every day, just so he could survive. Fearful for his own sanity. No, he was not a man of great promise and as yet unrealised talents, who'd been unlucky to have been trapped in this backwater town where his talents went unrecognised and opportunities were non-existent. No, he was maybe not talented or promising at all. All these years telling himself he was really an undiscovered European art-house film-maker. But face it – he hadn't even looked at a film script in three years. Hadn't made a film for seven and even that had been inconsequential.

He had in fact grown rather comfortable in blaming everyone else for holding him back. As bad as those neds in the schemes who smashed their own windows and graffitied their doors knowing that the council would get them a new house. Who didn't even bother looking for work any more, because there was no point.

He'd grown complacent. Become, actually, rather proud of his resentment, smugly secure in his little hatreds.

And what was Meg? Not a shining light of hope for a new future. Not at all. She was this incident he'd invented to up the ante on his self-loathing. To give him the final excuse to give up on everything. Six weeks till she would come.

The bus home and the world was trying to prove how shit it could be. These two women in their thirties in worn-out high-street fashions, on the seat across from him. A little girl who wouldn't sit still on her mother's lap. Dressed all in pink. Aged four probably, by her height, but she has a dummy in her mouth. A pink dummy. The mother with pink lipstick thick on her lips. The kid tries to speak, this dummy in her mouth.

'Mwaaa, mwaa.'

'Fuckin' sit still, Chelsea. Fuckin' shoosh.'

Seven stops to go. The kid is called Chelsea, like the Clinton girl. His guess was they came from Pilton, the scheme the government had tried to forget.

'Mwaaa, mwaa, mama.'

The kid reaches for something in her mother's bag. Mother slaps the kid's hand. Kid cries – dummy in mouth, almost choking on it. Four years old.

'I said no and you keep on fuckin' goin' on at me, just fuckin' shut up.'

He turns his head. City of self-pity. City of state dependence. Of three generations of unemployed. Grandmothers aged forty-five. He tells himself it is not just here, it is happening everywhere.

'Fuckin' leave it, Chelsea. You're doing ma fuckin' heid in.'

Another slap. The kid crying. Tom wanting it to stop. To stand and shout 'Stop!' Tell the bus driver, call the police. This is child abuse. Hitting your child in public is illegal now. Take the fucking dummy from the kid's mouth, let her speak, teach her how to fucking speak. He remains seated, he says nothing.

Five stops. The kid crying and now the mother is hugging her.

'Ma ma, boo boo.'

This mother takes out the dummy, sticks a bottle in. Bubbles inside it. Orange. Irn-Bru, Tango in a feeding bottle. City of single mothers. City of lost souls. Of despair.

'Baby,' the mother says. 'Aw baby am sorry, gies a hug, aw baby.'

Clutching Chelsea to her, kissing her head, stroking her back. The kid quiet in her arms, tears turning to fizzy-bubble hiccups. The abusive cycle of punishment and then sugar-sweet hope.

His son can't speak and it is all his fault.

Two stops. City of irreconcilable social difference. City of suicide. Ten per cent more than in the rest of the UK. Aids capital of Europe in the nineties.

'Wassa, wassa.' The little pink girl pointing out the window.

'Whit? Stop fuckin' gettin' in my face!'

'Wassa.Wassa.'

And he sees what Chelsea is pointing at. And it takes him back to Sean, years before. Hard to describe to a child, but he would have tried with Sean. A warehouse – windows boarded up. To tell his son about post-industrial decline. The British Empire.

'Fuckin' sit down. Shut the fuck up.'

The slap again, this time to the face.

The child screaming and he could scream. He has to do something. But it is his stop and he is up, having said nothing. Waiting, cowardly, in the space by the door which you are not supposed to cross, not speak to the driver, waiting.

City of lost dreams, of escapism in addiction. He would never hit Sean.

Out, three streets from his street. A drink. 'Edinburgh, City of . . .' The image is pure in your head. Think of Meg, hope of happiness. You don't need that drink.

Passing the off-licence. Haddows, City of Shadows. City of every passing sign – of Poundstretcher, of Cash and Carry, of

Sunbed World, of Your Cheques Cashed Here, of Lucky Time
Chinese Takeaway. Of Meg. City Meg could never live in. And
that was the horror of it. To try to get her to stay, he'd have
to do the same thing the corporate clones were doing. Searching
for a word of positive spin on this city.

City of. City of . . .

That was it. Kitchen. The duty-free bottle in his hand. The
seal cracking open. Just a shot, he wasn't drinking again. Just
the one. Two years of carefully monitored moderation. Counselling and a calendar on the wall with dry days marked in red.
And Morna – measuring out permissible units of affection. Two
years since the divorce, and liver damage, the warning from the
doctor. God, to just have Morna's touch on his shoulders –
another reason to get drunk. Six weeks till Meg came and six
hours till bed. It was OK, just tonight, a minor relapse. He'd
stay dry, it wasn't like he was damaging his future. Just the one
glass then. Just the one.

Call

'Edinburgh, City of . . .'

    'Yeah, I know, you keep telling me but . . . but of what?'

'No, that's the point, there's no –'

'Is there an echo on this line, or –

'No, listen, this IS the joke. OK! There is no last word!'

'I don't get it, I'm sorry. Tom, are you OK?'

'They call this a fucking concept! People get paid to come up with a concept that has no concept, I mean for fucksake!'

'You sound . . . you seem a bit . . .'

'Here's me trying to explain a joke. Rule number one, never explain a joke. You know I sent you three texts, and rang your landline?'

'I told you I was in the garden. What's the big deal?'

'Forty-five minutes. I sent you three texts and one email.'

'There's no signal in the garden, you know that. And my wireless connection . . .' [Silence.] 'My You, are you drinking?'

'Not really, just a wee dram – Christ, if you'd been through a week like this you'd . . . Anyway, I was in another stupid meeting, right, and I kept thinking of you.'

'You sound stressed . . . As long as you're OK. I want to talk about things.'

'OK, things I can do.'

'No, but our second day together, I'd like to talk about that.'

'You know, this meeting today. I was sitting there, thinking, all the time. Just thinking of your face smiling at me from across the table, your legs underneath, you slipping a foot out of your shoe.'

'Tom?'

'You're here with me, in Edinburgh. We're sitting across the table from each other at this corporate function. The others

are chatting and brainstorming, I'm taking out my little manicure set.'

'I don't feel quite up for this. There's so many things we
have to discuss.'

[Silence.]

'It's like a scene in a movie. Can I just tell you?'

[Silence.]

'Why is it I just know this is going to be pornographic?'

'Are you ready now, my Meg?'

'OK, OK. So we're attempting phone sex again?"

'This little leather thing, with a spine like a book and inside
are tweezers, a nail clipper and nail file. I have it in my hand.'

'OK, just let me get in the mood.'

'Yeah, OK, you're sitting there watching me take it out. Open
it up. You can tell I'm up to something, something bad.'

'OK, I'm going through now.'

'That's right. Get yourself into bed. Put our eye mask on.
Put your hands in your panties.'

[Footsteps. Silence.]

'OK, the eye mask is on now. I'm lying down, nothing here,
just your voice.'

'OK, this meeting, so they're chatting and laughing and
they – '

'Wait! I thought you said you'd be working late. You're not
jerking off in the office, are you?'

[Laughter.]

'No, home now. So. We're in this restaurant overlooking
Leith docks and they're all talking about Edinburgh, City of
. . . what a great advertising concept it is and –'

'OK.'

'You see it, some chichi pseudo place with pish wine, really
pretentious? You see it? You got your eye mask on?'

'Yeah, I see it now. You're trimming your nails.'

'You touching yourself, you stroking your clit?'

'Yeah.'

'That's right, I'm trimming my nails and I'm not even
throwing you glances, but I can feel you watching me and you're
shivering, all the way down to your pussy, because you're not

wearing any panties, like I asked you, and you have a dress on and no panties and it's just your pussy there, touching the cold metal chair.'

'Right ... they don't even know. You're filing your nails so carefully and ...'

'They have no idea, because I'm making them laugh, telling them how wonderful their advertising concept is. And they're thinking I'm such a great guy, and the nail filing, they don't even notice it, it's like someone with a toothpick after a steak, like folding a napkin, and your pussy there, naked on the chair.'

'It's getting so wet. I want you to touch me.'

'But we can't. You have to sit there and watch me filing my nails. Making them smooth, holding them up to check, running them across my wrist, to see if there are rough edges, because there can't be. Not for what I have planned for you later.'

'The things you do. I'm shivering. They've no idea how wet my pussy is. I'm touching it now.'

'That's right and you have to be good, you can't give the game away, you just have to sit there with your soaking aching pussy, that's maybe staining your skirt and not stare and not think about what you are thinking about.'

'You are, you're going to, aren't you?'

'Later in the hotel.'

'Yes, tell me.'

'I put the mask over your eyes, you're going to kiss my finger-tips, you're going to check their smoothness against your lips.'

'So wet. You're touching your cock, aren't you?'

'It's hard, so hard. You sat there all the way through the meeting, watching me, knowing what's coming to you. You know, don't you, why my nails have to be so smooth?'

'My God, yes.'

'We're in the hotel room. There's a view of Edinburgh, the castle, the festival, but you can't see it because you're blind-folded. Your hands are resting on the windowsill. I'm licking your wet, wet pussy from behind, my cock is throbbing, you have to stay like that, legs apart, your lovely long, long legs, people pass by in the street, they see a woman with an eye mask. I'm putting one finger inside you, and another. You're so wet. Do you want more?'

'Yes.'

'You're so wet, they slide inside so easily, you're sucking them in. Two fingers, three.'

'I'm wearing my blindfold. My God.'

'All the way to the knuckles. You arch your back, you gasp as I push further in, the lips of your pussy pulling me in.'

'Oh God. You're going to . . . if you do I'm gonna . . .'

'You want me to, don't you?'

'Yes, please . . . please.'

'Aww . . . you're groaning, my whole hand inside you. You open for me, suck me in, I'm reaching inside you, making a fist, in up to my wrist.'

'God, oh God! Ah ah, I'm coming! I'm cuhhh . . .'

'Aww. Awww.'

'Aaah.'

[Silence.]

'My beautiful girl.'

[Weeping.]

'Are you OK, my You?'

'Yes, yes, sorry . . . I'm just . . . that was so . . . we . . .'

'We came together.'

'Yes, yes, I'm just crying because it was so . . .'

'So beautiful, yes, we are.'

[Silence.]

'You make me . . . I swear . . . this has never . . . only with you.'

'I didn't freak you out?'

'Beautiful, it was . . .'

'God, Meg, all I want, if you were here, we could . . .'

'I know.'

'I wish I could see you. Your sweet face.'

'I know, but it just makes it worse. Saying it. We have to . . . we have six more weeks, my You.'

'You booked your ticket?'

'I get in on the 26th. American Airlines.'

'You at the arrivals gate. I can't believe it.'

'God, I'm shuddering. Aww. Aww. God, I'm coming again. Aw, Jesus!'

[Whispering.] 'I miss you so much. I miss you, I miss you.'

'I know, I know, I do too, but how we going to manage if we talk about missing each other all the time?'

'I know, I know.'

'You, my melancholy man.'

[Silence]

'Six weeks . . .'

'Yeah, yeah . . . so many things to organise. Oh, did you speak to Morna, face to face?'

[Silence]

'Yeah, I told her.'

[Silence]

'God, sorry, don't know why I brought that up. I guess it's just so hard finishing with people. My God, I've always been the one to end it first. One whiff of failure and wooosh I'm out of there, you know how conflict scares me. God, listen to me, spoiling our wonderful afterglow. It really was the best sex . . . ever.'

'Really? But you're not even here!'

'No, really, you were wonderful. It was the best, you're the best, my You.'

Journal

Email

My You,
Why can I not come sooner? The date for my arrival is rather
arbitrary. Could it be that I am enjoying our time apart? You
ask me these things.

Perverse as it seems the longing for you has turned into a kind
of blissful intoxication. I caught myself staring out of the window
today at a blur of light on the pane and it took me minutes to
realise that it was my own reflection. I keep losing track of
time, losing myself to thoughts of you. The daily waiting to
speak is no longer emptiness. It has become a sensation in itself,
a hollow inside me, that sounds like an echo chamber in an
instrument.

Is a long-distance relationship not maybe the solution finally to
all my insecurities and fears? To respect the distance that is
between two people. Not to suffocate but to hold each other at
arm's length, so that desire can never be sated. Not the stale
state of conjugality, but eternal renewal. Banality held at bay by
endless departures and arrivals. Not the boredom that sets in
when two fight over domestic details, not the compromises on
both sides which whittle down both to a body that is lesser than
even one. But a constant refuelling of desire, the processes of
waiting and then the rediscovery, finding each other anew.
Improving oneself in isolation as if dressing for a date. The
anticipation of the rendezvous replayed over and over again.
Maybe the only way to stay in love is this, through enforced
separation. As a friend once said to me, if I ever married I would
have to live in a separate house from my husband. Our love is

so great that we require different countries! And Freud said that
an obstacle is always required to heighten libido – when none
exists man invents one. In our culture of instant gratification is
there not something of value to be learned from being forced,
for once, to wait? I am reminded of the story of the lover who
had to wait all day to see his beloved, and so he walked the
streets, giddy with the pains of longing. When the appointed
time came, he went to her door, but just as he was about to
knock, he withdrew. It has always perplexed me, was it that he
preferred the dream of her to the reality or that he was afraid
she would not live up to the dream?

I dream of you as I wait.

Your You.

July 19
His email reply was so brief.

> Don't know this voice. Doesn't sound like you. Can we talk on
> phone instead?

Hurt me. But yes, he is right. He didn't say it but I know my
email was pretentious romantic. He didn't comment on a single
thing I said, then was silent, almost embarrassed for me on the
phone. I feel such a fool for having sent it. I *did* feel everything
I wrote, it just came out wrong. He must think me this pseudo-
poetic idiot. I won't spend another day indulging myself like
that again. Email is wrong for us. Ashamed of myself now.

Back to work. I've given up any hope of finishing off *The
Twelve Stages of Love*. It is truly terrible. This journal also. Had
this idea that I might show him what I've written so far, to ask
for his help. But how can I? Will he reject it too? Why can't
I just be cool, in the moment, like him. Why this need always
to analyse? Spoiled child taking a toy apart to find out how it
works, only to be left surrounded with broken pieces. And the
ways I've described him. Would it hurt him if he read it? Well
past bedtime now. One last try tomorrow. Must write from my
heart. If I can't, then all this effort has been waste.

July 20
Our last days together. They flood me, scare me. I have to stick
to an order. Start at the start.

Second date – third day. July 1.

We were sitting at an outdoor table in the rooftop restaurant of the Gramercy Park Hotel – view of the East River, the
Brooklyn Bridge. White linen tablecloths and an ever-attentive
waiter with authentic French accent. Tom joked about it all,
said it wasn't Edinburgh that was for sure. And we had both
laughed about this expression the event had summoned, that
we'd both heard somewhere before – 'erotic repertoire' or maybe
'symbolic repertoire' – and how it maybe came from Kundera
and how our vocabulary was so similar even though we grew
up on opposite sides of the world.

'I'm sure it's symbolic repertoire,' I said. 'That different lovers
get summed up in an image, a word. Right? Like sometimes I
see a four-by-four and it reminds me of Jono. Or say a jogger
and –'

'– and Jake, he was your last guy right?'

'No, Jake was Joy Division and bourbon. Jogging was Ted.
But your ex-wife? She was what? I mean as an image?'

'Hiking boots probably. We have hills in Scotland. You know,
hillwalking?'

'Mountains I can relate to.'

'She did Munros, that's . . . sorry . . . They have this name.
Like halfway between a hill and a mountain, everything in Scotland is only half of anything. They're called Munros. God knows
why. Some guy, nineteenth century, called Munro probably.'

'Mr Munro.'

'Yeah, never could understand why she dragged me up so
many. All this effort to pose for your achievement photo with
all the tourists, then to just have to . . .'

'. . . to climb back down again?'

'Right, exactly.'

And we did that – finished off each other's sentences. Which
has always annoyed me with men before. (That controlling need
of theirs.) But with Tom it makes me smile – I should like him
to finish off all my next sentences for me.

The above – no good. Comes close to what I remember we said, but I'm always the first person to tell a scriptwriter that their dialogue is unrealistic. And the female voice seems to be just leading, asking questions. Like a writer trying to find the subject.

The waiter hovered. We were holding hands, circling thumbs, the menus unlooked at. The waiter gave us time.

'Anything else in your symbolic repertoire with your ex-wife?' I asked.

'Big pants.'

'You mean like what you call "trousers"?'

'No, no, I mean knickers. Big ones.'

'Ah, I have big knickers.'

'Yes, but you also have thongs, garters, frilly Victorian thingies, these things I'm assuming, or maybe hoping for. She only ever had big pants.'

'Kinky!'

'Uh-uh – denial. She had this idea that if she wore big pants they'd support her buttocks and keep them forever firm – like a retirement plan. Like when she was seventy she would maybe pull out a thong and say, look, I've done it.'

'Funny. OK, what else. Food?'

'Right, like, shall we? I mean eat.'

Can't recall the exact negotiation of ironic national difference that led him to order the Aberdeen Angus steak, rare, and me the sushi. Some joke about flying Scottish cows round the globe for the slaughter? Mine maybe something to do with fish not feeling pain, cold-blooded, like I am. The waiter took the order and Tom added another bottle of Chardonnay and we went back to the handholding across the table, sensing that when the waiter had turned his back we could be that bit more naughty. Stroking wrists. Fingers along arteries, sensing the importance of blood. Sushi and Angus steak. Raw and rare. I said something like:

'Isn't it funny though, you know? Like you said, you've had so many lovers – and symbolically, you know, you'd be reading a menu and you'd think, Beef, I can't eat beef because of Jason.'

'Or the fish because of Fiona.'

'Or the foie gras because Paul loved foie gras. Or the lamb because of –'

'Larry!'

'Larry?'

'Hand puppet. When I was a kid. BBC. Kids' show, like mister-the-lamb. Larry.'

'Larry for me is Sanders.'

'Sanders the Lamb?'

I had to kiss him then, even though the executive lunchers at the next table were staring. He stroked my neck, his knuckles deliberately brushing against my nipple. He pulled away. Picked up the menu.

'You know, you're right. I mean. Look – goat's cheese, right? Goat's cheese is Morna. And tarte Tatin is Sheila.'

'Your ex? We could skip dessert.'

'No, dessert and bridges were Lizzie.'

'You never told me about Lizzie. What's the deal with bridges?'

Two pages of dialogue written, but still I haven't even begun to set the scene.

START AGAIN. Further back. A day apart since our last encounter. I had been anxious about seeing him again. He'd mentioned in passing that he had another week here. Note: Stendhal says the waiting period is the one in which the lover grows in the imagination. 'Crystallisation' he calls it. (An old salt mine in Germany. You lower a branch inside – a month later you pull it out and it's encrusted with salt crystals like diamonds – a metaphor for the romantic imagination, how the image of the beloved becomes diamond-like through absence.) Silly. Nothing like that. I'd assumed we'd never see each other again. I'd get a goodbye text if I was lucky. I'd send him a 'see you around'. At 5 p.m. I got one from him.

Haven't washed in a day, can still smell you on my face. Xxx

Perverse. The man was a pervert and a European. (The two being equivalent.) The next day I'd been staying at Sally's place, was planning to head home to Fire Island. I decided to stay another day. No rush to get home. I didn't say 'because of him'. Texted him back out of mere curiosity. We swapped a few and I set the time at the restaurant the next day. Getting ready I was struck with melancholy. What was I doing? I'd stopped second dates years ago. Sally said I seemed absent-minded, dreamy. And yes, I'd let my plans drift. So unlike me. Day two – stage two. Wandering through parks and streets dreaming of the caresses of the beloved. NB Kafka drew this stage out for eight years with a woman he'd met for an hour! A thousand letters. Remnants of the rituals of courting. Courtly love. (Courtney Love – Tom would laugh at this – we are all whores now he would say, there is no second stage, no longing, everyone fucks on a first date now.)

But I did wander that day before he called! Couldn't eat (Stendhal – a sign of the first stirrings of love). Laughable. No, I couldn't eat because I was hung-over. Or face the drive home for the same reason. But still, I did walk around Gramercy Park staring at people. Empty feeling in my stomach, melancholy. *Post coitum, animal triste*. Ate falafel for the first time in years, spent an hour in Union Square just staring at people. A young couple, office workers on lunch break holding hands while talking to other people on cellphones, a woman looking round and waving to a man in a suit across the park – a blind date? A bag lady rummaging through trash. The faces of so many races. The Flatiron Building, bisecting Broadway and Fifth. Thinking about Broadway, how it was the only diagonal cut through Manhattan's grid – ancient Native Indian path. How people found it beautiful because it broke with the mathematical order of the city. Thinking of the energy that built this place, of how much energy it expended each day just to be itself. Had I thought of him at all that day apart? No, I was looking at people – in awe of a thing I took for granted – maybe seeing Manhattan through his eyes. He called at around five. I decided to stay another day. Be so nice to believe I went through Stendhal's second stage of love, but I strongly suspect it was just a hangover. DIGRESSION!

Yes, as I finished dressing to meet him, I looked at myself in the mirror and I was back there again – the smell of us on my second-day clothes. I told myself it would be OK to break my rules just this once. GET BACK TO PLOT.

OK, the restaurant. The whole experience had been extremely erotically charged, but I can't write erotics. This is my problem over and over. I'm cold, surgical, taking a body apart to find the heart.

How had we even got to holding hands?

Damn it. Dried up again. Should maybe call Sally to talk all this through. No. Know what she'll say: This whole long-distance love affair is just some product of my romantic imagination, of writer's block – I should give it up, and him, and go back to script doctoring. 'Really, Meg, you can't turn this guy into a movie.'

YES, that's it! First thing he said day three – like at the airport.

'It feels like we're in a movie.'

START AGAIN.

Too late again but some progress. Start again tomorrow.

July 21

His call today, laughing about how little we could remember. He said, yes, we had been talking about movies.

New Word Document.

Rooftop café – view of Brooklyn Bridge. Him in beaten-up suit – shades on, smiling to himself. Me self-conscious. Was it the place? Or my dress? Fear that he was judging me. He seemed not to notice that I was wearing exactly the same outfit and I worried that my scent was a little less than fresh. (I'd sprayed deodorant all over the inside of the dress.) I couldn't see his eyes because of his shades.

'What? What is it?' I asked.

'Jesus, I mean, look at me sittin' here.'

He'd put on some kind of Scottish version of a Brooklyn accent.

'In New Yoik City sittin' wit da most beautiful dame in da woild.'

God, really. I was a mess. He looked over his shoulder. Taking my hand conspiratorially.

'C'mon, a lowlife like me, is dis for real? Someone's filmin' us, right?'

Him making an act of turning up his collar and trying to look inconspicuous, then leaning in closer to whisper. His accent was more Bronx. (Pretty damn good for a Scot.) Me trying hard not to laugh.

'I mean, don't look over da edge but dose tings down dere, right, dose yellow cabs and da goddamn Brooklyn Bridge, gee, I'm feelin' like Serpico here or Ratso or –'

'Pat Bateman?'

'I was tinkin' more Travis Bickle. I mean, dis must be a real problem for all youz in dis crazy city. You know, feelin' yer in a movie all da time. You sure nobody's filmin' us here?'

What was that thing he said next?

'And what's dis? I'm hearin words in my ears telling me what to say, cos it's a second date, right. Dere's dis scriptwriter guy, sittin' on my shoulder, sleazy lookin' muthafucka, feedin' me all da lines for da classic second date an I'm fightin' him here, so, my apologies, dis is gonna be . . .'

That next thing he said, I'm sure it was that.

'. . . THE WORST SECOND DATE EVER.'

Laughing to myself now. Yes – his line. The worst second date ever. Yes, I had been anxious about seeing him again – the burden of the second date. Those awkward unasked questions: Was I just drunk last time I saw you? What did I find attractive about you the first time? Whatever it was, my anxieties had been choked by laughter and the fact that no matter how self-conscious I'd felt, he'd been there first making a joke about our self-consciousness. The worst second date ever.

The waiter brought the Chardonnay and there were more playful theatrics in the tasting and pouring, his Ratso Rizzo Travis Bickle accent that he seemed almost too scared to drop. He clinked his glass against mine, sat back and stared at me. I still couldn't see his eyes.

'Yeah. So yeah mebbe dis date'll be so bad dat it'll be our last.'

The way he switched from cocky Bronx boy to paranoid Scot.

'I don't really think that that's usually the kind of thing, typically, that men say on a second date.'

'Really? OK. OK. So if we're gonna do dis scene, what should we be sayin', typically? Now dat we're in dis movie called da woist second date ever.'

'Well, you know. Typically we should be making small talk about art, music, things we have in common.'

'Naw, people do that on da Internet now. Tick da boxes, before dey even meet anyone – you know: I only want to meet someone who's into Dvořák and the Clash and *The Da Vinci Code*.'

'You read *The Da Vinci Code*?'

'Naw, but da Clash was OK.'

'The Clash are superb.'

'American dames always say dat, dey were OK, no big cheese.'

'Cheese? So what was your worst second date ever?'

'Well, you know. Done it too many times to remember.'

Then he was back in his normal accent again, which I preferred.

'You know the routine – you find out this one book that changed both your lives. This one city you always wanted to visit. That is the same as mine. The –'

'The one movie that made you both cry.'

'Right, right, the one song that we both love that will become our song.'

They were playing Euro-ambient, vaguely corporate-sounding. He laughed at my listening face.

'OK. This isn't our song. Right, right, so movies, books, the whole –'

'Romantic repertoire.'

YES! So that was where the line had come from. Not this academic thing, just this throwaway thing I'd said. Or had it been him? Give the line to him.

'Romantic repertoire,' he said.

'It's a cliché now.'

'Touché. Here's to cliché.'

No, I'm getting off the subject again – playing with words. It had not been like that.

'OK. So give me ya woist. Let's trash an' boin dis date and see which way da chips fall and da wind blows.'

Too much. Chips in the wind. Mixed metaphor. DELETE.

'The second date is always the worst because each person reveals their erotic past and their demands for the future. It is all analysis and assessment, the interrogation of cultural and sexual history.'

DELETE. Getting my genres mixed up again. Keep it simple, stupid. Too dry and he had made me wet. I need another line from him. The worst second date ever.

'OK, you first.'

'OK. Cobain, Richter, Antonioni, Naples . . .'

'Bach, Holzer, Godard, Paris. I once went to the *Deux Magots* to see where Sartre and de Beauvoir . . .'

No. These things were said but not like that. (If only I could have recorded our conversations!) How had I ended up walking downtown with him, hand in hand? Back to his hotel room?

Set the scene.

Second location. Dinner done. Second bottle of Chardonnay finished. His hand in mine walking toward Union Square. A couple in front of us, twenty-ish. Him black, her Hispanic; he was wearing her clothes, she his. Very Williamsburg.

He said: 'So, this is the worst question ever – you must have done this before, with someone else, this walk, right?'

Yes, the worst question to ask, every love must be the first, the only. But his smile.

'Well, actually, yes. Twice before. Actually, no. Maybe more.'

'It's good, it's all good, as dey say in Nu Yoik. I knew it. My God. So what happens to us? Us old people who've done every-thing before?'

'I guess you can't go there twice.'

'Lightning never strikes, right? But here we are, and this is, what, your fourth time here, hand in hand? And our second date.'

'So your hypothesis on this terrible condition of holding hands is what, exactly?'

'OK, so every lover detracts. Reduces what's left. There can be no more sushi or Bach or walks in Union Square, no more –'

'Sonic Youth or Meredith Monk or Jackson Pollock or Aberdeen Angus.'

'Or bathing in a lake at night, or scented candles in a bath for two or –'

'– or reading from Shakespeare together in bed, or –'

'– or slurping miso soup from the same bowl.'

'God, how many times have I done that?'

'Miso is new in Edinburgh.'

'Sad, so every lover diminishes the ... possibilities still open ...'

'Maybe I should just get a cab,' he said.

No, I said, you're funny, this is fun. Walk with me.

'Sure,' he said, 'but I dunno – what's left? Things not done before.'

'Such as?'

'Like skydiving or fucking eight people at once or maybe going to McDonald's and listening to Guns N' Roses' fourth comeback album and forcing yourself to cry into your free gift and fries.'

'We'd have to ride the A train for an hour to find a McDonald's.'

'Tell me about the guy in Union Square.'

Walking in circles through the trees, and I knew from before that the guaranteed way to ruin a date is to talk about your previous loves. Every man has to erase all other men, has to hear you say he is your greatest lover, the smartest, most successful, best-looking, with the biggest dick ever. Trying to force it from you with a squeeze of the hand, by an offhand recriminatory remark, by a sudden lack of interest in you.

'We should do something else. This is getting weird,' I said.

'I like weird. I am weird. Seriously. As an exercise in exorcising demons. I'm only here for five more days. I want to do it. Who gives a fuck about the Empire State, the Guggenheim? Gimme the grand tour of past lovers, I want to see where you danced with Jake and kissed Toby and drank miso with Jobe.'

'Who's Jobe?'

'Sure, whoever, whatever,' he said with his ridiculously endearing Bronx accent.

This kind of talk – terrifying. This confessional mode that in any normal relationship could take years to get through. It pulled me again into the centre of the square.

'You sure you're OK with this? You're not going to freak out on me?' I asked.

'Hit me.'

There were buskers playing. Five or more. Couples everywhere. A sign saying don't sit on the grass and maybe a hundred students and office workers sitting on the grass, listening to the bands playing. Sounds of neo-folk, bangra, salsa, rap.

'OK, his name was Jose. He was an experiment. An Internet blind date, maybe six years ago. We met at the statue in the middle.'

'The one right there?'

'Yeah. Just a one-night stand. He had broad shoulders and was full of ambition, that was about it. Jesus. I'm not off to a very good start here, am I?'

'Beautiful. Gimme more. Round here. Any more romances in Union Square?'

'Just a casual fling. The restaurant over there. Steak Frites. Maybe four years ago. His back was too hairy. He was an aspiring scriptwriter. Wrote sci-fi.'

'Name?'

'Fredo. Third-generation Italian. I was going through my Latino phase.'

'We take a left or a right?'

'Well, where we just came from. I have this terrible confession.'

'Go on.'

'The restaurant just across from where we were. I dumped Johann there. He was German, obsessive.'

'*Oy vey!*' Tom shouted, laughing. And I'd thought just then, to love and love just once. To be like Fredo, to be looking for a wife. A life with a wife. Like Italians from a hundred years ago. But it was dumb, as dumb as Fredo. '*Bambini. Molti bambini.*'

Tom pushing me on, giving me the courage to lead him through my past.

'Jesus, and there's the whole Upper West Side and the East – right – I see you walking in Central Park with a Jewish intellectual, pointing out the place where John Lennon was shot, to some tourist guy from Liverpool.'

And he was spot on. Yes, I had done those things – well, almost. The intellectual had been from Harvard and turned out to be not so smart. And the John Lennon spot I'd done during a brief affair with a visiting lecturer from Cambridge. I was anxious about where this train of thought would lead us.

'OK, we'll take a right and head into Chelsea,' I said.

And I led him past the brownstones, and the muscle-bound men with poodles and the superwaifs with Great Danes. Him laughing at every little thing I pointed out. The details, the demographics. Telling him how Manhattan was split up into types of person in different neighbourhoods. Him telling me that Scotland was so different, because it was all the same. Poverty and more poverty. To Sixth, to Seventh on 14th. Standing before Le Singe Vert.

'John and I used to go here and lunch, he was married. Gay and married. I mean, like to a man. We had this hotel on 21st. We did "lunch".'

'God, you're incredible.'

And I couldn't work out why then – so light-headed. Bouncing along leading him by the hand. Something liberating, maybe, about having the worst second date ever. What was motivating him? I couldn't stop.

'God, the Village. You'll love the Village. It's so Paris, so gay. Bleecker Street. I have to take you to Bleecker Street.'

Along Twelfth to Eighth. I explained how decades ago it was this haven for gays and artists and how there had been transvestites on every street corner selling their wares, but now all the old radicals had become landlords and they were trying to clean up the area, force out all the young gender-benders who were like they once had been. I found the café in Bleecker Street that I'd thought might have been the one in the Joni Mitchell song. The one about finding someone to love, in a Bleecker Street café. 'Tin Angel', I think. Told him of how I sat there thinking of that song, week after week, those first weeks after moving here, age twenty-three, when I'd given up on men. We went inside and it looked more straight now, studenty. Twenty-somethings all sitting solitary at their laptops. We paid five bucks each for takeout skinny lattes

and I told him about Yvonne and my three months with a
woman.

'You were a lesbian?'

'For a bit. I couldn't deal with the lentil bake.'

Him in hysterics. I had made a joke. How long since I'd
made someone laugh?

'You're being very brave,' he said.

Maybe I'd wanted to stop right then. But his proposition had
turned into a mission and I'd whisked him on. I had to find
the park. Stonewall Park. He'd been taken aback at the sight
of the sculptures. Lifesize humans. Two women kissing, two
men sat together on a bench holding hands, bodies cast in
bronze. Told him it was the only gay public artwork in the
world. That it had been almost impossible not to have at least
tried to be gay in New York in the early nineties. That he just
had to picture it. Fifth Avenue and the demonstrations to open
the world's eyes to Aids. The number of people in the Village
that had died. He told me he wanted to sit there on the bench
next to the kissing women and think of me aged twenty-three
with Yvonne, but I'd decided to move on because there was a
bum on the facing bench, eyes sunken in sleeping sockets, the
sickness written on his skin.

Then it was down and back across Houston to Soho and I
sensed he was tiring.

'You want to stop this now? There's rather a lot to get
through. You must think I'm a total whore. Most of these things
only lasted a month or less.'

'I want to see it all.'

So Soho and I told him of my pad there, how I rented it out
for the summer, it brought in about 65K. And of Jacob, the
older man I had known, yes, in that sense, the artist who'd
never quite made it, but had got in early before the gentrifi-
cation and converted his loft by himself. Worth three million
now and he'd given up on his art and sublet and didn't have to
work any more. How he used to take photographs of me after
we'd made love; he was going to work them into canvases but
I never saw him paint. Probably '97.

He smiled, and squeezed my hand. 'Onward,' he said.

The Lower East Side and all the incredible antique stores and the little ultra-trendy boutiques that only ever last six months and Chaz, the graphic designer – only twenty-two, my younger-guy phase. Tom had fallen silent, my feet were sore in the stupid heels. He asked me about all the acronyms. LES, and BoCoCa and Dumbo. I explained it meant Down Under the Manhattan Brooklyn Overpass. Told him about the new one – SoHa – South of Harlem.

'I need names of men.' He was flagging, but I sensed I had to get this done. For myself. To exorcise them all. My obituary list of lovers.

Canal Street and Thomas. Nolita and Eric.

We were heading south toward the Financial District. I told him about Jerry the trader, five years ago. He worked in Morgan Stanley, three hundred deaths at Morgan Stanley. He hadn't called me back. I had forced myself to assume it was just the usual – that he wasn't that into me – a one-night thing. I'd never had the guts to look for his name on the 9/11 memorial website.

More, Tom wanted more information. What did Jerry look like? Was he tall? Did he work out?

All around us, the fake Greek columns of the court buildings, the spotlights turning on as the light faded. He wanted to see Ground Zero, but I insisted on Brooklyn Bridge – it wasn't too late. We could walk it, I said, the view from halfway, even to native New Yorkers, was still incredible. I'd done it with David before, he lived in Brooklyn Heights, across the way, two doors down from Norman Mailer. My feet were sore. We could stop this whole thing now if he wanted. But no, he wanted to go on. Heading to the walkway. The game turned morbid, obsessive, his questions interrogatory. So, David? Did he want to have kids with you? What was his salary? Did he go down on you? Did he make you come? I had no desire to tell him any more.

A sudden jerk from his hand. He'd stopped dead in the middle of the street. I turned, his arm shaking, face hidden from me. Sobbing.

'You OK? My God, I'm sorry.'

I led him away. A taxi blaring at us.

'Let's go on. Show me Brooklyn and David.'

'No, no. You should go home. You're tired. I'm sorry I've been talking and –'

'I need to see where you fucked David.'

'God, why are we even doing this?'

'Sorry. Just this theory . . . I'm only here for a few more days and . . .'

'Tell me.'

'That I'm burned out, I guess. Too jaded to love, I can't walk the same streets again – seen it all before, all the clichés. It's just a theory . . . No, that's a lie.'

'Tell me.'

The joggers ran past us, tourists' flashing cameras. He raised his eyes. Long silence. Tears on his face.

'I'm trying, really fucking trying here to make this as bad as I can for you, so I can walk away . . . so I can . . .'

'Tell me.' I kissed his cheek. He got his breath back.

'. . . so I can stop myself falling in love with you.'

I cannot cry when someone cries in my arms. My first instinct is to run. But he held me tight, and I felt guilt, that I had led him to this. More, that he was crying for me. I got him a taxi, but still he would not let go of my hand. Twenty-five blocks together and his crying hadn't stopped. The strength of that hold led me back to his hotel, his room. I am weak, maybe, to the stronger power of weakness shared. So long since I had acknowledged any weakness in myself.

He wept as we made love. So urgent then so gentle then so angry, like not one man but many different men. And my tears came as I came. And I held him through that night and wept alone then for this man who had cried my years of hidden tears for me. This man who was many men. And I have known too many. A sad happiness as I gazed at his face. This worst second date ever, that would put an end to second dates for ever.

Need to call him now. Too late. 3 a.m. my time. 9 a.m. with him. He will be at work now. He has a lot on his plate right now. He said he was going to see his girlfriend and end it with her. Stupid, to work this late. I'll need sleeping pills again, earplugs, eye mask. His eye mask. Our third day together. Days it'll take me to write about it. Day of a man in my home, on my island. Night of making love blindfolded.

Day of Wee Fibs

Meg was always talking of days: our day of this; our day of that; our first – our last. Three weeks of this now and, well, Tom was having a wee day all of his own. Day of sneaky wee fibs, he told himself, as he took a tiny wee mouthful of breakfast voddie. The wee fib that was necessary to face the day. The wee fib that if he hid the bottle on top of the fridge then Sean wouldn't see it later and there would be no evidence, therefore no real problem. Another three texts from Morna asking when they could meet up for their talk – and another wee fib, a text back to her saying for the tenth time, *Probably tomorrow x*.

And the x at the end was a fib, as much as the promise to meet up. He'd have to keep fibbing to her until she got the message. And the wee fib he'd told Meg last week, that he'd already confronted Morna. That was a big fib and it required the decanting of another shot into the wee hip flask.

And work was the biggest fib of his life, that was a given. He discovered on this day of fibs that the excruciating platitudes and puns of McGregor were actually endurable, nay enjoyable, if you had a wee fib behind his back. The potential sneaking out to the corporate bathroom for only the second wee glug from the hip flask. The peppermint antacid tablet chewed up and spat back out again to cover any possible smell of the voddie. The jaunty way he even managed to make a few wee jokes in the office over the Edinburgh, City of . . . campaign. City of sneaky wee fibs.

The only thing not a fib all day nonetheless rested on the back of a fib and was hidden by a fib. Yes, to his fellow workers it looked very much like he was making shortlists of catchphrases, taken from the hundreds of hours of transcribed market research interviews I-Com had commissioned. Yes, he told himself, even if you stood right behind him, you'd see the bullet points, the sheer volume of text on the screen, shrunk down to nine point – and you would think, 'Aye, Tom's hard at work today.' He'd even named the file 'City of . . .' in case anyone checked the desktop, and he'd cut and pasted a page of corporate doublespeak at the top, just in case any of them got nosy when he nipped out to the bathroom, with his joke about that curry last night. But no, it was a cleverly constructed fib, a very necessary fib to hide the fact that Tom was in fact having a very honest confrontation with the truth.

Staring at the screen, checking to see if he was being spied on.

WHAT TO DO WITH MY LIFE
1. *Become an American citizen.*
- Apply for a work visa. Six months long. Approximate cost $1,500.
- Move in with Meg on Fire Island. Contribute to her household income – about $2,000 a month.
- While working in US apply for Green Card – cost $3,000.
- Marry her – apply for residency. After a year of living together we will be tested to see if we're a legit marriage. Then get my American passport. Cost $2,000.
Problems:
- Post 9/11 US visas are hard to get.
- Having to find work in New York before applying for a visa. Will need a US sponsor or employer. How to start that? Google jobs in NYC.
- Having to fly back and forth to the UK as I move from visa to Green Card application status. If I overstay, will be penalised – forbidden re-entry to the US for nine years.
- What kind of work could I realistically find in America? Visas demand that you are doing a job that an American couldn't do, that you are 'special'. (I am not special, anyone can do the shit I call work.)
- 3 x international flights. Visa lawyer. Immigration lawyer. Est cost $8,500. Shit.
- Would Meg agree to marriage? Would it be confusing for her, having this almost marriage of convenience so that I can get resident status?

- Leaving Sean behind. It would be in legal terms abandonment and Sheila would sue for compulsory childcare contri-
  butions. A quarter of my salary. Six to seven thousand. Plus
  legals split fifty-fifty. Another 3K.
- Sean. Missing him. No longer being a father.

Back to the bathroom and it really was only his third tiny
sip and another wee fib – that the guy in the mirror was looking
fine, not hung-over, not wearing the same shirt for the last
three days. Meg's hickey long gone. That this was just a wee
phase he was going through until he'd sorted out the life plan.
That as soon as he'd cracked it he would never touch another
drop. That he wasn't on the same slippery slope that had led
so swiftly to the destruction of his marriage.

Ho-hum. He was back at his desk, smelling so peppermint-
fresh, and not even tipsy. Resisting the urge to do a funny wee
dance and kiss McGregor on the forehead. Back to the business.

2. *Meg moves to Scotland.*
- She will apply for a UK visa. (NB A lot easier for an Amer-
  ican to get a British passport.)
- We will get married.
- She will live with me in my flat and help in raising Sean.
  Problems:
- She would be leaving behind all her friends and her career.
- I would need to get a bigger house so she could have her
  own space. Will actually need to get another fucking mort-
  gage. Can I? When I'm still paying into Sheila's?
- Scots don't like Americans, she would find it hard to make
  friends, she would be lonely.
- Possibly living with a woman again, day in day out, would
  be too much to deal with.
- In time, the weather and the culture (lack of) would depress
  her.
- She would find it hard dealing with Sean.
- Sean might make a point of rejecting her.
- Meg might reject my proposal.

Three hours of black coffee, sobering up, fibbing to McGregor about how well the City of . . . project was coming on. Maybe not fibbing to himself any more that he was OK to drive. To drive to pick up his son from school. No, that was a sobering thought – facing his son on a day when he'd been making plans for leaving him. The new Pro Plus caffeine tablets – they give you GO – with water and another two Rennies to kill the heartburn caused by the Pro Plus. Three thousand milligrams of caffeine. Why even bother, he'd only had three tiny wee sips?

But there was that wee swerve on the corner of Leith and Waterloo (funny the way he'd been dropping the word 'street'), that wee bit of mistiming, that close scrape with the oncoming car as he turned right to park outside the school. And there was the feeling as he sat on the usual concrete hippo that any minute now he could be violently ill. A few more peppermint Rennies would sort him out. No more driving today, he'd walk home with Sean – in fact, call the ex and ask if Sean could sleep over tonight, even though it was supposed to be next week. She'd be pissed off at the break in the schedule that he was supposed to be getting back into now that he was back after America. But hell, there was no way he could turn up at her house even slightly tipsy – she'd developed a nose for it over their years. She'd sniff it and press charges for drunk-driving, endangering the life of a minor. More legal action, back to where they'd been years ago. Breathalyser, car impounded – fine of a thousand. No, he needed the car for Meg, to show her the sights, the festival (just starting this week, he should get a programme). No, get the hell out of Edinburgh, take her to the Highlands.

No, no driving. Not worth the risk. Sean would stay the night.

Another wee fib, that he was not picking up his child from school after three units of alcohol. Another, that he was not feeling guilty and sick to his soul at what a worthless piece of self-pitying shit he had become.

And then there was Morna, so many fibs to her already, and fibs to Meg about her. There she was heading right for him now, striding up through the play park. More fibs to tell. His mother had said a fib was not the same as a lie, more a peedy wee thing. An' grown-ups tell wee fibs aw the time, just so we can get on way oor lives, eh? Yer dad just likes a wee drink, son, no a problem.

Wee fibs rehearsed now for Morna: I've been working long hours – food poisoning – I'm experiencing some kind of prolonged postponed jet lag – been in London all this week.

He actually thought of turning his back to her. Trying to look invisible. Of maybe picking up his mobile – pretending to be on an important call. Actually working out the wee fibs as she walked towards him. Mobile phone out in his hand. Doing just as planned. To make it convincing he had to be mid-sentence as she arrived.

'What do you mean, you can't find the file?'

His hand in the air to tell her – just a minute.

'No, I left it on the desktop, marked urgent.'

She was standing, arms crossed in front of him. Saying:

'Ye no think it's aboot time ye telt me whits goin' on, eh?'

He covered the mouthpiece. Mouthed: 'The office, OK?'

'Yes, but those files have to be in London by start of play tomorrow.'

He was overdoing it. That one glance he'd shot her, to check if she was falling for it, had no doubt given her a glimpse of the fibber he was. The bells, the bells, saved by the bell. The kids screaming out the doors. A minute more of this pretence and he could be away with Sean. But she was in a mood, so unlike her.

'Ye could at least huv the guts tae tell me, eh? S'no like am a fuckin' eedjit!'

'Wait, wait, someone's talking to me here, can you give me a second?'

'If ye've been shaggin' in New York, ye should've jist tell me. Three weeks and all ah'm getting is this – speak the morro, see you the morro shite.'

'Look, Morna, I've really got to take this call.'

Liar, pants on fire. Fibber fibber, worry 'bout your liver.

'OK,' he said, 'I was just thinking, we should have an evening together. Talk about things. I was thinking, Friday. OK?'

'Ye said the morro.'

'Yes, but something's come up at –'

'Aye, the office! Please yersel.'

Her son in her arms then and moments after Sean was by his side. Ian chattering away about some football score Sean had got on his Game Boy.

She was pacing away. And he was shouting 'HELLO, HELLO, you still there. OK, yeah, so can we do FedEx?' down the phone to this person that didn't exist.

'I'll call you,' he called after Morna. 'Tomorrow.'

The fib had exhausted him, and Sean exhausted him more, and the fib he'd told Sean so they wouldn't have to even try to talk in their three hours together – that he had work to do at the laptop. Back home with Sean next door, logged on to Second Life again. Tom fibbing to himself that he wasn't being negligent as a father. Those hours when he could have had quality time with his son, spent instead in fearful negotiation with the needed voddie, while Sean ate his pizza alone, and he worked over point three in secretive nine point.

3. *Dual countries*
– Spend five months a year with Meg in New York and she five months in Scotland. Make it winter in New York – more sunlight – less depressing. Two months a year apart which would be healthy for us both, giving us space and maintaining that air of difference and distance that I sense she needs.
  Problems:
– Sheila would never agree to me spending that much time away from Sean.
– She'd want at least some financial recompense for time I'm not putting in on childcare. Three days a week. Forty pounds a day for a childminder. One twenty a week, 26 weeks. Nearly 3K.
– I'd have to break it up more. Do it a month at a time. One month in Scotland, one in America. Five flights a year. Five thousand pounds.
– How the fuck can I pay for all this? Have to make more money. Climb the corporate ladder – become a fucking entrepreneur.

- The stop–start nature of it all. One week fearing departure gate episode yet again. One week of getting to know each other again on rearrival, strangers, five times a year, each.
- As before – will miss Sean.

Another wee fib, when he was done, that he could engage with his son, maybe even ask him what this thing was he did online every Thursday. Guilt drove him through.

'This is Second Life, huh?' Sean nodded from his seat at the computer terminal. Tom, reaching for the seat, positioning it carefully behind Sean.

'Sure it's beyond my comprehension, but why don't you give me a lesson.'

'S'coo . . . coo . . . cool.'

There were 85,197 online now. Avatars. An island in the middle of an ocean.

Tom sat there, studious. He was not going to think about the drink and the many symbolic resonances that this other world had for his son. No – sit and learn something for once.

'I . . . Aye . . . Eyela . . . Eyeland.'

'Yeah, pretty sparse though, the island huh?'

On-screen – not quite what Tom had expected. The links he'd checked out told him Second Life was a total virtual world, that people from all over the globe were spending up to six hours a day in this place, that this was the future.

It looked like a cross between an architect's virtual simulation and a computer game from the 1980s. Chunky, slow-moving graphics. Some kind of fenced enclosure. Schemata of trees and beach houses beyond. People moved by jerkily without seeming to see each other. Eight of them. Avatars. The word meant 'incarnations of divinities on earth'. There were only so many forms to choose from, twenty or so, but you could 'personalise their characteristics'. There were two by the fence in front of some kind of flashing instruction icon on a video screen surreally standing solitary on the beach. The icon had a dollar sign. Said BUY HERE. The two closest avatars looked remarkably similar. Floating banners above their heads said their identities were Bounce Sinatra and Neo Depp. There was a sound

through the PC speakers of waves breaking on a beach. That
was all that was remotely real. But incongruously so. Something missing, between eye and ear.

'So who's your avatar?'

Sean clicked on the icon, some schemata of a young gothic
cyberpunk man called Ziggy Cruise.

'This is your friend?'

Sean laughing.

'Nuhh, no, no, thi . . . thu . . . this is, this is muh . . . me.'

Too many questions for his son then. 'So where is this? I
mean, is it based on a real place?' 'So why is this cool?' 'You
know any of these people?'

Sean laughing, clicking, moving forward through the virtual
beach houses and some impossibly placed cinema complex on
the edge of a cliff. The banner said $9.95 to sit in a virtual
cinema with others. Things he realised then: that the world
brought closer by technology was a lie. That nonetheless he
was closer to his son when doing this than in the real world.
And this was not so far from how it was with Meg.

The sound of the ocean.

'Muhhh, mooo, vuh, vuh.' Sean wanted to show him the
movement options. Then pointed at the icon. And his avatar
could move, shout, laugh, sit, wave, shrug, hug. No click-on
banners for fight, insult, reject, fuck, wank or drink – although
a sign said 'Virtual Drink Here'. Just Hi and Follow me and
Will you be my friend and This is a private area and Please
click on the icon to buy credits to enter.

The sounds of the virtual waves rolling in.

'Sean – can we make up someone for me?'

'Shu . . . shure . . . Dah.'

Half an hour of mute amazement then as Sean picked a
generic avatar and went through the shape-shifting transfor-
mations to shrink the height, add a beer belly, a beaten-up suit,
stoop the shoulders, laughing to himself all the time.

'This is me, you think this is me!?'

Sean laughing. Another ten minutes and Tom's avatar had a
name and a password. Tom Bogart he was called. Tom asked,
why Bogart? Sean couldn't explain, must have been something

to do with one of Tom's many impersonations. Tom stood back and watched Sean's back shaking with laughter as he navigated this semblance of his father round the desert island.

This thing troubled him now. He had told himself he'd left his wife and come back for the love of his son. But almost an hour in his son's company had him doubting it. The thought he was fighting before it reached its end. The opposite of the thing he'd told himself over and over, that the magazines tell you. You leave a partner but never your child. But his son had left him already.

Maybe his broadband was too slow. No interaction. The people on this beach walked past without even seeing you.

The fib to the ex about Sean staying overnight worked a dream. Another hour and Sean would be in bed on the futon, teeth brushed, spare pyjamas on. Another wee fib that watching his son asleep in his home did not upset him. He'd get him to school on time tomorrow. Tom alone now with an hour to kill till Meg called. Another wee fib. That he would just have the one to calm his nerves before she rang.

All the fibs would end now. He was back at his laptop in his bedroom, working back over point three. Maybe he and Meg could come to some kind of sophisticated modern agreement. It being a lonely game, this long-distance love, and maybe she'd need a man for hugs occasionally, and he'd be OK with that, and it would solve the Morna problem and he was sure Morna would be OK with that too. Just hugs – no sex. The day of sneaky wee fibs over now. No more. Yes, when Meg called he would propose this to her as a solution.

Trembling before the fridge. No more fibs. No more voddie. Think of her here, seeing you drunk and passed out. No more fibs. She is your only hope, stay dry for her. The image of her in his kitchen, preparing her organic muesli breakfast. Voddie bottle in his hand.

The smell of it as he poured it down the drain. For her. The last half pouring out. Such a waste. He stopped. Just one more. One last fib. One to calm him before she called.

Call

'My You ... But isn't it weird, our first day on Fire Island and we didn't take any photos.'

'I did, they're on your phone, you keep promising to send them to me!'

'Did I? I'm sorry, Tom.'

'I keep asking you!'

'Sorry. OK. I have a confession to make.'

'Tell me, my sacred sinner, of your transgression. You have been a bad girl. Tell me of your sins, say ten Hail Marys, three hundred Lady Madonnas and two Strawberry Fields Forever.'

'Tom, are you drunk?'

'I've had an elegant sufficiency.'

'That was Wilde, right?'

'I'm in a wild mood, yes.'

'You see, we get talking like this. You do this to me all the time. It's like random access. Someone should be writing all this down. What I was going to say was – Wait, this is important. If you're drunk, I'm going to have a drink too.'

'I'm OK, not too drunk, hello? [Silence.] My You? Shit!'

[Silence.]

'OK, I have some wine now. Where were we?'

'Hey, Meggie, I ever tell you – my dad, he was a . . . used to cry all the time, big slobbery kisses, failed writer, total alkie.'

'Yeah, we talked about our parents.'

'Couldn't write when he was with my mum, kept walking out on us. Oh boy, then he could write, the fucker, he'd get wasted, all alone and fucked up, then he'd write these romantic poems to my mum.'

'That's really sad.'

'Makes me sick, fuckers like him, all in the name of so-called art.'

[Silence]

'OK . . . I hear ya. You OK, Tom?'

'Me, fabulous, bees knees. Sorry, Meggie mio, what were you going to say?'

'It doesn't matter now.'

'No, no baby, never mind me. Tell me your secret, please please do.'

'You sure you wanna hear it?'

'Your dirty little secret. Do tell.'

'Jeez, ahmm. Actually, I've forgotten already.'

'Nietzsche says it's a sign of a healthy mind. A power, a skill, to forget. You should practise it, he says – forgetting.'

'Really? Wait, I've got to write that down.'

'Hello? God in fuck!'

[Silence.]

'I'm back. What was that again?'

'What?'

'What you just said. Forgetting is a sign of a healthy mind. It was Nietzsche.'

'Did I? OK, OK, yeah. So people who are always redigesting their past. It's very Scottish. Something to do with indigestion. Scots have the worst indigestion in Europe. That's a fact.'

'Wait, slow down. You're giving me heartburn.'

'I don't know. Depends on your dirty little secret. Your confession. I'm still waiting.'

'OK, you wanna hear it?'

'Your audience is captive.'

'OK, well, see, our day at Fire Island. Our first day on Fire Island.'

'I'm a Scot, like an elephant, we don't have elephants in Scotland but I never forget.'

'You see, this is my problem. I dunno, maybe it was just that we were so . . .'

'We were, weren't we? So drunk.'

'No! So absorbed in each other, I dunno, I can't remember a thing.'

'Really? I remember it all, every word.'

'God. I feel so shit, this incredible day and it's all just a blur.'

'I remember the blur too. That was the best bit.'

'No, but I want you to tell me. I mean, maybe that's what couples do, they remind each other. I feel like an old lady already. Tell me about our first day on Fire Island . . . Jesus, I must have dementia.'

'OK, OK. You ready?'

'Go for it.'

'OK, we got there early. I was tired. Needed a wee snooze. You agreed, but just a wee one you said. I'd just taught you the meaning of wee. You thought it meant a pee-pee.'

'What then?'

'Well you got up and you said the place was a mess, everything was a mess, your hair and wardrobe and the kitchen. You were talking about your routine.'

'Sounds like me.'

'You said you needed to go for your walk.'

'Yuh.'

'We were out the door and you were walking ahead of me, and I felt like . . . You were five steps ahead, all the time. Over the dunes, the beach. I got this sense that you didn't want me there.'

'My love.'

'No, not that I . . . I kind of got an idea of what was happening.'

'What was happening?'

'Well, I thought it had been a while since you'd had a guy sleep at your place. It was weird for me too. Waking up beside a woman, waiting for her to get ready in the bathroom. Like usually I just leave before all of that. Habits, grumpiness. Sorry, I'm talking about you here.'

'We were walking along the beach and?'

'No, nope, lost the point here.'

'We were on the beach, Tom. How did you feel?'

'Seriously? You want the cute version or the pre-analysed Freudian?'

'The real one.'

'I felt, I dunno, I thought maybe you should chill out and be a bit more courteous. I was thinking there are certain social

graces around the post-coital breakfast. I dunno, I was thinking
that you wanted me out of there . . . asap.'

'Confession . . . I did.'

'Bitch.'

[Silence.]

'I take that back.'

'But how did it change? How did we end up?'

'. . . In that kiss by the water.'

'Yes, that. How did that . . . ?'

'I was walking behind you. I was looking at your ass. Your
great ass. I was thinking, that great ass doesn't want me here.
That great ass doesn't want any man here. Maybe I thought
that to make myself feel better.'

'Go on.'

'I was thinking that that ass, those legs, that back, walking
through the sand, was walking away too fast and I stopped
chasing. Just stood there and you walked away and I'd been so,
the word – not obsessed. I just gave up. I don't know, I was
thinking, Give up. Look around, and I stopped.'

'This is beautiful. Keep going.'

'What's that noise?'

'I'm typing up what you're saying. You OK with that?'

'Yeah, no, not at all . . . A couple of V&Ts and I talk for hours.
OK, I was standing there and then there was the sand. Yeah, it
was hard to walk anyway. Anyway, I just stopped there and your
back and the sea. Is it the Atlantic? The waves. Birds too. Orange
beaks – oystercatchers. Don't know. Seagulls. They sounded
different from the Scottish ones. Someone told me they have
regional accents. Don't know. I was just . . . Wassa? Is that you
typing?'

'Is that a problem?'

'Yes it is. I dunno. Who cares. OK, OK, now I'm getting
lucid, I'm going to go off on a rant. You OK with that?'

'I love your rants.'

'OK, so . . . you see . . . the thing about nostalgia is that it's
usually, in a healthy person, about things past. Like the other
day you were telling me off for wishing you were here, and so
now it's my turn and I think you should stop being nostalgic,

because it implies that we're over . . . I mean, don't you think it's kind of sick mulling over those days . . . when we're actually here right now in the now?'

'On the other side of the world.'

'Don't you think . . . ? OK, OK. I'm being paranoid.'

'You are actually, my You.'

'We should fuck.'

'Well, how, Tom?'

[Shouting.] 'I just need to see your fucking face!'

'I know, I know, mee too.'

[Silence.]

'Maybe . . . if we get webcams? Seriously.'

[Silence.]

'God, listen to us.'

Journal

July 21

We talked late into last night. (He'd called me back with
insomnia – had given up on trying to sleep.) I totally forgot
how early it was with him. We finally said our goodbyes at
about 2.30 a.m my time. It must have been almost time for
him to go to work! Feel guilty for not properly telling him
about the writing. It feels like I'm betraying him – but what
can I do? Must see it through, and find a way to ask him if
it's OK.

FIRST DAY FIRE ISLAND. DAY THREE. Our arrival.
The walk home. Him going through all my things, being 'nosy'.
The garden. Our song. Making love with the eye mask. Too
many details.

Have got to tidy up all the last loose ends on *Fatal Love*, so
I can find the time to do this. A script report is due by five
today. Josh is mad at me, says I've gone off the rails. Damn
him, I don't care. Been through my accounts today and I
REALLY CAN afford to do this. Give up work for three months
and fly to Tom twice in the next year. Have to work on this
terrible script now.

July 22

Fatal Love is put to bed and Forward Features are happy – three-
hour consultation on the phone, line-by-line edit, following email
– 9K. The cheque's in the post. At last! Tom laughed so much
when I read over my notes. I really think he should work in film
again. He has a better eye than me for detail and character. I am
all structure and critique. I can never create anything new, only
empty architectures waiting for people. He had me in hysterics
with his stories of these appalling corporate videos he has to do.
How there was this publicity campaign in the nineties to promote

Glasgow – Glasgow's Miles Better – some picture of a smiley cartoon character. How the – what did he call them? the *neds* (it's some horrible derogatory term for the underclass) had subverted the slogan. 'The ironic genius of the dispossessed,' he said. They turned it into the name of a form of ritual mutilation – gang fights with razors – they held you down and slashed you from mouth to cheekbones (God, do they really do this?). All these guys walking round with scars-for-life carved into their faces. Anyway, so this is what they call the Glasgow smile. 'That better now mate, you laughing?' I feel all my social conditioning fall away as he makes me laugh about things so terrible.

I told him it would make a great film, I'd write it for him to direct, it would win at Cannes. He said I should know by now he's just a hack. His humility as always. I really do believe he should direct again. He can see through people and effortlessly finds images that say more than words.

Can't stop fussing over *The Stages of Love*. Thought a reread might get me kick-started into writing of our first day here. I found this.

STAGE TWO: SECRET LANGUAGE.
The lover experiences the physical symptoms usually associated with euphoria – dizziness; intoxication; absent-mindedness; hypersociability.

In the company of the beloved he is enthralled by perception itself. He finds in everything they share an unfolding pattern, a secret code that connects them. He discovers beauty in the smallest of things and must share them with her. A song half heard in passing is no longer just a song but 'their song'; a tree becomes a symbol of mortality; a place they sat becomes 'their place'. The meanings of words seem to fall away from things. Every object must be renamed together. They call each other by secret names. However, the lover must deny the degree to which he falls back on the history of romantic language to express himself. Poems, songs, films, drama, the entire history of romance is there for him to use, but he must reject it all, find something unique and spontaneous. His affections cannot be clichéd. When the beloved is not in his presence he does not feel loss, because in this stage the beloved is for him everywhere – is the very language through which he is seeing the world anew. However, as a result, the lover's perception of the exterior world is diminished. He has poor coordination. He walks about 'as if in a dream', bumping into things, forgetting things that need to be done. The lover breaks his routines, is prey to sudden irrational acts, all in a kind of intoxicated fascination with relearning the world.

Outcomes: unfortunately, the intensity of pleasure experienced at this stage is in direct correlation with the extent of trauma caused later. The problem with the intoxication of the private language is that increasingly the lover finds normal social talk impossible. The world outside does not understand. Songs are just songs, places are just places. The world seems not to notice or care. In creating a secret language and repertoire of intimate symbols, the lover has set himself against the world.

I wrote this in 1992 and it upsets me now. It was based on Michael and, later, Isaac. I cannot write today.

July 23

Our day three. Our secret language. July 2. Our secret name. We got the ferry and were holding hands on the top deck. I was telling him the whole history of the island.

No, but it's incredible. Used to be this haven for writers and artists in the sixties, now they're like eighty, the oldest gay community in the United States – Cherry Grove and the annual drag queen beauty pageant, the path mosaics and murals. And there's this old Buddhist couple, just down the path from me and they speak to no one. It's like everything extreme in the world on one little island. And my shack, it's lovely, you can smell it before you see it. The rosemary bushes in the garden. The last owner was called Rosemary too. I painted the sign myself on a piece of driftwood – Rosemary Cottage.

I said these things.

The ferry docked and we walked, hand in hand, along the sand paths. And his face, amazed. Pointing out the shacks, asking who lived there and there, how much did it cost? And I told him there were millionaire mansions all round Ocean Bay Park and Cherry Grove, but where we were headed, down the beach, was almost retirementsville. So quiet, the houses no more than huts. A few old hippies, like Old Pete, who braved the elements all year round. Tom couldn't stop raving – Who'd expect it here, just sixty miles from New York City! Look at that shack – that other one, so dilapidated. People paint their own houses! – look at that flower garden. Asking me how things worked, did people know their neighbours? And I told him how three years ago, when the storm came and the power lines were down, Augie went from house to house handing out the handmade candles he usually sold to the tourists for ten bucks a piece, that Old Pete made a huge bonfire and everyone for miles came round and we all brought whatever had been in our defrosting freezers and barbecued it, stayed up all night, and Josie brought over some weed from her garden and we all sat round bloated with veggie burgers till dawn, then we ran down to the beach to skinny-dip while Josie danced naked on the dunes and Eric played guitar, and lots of these summer sharers, just kids, made drums out of things they found on the sand. An old oil drum, a plastic bucket. How I loved the hippies.

'Let it be, let it be.' We were singing all the way up that long sand path.

We stopped at my gate, then he was singing, 'Parsley, sage, rosemary and thyme.' Kissing me. Telling me this place was like some kind of heaven, haven, playing with words. I was telling him the water supply was not so great and the deer that looked so cute carried ticks that had Lyme disease and it could kill. I led him inside and he couldn't stop ranting. His parents had been hippies, he said. If they could have just lived here and not in a shithole town in Scotland. He was running round inside, laughing, picking things up. Pointing out my collection of paper-weights, my Victorian dollhouse, the little pipe cleaner me that my aunt's daughter's daughter made for me.

'Looks just like you.'

He was saying I was an eccentric. Victorian kitsch and hippie throw rugs and Vivienne Westwood – a woman of contradictions – all he'd ever dreamed of – but he'd maybe got here at just the right time. Before I became a mad spinster.

He was at my wall of photos from the last ten years, asking who's this, who's that. A moment then when I felt anxious. My private wall, me with so many friends and lovers. And I had not thought of that, had never brought a man back before. Never thought my cottage might be some kind of mausoleum. But he was joking, jumping about, pointing at the photos – 'He's cute.' 'God, your hair was so short.' 'You were how old then?' 'Jesus, you were blonde?'

His enthusiasm was freaking me out. Ranting manically about how peaceful it was here, the sound of the waves, how silent, his overexcitement destroying every possible moment of silence. I wanted him just to sit. I thought it might have been a mistake to invite him here. He asked if it was OK to smoke. Outside, I said. Minutes then, watching him through the window, reeling from the shock of his presence in my home. Things he had touched he'd not set back in their right place. My shell box, the pine-root sculpture that I'd found on the beach. I had to sit – tell myself it was OK.

And it was before me, that I had never before passed a day with a man in my house. It was almost midday, we'd snacked on the way, in the car. How could I pass the time with this all-too-foreign man? We could walk the beach, we could prepare a salad for later, we could head back to where we'd come from and go to Sal and Sheila's store for some groceries. He told me his ex-wife was called Sheila, then fell silent.

Gap in order of time. Forgotten.

We made love. I wept. Talked after about how it confused me, this crying. New to me. I tried to analyse it as he got dressed. This terrible need I felt then to share tears with him. His back to me as he dressed. That was maybe why I turned cold on him.

'Look,' he said, 'how about a stroll down the beach hand in hand? Too kitsch? Maybe we could get drunk and pretend it was our first time.'

I was silent.

We walked along the beach and I was pacing ahead, angry

over the weeping. Resenting him for making me cry. Confused, talking only of how much he'd upset my routine. I was a mess and blaming him, as I kicked the waves. So much vulnerability he'd opened up inside me. Yes, he was right. I wanted him to leave. Hating myself for thinking that. This hollow ache. He was thirty feet behind me and I told myself that I had to find a way to make him go – had to get back to the cottage. The next ferry was at two thirty. He seemed oblivious to my feelings, was still joking, planning our next few days.

I asked if he was worried that they'd miss him in New York, meaning to suggest that he should be thinking about the ferry time. He said he'd made the call and the technicians would take care of it, nothing more left for him to do but make a few more calls till the flight home at the end of the week. The end of the week! I had only invited him for a day. I needed time alone. I made up an excuse, any. I needed to do a bit of work in the garden, I said. To turn the soil. It backfired. He was up on his feet and saying he felt he was a gardener today. Somehow his manic energy caught me off guard. At least it would kill the time till his ferry. I do recall telling myself that. (You wanted him to leave, remember – ferry timetables).

It was hard work, he said, he'd taken off his shirt, was digging away. It made me sad, that what he was doing was pointless, because only an hour ago I had wanted him to leave – that he must have once had a garden at a house with his ex-wife and child, that maybe he was digging so intensely because he was trying to avoid facing home – facing me. Digging himself a hole.

That was when our 'secret language' started.

'Is this coriander?' he asked. 'We call it cilantro.' 'And this is rocket, right?' 'Arugula,' I said. 'OK, for Christsake, that's fucking parsley.' 'I guess it is,' I said.

We kept digging.

Trying to remember the things he said as I look out at my garden. (Makes me sad now that all trace of his work has gone already.)

'Too much sand, yer right. Ya really need some shite here to make some loam.'

He'd been talking in Scots again. Shite, sheet, she-ite, loam? I'd asked.

'OK, loam is just, you know, fertile soil. Shite is shit. In Edinburgh we say 'away an shite'.

'You do what?'

'If someone pisses you off or you think they're winding you up, you say –'

'Sorry . . . "winding you up"?'

'A wind-up, c'mon, you must do it here.'

'I don't think so.'

'OK, a wind-up's when you say something deliberately to piss someone off. Like they're racist and you tell them about this Paki bird you're shagging.'

'Sorry, Paki?'

'As in stani. C'mon, hen.'

'Hen? I'm sorry, I don't think I'm understanding a single word you're saying.'

We sat then in the garden and he explained it all. Pakis and hen and the wind-up. I told him that all of these things seemed a bit scary, sexist and racist to me. He said the essence of British humour was to poke fun at difference. I told him difference was taken very seriously in America and was no laughing matter. He said that that was why Americans couldn't laugh at themselves. I said that was why we found Europeans laughable. He said you got me there. A debate a bit like that.

This ridiculous hour spent learning each other's words, sat there with our gardening gloves on, and somehow I wanted him to stay.

'Ye takin the piss, like.'

'So what? You say "like" at the end of a sentence. What does that mean?'

'Well, like it means, like, know what I mean.'

'Like they say in California too, like, uh, like – get my drift.'

'So what's a drift?'

'Something to do with surfing, I dunno.'

'We don't really surf in Scotland, but.'

'So what's that, that "but"? Like an ass? Like a butt?'

'Naw naw naw, in Glasgow they say "but" at the end of sentences.'

'What?'

'Like, ye know whit a mean, but.'

'But what?'

'Like that's just the way it is, but.'

'But what?'

'C'mon, yer bein' im-fucking-possible here.'

'I'm being what, but?'

'We do that, split words up to put fucking in the middle. Fan-fucking-tastic. In-fucking-credible.'

'Inco-fucking-herent?'

'Well, maybe not that.'

The whole rest of the day, us swapping accents, me trying to be Scottish, him American. The guilt gone, no thought of the time and the ferry, just going from one line to the next.

Tele-fucking-phone. Micro-fucking-wave. At times I thought I'd taken it too far but there was no end to his laughter. Every object in my house renamed. Com-fucking-puter. Fax ma-fucking-sheen. Him telling me that a little more on the 'a' and a downward turn at the end would make it more Edinburgh, that at the moment I sounded a little too Highland with my upturned lilt. Such laughter.

'You got a problem with yer swear words there, doll,' he said. 'Some kindae com-fucking-pulsion.'

'Yeah, I should, I should . . .'

'What? What?'

'Shh . . . should take it to my psycho-fucking-therapist.'

Dinner was chick-fucking-ken, and he told me that 'ken' in Edinburgh meant know, as in you know what I mean – ye ken. We drank Chardo-fucking-nnay. And every word he said had a like in it. Like fuckin', like know, like what ah fuckin' mean, but. We got all mixed up. Like fuckin' con-fucking-fused but. (Definitely not what Stendhal meant by secret language – renaming the world together!)

How did it happen? It was late then, the ferry long gone. No sense of a decision made. He was going to spend the night.

My bedroom, undressing, giggling like teenagers, reaching for kisses and words in our swapped languages. Naked and calmed, he kissed me from my face to neck, breasts, stomach.

I felt drunk, giddy. He held my hips firm and went down on me. His tongue circling my sex. Then his body started shaking. It was laughter. He was trying to say something, apologised for trying to speak with his mouth full. He kept apologising, going down was a serious business, no place for laughter, but the word had just come into his head, he said.

'Tell me. What?'

'Tuhhh, tuhg ... God, I'm sorry.'

A moment when I worried he was laughing at my body.

'Tongue!' he said. 'I come from a small village three miles from this fishing town called Tongue.'

'No – seriously?'

'Yeah, it's on the north coast, above the Highlands. We could go some day, my folks still live there. There's just one other Tongue in the world – Australia.'

'So like, no, it's really called Tongue?'

'Yeah, spelt the same and everything.'

The sentence in my head, I could hardly get the words out from laughing. 'So you say, what ... "I come from Tongue"?'

He was weeping with laughter

'You ... you do ... most women do!'

Falling about on the bed, hysterical.

'Wait, it gets worse.' His face wet with tears, he could hardly catch a breath. He'd set me off again, laughing at him laughing.

'Cahh ... car ...'

'Car?' Like we were stoned, random words, falling over. What the hell was he talking about? I didn't care, hadn't laughed like this since maybe grade school.

'Sti ... stihh ... stick ... ers.'

I saw 'car stickers'. I Love NY. I Love Brooklyn. The little red graphic heart where the word love should be.

'No – no – fucking way.'

'Yes – total way, sponsored by the local council.'

'No! On the bumper of your car?'

'Yeah, yeah, my dah ... my dad had one.'

'Jesus ... No! ... I love ...'

'Yes ... I Love Tongue!'

July 24

Sent him an email with our jokes on it. A joke retold is not so
funny any more, he said. That, actually, the town of Tongue
was a depressing place now. Only one fishing boat left – fifty
years ago there had been a hundred. He apologised for being
morbid. He was just tired, he said. It had been getting to him
that all he had to look forward to in his day was talking to me.
Like he didn't actually live in Scotland. He was sorry.

This change that happens within him. So quick. I am not
there with him to witness it. So many things in his day I cannot
see. I sleep through his day, we talk in his night. My laughter
now makes him melancholy. Makes him miss me more, he says.
He has not laughed for days now. The phone is not enough.
He finds my emails alienating. My text messages too frag-
mented.

Our day is not done yet. I have not written of our night of
the blindfold – the eye mask. Am sad today thinking of his
sadness. I googled Edinburgh after he hung up to try to see his
city for myself. Maps. Satellite pictures. It looks so beautiful.
The International Festival will begin soon. A million foreign
visitors, three hundred shows, art, theatre, dance, comedy. He
says that the locals find it a nuisance. I am struggling to understand his sadness. He tells me we were alive in every second
on Fire Island, but now we are six hours apart. Will try to write
tomorrow of our perfect night.

July 25

Phone sex again today – his car – he was driving me naked and
blindfolded round Edinburgh. He makes me come with whispered words. Terrible questions after he hung up: Is this all I
have ever wanted? My eye mask, our ritual. I'm in darkness and
he tells me of how he touches me and I'm there with him.

'*Love depends on uncertainty and distance.*' Stendhal in his book
called *Love*. '*Certainty kills love.*' Ibid.

The old fear has kicked in again – that I am in denial, that
this is all a fantasy, that it takes a man to make me feel whole.
Hole of a woman. Ashamed of how he makes me feel. (Feminist
guilt.) Can tell this to no one. Appalled at myself.

TRY TO WRITE ABOUT IT. No one is watching/judging.

The blindfold. My friends would be horrified if I told them. I can see it as they would – you have blindfolded sex because you cannot face emotion. So lonely now. This thing so intense and I can tell no one. He makes me cry. I cry when I come. I cannot explain this. Sex is many subtle negotiations over what is essentially rape, my friends say, quoting Andrea Dworkin. Men are violent – yes, he was on day five: the bridge. Am so confused. These things I can't write. Everyone will hate me.

July 26

Our call. I feel he is putting on a brave face, something is troubling him, he won't tell me what. All there is to do is press on. WRITE IT.

July 2. NIGHT OF THE BLINDFOLD.

The sex thing had been impossible because of the laughter and we joked about that too. There had been too much negotiation of sexual positions after the laughter and I felt, I guess, some kind of fear of letting go of that effortless humour, and sex seemed like an exercise in grave purposefulness. And he had been too drunk again, he apologised, and we joked about that too, and then about how laughter and erections didn't go together. He was snoring again, and it was so late, the sun coming up and I can never sleep when it's like that. I had always meant to get an eye mask. He had this free air-travel one in his bag which was beside my bed, I'd noticed it when I'd been fumbling around for his condoms. I hunted round in the half-light and took the eye mask from his bag and fastened it round my head. It was well designed, blocked out all light. I had spooned my knees behind his, set my hand on his pelvis, fingers hanging over his beer belly.

I could have cried then behind the mask. For the many times I'd spooned with a man after a day of doubts, accepting less. The doubts descending again. That all we had joked about really was our cultural differences. That those things would disappear if we spent any real time together. That I was starting again with another man, always starting again.

The night of the eye mask. How life changes come about by accident. Try to write of it. What you felt.

'I cannot see. I don't want to see. If I see I cannot lose myself. Make me blind. Make me hear and feel. My love, my love.'

DELETE.

It had happened by accident. His complimentary international flight bag. A micro tube of toothpaste, mini toothbrush, and this thing, this eye mask.

(An experience close to what is called Zen. How could this simple piece of nylon have transported me to this place I had only heard of?)

Sociological analysis and now this New Age mysticism. The closer I get to the truth the more my voice breaks into different voices.

DELETE SELECTED SECTION.

It wasn't a blindfold in the literal sense. Nothing deliberate about it. I was woken by his kisses and hands on my breasts. His fingers running down my stomach. His tongue circling my sex. I was half asleep, maybe he was too, dreaming of some other body. Disoriented. I'd fallen asleep as the sun was rising but now it was dark – had I slept a whole day? Realising then – the eye mask was still on. I reached to take it off but somehow his hand found mine then was leading it to my breast, telling me, without words, to touch my nipples. I wanted to be free of the mask, but the dark was as warm as his tongue, as deep as his gentle fingers. (I have always had an aversion to sex in the dark. It being always a denial – fear of looking – I need to see this act to believe it at all. To hear a man tell me what I look like – seeing his excitement arouses me. In the dark I think only of two bodies who cannot face each other.)

The sensations.

Like chasing an eyelash across the skin of your retina. Like squeezing your eyeballs (as a child) so you could see the stars. Like near drowning. Mute beauty.

Too poetic. DELETE ALL.

I'm sure now he didn't know I was still blindfolded. That if he had, he'd have apologised and helped me take it off. (Would have removed it myself if the feeling had not been so intense.)

Sounds were louder. Every breath. His sounds animal, hungry. Feeding. The smell of my sweat, my sex. Sound of my own breath, aroused at hearing it so loud. Each pore open, listening in the dark. Hearing lungs filling and emptying, quickening, tasting air, blood in veins, heartbeat in my throat, muscles in my legs tightening pulling my knees up, wider as he delved with his tongue. Us passing into this deep dark place, expanding, filling the room, opening for him, wet, so wet, pouring out. Hearing for the first time this body gasping and pleading and breathing and moaning so loud, this man whispering, every sound, sensation amplified in the dark. Until the screams shot through our flesh. I was crying, howling again and again, hours it seemed on this plateau, these peaks – abstract, shapes in the dark, sounds of a woman crying, begging, screaming again and again. Feeling her in my spine.

Terrible clichéd attempts at poetic language.

DELETE. BE HONEST.

OK. Sex with men before was always the instruction manual. The candlelit dinners, then playing amateur gynaecologist – Lift my pelvis so you can hit the G-spot – massage my clit at the same time – look into my eyes – don't close yours – I find it alienating – so many instructions given – so many men shrinking from my maybe contradictory demands. 'I come with an instruction manual,' Tom said. 'I mean, really, only usually manually.'

LAUGHING NOW. How is it possible to have sex with a man and laugh at sex and still go through with it – then cry? NO, THE LAUGHTER WAS AFTER. I feel as awkward now as maybe he felt when he'd opened his eyes and saw I'd been wearing the eye mask throughout. (My prudishness maybe.) Write it!

This abrupt change from the intensity of the mask, to the room filled with light and this thing threatening to happen. The need to talk – tell him how beautiful it was. That would destroy it all. (To have to return to this world of objects examined in talk. Cold light of day.) I couldn't stop weeping. He'd said:

'I'm sorry, baby. You OK? I didn't realise. Hope you don't

think I'm into that kind of thing . . . Jesus, I'm such a dumb fuck. Guess I had my eyes closed – didn't even notice . . . are you OK?'

I'd kissed his fingertips, tasting myself, brought them to my breast to make him feel my heartbeat, touched his lips to say don't talk. Shook my head, nodded, couldn't speak, wouldn't let myself. I took the eye mask and held it over his eyes. Then pulled it away. Trying to tell him through touch. His eyes looking for answers in mine. My hand again to his eyes with the mask, holding it there, seconds, kissing his knuckles. Him smiling, not sure what I was doing, playing peek-a-boo.

'What, what is it?'

I had to be strong. Told myself that. To not let go to laughter. Make him feel this thing that was more. Without words. I lowered the mask from his eyes. Do you understand now? I tried to ask with my eyes.

'Yes,' he said. 'I see. I see now.'

'I see you too.' I lay back, putting the mask to my eyes. 'I see you too, my You.'

'S'a good name. You. Sounds like Eustace, like useless.'

'Letter U – my You.'

'I am your You.'

'Yes, you are, and I am yours too.'

Yes, that must have been the night we invented our love name. Both the same. You and You. What am I now? Half a you? We make no grammatical sense. We are nonsense, but I am tired of sense. My You. My You. I see you now.

Speech Therapist

A house. A star. A car. An apple. A landscape. Five cartoon images placed in front of him.

Tom had left work early to get there on time. All this week fighting the voddie. The calendar had dry days drawn in advance then crossed out. A few wee secret shots of voddie today at work, black coffees and six Pro Plus tablets so he could drive. The whole day preparing for the humiliation of sitting with his ex and the child psychologist. She'd texted from work. She worked long hours now. Had to, she said, because he was behind in child-support payments.

Working late. U meet Sean @ doctor? Will drop him off. Tell me results. Bring him over @ 7.

The meeting with the child psychologist was four thirty.

A house. A star. A car. An apple. A landscape.

Tom had got there just on time. Had driven round the massive NHS complex, trying to find the Psychology Department. He'd tried asking people but they were patients not staff. A woman, ancient, white-haired, yellow skin, in a wheelchair being pushed by a young Asian woman. He'd rolled down the window to ask, but seeing the pain on the old woman's face, the foreignness of the other, had decided it was best to try to work out the directions himself.

The Psychology Department was this big solitary concrete block a hundred yards from the ancient Victorian hospital with its horrible modernist extensions and scaffolding that spoke of more expansion. My God, were there so many sick people in this country? Of course there were. This country loved its sickness. It was what the Scots call Scottishness. Car park. Floor 5. Room F. He'd had to run to get there on time. This was Sean's fourth test now. The ex had called him to discuss it all, to remind him and run through the correct language. They must not let Sean know what was really going on. He was 'special', she said, not 'special needs'. He'd laughed at the time. Sean had bought special powers on Second Life. Sean could fly. Sean, with the help of the translation program he'd down-loaded, could chat in Japanese and Arabic.

He got there ten minutes late. Sean was just leaving the room. Tom didn't know the procedure. The man at the door introduced himself as Dr Foster – was not wearing a white doctor's jacket. Foster. Meg's middle name.

'Sorry, I'm maybe a little late.'

A house. A star. A car. An apple. A landscape.

'No, no, not at all. Sean and I have just finished up.'

'So, I don't know. I mean, what we do now?'

Sean's hand reaching for his.

'Dddaaah, it's co . . . coooo . . . cool.'

'Well, Sean and I have had a good long chat and –'

'You want me and Sean to come in together?'

'Not at all. Sean has his computer magazines.'

Tom turned to Sean.

'You OK with that, kiddo, you cool?'

Sean nodded.

'Sean's been telling me all about computers and –'

'Hay . . . hay . . .'

Tom watched as the psychologist waited till Sean finished the word. The word was in Tom's head – haven. The place where Sean met his virtual friends.

'Hayvuhh . . . hayvuvv . . .'

Haven, Tom wanted to shout.

'I'm sure Sean wouldn't mind waiting for just a bit while we speak. Tom, isn't it?'

'Yes. Tom.'

'Be just half an hour, Sean,' said the shrink, call him Foster, find out his first name so he can't control you. Him with a second name, you with a first.

The room was exactly like Tom expected. Old wooden book-shelf with many tomes – behavioural science, even some Freud – cheap NHS Formica version of the therapist's desk. On the wall a beach sunset. Not an original painting but a photograph of a painting of a sunset. As Tom sat he'd already made his mind up. Half an hour of quack nonsense, then take Sean back home, not to log on to Second Life, but to do something more constructive.

The two chairs, the desk between. Tom was wittering.

'So the tests. It's not like, physiological, he's not tongue-tied, there doesn't have to be surgery?'

The calm of the man.

'We're not in the Victorian era now. No, rest assured that Sean's in every physical sense just like every other child his age.'

'And it's not ADHD? My wife, my ex, thinks . . . She also thinks it might be hereditary. I had a stutter when I was kid. I mean, can it be passed on?'

This Foster, this doctor, took his time. No doubt some cleverly constructed ruse to put the client – wasn't that what they called them now? – into a state of calm confidence before the bad news. Fifteen months waiting for these appointments on the fucking NHS. Who's going to pay for BUPA? the ex said. No, Tom was not calm.

'We're fine on all that,' the doctor said. 'All the tests done. Sean does not have ADHD and stuttering is not hereditary. In fact, you should know that his knowledge of maths –'

'I know, the kid's a genius with his computers. But I was worried that it was maybe –'

'No possibility of autism. Sean's mother has already alerted me to this. No concerns there.'

'Thank God.'

'Tom. What I have to tell you is that your son is exceptionally bright for his age. His written sentences, his grasp of grammar.'

Tom couldn't hold it back.

'Written, yeah, I know, but speaking.'

A house. A star. A car. An apple. A landscape.

The pictures laid before him then, after the explanation of the test. Tom was resisting, going back through the entire history of what he knew of psychology. Freud was dead and everything for him was sex. Angered now at this dumb sub-

Rorschach test that he, if he'd been a better parent, would never have let his son be subjected to.

A house. A star. A car. An apple. A landscape.

'I simply asked Sean to write what he felt beneath each image. The first thing off the top of his head. His writing skills are advanced. He did the whole test in less than a minute . . .'

A house. A star. A car. An apple. A landscape.

'. . . Some questions though over his word association. I was hoping you might help.'

Get this over and done as soon as possible. Sean was waiting beyond the door, on the NHS sofa that was three seats together with metal armrests that separated them.

Under the picture of the house Sean had written LONDON.

A star. Sean had written HOLLYWOOD.

A car. Sean had written THURSDAY.

An apple – TWO TOWERS.

A landscape – BOGART.

'Well, they're cryptic to say the least,' said Foster. 'All Sean told me was that Bogart is something to do with some kind of computer game.'

'Yeah, he's this avatar Sean made for me. Bogart.'

'An avatar?'

'Yeah, it's this computer game thing. Second Life – that's what it's called.'

The man had the audacity to take some notes.

'This obsession with computers . . . I try to discourage it as much as possible.'

'The Two Towers though? Unusual response to a picture of an apple.'

'It's *Lord of the Rings*. You know, the second movie. He's watched it maybe twenty times.'

'Of course.'

Sick of this whole hidden-agenda scenario that was every encounter with the NHS. These fuckers did these same tests on junkies and had at the end of their thirty-minute session decided on whether or not to sign that paper, pre-prepared on their desk, that would place your kid, or you, in care, for ever.

'But to go back to Bogart?'

'Well, Sean's never seen a Bogart movie. It's just this name he came up with for me. Online. I don't think it means anything really. I mean, there's only so many second names you can choose from in Second Life. Names of film stars.'

'I see.'

Hollywood he'd managed to have dismissed as just the usual childish obsession. London and Thursday took more work but he got clear of them without having to suffer too much prying.

The handshake and the card with the time and date for the next consultation.

'Fine, well, I shall be writing to the school to say there's no need for special-needs treatment. We'll work on some behavioural exercises, next time he comes. I'll send an appointment schedule.'

Tom was out and Sean was setting down his computer magazine. He would have liked to take his son's hand but Sean was too old for that now. Tom led him out as quickly as he could.

A man of thirty in a wheelchair and respirator in the lift with them, his body given up on itself. The lift door opened at ground floor. Out and the sickness was queuing in the waiting area by reception, the white sweating faces behind the reception desk too tired and bored to care. He was going to go BUPA. God knows how. It was natural for the body to be well and to think you were sick from the start was a sickness. Fifteen years as a Marxist and one week in New York and his entire ideology reversed. Fuck the NHS, fuck the cradle to the grave that brought the grave on quicker. No, illness is not your fate. Grow up. Be well. For fucksake. This entire country that made itself sick so England would take care of it. My God, he was George Bush now. He was Thatcher. He was grabbing Sean's hand, dragging him out of this hell.

Across the car park.

A house. A star. A car. An apple. A landscape.

LONDON. HOLLYWOOD. THURSDAY. TWO TOWERS. BOGART.

He headed west to drop Sean off at his mother's. The drive through the privately owned tenements, the slightly bigger gardens that all the locals thought made them better than everyone else. Finger on the buzzer and the usual 'Hi, we're here' through the security speaker. She never came down to meet his eye. They both preferred that. She would buzz Sean in then he would be away.

But today she was at the door. 'Saturday,' he said, 'two o'clock, it's fine,' without meeting her eye, and then was on his way through her garden, heading for his car double-parked with the hazards on.

'Tom!' she shouted after him. He turned obligatorily, she was his ex-wife after all, they were polite to each other now.

'What, my love?' The words, he caught before he said them. All that came out was a 'What?' – 'What's wrong?'

Staring at her as she stared back at him over the garden now filled with toys from younger children in the same block.

Something told him he'd have to move closer, her face at the door. Sheila. Sheila was happy with the way things were with the childcare now. He'd heard this from other people, friends of friends, not from her directly. She had a new boyfriend now, Jason, he had three kids and lived two blocks from her. He was divorced too and Sean played with his kids. Tamara, Becky, Phil.

'What?'

Standing on her front doorstep. Looking at her. He never looked at her. This rule he had about that. Only the eyes, not the rest. Not the wrists, the arms, the neck. He was looking now at her wrists, her arms, her neck.

'Well, I think, don't you?'

'What?'

'Well, Sean's told me about her.'

Every word in quotation marks as he said it. Every quotation mark a question.

'What?' 'Sean told you?' 'About her?'

'I'd rather have heard from you first.'

'Well, I'm sorry about that but –'

'So, she's from New York?'

'Well, yes, in fact, she is.'

Her fingers on the edge of the door, opening it further. Don't look at her. That thing she's doing now, the swing of the hips.

Just to torment you. This new spontaneity she's found since the boyfriend. Her dyed-blonde bob, her newly visible waistline. Her clothes which were now Armani not Gap.

'Well, I'm OK with it but I'd rather have heard it from you first.'

'What, is there a problem here?'

'She's coming to stay for how long?'

'A month, we're just going to see what happens.'

He felt like a kid with a stolen toy hidden away. He'd said, 'We're just going to see what happens.'

'Well, that's great.'

Great, is it great? What was she really saying? Three years apart and now she was telling him things were great.

'Well, I'm just glad you've found someone, but, seriously, New York?'

And he saw where she was going with this. This way she made him second-guess the thing she hadn't said. This thing she called diplomacy, which was feminine coercion.

What? he wanted to shout. 'What?' he asked quietly 'What's wrong with New York?'

'Well, as long as you know what you're doing.'

'What, what am I doing?'

'Well, it's the same pattern all over again.'

'What?'

'Come on. I shouldn't have to tell you by now.'

'What?'

'London, Dublin, Paris?'

'So?'

'OK, you don't want to talk about this.'

She was closing the door. 'Fine, I'll drop him off Saturday.'

His foot in her door then, an invasion. 'No, sorry. No, but what are you saying exactly? What?'

'Well, I just need to know that you're not going to run off again.'

'Oh, for Christsake, come on.'

'Sorry, it's just this pattern with you. My therapist says.'

'Great therapist – you talk about me. Wow, great, I should get one that lets me talk about you.'

'Muhhh, muuuh,' Sean was shouting from the hall. 'HA . . . da.'

'This isn't the time or the place,' he said.

'DAH, DAAA, DAAAHD.'

'Come on, we're –' He stopped himself short. He shouted through the door to Sean.

'It's OK, kiddo, we're not arguing, just having a grown-up talk.'

Her face then, for him having shouted into her home to her son.

'You've no idea, have you?'

'What? I have plenty of ideas.'

Something unsaid in her eyes that made him want, as he'd wanted many times before, to just touch her.

'No idea,' she said. He sensed what was coming. 'How much your son loves you. If it wasn't for that, I would have long ago –'

'Please, Sheila. Sean's just there behind you.'

Her voice lowered. 'If you run off again, I swear –'

'I'm not running anywhere. I'm here.'

'– it'll get legal, don't think it won't.'

'C'mon, we're upsetting Sean now, c'mon. I'd never leave him.'

'No, not like before.'

'Do I have to do this again, do I have to explain?'

'You explained nothing.'

'Look, Sean is just standing there.' He shouted through the hall. 'It's OK, kiddo. Put on your video.'

'God,' she said, 'listen to you.'

'Look, this is exactly the wrong thing to be doing in front of him. The speech therapist said that.'

'God,' she muttered under her breath.

He wanted to turn away, the garden path before him. But he had been the one that first walked away. The neglectful father. This debate he'd suppressed for so many years that he'd felt so immediately in those first years of separation. This argument he'd never articulated before. That in those years of marriage had him moving from country to country to try to build their family in a better place. Not here. He had wanted his son to grow up in a multicultural society, in the New World, to believe in himself, because he knew what it was to grow up here. And he had as a child been an outsider and bullied and he, too, had developed a stutter. And even his own father had been the same. For three generations his family had wedded the English and the French and had travelled because they wanted something more, wanted out. He was sorry for trying and failing to bring his child up in another country that was challenging, threatening, open and other. To bring his child up with questions not the same old answers that were always what street you lived on, who your parents were, class difference and income, what football team you supported, Catholic or Protestant. Blue or green-and-white faces washed whiter with bigotry.

Still he was standing there at her door.

'He blames himself, you know that, you must.'

'Christ Almighty.'

'He thinks his stutter is to blame . . .'

Unfinished sentences. God, he knew where this would go.

'. . . for us.'

'Stop it. You have a boyfriend, I hear this from Sean every day. Jason did this, Jason did that.'

'Stop.'

'Stop what? Like he doesn't know every fucking thing already'

'Shh. He's hearing all this.'

She regained her composure.

'It's great you've got someone who cares for you . . . Just . . .'

'I'm not moving to New York, if that's what you think. Jesus.'

'OK. I just needed to hear that from you.'

'I'm not running away again.'

'OK, that's good. I just needed to hear that . . . OK, be here on Saturday, 2 p.m.'

'Fine, two.'

And don't let him do any more of the computer stuff. Oh yeah, and he's got the child psychologist again next week.'

'Got that on my list. It's fine. OK. Bye.'

'Bye.'

A house. A star. A car. An apple. A landscape.

Tom walked away, turned the corner and got into his car. A second before driving.

LONDON. HOLLYWOOD. THURSDAY. TWO TOWERS. BOGART.

Not isolated words but a sentence. A whole paragraph came to him. Sean talking in his head without the stutter.

'We moved to LONDON when I was five, my dad wanted to make films, like in HOLLYWOOD, he had this big job offer in New York to be a film director. He showed me the pictures of the Empire State and the Brooklyn Bridge and told me we'd be going there soon. But I was scared and wanted something to happen so we wouldn't have to go. Then the TWO TOWERS fell down. And they argued, and when my dad's job fell through it was my fault, cos I'd made it happen. I'm sorry, Dad – I made the towers fall down. I see my dad every THURSDAY now. I go on to Second Life and my dad does these movie voices, so I called our avatar BOGART and Tom cos that's his name. Tom Bogart is the name of our avatar.'

The off-licence on the way home. Vodka and Schweppes. Quick transaction. Home. In the door. Three deep mouthfuls. Yes, it would only make things worse, but he was logging on to the PC, with his new password for Second Life.

The island on-screen again, ten people with celebrity names walking the sand, between the flashing banners. The sound of the ocean. Tom clicked on Sean's icon, Ziggy Cruise, the password was pre-saved. It took a while but he found the toolbar with the speak command and clicked on Speak History. The date – the last day Sean was here. Tom clicked Open.

ZIGGY CRUISE: Gotta go now, my dad's waiting.

DEDE DEPP: My dad's a weirdo.

ZIGGY CRUISE: Mine's OK. Not weird, just a little wired right now.

DEDE DEPP: How so?

ZIGGY CRUISE: He's got this girlfriend in New York. It's some big LURVE thang. You're from New York, right?

DEDE DEPP: Close, Cruise boy – New Jersey.

ZIGGY CRUISE: SO cooool. Gonna run away when I'm fourteen.

Tom scrolled down. Ten pages of his son talking. Quickfire, cynical wit, a voice Tom had never heard from his son before. A voice so like his own.

It was starting again. The pattern as before. The sense of things closing in. The fear of which only made it come closer. The tears turned to howls. The howling was what happened last time, just before he ran. The howls that had to be drowned in vodka. It was happening again.

Call

'My You, what's wrong? Why are you crying?
'Sss ... sorry ... I ...'
'Aw, my love, tell me.'
'You ... you say you're trapped. You have no idea.'
'My You, it's OK.
'Wha ... What I'd give to be able to live with you in New York.'
'Shh now. Don't talk like that, you have Sean.'
'Sean has his mother, I'm just a babysitter.'
'You know it freaks me out. I told you about my dad.'
'I know. I know. I know.'
'You're a good father, I know you must be. You're going to stay with Sean.'
'I know ...'
'I'm not going to be the woman that takes a man from his kid, I couldn't face it. I hated my dad's second wife. I couldn't do that.'
'What are we doing, Meg?'
'How do you mean? We're talking, you're fine.'
'I just wish you were here, I wish you could come sooner. I'll pay for your flight. Put it on my card, you could be here the day after tomorrow.'
'I know, my You, I'm just. I'm not like you. I can't just jump into things. I need this time to get things together, to process. You're a bit of a whirlwind. These things take time for me. If I go in deep too fast I'll just freak out. I just need this time alone. Besides, I've got stuff to work out with my work and property and –'
'OK, understood, I'm cool now. Sorry.'
'My You. You know, it's not so bad like this. I was just thinking I have this friend, Annie, and she has this issue with her guy.

[Silence.] She's a morning girl, like me, only ever horny when she wakes up, most women are, I think, but he's always grumpy in the mornings and comes too quickly cos he's an afternoon guy, just like you. And by the time he gets home, she's exhausted and then he wants to have sex. They're arguing about it all the time. Practically getting divorced because of it. [Silence.] So, you see, it's not so bad. I'm in my morning and you're in your evening and we're in sync, it's funny but kind of perfect really. I told her she should get a long-distance lover. In many ways our set-up is perfect.'

'You think this is perfect!?'

'No, no. Don't get all grumpy, my love. My evening man.' [Silence.]

'So how long are you going to stay for when you come?'

'Well, the return is four weeks after, but I paid a bit extra, so I could change the date, I mean indefinitely, I have Air Miles with American, up to three months . . . if . . .'

'If things turn out all right. Yeah? Maybe we should just play it by ear.'

'Don't say that. God, you want me to come earlier, now you're saying I should leave earlier! [Silence.] Tom, what's going on? You're self-sabotaging.'

'No, no –'

'You are, I do this myself. Talk to me. [Silence.] You're getting insecure again, you're thinking, what if she doesn't like me any more, what if she hates my city. I know this, God, I've been through this before.'

'I'm just worried about, I mean, how we do this in the future.'

'Well, like we agreed – we see each other half the year, maybe eight months. Three return flights, I told you – I can pay for your flights to New York.'

'But I mean, for years, how can we . . . ?'

'Well, of course, ultimately there has to be some kind of choice, but don't you think it's a bit early to be thinking about that? Not that I'm –'

'You won't want to live here.'

'There you go again, self-sabotaging. I might, I might move to the UK, permanently, I might even get a job there, nothing to do with you. In London or . . . Edinburgh is amazing, I've seen so many pictures, and the festival, I'll get there just before it finishes. The Wooster Group are performing, you know, from New York. We just don't know. OK, my You?'

'Meg . . . I'm sorry. I want you here as long as you can stay.'

'You're not exactly selling me on this.'

'Sorry . . . I'm just . . . You're right, self-sabotaging. I just want you here with me all the time. I just thought it would sound needy if I said it.'

'My You, you always talk in opposites.'

'I want you to live with me here. We'll buy a Scottish castle and be king and queen over all we see.'

'My You . . .'

'I'm sorry . . . I . . .' [Crying.]

'My You, it's OK. It's OK. Talk to me please. Tell me a story.'

Journal

July 27
Finally, I calmed him. No matter how fraught we become our phone sex seems to ground us. With my blindfold on I can see – everything opens up. In our fantasies I am always the passive one but I feel empowered. (God, such a feminist word – all that is no use to me now.) Just realised that this journal is becoming something more. The observation of tiny emotional movements and shifts in a day. I write – blind to judgement (maybe over-analysis has crippled me in the past). This is so much better than any fiction I've written before.

Just been experimenting with script format. An idea – that the phone sex could turn into sequences in a film.

INT. BEDROOM. DAY
She lies on her bed with the eye mask on, the phone to her ear. We hear his voice down the line. The tinny crackle. His whispers.

> [HE]
> You're sitting in my car, in the front seat beside me. You're naked beneath an overcoat. Wearing nothing but heels. You have your eye mask on.

Cut to:

FANTASY. INT. CAR. DAY
The car passes through the city of Edinburgh. Blindfold on. She sees nothing. From the driver's seat he tells her what he sees, as his free hand parts the coat and finds the soft flesh of her thighs.

[HE]

> We're on Princes Street now. Thousands of
> people, tourists. No one can see you – see what
> I'm doing to you. Spreading your legs, touching
> your pussy. We're passing by the cathedral now.
> There are buskers playing guitars. A bus beside
> us at the lights. They could see you if they were
> looking but their eyes are on the sights, the
> castle, the park, we're surrounded by thousands
> but they don't see you, you can't see them. I'm
> stroking your clit. You're getting wet.

His fingers move inside her. She throws back her head, resisting
the temptation to take off the blindfold. The humiliation of
being seen like this, surrounded by strangers. It excites her. Her
breath quickening. He takes his hand from her as he puts the
car in gear. They drive on.

[HE]

> I'm driving out of town now. I'm going to park
> in a supermarket car park. When we get there,
> I'm going to put your seat back and fuck you
> in the car park. You have to keep your eye
> mask on. There'll be hundreds of shoppers all
> around us, and I'll be fucking you right before
> their eyes. You will resist. I will hold you down.
> I'm going to cover your mouth so no one can
> hear you when you come. The car doors are
> locked, you can't escape.

He said all these things, but when I see it written down . . .
My God, I'm a pornographer! We are *Last Tango in Paris* –
First Waltz in Edinburgh. Is this really me? I have the bug now,
can't stop.

I am calling them 'He' and 'She'. Feel better about this. The
story taking shape is based on us but is not us. It's not like I'm
betraying him. Tell yourself that, Meg. God, I could go back
through the entire journal and turn it into a film!

Just texted him a quick message.

Nite nite, my love, hope I didn't upset you tonight. You inspire me so much. You are a genius. We are the best movie ever never made. Love you x

July 28

Things are coming into sync – tonight he talked of Sean and I need to write of our day four – DAY OF HIS CALL TO SEAN. Be good to get all of our days written down, get beyond the Tom and me to write about He and She. Have spent five hours today converting our first days into script format. It's brilliant. His dialogue is fantastic. Of course I've changed bits here and there but I really feel I'm on to something here. It has to be my little secret until it's done. A crazy idea, a gift to him, that from our days together a script will come, a script for him to direct. How impossible and beautiful that would be, for us to make a film together about our love. And all this from his tiny bits of encouragement. Is it possible that two people can inspire each other so much? Been finding it hard to hold back with my questions to him. Pushing him for more information on the day of the call to Sean.

All I know is:

Sean is ten. He goes to a state school. (His mother wanted to go private but Tom could not contribute enough financially.) Sean is a genius at computer programs. He is getting medical/psychological help with his stutter. Tom blames himself for Sean's condition. Sean's mother is Sheila (39) – medical adviser for the NHS. Tom walked out on her three years ago because of 'differences'. He won't explain what they were.

My enthusiasm seems to upset him though. I try to explain how much beauty there is in the tiniest of details, how I need him to remind me of every little thing. Long silences down the phone.

Our fourth day. July 3. Write of how his call to Sean upset everything. Second day on Fire Island. Day after the eye mask – day of the beach walk – he went through all my CDs. (Good, you forget your self-conscious imposition of structure when you just record – stay true to that – keep it simple, stupid!)

After the walk, he'd asked me to help with the time-zone arithmetic. He said that if he got it half an hour too early Sean's mother would pick up and say Sean was having his dinner – call back later. If on the other side of the hour, she'd say, too late, he's in his bed, call back tomorrow. He had to call Sean before he went to bed. 8.30 p.m. 2.30 p.m. our time. He had to call Sean.

It's all coming back. We have slept late, a nibbled breakfast of rice cakes. I am impossibly happy after our night of love-making. Singing to myself before the mirror, for once not seeing my face as a map of flaws, but glimpsing myself as he saw me the night before. Ridiculous playful mood. I finish my facial scrub and moisturiser and come out of the bathroom and he is there, sitting staring out my window. I have an idea, a surprise, a game I used to play with my dad. I tiptoe in, trying not to laugh, and stand behind him putting my hands over his eyes. Masklike, to remind him of our game with the eye mask.

'Boo! Guess who?'

He shrugs, his hand reaching to pull my hands away.

'Play the game! So you have to tell me. Am I happy, sad, angry, melancholy, surprised or whatever? Keep your eyes closed!'

I carefully keep my hands over his eyes while I move round to face him. I put on my sad face, say, 'So what am I now?' Pull my hands away from his eyes. He doesn't get it. Any of it. His face sadder than mine. I put my hands over his eyes again. My happy face.

'So am I angry, silly, melancholy, happy?'

I pull my hands away.

'OK. You look . . . I dunno. Melancholy?'

'No, silly!'

'Beautiful?'

'No, that's not on the list.' I pull my happy face again.

'I'm sorry,' he said. 'Crazy maybe.'

The longer the game went on the more it undid what I'd meant. He hadn't even tried to guess properly. I felt like a fool. He held my wrist as I reached again to cover his eyes.

'Meg, can we stop this? Please.'

Melancholy man after a night of letting go. Staring out my window.

'I play this game with Sean. OK. I have to call my son in a few hours.'

All morning it haunted us. He had to call his son at two. We had three hours. This time I wanted to celebrate and be as light as a feather, but was pulled down by the weight of that impending call. That morning I behaved so strangely. So much need, dancing round him trying to cheer him up. As if I sensed that our night was going to be erased. Yes, I resented him for shutting down on me. Resented him more for turning me into what I became that day – stupid needy kid, fighting for Daddy's attention.

July 29

Just off the phone to him. The Sean and fatherhood issue won't leave us alone. My mistake, maybe, that I'd prepared this speech that I'd never come between him and Sean. It backfired horribly. He said (and I couldn't believe this) that maybe he wanted me to come between him and his child.

Am up to day three in script rewrites now. He and She. She is not as wholesome as he is. I have to rewrite her as a character with some kind of life, she can't be a writer – what do writers do? They write. So dull! Maybe she works in PR? I tried to remove the child from the story, thought it too melodramatic, too *Hiroshima Mon Amour* (note: we talked about that on second last day). But still, if there is no child then there is less dramatic tension – nothing really to keep him there. Feel bad about this now. The simple narrative solution for two in love is to go to each other. But to create a great timeless romance, to arouse greater passion, there has to be an obstacle. It is of course Sean, but I don't want the story to be too personal. I know so little about Sean. (Maybe that's for the best.) I don't want to put Sean in the story. Other possible solutions – he has a sick ex-wife, his father is dying of cancer. I worry that this story as it develops is too close to our own. Have to find a device to abstract it.

Tonight on the phone – I had to resist the urge to ask him more about our day. The music was loud in his flat. I kept hearing a glass clinking against his teeth. I'm sure he took the phone through to his kitchen at one point. Sounds of footsteps, of his fridge door opening. His music blaring. Sound of the unscrewing of a lid – I asked him if he was drinking. He said it was apple juice, he was on a health kick. But his words were slurred. He was blowing smoke into the mouthpiece. (He always smokes more when he drinks.) Lengthy silences. He went into this long diatribe about his father. How he chose alcohol over his family. I told him my father had walked out. 'I am not your father.' Him raising his voice – alcoholism ran in families, it didn't mean he was the same, life was hopeless if we were tied to repeating the past. Silences. How much was he drinking? I asked. I hoped he wasn't using me as an excuse. He said I sounded like his mother, the way she went on and on at his dad. Year after year. That I was lucky that my father had left. That he'd wished from age nine that his father would just drop dead. I had said something dumb, about personality types then, how drinkers were usually type four personalities, stuff like that. Silence, then, OK, he'd had just the one, he said, in the pub after work, it had been a fucking hard day. I can't talk to him when he's like this. He was drunk.

Perhaps that is the script solution – he has a secret addiction he's keeping from her. Yes, he fears what she will find when she arrives in his country. I want this story to have its own logic, divorced from ours. Our true life story is just the start. Act One they part. Act Two is their time apart. I need to find a narrative strand that will be different from us. So, the possibility is that he is an addict, a hidden secret. That gives dramatic tension.

His dialogue from day two is great. He thinks he's Woody Allen but he's more Brando. Writing about him – he turns me on. Couples should do this for each other. He comes across as this brooding tormented soul. God, he will laugh when he sees my script pages. More to do now.

July 30
Phone sex again last night. His stories get darker and darker.

We were walking through a park on the outskirts of Edinburgh. Joggers passing by. He pushed me into the bushes, he held me down. Hand over my mouth, he fucked me behind a bush as a man stopped and watched. He whispered to me

about the man watching. The man was masturbating, muttering
to himself, six foot tall. I came again and again. It's OK, I tell
myself. The feminist utopia of mutual sharing and caring is a
lie. There is darkness in each of us. How strange to be liber-
ated from liberation.

Am up to day four in script format now. 'God is in the details!'
(Who said that?)

The aftermath of the blindfold game. Twelve midday, day
four. And he was saying sorry for being so grumpy, he didn't
mean for the Sean call to put a damper on our day. Post breakfast. Him pacing about, picking up my things, pottering about
in my kitchen, gazing out at my garden, then at my laptop.

He said maybe I should do some work. If I wanted.

'What do you mean by that?'

'Just, you shouldn't let me get in your way.'

But I wanted him to get in my way and he was pushing me
away.

'You want to do some work? Is that what you mean?'

'No, not at all.'

'Am I hogging the laptop? You want to check your emails?'

'OK then, when you're done with your own, Meg.'

I tried to log on but couldn't concentrate, I wanted to jump
up and kiss him, take him back to bed, for us to spend the
whole day suffocating all insecurity. My mind a mess.

Him then at my laptop – was maybe checking for emails
from his girlfriend Morna, from his ex-wife, from his job. He
had two more days. His flight was confirmed. I sat on his lap,
arms round his neck, smothered him in kisses, couldn't let a
single fear voice itself. He kissed me back but not in the way
I needed.

Then he was up making tea. I couldn't keep my hands off
him, had to fill that growing space between us. The seconds
when he would not respond, making me cling more. I was
pathetic, needy. I couldn't stop.

'The kettle's boiled,' he said, unwrapping me from his neck.
'You want one?'

'I vant you to make love to me,' I said in my best Marlene
Dietrich.

'I was meaning tea, I'm having one. You?'

To say such a banal thing like he was in denial over the last night. Knowing that I was weak making me only weaker still. Kissing him.

'Stop, it, you're going to scald me.'

A generous shrug, a little laugh from him, which only made me cling more.

My huff. Getting dressed, angry at him. Putting on my sixties pink minidress, leaving the door open, just a bit, to let him see. Checking over my shoulder, to see if he was looking. Him back at the laptop. Then throwing my dress off, in a tantrum, putting on just any old pants, out of spite. Catching myself in the mirror. Feeling confused then ugly, as he sat reading emails. Vulnerable adolescent trying to get Daddy's attention.

'So,' I said, 'a beach walk?' I had this idea – if we got some fresh air I could maybe shake myself out of this funk.

The sands toward Ocean Bay Park. My arm through his. Him so silent, smoking, blowing it away from my face. His face turned away. I was pathetic, I was textbook. Jumping about ahead of him, saying, 'Let's run, race you to the end.' His solitary, slow walk. I raced ahead, tried to show him the traces of sea worms in the sand, bits of glass worn smooth by the waves. I ran back to him and hung on his arm, tickled him to make him laugh, I sulked and went off ahead, came back and kissed him. Joker, idiot. Putting on the funny accents from the day before. My best Scots.

'Look, look, some sea-fucking-weed, some crab-fucking-shells.'

He smiled back. Silent, melancholy.

'What's wrong, my You?' I said. 'Let's go for a swim.' Up to my ankles in water, beckoning him. He sat on the dry sand, fifty feet away, smoked. Waving at me.

We reached Seaview and sat. So many young people, in bikinis, swimwear, all muscles and tans, there was a game of volleyball. Boys and girls flirting, showing off. All laughs and big jumps. Our silence not that of yesterday. Awkward. Look at them – bodies worked out in gyms, put on display. Invisible thongs. Skimpy bikini bras. Teenage breasts too firm to bounce. I could tell he was staring. I felt my cellulite sink into the sand.

It made me sick – the way the teenage girls always looked round after they'd done some athletic trick, to the boys. This sense that all I had done all morning was try to be a teenager, anxious for his desiring gaze.

I was stupid, I know. I had to do something. We were only ten feet from the edge of the volleyball court. The ball was flying to the back. I did volleyball in high school. I had to do something to lighten our mood, to show off even. The ball was heading out of court toward us. I got to my feet and dived for it, hands ready in volleyball pose. I leapt forward. I tripped, fell on the sand, the volleyball hit me on the head. So foolish. The kids were laughing at me. Old woman, they must have thought. Humiliated. Tom got up and took my hand, helped me up. Like he knew.

'C'mon,' he said. 'I should get back to make that call.'

On the walk home, he must have sensed something was up with me. He was being like I had been before, trying to joke it all away. A tiny tear in his jeans, and he ripped it wider.

'Touch my ass,' he said.

Him doing his catwalk supermodel moves along the sand.

'I want you to put your fingers in my ass tonight,' he said.

He had to call his son.

July 31

Our chat today cut short because Sean was waiting in the living room (it doubles up as Sean's bedroom) and it was past Sean's bedtime and bedtime story. I asked if I could say goodnight to Sean. I know, I know it was too much to ask, and I got what I deserved. 'Maybe next time,' Tom said.

The script is upsetting me now. The child is a daughter. God knows why I decided to make her six. In many ways she (her name is May) is so like me as a child. Weird, this started as a journal but now seems like some psychotherapy thing. My dad left when I was six. I'm now seeing it from the other side, from Tom's ex-wife's perspective – my mother. It makes sense that Tom has no friends. Although Tom tells me nothing about Sean I feel his son's need for him, like I did for my dad. Of course his son has a stutter – I became anorexic. Have to keep it away from our real story.

Just after midday with me now and the sun will be going down soon in Scotland. This constant readjustment I have to make. He is sleepy as I reach my full energy. I slept better when he was here. The pillow between my knees and the one behind my back can't make up for his absence. I'm worried I'm becoming addicted to sleeping tablets and valerian root. It is worse now. My insomnia. Maybe it's our story running through my head all the time. Last night I dreamed I was reading a page. The words were there in front of me. I woke and they were gone. I do the earplugs and eye mask but then the sound of my lungs and my heart remind me of him. I slept better with his snoring. He joked about it today.

'You should get a snoring machine – maybe I should send you a recording.'

I laughed, but then he started to speak again. We are so out of sync. It is my fault. I have brought this on with my little secret.

Just reread everything. Have decided to write our story without the child. It would hurt Tom too much. Location too – I have to set everything somewhere else. He lives in London, she lives in Australia. The time difference is better, eleven hours' gap.

Stop avoiding it, Meg – the phone call to Sean.

After the volleyball and the torn jeans, we were trying so hard to joke it all off. He kept checking the time. He had to call Sean in thirty. I could tell he was counting the seconds. No talk.

(Was it like this for my father when he called once a week? This anxiety before the call.)

Back home. Living room. 2.30 p.m. He was pacing, apologising for pacing. But still not really there with me, in his mind he was in Scotland.

'Is it OK if I use your phone? I don't have enough credit on my mobile. I'll keep it brief. I can give you some money.'

'No, no, don't be silly. The extension goes all the way to the bedroom, it might need a bit of untangling. Sure, great, call Sean from my bedroom.'

Then he was in my bedroom on my phone and I was hovering in the kitchen, the extension cable running between my feet, disappearing behind the closed door. Listening. Not quite at the door but close. These fragments.

'And how's Ian?' . . . 'You get my birthday present? . . . Yeah? . . . Yeah, cool. I'll play it with you when I get back . . . Say hello to your mum for me, I'll be back in a few days, OK? Just a few days.'

That moment when he was laughing with his child.

'Miss you. Love you. Bye.'

Hating myself for the cinematic cliché he would find in the kitchen, the mistress who eavesdrops on this other scene of a family. Evil jealous bitch frantically scrubbing pots. Pretending she hadn't heard the laughter. Secondary character. The polite prepared submissive face asking him how his phone call home was, as if she'd heard nothing. The nine-inch knife in the sink, his face at the door – plunging it through his heart.

Ashamed at myself now, for not being more understanding that day. How I withdrew the next – how that brought on the spiralling madness.

'So how's Sean?'

'Oh, he's . . . you know he has these things he does, I have to pretend to understand. Boys' things, computer games and . . .'

Watching him struggle.

'We were cool, he's a cool kid. It's . . . very hard to speak to him, I mean, not so hard on the phone. He has this stutter. The thing is when he's on the phone . . .'

'My granda had a stutter.'

It all came at once, flooded me. I told him I'd decided a while back that I would not make a good mother. A burst condom, when? Sixteen years back. Michael. I didn't give the name. (Know it upsets him when I do.) The morning-after pill and a day of babysitting Seb. This was in London. A moment, when Seb was running round as Katy and I tried to have a grown-up chat and the kid kept on and on, 'Mummy, Mummy,' interrupting everything we tried to say. A moment when I felt the rage surge in me. Brat, spoiled rich kid brat, fucked-up so much already. And even then I knew I didn't have the patience or tolerance to have children of my own.

I ran out of words. I cried. And maybe he thought I was

crying for him. But it was anger, and hating myself for being so weak. I had long ago decided I would never have a child and then in that moment I realised that if I was ever to have a child it would have to be with a man very much like him.

'I wish I'd had a child with you.' Like he'd read my mind.

What could I say? I told him it was very sweet of him to say it. Hating the all-American sound of my voice. He must have sensed my awkwardness.

'Or maybe your child is your writing,' he said.

'Yes, maybe. Maybe it is.'

Grateful for the get-out. For not going through the whole debate about my age and my time left and my family history and when it was I had made the choice to be without child and if I had ever had second thoughts.

It's 10 p.m. now. Tried taking the daughter out of the script but it doesn't work. It needs that dramatic tension – what else keeps the Tom character there in his country? If no child then he could leave. Be here now. This is not based on Tom, no, the situation is entirely different. Sixty pages now. A story that starts with us but is not about us. Pure fiction. It will free us so we can live beyond it. Maybe it'll have to have a sad ending so we can have a happy one.

August 1

He was drunk tonight, but funny, singing, along to 'our song'. Have to write about 'our song'. Day four after the phone call to Sean. After my tears. I'd sat down at the CDs – he'd been riffling through them, I had to get them back in alphabetical order. I was up to C when he leaned over me, took a CD from my hand.

'You know, the thing about women,' he said, 'is they rarely buy CDs for themselves. Seriously. Maybe chicks aren't as obsessive about bands as guys are.'

I was still upset after his call to Sean, trying to get things back as they should be.

'Honestly, you can chart a woman's entire romantic past through her CDs,' he said. 'See, such a guy's album, who was he?'

He was holding up *The Bends* – Radiohead. I gave him some mock-serious diatribe about how sexist it was, what he was saying.

'OK, it was Ted's.'

Laughing, he held up another.

'Jesus! Frank fucking Zappa?'

Sitting there doing my ordering. I told him not to feel threatened by my past.

'No, but seriously, Zappa? That's a pretty scary past.'

Yes, he was right, most of them did come from ex-boyfriends.

'OK, OK, that was Tony, he was, I guess, yes . . . a bit of a druggy, I told you about him already. It was OK, we used condoms.'

He was laughing, kissing my neck. A second later and he was back at it.

'But . . . *Pavarotti Sings Verdi*?'

Really I'd never thought of it before. Hadn't listened to so many of these in years, the two or three I did were on the top, Joni Mitchell, Cat Power. He stuck Pavarotti on, was singing along to 'Nessun Dorma'.

'God, put that off!'

'Not till you tell me who he was!'

'Nope.'

'*Vincerò, Vincerò, VINCERÒ . . . OWWW.*'

'OK, OK, it was Arturo. I think he must've had stacks, gave them to every woman he met.'

I hit the stop button, tried to cut it short.

He kissed me. I sat by the stack of CDs, no music playing. He was searching through them all. I let him do what he had to do.

'My sweet,' he said, 'don't fret. I was just thinking, you know it would be nice for us to have an "our song".'

DID HE SAY THAT OR DID WE FIND OUR SONG BY ACCIDENT?

Start again. It was me who said we had to find an 'our song'. That day I'd sensed his other life. He had to return. Yes, it was me who searched for 'our song'. By way of nostalgia. To mark it, to let him go.

He handed me my half-empty glass of Pinot Grigio, topped it up. I drank.

He was being sweet, I told him he was, but I said I had to confess, he was right, there was very little in my CD collection that wasn't already tainted by prior romantic association. So we turned it into a game, going through them all. One hand round my waist, his other holding them up one by one, his eyebrows raised, and me shaking my head. Dylan and Fatboy Slim and AC/DC. Nope, Jed, nope, Philip, Tom, a prior Tom.

'Shame on you!'

In a different mood, I would have felt this a violation of my privacy. But we joked about it all. My CDs in his hand, me raising an eyebrow, making him guess.

'Tracy Chapman? Jesus, I mean, was that your lesbian friend?'

The laughing and the kissing. I told him the lesbian was Bach – the cello solos.

'Fuckin', yes!' he said. 'I would have stuck with her if I were you, although potentially rather morbid, she must have been.'

'Yvonne, my God, yes, she was more than potentially so.'

Fifty or sixty left. He had become more appreciative, had most of these himself. Johnny Cash? Nope, that was Steve. Samuel Barber's Adagio? I don't want to talk about it. *Nirvana Unplugged*? Nope, that was Andrew. Poor Andrew. Fucking hell – what – Parliament, *Mothership Connection*: 'I'm thinking madam had a black lover or maybe some retro-geek from Williamsburg?'

'OK, so I was a slut.'

'No, no, not at all. Nothing wrong with a bit of ethnographic research, in the shagging department.'

We finished the bottle, he got the bubbly from the fridge (the Veuve I keep in reserve). I recall being worried that we'd drunk too much already, I have my rules. I nodded yeah, to hell with it. How could it be possible to have such fun psycho-analysing all the rotten CDs you'd hidden at the back for a decade? How was it possible to laugh after the phone call to Sean? I tried to regain my authority, but even the thought of that had me laughing at myself.

'Basically, so what you're saying,' I said, 'is that, and this is some kind of po-mo critique of consumerism, that there is only a limited repertoire of lovers' songs. Like every love story needs a soundtrack. Three million people weeping to the same song in that movie that they thought was unique to them, our song. So sad . . . Like, I mean, Whitney Houston . . . Nelson Mandela said her voice gave him hope in his many years in jail, and it's just this track, too crap to dance to – and I couldn't help thinking what a shame that the anti-apartheid movement had Whitney as a soundtrack, know what I mean?' TOO THEORETICAL. THAT IS NOT HOW I SPEAK WITH HIM.

'Nope, just like to hear some music that you love, that's all,' he said.

'Really, my collection is pretty limited.'

'Thing is though,' he was saying, 'if we did find "our song" it'll only be so long till they use it in some car advert. Everything of beauty ends up in a car ad. I once shot a car ad and we used John Cage and I thought it was cool at first but then I felt like a whore.'

After the laughter, it came to me. Way at the back – had to be there still – hadn't listened to it in nearly twenty years. Used to have it on tape then rebought it on CD. Never played it again.

'Or we could find something so overused and crap that it is kind of melancholy,' he said. 'I'm thinking here of Abba and gay nightclubs – a fifty-year-old guy, fifteen years back, in leather chaps, waltzing with a teenager in rave gear, to "The Winner Takes It All", totally out of time with the tune. Yeah, rather beautiful.'

Thirty or more old CDs and there at the bottom – *Treasure* by the Cocteau Twins. Uni, 1989. I kept it hidden from him as I took it out of its broken case and moved toward the player, him singing 'The Winner Takes It All'. The CD was in.

'Shh,' I said, 'just listen.' I hit play.

The first three notes and he whispered, 'Oh my God.' I shushed him, drank another mouthful. 'No, but this is . . .' I put my hand to his mouth. Shh. Giggling. He knew it too. '*Shhh*,' I said, feeling Elizabeth Fraser flow through me with the warmth of the wine. 'Shh' again, laughing at how it was all coming back. My old song, from when I was nineteen. My music that was just for me, solitary secret me. 'Shh, just listen.' I closed my eyes and drank in that voice that represented everything I'd been taught to distrust in the years that followed, studying feminism and linguistics, this music that I had turned against – this unbridled, romantic feminine voice, singing made up words in her own personal sensual ecstasy. (Note: The Cocteau Twins were this eighties avant-garde band that named themselves after *le grand artiste français Jean Cocteau*. I was so bloody pretentious!)

'*Ho do-kee mon um keg, ho me dono canop keg.*'

'It's nonsense, but I know all the words,' he said, humming along.

'Shh! Just listen.'

'*Evan evan oh canog ah nog, evan, evan ah ma dominin pow.*'

The song ended. He said, 'Stick it on repeat. Such beautiful nonsense.'

'It's really embarrassing,' I said.

'God, no, but you have no idea. Jesus, the Cocteau Twins.'

'Now you're talking nonsense.'

'No, no, but.' He was in fits. 'No, no, fuck, I saw them, at Glasgow School of Art, when was that? Nineteen eighty . . . what, 1989? Jesus. I can't believe you have this – I must've made so many copies, lost the original. Christ in fuck.'

I had hit the wrong button. The next song had started.

'No, no, put it back.' He took my hand. 'How could you possibly have this? Must be a rarity now.'

'Got it in the indie rarity section, at Joe's Shack on Twenty-Third and Third, three-for-one offer. Ten bucks the lot.'

'But my God, I was nineteen – a virgin! There was this girl who was a painter, a year ahead of me. A goth, did you even have that over here? I mean, like the Cure and winkle-pickers and dyed black hair and . . . people in black.'

I stifled a laugh, I had been a person in black. PIBs they called us in college, not goths. This story he told me:

'No, but she was into the Cocteau Twins. They'd maybe play one track at the end of the night and I would have been watching her all night, her hardly moving, not smiling or laughing or even drinking – the art school bar – like she was waiting. The Cocteaus would come on and she would just sort of step out like a sleepwalker across the dance floor, people parting for her, like they knew this was a religious experience. Like they thought, her dressed in black with her Siouxsie and the Banshees eyes and her Egyptian tattoos and her thigh-high black leather boots, like she would suddenly lash out with her black-painted finger-nails and slash someone's throat. But then she would dance – these tiny moves, shoe-gazing. And I'd be watching her as she stared at her shoes to the Cocteau Twins, and everyone else left the dance floor cos it was too rad or too slow, and she'd be there alone, focused on her feet, these tiny moves, like she was stepping on needles.'

He got up and showed me the moves. Funny.

'What was her name?'

'No idea.'

'You never dated her?'

'God, no, she was terrifying. Wait, I think I saw her at Sean's school. Like one of the other mothers waiting. She must be forty now. I didn't like to think it was her.'

'Sad story.'

'Yeah, but sadness was "in" in art school. Put it on again.'

I did just that, waiting for him to ask, testing him.

'Who was it for you?' he asked.

I think I told him it was no one, no guy in particular (not Michael, I didn't give him the name). It was my anti-guy phase, I said, after my gap year in Europe.

'*Evan evan oh canog ah nog, evan, evan ah ma dominin pow.*'

'No, but seriously . . . seriously, the critics said it was some kind of modernist invention of a new language. Like Joyce. She just sang what she felt, but . . .'

I told him I'd thought they were Swedish or something, singing in Swedish.

'They're from Falkirk, not even that, from Grangemouth! This tiny town just fifty miles from me.'

'They're from Scotland?

'Yes, YES! She went into this kind of ecstasy onstage, some said it was Latin or Gaelic or free jazz or smack . . . I guess you had to be there. I can't believe you have this. Put it on again. PLEEES.'

We were both drunk.

'*Evan evan oh canog ah nog, evan, evan ah ma dominin pow.*'

He was giggling. 'God, we use to sing to this, me and my mates. There's no lyrics, but we all had our own.'

I told him I'd had these theories about the whole album. Wrote them all down. About female supremacy and matriarchal culture. Funny to admit.

'No way! I so need you in my life, I so need you to put it on again.'

'*Evan evan oh canog ah nog, evan, evan ah ma dominin pow.*'

'No, no, just tell me what you thought the words were,' he said, kissing me.

'You really want to know?'

The retro guitar kicked in, the retro synths, just a few seconds. I let myself feel it. Turned it up. Singing in time. My words.

'*Even, even if I know, I know, even, even in, in the domino hour.*'

I told him it was something to do with the limits of male knowledge. The domino hour was the end of patriarchy.

'God, Jesus! Put it on again. You want to know mine?'

I had to know. I hit play again and he was singing in a falsetto girl voice, doing the eighties retro moves.

'*Evil, evil yeah, I gnaw I gnaw, evil evil at the dominant power.*'

For him it was a radical left-wing thing about the end of capitalism.

Hysterics then. He could hardly get the words out, how we both had thought it radical in some different way. Holding each other, as we fell about, fingers fumbling for the start button. Again. Again! Leaning on each other. Shouting as I turned the volume up.

'IS THIS REALLY OUR SONG?'

'IT MUST BE BY NOW!'

The laughter too, up a notch, two.

'BUT WE DON'T EVEN HAVE THE SAME WORDS.'

'WHO CARES WHAT THE WORDS ARE?!'

Screaming different words in each other's faces.

Evan evan oh canog ah nog, evan, evan ah ma dominin pow.

Evil evil at the dominant power.
Even even in the domino hour.
Even if it was nonsense, it was our song.

The CD on repeat all night, volume turned down as we made our slow gentle love.

The next day, back in the city again we were both playing our detachment game. This is my pattern – I feel needy, I pull away. I pulled away, maybe too far from him that next day. The day before his leaving. As if I would have preferred him to be just a song, a memory. The day when he threatened to kill himself.

Call

[Crying.]
    'My You. What's wrong?'
    'I can't fucking stand it. I'm going nuts. Work, everything. I need to see you now.'
    'You're lonely, that's all. You should maybe go out with your friends or –'
    'I don't have any friends.'
    'Maybe you're missing Morna.'
    'What are you trying to say here? Jesus!'
    'Well, no, I mean, to be realistic, you were with her for what? – a year and you're all alone. I dunno. I don't want you to stop hanging out with her. There's no reason for us to be hung up about these things. I mean, it would make me sad but I'd understand.'
    'For Christsake. This some kind of test? You fucking some guy in the city? That what you're saying?'
    'No, God, no!'
    'For Christsake!'
    'To be honest, sex isn't everything for me. I love our chats. If I had nothing else they would still make me happy.'
    'You're telling me to fuck Morna?'
    'No. No. Are you OK, my love?'
    'You have no idea. No idea.'
    'Tom! Please, no, I didn't mean that.'
    He could have hung up on her. Should have, but she'd spent the next ten minutes trying to undo what she'd said. She'd gone on and on, telling him that he'd got her all wrong, that no she didn't want an open relationship, it never worked in tandem with a long-distance one – she'd tried it before. Phone conversations became interrogations or it got perverse, telling each other about who you'd fucked this week. Revenge fucking it

became. Done it before, she said; she'd no idea how little that
consoled him. She'd gone all terminology on him. About how
long-distance relationships required more fidelity than live-in
ones. About how there was some guy she dated, in LA or London
or somewhere, and she could just tell by his face that he'd been
screwing around behind her back. There was a certain kind of
man, she said, who sought out long-distance relationships, so
he could cheat secretly, then the guilt would make him act intimate. How, she knew he wasn't one of those kind of guys and
she was sorry for having brought it up.

The phone long since set down. He was down. He rolled
over and stared at the ceiling. She'd no idea how she'd hurt
him. He'd wanted to ask her again to come to Scotland sooner
and she'd talked of the importance of appreciating distance –
how they could do this with texts and the Internet and she'd
send him an email to try to explain better, how this was a new
era, there was this thing called Skype, they could both download the software and buy webcams and watch each other
twenty-four/seven.

She hadn't wanted to do phone sex tonight. He needed something to make it all sync up. A wank. Some Internet porn – a
ten-minute search for a woman on the Net who looked a lot
like her. Key words: Brunette, Butt. No. The fridge – the half-
empty bottle of voddie. Echo of unscrewing of lid. He paused.
If this had been a night with Sean he would not drink. But this
was his third night alone and Sean was tomorrow and she had
not understood his need tonight. Nor felt it. He'd been staring
at a photo of her as she talked and for the first time felt the true
gap between them, in miles and in daylight hours. Thousands
of miles and her voice did not match the static picture.

The gap between sound and image collapsed as the cold chill
of the vodka melted into the hot burn in his throat.

Morna

The day was almost spent before Tom staggered out of bed. Breakfast, an absurdity. He checked for her email.

My beautiful You. So sorry about last night. Was thinking about that thing you told me about Morna. You were watching a film together. A Sean Penn. Curled up on her sofa. This scene where they – him and the actress – they were lying in bed together, after making love and looking into each other's eyes and stroking faces. Just like we did that night, my You. Then you went all moody and told me how you'd watched this movie with Morna. The night of our fight. You said you had to turn your face away from her because the film made you cry. Because you realised you'd never feel love like the love in the movie. That love was like, it was like a bank account, you said – how we spend it wildly in our twenties but then there's nothing but debt in our thirties. (You don't like your metaphors, I know, but it was beautiful.) You said you realised with Morna that you'd never look into another's eyes and have anything to share, because your love had been spent and you cried in my arms as you told me that – all you had left was barely enough for your child. That when you made love to Morna you both closed your eyes then when it was over you turned your back because you couldn't bear to share. My love. We cried when you told me and I am crying now writing this to you. Just know that an hour spent in each other's eyes means more to me than ten years of eyes met then lost. That I too have closed my eyes and turned my back in fear of seeing love and its lack. It was so brave of you to end it with Morna. Just realised how much she must have meant to you and how much you've invested in me. I will be with you soon.

My delicate dangerous love.

Meg XXX

Meg's email made it final. No more fibs. The confrontation could be delayed no longer. Almost a month of avoiding Morna at the school gates, postponing replies to her texts. Hiding away from her like a thief. It had to be done now. He texted Morna.

We have to talk today.

No work today so it was OK. He couldn't face waiting for her reply. Went out to the corner store to buy some fags and loo paper. Then to the chemist for some ibuprofen for the hangover, then to the supermarket for some milk and cheese. He'd kept on walking, trying to work out the strategy. He had to be hard on her. It was the most generous way. List the things wrong with their relationship. 1. The sex was never great – he'd never made her come. 2. She never spoke her mind, had this quiet downtrodden beauty which was supposed to speak for itself, but really how could they not talk when he had so many things unsaid screaming to get out? 3. She had put herself in the position of being his carer, his teacher. Had made herself indispensable. Texting him to see if he was sober, if he was OK. Encouraging him to cook big meals for them both. Urging him on to accept the quiet life. 4. She never laughed. She watched him laugh and smiled quietly. Like even laughter was something she had given up on. 5. She was not his intellectual equal. She'd never been to university, never learned how to ask questions – working-class common sense – with her it was always the same answer: accept things as they are. 6. Her singing. Doing her scales at her piano while he slept. This self-discipline of hers. Studying grade-two music, the same level as a ten-year-old. Futile. 7. Her whole working with backward children career – yet another way of telling him that life was suffering and had to be endured. 8. She had reconciled herself to a quiet life in Scotland. To living without ambition or anger, and now that he had met Meg, he knew he'd quietly been killing himself with Morna. The retirement plan, he'd called it once. He'd actually said to her: 'I can see us, aged sixty, growing things, pottering away in your garden, growing old together.' The problem was he was not even forty and Meg had reminded him that years before he had been driven by anger to achieve greater things. He could be that same youthful rebel again.

His feet heavier as each step took him closer to home, as if Morna had got his text and was already waiting there. She still had a set of keys, she'd watered his plants, her plants really, the ones she'd given him, while he'd been away. The keys in the door and there he was peering round the door to his own flat calling out Hello! Hello? For some reason he drew his bedroom door back slowly, as if expecting to see her waiting for him, naked. The bed – as he'd left it. Sheets curled into the human shape he hugged each night. The copy of *Men Only* lying next to his Bertrand Russell. He kicked the porno under the bed and headed to the kitchen.

Morna's pot plant still on the table. Rosemary. My God, how could he tell her he'd fallen in love with someone else?

Hair of the dog just to face it all. A mouthful and the stress was down and the abstraction had started. The dangerous phase. He could go for hours without food, forget to eat.

He was just about to start composing an email to Meg about the fear he had of facing Morna. But then he'd already told her that fib, that it was over already. His phone beeped. One message. The stupid hope that it was from Meg.

Just got yr msg. Was heading home. Over in 10. Morn XXX.

The waiting again. Not the same as with Meg. This dread that could only be calmed with another vodka. Minutes working over what to tell Morna. How to start?

One of her hairs on the rosemary plant. He picked it up. Her long black hair, falling over her breasts as she undressed. That he always found lying about, on his clothes, pillow, plates, days after she'd left. That he put in a little secret place on top of his bedside bookshelf. Twenty or so of her hairs by his bed. My God.

He checked. Another few minutes and Morna would be here. But as he ran through the list of her flaws again and the third vodka hit home, he had to admit that each accusation had also, in a way, been just a description of all the things that had, only five weeks before, been utterly compelling about her: her plants, her silences, her preference for hugging, her commitment to backward children, her melancholic voice, self-taught, singing her scales.

Her keys in the door and the familiar noise stopped him just before the thought that was finding words – 'Yes, I do love her.'

'Hiya.'

'Kitchen,' he called back. Draining his glass. To fill it again in front of her or pretend he hadn't been drinking?

'Went to Asda,' she was calling out. 'Thought we could do wir fave, brought the bubbly too.' Her long black hair then her smile. The heavy shopping bags dropping by her sides as she reached out for him.

'So, at last, eh, here's wur stranger.'

Glad to be able to hide his eyes in her shoulder.

'Actually, I could do with just one drink.'

'Aye . . . course.'

He thanked her and lifted the bags and started unpacking and cutting the veg, pouring himself another voddie, his back to her as she sat at his table and he fed her the usual questions about her day at work and she talked of some kid called Johnnie who was autistic but making so much progress. Her moving about behind him looking for glasses. Not finding any clean she washed them herself, then started in on filling up the sink to wash all of his dirty plates.

'Stop,' he said. 'I mean, just leave that to me. OK?'

Still he couldn't face her. Was cutting the onions, preparing their fave which was this boeuf bourguignon that he used to do with his ex, that Morna had loved even though she knew he'd done it before with his ex.

Pop of bubbly. The fizz and glug of glasses filling as he cut the onions.

'Cheers,' she said, holding the glass to him. Her eyes, through her hair. The fading daylight had thrown a halo round her head.

And he could've played it out, clinked glasses and kissed her cheek and sat her down quietly and explained. The glass to his lips, her eyes to his. He started to cry. Pathetic. He was always the crier with her and there she was setting down the glass as if there was all the time in the world and reaching for him. He stepped back.

'No, no. Sorry. I'm fucking sorry. OK.'

'Why doncha tell me whit happened in 'merica, eh?'

The table and sitting down and playing with the glass in his hand and still not meeting her eye and he hoped that all of it would tell her that she didn't need to be told. And then it was the bridge. Like he'd told Meg on that drunken night. The bridge. The Brooklyn Bridge. The Forth Road Bridge. Stuttering through tears.

'And I think – what am I doing here? That maybe this time, these three years, have just been this dream and how I survived and maybe I'm just still there, back on the edge again.'

Her shushing him, her hand on his shoulder, her moving his bubbly glass just a few inches away. On their second date, he'd confessed that a year before he had tried to throw himself from the Forth Road Bridge. That was the start of their romance.

'No, but I mean – just listen . . . I don't want to be here. I don't, I fucking hate all this and I just, I'm just afraid that I'm going to have to go.'

Her fingers through his like he was one of her backward children. And he was. Hesitating as before on the bridge. The fucking bridge.

'And this time here, telling myself it was OK, I think, God. God. I'm falling. These three years just a dream as I fall . . . this isn't real. I'm a ghost.'

She turned the oven off, took the boeuf bourguignon out, set it on the side. They might have it later. Her hands led him to his bed. Their bed of almost a year, and the morning-after pill she'd taken after the night when neither of them had cared. And how they could have had a child by now, if she hadn't said yes to that pill which he made her swallow before his eyes so he would know for sure.

Bed and bed was wrong. This was not the plan. Meg was going to call him around midnight. He was so weak. This was to be the night when he told Morna about Meg. This bed in which Meg would sleep, in less than four weeks. The familiar shapes of Morna silently removing her top, her bra, her back to him, her tiny waist, her curves, her modest way of climbing between the sheets so quickly to hide herself. Ten seconds and she would raise her face to his through her hair and run her hand over his chest. And it was as so many times before. Him lying on his back and just thinking about the glimpses of her beauty. And she asked, 'What?' like always and tickled him and asked again and laughed and he said, 'Nothing,' as always and she snuggled into his shoulder, her hair on his chest, her long legs curling round his, content in her belief that his lack of reply spoke more.

He had not meant to go this far.

'Look,' he said, 'you're right. I've had a few voddies and I'm basically . . . If we cuddle it's OK but not anything more.'

'You,' she said, pinching his ribs. 'So you.' These words were Meg's, not hers.

This wouldn't be the night when he told her. They would cuddle and sleep and maybe next week he would tell her it was over. He had turned his mobile phone off. Unplugged the land-line.

Morna's body against his, her hair on his pillow. It flashed before him as he fought her habitual warmth, her chin nestling in his neck, that maybe this was as good as it could get. To sleep well in Morna's arms and dream of Meg.

Morna's hand holding his gut, reaching down, between his legs.

'NO!'

His whole body jerking upright spitting out the word. Her face. As if slapped.

'Look, no. OK. I have to tell you.'

His eyes closed but a sense of hers on his face. Shouting 'Look' but not looking.

'Look. Look. The woman I met in New York it wasn't just some fling . . .'

'S'OK, I ken awready.' And hugged him tighter. 'S'no big deal. S'no the first time. We are what we are, an' all that jazz. I get it, it's fine.'

No, he didn't want to be understood. Meg wasn't understand-able. Everything in his world was only too understandable.

'S'OK. Dinna even wantae know, Ah'm no' exactly goin' tae ask ye to stop yer nonsense, ahm ah? Jist make sure ye wear a condom in future. Eh?'

So easily she could absorb it all. He could have broken

down, confessed about the little slut from the nightclub that night a week before America. She forgave his one-offs. She had decided Meg was just the same. She was stroking his shoulder.

'No. Listen. Don't touch me, OK. New York. I know it sounds crazy. It's fucked up. But New York.' He couldn't force the words out.

'So, you fucked her,' she whispered. 'Fine. Just spare me the details, OK?'

She didn't think sex meant much. Her hands pulling him into spoons.

'Shh,' she said, 'snuggle up. We'll talk aboot it in the mornin.'

No, there could be no snuggling. A hundred things to explain. How this lover had a name and it was Megan Hunt and she worked in the movie business, but it wasn't about movies and his failed ambitions, it was more that for the first time in his life he'd felt understood, that all the things he'd said to Morna that she thought witty were actually really sad, fatalistic, and with Meg, there was this hope that he could stop being a smart-arse and really make something of his life.

'Shhhh.'

That was it. Final. Her shh was death.

'Morna – I think you should go now.'

'C'mon,' she muttered, 'sleep.' And she had this all worked out. This American thing would pass. She maybe even loved his infidelities, proof that the world was as dark as her hair, proof that he would come back again because there was understanding in the sharing of darkness.

'No, no. I'm going to sleep on the sofa.'

Her hand pulling him back as he tried to rise, bringing his fingers slowly, strongly to that place of her wetness. Her moan. Moaning Morna.

No, he would not. He would not.

'I'm in love with her,' he said. 'Her name is Megan.'

She raised her voice then – glimpse of her violent past, self-harm, abusive men.

'Look! It's fuckin' OK! Just FUCKIN' SLEEP! OK?'

He lay on his back as Morna lay silent beside him in the

enclosure of quilt and sheet that he had wrapped around her so they couldn't touch.

He must have dozed off and Meg had no doubt texted and tried his landline. And he was confused. Because this was meant to be the end and he had told Morna everything but still she was sleeping beside him. To these things that were life-threatening to others, Morna said, 'Just fuckin' sleep! OK?'

A moment in the night when her hand had reached, in sleep, between between his legs. And he had grown hard and rolled away. No sleep all night. Waking every time she moved.

Around four. Her musty breath and hair and scent of rosemary and fags. No sleep. To just fuck her. Meg wouldn't know. To get her to wank him off. That was surely OK. Not betrayal. No kissing – eyes closed. He'd tell her this was the last night, ever. She was asleep and it was all wrong but all wrong turned him on. He pulled the covers back to reveal her waist, slowly, then her arse, her long legs. She was asleep so he jerked off. Tried not to wake her with his movement. Six inches of quilt between them. No, no. He pulled away at the last second, shooting over the sheets. Morna was asleep. There had been no touch. No infidelity. Meg didn't know.

But as he rolled away from her, he sensed her movement in the bed. She had not been asleep at all. She was up and dressing now. He closed his eyes and tried to picture her. Searching the semi-dark for her panties. He pretended to be asleep.

Her feet left the room. There was the smell from the kitchen of her every morning fag. She was in the hall then. Keys in the door. He waited to see what the noise would be. Would she post them through the letter box? If she held on to the keys then she would be back. They clunked through the letter box, then hit the lino.

So it was done.

The compassion of the woman. She'd let him go without an argument. She'd always known this would happen.

Seconds ticking by. Sound of her feet down the steps then he was alone. Staring at the curtains, second-hand Habitat. A car starting outside. Her car, pulling away. It was done. 6.45 a.m. Half awake. This silence. Like waking to the sounds of a

foreign city. Like being a child on holiday with your parents.
After they'd carried you from the plane, the train, the taxi.
Waking and the birds sounded different. The seagulls in France
like children crying. Foreign sounds. Not scared, just listening,
adapting to the dimensions of a room, unknown.

A car radio, voices distant. A click of heels from the flat
above. A voice down the street seeming to come from some
stadium where there was no stadium, echoing along the tene-
ment walls. A sound of cheering. Football replays on video
maybe. A pigeon cooing. Tiny glimpse of early blue light where
the curtain rail had come away from the wall, which he'd never
got round to fixing. A plane passing. The gulp and gush of the
hot-water boiler downstairs.

Time was there again. A substance like air. Not just a measure
of events, but all the spaces between.

Meg would be worried that he hadn't called last night.

A van passed. Diesel engine. Not the fear of being left alone
in his room. He was part of it, it was part of him. Meg was
part of him now in this waiting. This hour. She would be trying
to sleep, anxious about him. Days and weeks of this. This room,
this sense of time stretching ahead waiting for Meg and their
many future anxieties.

But waiting could be this thing not endured but adored. He'd
text Meg in ten to see if she was still up. Ten minutes made no
difference. He could call her right now but he needed this time
just to breathe. He would witness Edinburgh as sounds. The
simple beauty of just this. Not afraid any more to be alone with
time. There would be no more wasting of it, killing it. Morna
gone and her gift had been guiltless and he loved her more for
that. The flap of birds' wings. A car reversing. A plane overhead. A child crying in the neighbouring flat. The breeze
through his curtains.

Dawn and the dawning. He sits there in his bedroom, looking
at his things. The aerial for the bedside alarm-clock-stereo
made out of a coat hanger, that he, every day has to change
the position of to get a signal. His favourite pair of Levi's that
are too small now that he has grown a gut. The broken things
that you can't throw away. Like his car with the slow-leak

puncture that he pumps up every three days and can never get round to fixing. The bathroom shower head that soaks the walls that he has not got round to tiling. The way he wipes the walls down with a cloth. He has come to love these strange rituals that waste his time. The viruses on his PC that call up random porno sites and life-insurance offers. The shoelaces that keep snapping. The wedding ring he carried on his key ring after the divorce that now sits on Meg's finger. And Morna, he will be seeing Morna again twice a week in the playground, and there will be a way to recycle that too and make that work. Nothing is ever resolved, he told himself, there is no end to anything, even death lingers, gives back life.

Staring at the bedroom walls, painted red by the last occupants.

It was seven o'clock now and he just needed those few more minutes to compose himself. So late with her now, a few more minutes would make no difference. And she would ask if he was OK and why didn't he call last night? And he would tell her about the sounds and pigeons and car doors and morning coming to itself in this city of broken things. They would lie in bed together in just less than a month and listen together to the sounds of the waking day as if they were children on their first day in a foreign country.

He turned on his mobile phone and texted: *Sorry late – r u awake, my love? xxx*

The silence was changing now. The dying echoes of his breath in the room. What if Meg didn't reply? The heart now accelerating. The need for a drink to calm the nerves. Madness starting from nothing. Ten minutes ago he was philosophising about his freedom and now the empty room was terrifying. Minutes and no reply. He plugged in the landline – two voice messages from her, increasingly anxious. Where was he? Why hadn't he called? Another saying goodnight, she was tired, worried, but she had to sleep now. 'Goodnight,' she said. Goodnight as he stared at the morning light.

Journal

August 2

Woke late after a sleepless night worrying about him. Flashback to our night of fear – the bridge. Put my earplugs in. The phone might have rung all night for all I know. One answerphone message from him. Explaining. So many sorries – he left the phone off the hook, his battery was out of power. Feeling down now. Full of doubts. He didn't want to speak last night – that's what I feel – he's sick of me and my prying. I wanted to call Sally and talk about all this. Then Josh called at three. Cheered me up. Wants me to come to Manhattan. Fine. Tom has a day without me, I can do the same, it's not like we're tied to the phone!

Josh won't let me go, he said, has another three scripts lined up for me this year. One of them a low-budget indie but very promising. I told him, no, I was working on a private project. So many questions from him then – said I was primed to go it alone, if it was a novel he had connections with HarperCollins. Poetry and he'd had lunch with Simon from Bloomsbury last week. He makes me laugh. He won't let me go, he asks, have I been approached by another agency? Is that the reason for my silence? He'll cut his percentage in half, he said, if I stick with him. *Fatal Love* is with Fox now, a big scandal, they fired the writer, he took the liberty of showing my script notes to them, they wanted me on for a dialogue polish – 85K. He said. 'I want you back, baby! To discuss future projects.' He had me laughing for thirty minutes on the phone. Funny how I need Manhattan and all of its nonsense. Am I really so superficial that I need to ask the world to tell me how fabulous I am? Yes, maybe I was glad to hear an enthusiastic American voice again after the Scottish silence.

A second glass of Chardonnay at my laptop and I am sitting here thinking, yes, these seventy pages might be the reinvention of the modern romance. Our story is different. A bit po-mo.

This couple, so afraid of repeating past mistakes. Their second date and they discuss *Kundera*. On their third it is *Kramer vs Kramer*. The fourth, *Before Sunrise*; their fifth – *Hiroshima Mon Amour*. This couple who measure themselves against the history of cliché but still find something spontaneous.

Our seven days contain more than seven years.

Laughing at myself now. 'What a sell-out,' Tom would say. I hear his voice and he makes this a joke.

The pitch: two people, unglamorous, nearly forty, fall in love, stay in love across the great divide. No crisis. Just love, enduring, profound, impossible and beautiful in its impossibility. The studios would want a suicide or a fatal incident. Love cut off in its prime. Is that really all anyone can stomach? Is the world so deprived of love that they have to do *Romeo and Juliet* every fucking time? *Sylvia and Ted, Sid and Nancy, Kurt and Courtney, Michael Hutchence and Paula Yates*. Suicide and nostalgia.

Fade to black, the music rises, the angels descend, as he says.

Tom will hate it but I agreed to meet Josh in Manhattan the day after tomorrow. Will spend a day in the city. Have to leave early. Hope he's OK about it. Hope I'm not doing this just to spite him for ignoring me last night. So much to tell him. Must call him before bed.

Email. August 3

My love, I know you don't want me to go and Manhattan has bad memories for both of us. Late now. Tried to text and call you. No reply. Had to turn our song off. I've been howling along to the Cocteau Twins for the last half-hour, the CD on repeat. Our Treasure. Torturing myself. Trying to hold her long notes and running out of breath, laughing at myself. She is so beautiful in a way I will never be. You make me beautiful. We are such an incredible story.

Love You. XXX

PS I'll miss our daily phone routine when in Manhattan. Will try to call you – your a.m. I'll be at Sally's.

Echo

'You go first.'

'No, you.'

'First, I'm calling . . .'

'Sorry? Why are you on my mobile, Meg? It's really loud, where the hell . . .'

'. . . from a payphone in . . .'

'. . . are you?'

'. . . Brooklyn. I left your landline number at . . .'

'OK. You're what? Where?'

'. . . home. I had to . . .'

'God, this is hell. You talk first then I'll listen. OK?'

'. . . bum a quarter from this woman. For the payphone. I have to go and meet . . .'

'You got a quarter from a bum? What? What's that noise?'

'. . . my agent. You there? I have my calling card but you still need a quarter to make the call. It was an ambulance. How was your . . .'

'You're standing in a phone booth?'

'. . . day?'

'Meg, all I'm hearing is myself then you seconds after.'

'. . . on my way to meet my stupid agent, he's worried that I'm . . .'

'There's too much noise. An echo.'

'Tom, can you hear me? I'm near the Brooklyn Bridge. I wanted to ask you about the bridge. Remember the night we had that big blowout? Our second-last night. You were . . .'

'Are you in Brooklyn, Meg?'

'About bridges. Tom? Can you hear me? We're overlapping again. I was trying to remember the argument we had – on the bridge. The night we got drunk. On the fifth day. When you scared me on the bridge.'

'Meg, the noise – I can't.'

'Sorry. Are you OK, Tom? You sound . . .'

'This fuckin' echo on the line. The delay. What is that?'

'. . . upset or . . .'

'Shit! Can you try another . . .'

'. . . angry at me.'

'. . . phone?'

'Hello? We keep overlapping . . . Why are you shouting . . .'

'Try another phone!'

'. . . at me? Yes, sorry. OK, yeah, I'll try another phone.'

Now Tom was anxious. She'd hung up. Would she get back in her car and wait till Manhattan to call? Jesus. It was only 2 p.m. –8 a.m. with her. She'd called him on his mobile in the office and how could they talk intimately from the office? And no calls this morning and his texts to her not replied to and then this vague memory of something she'd said warning him about possible connection problems in Manhattan, maybe even days or weeks back. God! He called her mobile.

'Hi, this is Meg, I'm not available right now, please leave your number and I'll get back to you.'

Customer Care

She was in a Manhattan hotel room with a tall good-looking black American man. She was lying naked on the bed blind-folded, and the man was standing back, watching her. It was his fault for putting these things in her head. That was the one thought that destroyed his last hour since she phoned. He couldn't email her and, damned fool, he should have asked her for Sally's number.

Three thirty p.m. and he called it a late lunch. The final day before the big meeting on Edinburgh, City of . . . and he'd failed yet again to come up with a single word to finish off the impos-sible sentence. McGregor was getting impatient to see the results of all of Tom's research. Was saying it would cost more, and they were always conscious of costs, but they could call a last-minute brainstorm with the Black Agency and their creatives . . . It would eat into their profits but the team there were shit hot and they'd got the *Daily Record* and the last Bank of Scotland corporate and the Department of Sewage. No, Tom said, he had to do this alone. Trust me, he'd said to McGregor, I'm close, really close – 'We do this ourselves, all or nothing.' And McGregor must have liked the sound of that, the sound of money dropping through a hole into his own pocket, the savings.

No call from her. Freaked out by her lack of communica-tion, he had a quick double at the Lion and was walking past a couple of fashion places feeling sorry for himself when it came to him that the only way to cope with this was to take a more positive approach. Shopping is the answer to everything, she'd said. He needed a new shirt, she'd be dressed up for her meeting – so be it. He'd put her call behind him and take her cyber-shopping. Almost 10 a.m with her now. He texted her.

Hope yr meeting is cool. Sorry for freakout. Can we text now? Am shopping 4 nu shirt, need yr advice. Think Corporate Me. Style???

No reply. Something wrong with his phone. He headed into

the American-style shopping centre, thinking it might ground
him in her world. Into Gap – nothing much caught his eye.
The next was Diesel. More her than him. Way out of his price
range, but what he needed was a change. To turn up for this
prep meeting today, then the grand slam tomorrow, with a new
funky outfit that spoke of the new funky Edinburgh. And give
it to them – that one word at the end of the sentence that would
be … Edinburgh, City of … He was feeling intimidated by
the choice of styles and the price tags and was about to give
up on the prospect of self-transformation through change of
attire when his phone beeped.

Cum over

It made no sense but was horny. The text had maybe been
cut short – cum over my tits, my face. She was probably shopping, looking at bright colours, maybe having a coffee, smiling
at young lovers on Fifth Avenue. Maybe she'd been writing a
longer text and hit send by accident.

*Yes I want to come all over u. We r shopping together in Edin-
burgh! 2 funky shirts B4 me. 1 grey 1 blue w/ gold stripes. Which
do u prefer? Xx*

Five minutes waiting and the Diesel salesperson still holding
the two shirts, irritated by his indecision. Tom was just about to
walk out when he got her text. The wonders of intercontinental
telecommunications. 'Bringing the world closer.'

The same again.

Cum over

In the changing room with the two shirts he texted again.

*You want me to come over u? Am in changing room now. My cock
is getting hard. X*

Waiting, then undressing and sniffing his armpits and being
none too impressed and then worrying they would charge him
for stinking up their haute couture. And the sight of his gut
in the mirror. Still no reply. He tried again. It was hard to
text one-handed while fastening the shirt buttons and trying
to wank. His cock, like Meg, wasn't responding. He typed
again.

*U are here w/ me in cubicle, on yr knees, sucking me. What u
think – the grey or the blue with stripes? My pervert wife. Xx*

He tried on the second shirt, not seeing himself in it at all. Waiting then, and the shirts were too fucking expensive anyway. She hadn't replied. Maybe his last text was too vulgar. And he shouldn't have said *pervert* or *wife*. Or the signal had been weak in the cubicle. Nine slow painful minutes waiting for her to text or call. Then he was out on the street with nothing to show for this endeavour and still wearing his old stinking H&M and thinking that she had maybe worked out just how tragic he was, afraid of investing in a £75 shirt. He was heading back to the office and it had been twenty minutes, and he was getting himself into a state, worrying about what might be wrong. All his mobile screen said was MEMORY LOW. He was about to give up on life when the phone beeped. Forty minutes late. New message. Same as before.

Cum over

Panic starting now. He installed himself at his desk, McGregor and Stephanie eyed him suspiciously. He did his best to look busy then texted her back.

My love, didn't get a shirt or cum or anything, dyin to speak xxx

But the message wouldn't send. He pushed send again and again and the damn thing was still in the outbox and no tick to show it had gone and now a symbol on his screen like a no-entry sign and a new message from Virgin. INBOX FULL – no incoming or outgoing messages. He needed to call Virgin Mobile or the Carphone Warehouse right now to find out what was wrong with the fucking phone. Or delete some of her messages, that might do the job. He opened up the inbox and there were fifty-two old ones from her; nineteen from Morna, two from the ex. Deleting the Mornas. Bossman McGregor was there. 'Meeting, people, now.'

And 'cum over' sounded like a text to a lover in Manhattan. Like she'd sent him the wrong message by accident. How many times had he done that with Morna, when drunk and at 2 a.m. trying to text Marcia or Maria?

The next three hours were flow charts and questionnaire analyses and demographics and the pressing question of what the slogan would be. Edinburgh, City of ... No, he wasn't feeling guilty over having done absolutely no work on the project in the last four weeks, spending his time secretly calling Meg long distance on the company line, texting and emailing her in working hours and typing up his many strategies for their future. No, fuck that, he was freaking guilty about last night with Morna. In the midst of the meeting he texted again.

I can't cum over. What u mean?!!

Six twenty-three and the meeting was over, with Tom assuring McGregor that the research was excellent and that by tomorrow, for sure, he would have the slogan, no need to be commissioning other creatives in other agencies. In fact, the questionnaires and the buzzwords today had confirmed a line of thought he'd been working on for weeks, which would be a real gem. He would have a big surprise for tomorrow. All of which was a lie.

But even after the climactic ending there was still the office. He couldn't let himself be seen fussing with his phone, so he called it a day and headed out and was deleting Morna's texts as he walked. Jesus, two hours and no reply from Meg and him unable to send any of the ten he'd attempted. This damn fucking phone. Morna and the ex deleted but still it said INBOX FULL. UNABLE TO SEND OR RECEIVE.

Running up the steps to his flat. Landline in one hand. Mobile in the other, reading her mobile number from his screen. Ringing, ringing – her voicemail. He dialled again, she was maybe in her meeting or 'doing lunch'.

'Hi, this is Meg. I'm not available right now; please leave your number and I'll get back to you.'

'Jesus, Meg, my love. Don't know what's wrong here. Can't read your messages or send. This fucking mobile. Didn't buy a shirt. Been trying to text you for six hours. If you're there, baby, if I've offended you in any way? Jesus, where are you, my love?'

Text her. He was tearing through his drawer of bills and bank statements looking for the number for Virgin Mobile and the Carphone Warehouse. She was in Manhattan to meet her agent and she'd flirted with the guy all night at that party. Fuck. The last mobile bill, finally. Dialling.

'Hello and welcome to the Carphone Warehouse helpline. Our office

*hours are nine till five thirty. If you are calling outside these hours
and have a technical enquiry then check out our website.'*

Fuck websites, he needed to speak to a human. Her agent
would be plying her with drinks and she'd be wondering why
he hadn't texted. Jesus Christ! Was she really sleeping at Sally's
tonight?

*'Hello and welcome to Virgin pay as you go. If you would like to
top up with a top-up card, press 1. If you have used a credit card with
us before, press 2. If you are interested in any of our new promotions,
press 3. If you would like to speak to a customer-care representative,
press 4.'*

Four. Thank God.

*'We are sorry but due to a high number of callers we are unable
to connect you to a customer-care representative. Please continue to
hold, or visit our website at virgin.co.uk and click on FAQs.'*

The fucking world was a recorded message now, cryptic maze-
like computer-operated systems that led you back to where you
came from after paying one pound a minute for the privilege,
with this soft educated female voice and that gentle lulling wallpaper Vivaldi that became increasingly terror-inducing as it
repeated itself. *And why not visit us on www.virgin* ... A human
being please, for crying out loud.

Her agent had insisted on another bottle of Veuve, and
insisted that their relationship was based on mutual trust and
would she like to come back to his to look over the details of
some new contract? A drink, yes. Big one. No mixers left. Double
straight.

Sitting on the ground, Vivaldi in his ear, trying to suppress
the rant. The problem with international text messaging was
that it gave the promise of immediate response and contact.
She may have been out of range. Her battery might be down.
Virgin might not be talking to Verizon. She might have it on
vibrate not ring and it was in her bag shoogling away unnoticed.
But then the fear. Had she chosen to turn off her phone because
you were disturbing something more important than you? The
problem with text messaging was that in many ways it was an
exact representation of what was wrong between women and
men these days. So many real conversations like text messages

now. Short-cut jargon. U r cute. C u later. Luv u. Xx. The problem was long sentences, and long-term commitments, were already out of date.

Are you with your agent? Call me as soon as you get this. XXX

Vivaldi's fragment of a season yet again and thank you for holding. He reminded himself of the way things were before texts. That silences were not threats. That your beloved spent hours in the day doing what she had to do. Her agent was fucking her blindfolded, she was having an orgasm. More vodka.

Still on hold. Maybe – if he tried deleting some messages. Her archive.

Tom. Feel like crying tonight. All things seem incredibly sad in the world. Want to lie in your arms for you to kiss my tears. X

My love. I can't wait to speak. X x

My You, I couldn't sleep. I was so cold on the outside though warmed by our 2 hour conversation! We're going to be poor but happy. I want to kiss those lips, pry them open and hide inside. Goodnight. X

I want to be in your time in your head, in your body in your bed . . . of course I can't sleep. Call me now. Please. X x x

So hard to delete anything. All there was to show of their first month apart. Every day, text, mood. He had to be pragmatic. Memory was full. Some messages very brief. Just check-ins on when it was OK to call.

Having a walk at 3 so could speak now briefly or at 9 your time? Xxx

You gonna ring in ten? XXXs

Are you free? I'm gonna call you now OK?

Sorry, babe. Went out of range. Late now. Will speak in morning. Xx

Hard, but they had to go. He was punching the select then delete buttons, leaving only the long memorable ones. Sipping his third voddie and still waiting for her to ring. Those texts he could never delete.

Every day when I come out of the daze of chores and work I marvel anew that you exist. My soulmate, my laughing man. I'm gonna write you a big fat email now. X

The others that told him she was just like him.

Sorry for my slightly hysterical barrage of messages. Put it down to extreme exhaustion. I was just looking forward to speaking to you! I know it's the middle of your day. Excuse my craze. I can try you your nite. 9 or 10? Don't go to sleep without me tonight. X

The deletions had no effect. MEMORY FULL, the screen still said. An old phone, three years now. The pics she'd tried to send had probably jammed his memory. OK, OK, it was expensive but the time for this pussy-footing around was over. Landline calling her internationally again.

'Hi, this is Meg, I'm not available right now, please leave your number and . . .'

Just one text from her in all this time. *Cum over.* And no reply to his many questions over what she meant. Food could wait. He was supposed to have Sean tonight. He made a call to the ex, postponing Sean's weekly sleepover – any excuse, the first one off the top of his head, he had a big meeting tomorrow. There was nothing else for it. More vodka and Vivaldi and waiting for the customer quota to die off at one pound a minute. He was back on to Virgin and the queue for customer care. Why could they not play the whole fucking *Four Seasons*? He was stuck in this eternal loop of Spring, with this languorous female voice thanking him for his patience. He was in the kitchen, phone jammed between neck and shoulder as he tried to wash some dishes, as he contemplated a coffee and filled the kettle. He'd taken the landline and the mobile through to the toilet, because he needed a shit. He'd set the mobile on the cistern.

Even as he'd done it, he'd thought – mistake. That if she rang when he was at his business all she would hear was this weird animal grunting and she would hang up and if Virgin picked up it would be the same then he'd have to redial and be back at the start of Spring again. He'd never taken the mobile into the toilet before for obvious reasons. It happened like a déjà vu. The voice on the phone: '*Hello, this is Virgin, how can I help you?*' Heard above the noise of the flushing. A confusion of wires and phones. Déjà vu. It happened like so many things in his life. Tragic, foreseeable, but unstoppable. Somehow his finger fumbled from the toilet roll and hit the side of the mobile and the thing fell – horror-show slo-mo B-movie close-up of the moment of impact. It fell like it was trying to tell him something. It fell into the shit that was flushing.

The City

My love, this place terrifies me now. Scared of meeting my agent. Sent you six texts. We haven't spoken since the street – it was awkward. Why aren't you replying? Where are you? XXX

Twelve forty. Trying to park off 52nd. No texts from him. And she'd run out this morning to catch the ferry forgetting to take the Post-it note that had his home number on it, and the number wasn't on her cell. God knows why? Because it had become routine to sit there and read from the Post-it as she typed it in. She knew the numbers but they seemed in the wrong order. Different voices were telling her different things – to retry the area code, that no such number existed. Just one digit was wrong maybe. She scribbled them all down and tried to reassemble the twelve digits. Why the hell hadn't she typed them into her cell? She'd tried to reply to his texts, typing: *Come over me, I'll wipe your sperm from my breasts with your new shirt. I want you here with me. So scared of this day. Xx*

But the phone said insufficient memory.

It was all her fault she told herself. No call from him last night and then the terrible panicked echo on the payphone and now this text nonsense. A day and a half since they'd spoken properly. Something had been wrong with her texts. They said not-sent. This should not be scaring her as much as it was.

Her phone rang. She waited for a gap in the traffic and fumbled in her bag. She almost dropped it reaching for it. Almost skidded into the back of a limo. Didn't even look at the sender, held it to her ear. It kept ringing. She hit the pick up button – it was still ringing. Fuck. It was her alarm-call from the day before. She'd set it for half an hour before she was going to call him. Fucking cells.

His last text had seemed so random, something about a shirt

and no reply to her replies. He usually replied within seconds.

So she was frustrated as she parked the car in the under-ground lot of the appallingly affluent ultra-chic hotel where her stupid bloody agent, whom she'd been so fucking weak to agree to meet, had arranged a cocktail lunch to discuss her future. Fuck him. She had it all prepared. If he wasn't going to allow her time off, her career could go to hell and him with it.

God, she hated this now. The corporate-clothed ethnic slaves that helped you out of your car, the obligatory tip and the smile. And it was all Tom's fault – his attitude inspiring her to see the world again through the critical eyes of a writer. His fault for not calling or replying to her texts on this day when she so needed his reassurance because she might just be about to tell their story to the world or decide never to tell any story and end her career for ever.

On the up escalator to the restaurant, passing the fake Greek columns, the modernist glass windows, trying not to think about Josh in his Karl Lagerfeld with his manicured nails, waiting for her, and how she so needed a single word from Tom to give her the guts to do this. To face down a Hollywood agent. To have integrity.

She tried calling him again in the elevator.

'*The number you are calling is . . .*'

Silly to even think of it but it had to be Morna. He'd told her before she had a history of hospitalisation. And he was weak like that. Felt lost without feeling guilty about something. He'd have met up with Morna after work, gone back to hers, got stoned. Right now, after six his time, he was with Morna. It made sense, her writing these last few days had revealed how insecure he was.

Elevator. Check the outbox, the things you sent him. First the sexy one then:

> *My love. No reply from you – was I too rude? Am meeting agent – going to end it all with him – like you did w/ Morna – thinking of u – seeing u everywhere – want you to text me something lovely. Now. Xxx*

My You. Do my texts work from here? Tell me if you get this. R u
free? R u with your kid? With Morna? You haven't answered all day.
I'm off to my meeting and have left your landline # behind. X

My love. I can't stand this. R u angry with me? I'm sorry if I was
needy with you. Sometimes I don't know how 2 make u feel better &
I want to but am powerless . . . x

Why aren't you texting me? My number in Manhattan at Sally's is
212 414 8756. Our phone call confused and worried me. I'm driving
now. Please text back to say you're OK. Please. XXX

Hate this. But if u don't respond it makes me feel like a stalker.
Whatever I said to offend you will u answer? B honest. XXX

No, she wasn't panicking. When she panicked and talked and
talked he would tell her 'Shhh'. As to a child. When he touched
her breast and told her her heartbeats were too fast, she did
feel like a child, scared and jabbering away. Shh. And maybe it
was because her new writing had brought up the issue of her
childhood and her dad and if her dad hadn't have left, and
maybe if she hadn't had to be mother to her mother when she
broke down, then she would have been able to Shh.

The right floor. The restaurant ahead. Josh waving to her –
arms wide open.

'Look at you, my sweet. Do you really hate me that much?'

Hugging and kissing the air by her ears. Taking her hands
and leading her to his table. Ordering Veuve.

'Don't tell me, I know. Forget the Fox job. I always knew
you'd do this sooner or later. In fact, I like that you've not been
returning my messages. Cos I know, I know, you've got some
magnum opus simmering away. I can see it on your face. Look
at you. I'm on margaritas. You want one? Seriously, they're not
so hot but the maître d's a stud, don't you think? Oh, my sweet,
everyone is talking about your new hermit life. "Our new
Salinger" – clever move. So good to see you. Tell me all.'

Shit

No thought of hands in your own shit. Thoughts only, and this amazed Tom afterwards, of the architectural layout of a shit pan. The smooth gentle ceramic curve that facilitated the easy passage of your passage. The bend upward then down into the fathomless depths of an entire city's communal crap. Microseconds after the flush and a mobile phone was about the same size as a shit. And even though there was shit there too, enough for the world to marvel at, even though that was the case – This is the case, he told himself as his wrist bent round the bend up, into some situation that was not designed for man, and caught its edge and other things, unspeakable. Even though that was the case – a sense of joy, something that the average man could not grasp, to save joy from the back passages of human waste, that you had fought, and then retrieved this plastic object that had every name and every number of everyone you ever cared for within it. Yes! He pulled it out, thanking God and shit and its slow passage and maybe even that big one that had blocked the smooth transit of everyone he'd ever loved into oblivion. And held the thing, the phone, wet and shining and as resplendent as a newborn child, but still covered in comparable unspeakables, up in that air and shouted yeah fucking yeah.

But after it had been rinsed under the tap, the thought of water and electronics. There was this moment with the on switch, as if asking the world of high technology to forgive his all-too-human failings.

It was dead.

Fifty text messages from her saved. All lost. Any way of texting her dead. And she wasn't at home. Maybe she'd texted him the number of where she was going to be tonight. He had only her landline number but she would not be at home for another thirty-six hours.

Jesus and technology. He washed the shit off his hands. Oh yes, but there was still a redemptive metaphor. An anecdote to tell her when it was all done and the phone dried out or maybe a new phone bought.

'I searched the very bowels of the earth for you, my love.'

'I crawled through the shit for you, baby.'

OK, it wasn't as romantic as he'd first imagined.

There were things to deal with, practicalities, proctologies.

Nine a.m. tomorrow morning, Princes Street, he'd walk into Carphone Warehouse with his credit card ready and the SIM card from the dead phone, and beg them to test it, try it to see if it worked in a new phone, and then he would buy a new one so as retrieve Meg's numbers and messages. A funky fuck-off phone with the ability to take photographs like hers. One even better that had video capabilities so he could see her when he spoke to her. With an infinite memory card so he would never again have to delete any of her messages. But that was tomorrow, and it was only 8.30 p.m., and too early to sleep, and there was his big meeting tomorrow over Edinburgh, City of . . . and he was alone, so alone, and the vodka bottle was empty now and he needed one more, just one more to help him sleep through this long wordless night, waiting for her to call his landline.

Email her. The offie, the new bottle and half of it drunk and typing.

My love, the shit has hit the fan. I am in the shit.

Another three paragraphs another three emails. No good, he was ranting to himself, the bottle done. She'd said she didn't have Internet access at Sally's. It would be the longest night.

Journal

August 4

Just back. Sally's cooking dinner. Three hours of Josh and sushi and Veuve and his plans for me and his questions. I excused myself – the toilet – to check my messages again. I tried calling Tom's cell. No response. Sent him a message.

Don't have your home number. Your mobile is turned off. You're either not answering by accident or by choice. You'll have to call me at Sally's 212 414 8756. XXX

So confused when I went back to Josh's table and his vague flirtations. So tired of moviespeak. That was all you left me with, my You. All our plans shot down by your lack of response. I drank too much. I needed attention. Josh gave me that.

'So, my sweet. I won't tell a soul. An album or some haiku?'

'It's really just a journal right now.'

'Excellent. Tell me, do.'

My gut instinct was to say nothing, to thank him for the opulent free lunch, but then I was thinking of you, in some pub in Edinburgh with Morna or some other Morna-like woman. Thinking about your drinking. The night on the Brooklyn Bridge. Trying to fight this impulse that told me you'd betrayed me. Telling myself that it was OK, nothing had happened, but still resenting you. Telling myself that telling Josh our story wouldn't be a betrayal. So I said:

'It's a love story.'

'Really? A good one, I hope, though, not like our last few.'

'It's about long-distance love. How it's all we can believe in even though it is impossible. All we have left to live for now is the impossible.'

Even as I said it I knew it was one of your lines, my love, not mine. But Josh was off, raving about the potential of the project and how Warner Brothers now had a fiction wing and there were clever strategies to bring out a novel and screen-play at the same time, mutually supportive, and possible inter-national co-production deals for such a story and how Kate was looking for a really challenging role like this.

'Blanchett?'

'No, silly. Winslet.'

And how it was just a quick cab ride to Chelsea and he could make the phone calls there and then in his pad while I basked in the glory of such a great concept. I had been weak. I went back to his.

He'd opened some more Veuve and put on Miles Davis. That was it, I knew where this would lead. I got out of there asap. He says he's gay but he's ambiguous about everything. Telling him I was sleeping at Sally's tonight and right now all I had to do was find a phone.

'You can use mine,' he said.

Why haven't you called me, my You? Where are you?

I'm sorry for telling my agent about our story. For not telling you sooner. We are a great story – I will never sell out on you, my love. I'm tipsy. Where the hell are you? It feels like you're punishing me for talking to Josh. It wasn't like that, I promise. Our story is ours. I won't tell another soul unless you want me to.

Have to go to dinner now with Sally and all my friends, downstairs. My cell is low on power. Taking it with me.

Pub

And of course, fate being what it was and him being fated to a life of crap, his only record of her mobile number was on the SIM card that was now deceased. After an hour of sitting waiting for Meg to call his landline, another hour of typing emails to her then realising he was too drunk to type, Tom had gone through maybe twenty worst-case scenarios, putting himself in her place – what would she do if she'd been under pressure with a meeting and had gone these many hours with only one cryptic message from him? All the conclusions led ultimately to the same end. She would hit the pub.

But he wasn't just drowning his sorrows. Oh no, nothing of the sort. Time was up, he had been neglecting his responsibilities. Tomorrow he had to finish that impossible sentence, so he was in fact conducting extensive market research on Edinburgh, City of . . . hoping that by some miracle some drunk with a quick turn of phrase could give him the buzzword.

His other question for the masses was on the possibility of sustaining a long-distance relationship without a fucking mobile phone. And for his purposes tonight he had picked not some chichi pseudo place but the real deal – the Arlington. A genuine un-working man's pub. The kind of place where people fell over and stayed down and no one batted an eye. Why? Because he needed a challenge, because he needed to be distracted, because it could be dangerous. Because Meg had not called. Because all hell had to be unleashed.

There were Archie and Johnnie at the bar, both late sixties. And neither of them was really taking to the corporate brainstorming technique he was trying on them.

'Edinburgh, City of . . .'

'Whit?'

'Go on, first thing off the top of your head.'

'Well, it would hav been ma hair but that wis long ago, son!'

'No, the first word you can think of. Edinburgh, City of . . .'

'This a joke, like? Cos ahm no gettin' it. Listen, son, I hope yer no takin' the piss!'

Ah yes, the ever-present threat of violence. Bring it on, he thought, let's see how shit it can get. 'Another pint an' a chaser?' 'Aye. Same for you, Johnnie?' 'Aye.'

'No, but seriously, son, you tellin' me you get paid tae dae this? Just sittin' on yer arse aw day tryin' tae come up wae wan word?'

Old Archie laughed so hard when Tom told him yes, Tom worried that the old guy was going to swallow his false teeth. Once the old fossil had regained his composure he was shouting out to the rest of the bar, 'Quiet please, quiet.' Indicating Tom as 'this young gentleman' and explaining Tom's question.

'So we're lookin' fir wan word. The winner gets a drink and a tenner.'

Amazing – the sudden animated unity in this crowd of what he assumed were solitary drinkers. Suddenly it was *Who Wants to Be a Millionaire?* This incredible inversion of an ad campaign, with the creatives replaced by alcoholics.

'C'moan. Edinburgh, City of . . . ?' shouted Archie.

'Shite,' shouted one. 'Whisky,' another. 'The Scottish Republican Army.' 'Lapdancing!' 'Doleys.' 'Snobby English cunts.' 'Hearts!' 'Albion Rovers!' 'Shortbread.' 'Pakis.' 'Fuckin' tourists.'

It was over as soon as it had started. Archie announced himself the winner and blagged another drink off Tom and the sub of a tenner and they got down to Tom's real problem. After two more pints Tom was officially the old guy's best friend and the ancient arm was around him and what was his problem? Tom warned it would take a lot of time. But what did he have to go home to now, but more waiting for that call? And it was no doubt fate that intervened and made him lose his phone so he'd finally have to confront this question. And it was maybe that the old man looked a bit like Hemingway with his nicotine-stained white beard that gave Tom the guts to keep on. The fundamentals. The four or five possible solutions for a life with Meg.

'Go on,' Hemingway said as the barman brought him another top-up.

Tom went through point one. Meg moves here. Old Hemingway just shook his head, then lifted his drink to his mouth in that stoic timeless way Hemingways do.

Tom told him point two. Move to America. Old Hemingway told him, 'Aye, bit the son's a problem though, eh? Aye, bein' a faither . . . huv three bairns masel, grown-up now, course, all lassies.' Naw naw, it was fine he wasn't boring him. 'Go on . . .'

Point three. Dual citizenship. 'Aye, aye you have a point there. Bit she might change her mind. Go on,' Hemingway said.

Point four. The long-term view.

He was thirty-eight now. Sean was ten. Six years and Sean could leave home. Eight realistically if Sean went to college and he really should. Eight years then. He would be forty-six. Emigrate to the US. No guilt over fatherhood – live with Meg and have his bones buried beside her in some plot on Fire Island, New York State.

'Now yer losin' me there but I can sort o' get it,' Hemingway said. 'Is she, how ye say it noo, is she a darkie?' No idea what Hemingway was on, Tom tried to speed it up, before the old man got started on the Jews.

Point five. The perverse option. They would see each other when they could, a month here a month there, and take lovers when the need arose, when the phone calls weren't on time, when the alcohol spurred the need – but tell each other everything. Hours on the phone describing sex with others as they had phone sex. Years. The only non-delusional way to be together while apart. Make them stronger. Meg was, after all, a sophisticated attractive thirty-eight-year-old New Yorker and, as she said, she got depressed and started to hate herself when she went more than a month without sex. They'd draw up a kind of contract that allowed them to fuck others on the condition that they were the primary relationship. Like De Beauvoir and Sartre. This had not been discussed yet.

'Aye, but I see problems,' Hemingway said. And Tom listed the foreseen problems: he couldn't stand the thought of her with someone else, and men in New York were so much better looking; he feared his descent again into casual sex, the long nights spent chatting up overweight girls who worked for the NHS, trying to take an interest in what they said about reality TV, having to watch reality TV so he could score. Like tonight, he would be without phone contact, and if he shagged some bird the guilt would kill him. The phone calls would turn into interrogations. The hours between text messages – filled with paranoia. Telling each other about lovers would become a perversion. A competition – I missed you so much this week I just had to fuck three other people. It was no longer about fucking. He'd rather they were celibate. He was for the first time in his life facing celibacy.

Hemingway looked down at his fifth pint, stroking his ancient beard.

'Simple,' he said, taking his time. 'Sorry tae say it but you're no gointae like it. Was in the army masel. Had a lassie masel in France, ye ken, the war. Had tae come home, ye ken, fuckin near killed me it did. Sayin' goodbye tae her at the boat. Ye cannae imagine. No a day ah dinnae think o' her face, on the fuckin' pier. Murder any cunt tae get a chance tae get back there wae her again. This is ma point, son. Ye huv tae make tough decisions. Huv tae huv wan clear answer and just dae it.'

'Yes, yes, of course. Go on.'

'Well, there's yersel and yer American lassie and yer ex-wife and yer boy right? Yiv got tae face the facts, son. It's as clear to me as day.'

'Tell me.'

Hemingway looked over his shoulder then leaned in to whisper: 'Wan of ye has tae die.'

Journal

August 4

Nine p.m. Sitting here in the spare bedroom at Sally's. Kid's bedroom, Charlie's at her dad's tonight. The girls are partying downstairs. All around me neglected Barbies and cuddly toys, posters of boy bands. Charlie is eight, but already surrounded by images of sex. I have to sleep in this room. He still hasn't called or texted. I just tried his cell again. Still no reply.

I knew I couldn't face socialising tonight. Feeling guilty for telling Josh too much about my journal. It's almost like Tom knows and that's why he hasn't texted. But still, he should have sent me a text to say where he is. I'm OK, I would normally be OK given this situation, but I know how much he needs and craves my calls. His love for me is obsessive. Silence in an obsessive is bad. He has turned against me. I just know he's hating me now. He's probably freaking out like that night on the bridge.

They've turned up the music downstairs, I'm sure they have, just to prove their point. I should have gone to a hotel. Should have been more wary when Sally texted to say she was arranging a little get-together of 'The Sisterhood'. I'm so stupid, drank too much. The big meal. The low lights and Nina Simone. Carmella and Jay and Becky feeding her baby and then all coochee-cooing, and no males there to break the growing tension. Dessert was done and I'd kept checking my cell every ten minutes for a message and the others had seen, so when Sally set down her glass in that little silence she knows how to play so well, and when she asked, So how's Tom, it meant more than I'd feared, because they knew. My friends.

The coven, as he called them. Our night here. The hundred questions they'd asked him. His angry screaming crazy fit on the Brooklyn Bridge on the way home. The night he'd scared me.

Where is he now? My cell is dying. Have to stop texting him, it uses more power. Will try again in an hour. Too late to get to an Internet café. Sally has broadband but it's downstairs in the party and there's no way I can sit there online as they look over my shoulder with their questions. I sense something awful is happening to him.

Write of that night. Keep writing. He knows you're at Sally's, he hates Sally – this may be the reason why no texts.

We'd woken late that morning. Him melancholy again. I sensed that Fire Island would be too oppressive for us both. We'd already walked all the walks. We would be sad going over what we'd already done. I had already agreed to meet Sally, weeks before. I really couldn't get out of it. I thought, since he was leaving the day after next, it would be more stimulating to be back in Manhattan. He'd come here with no changes of clothes (was wearing the same socks for the third day, all his stuff was in the hotel). So it was agreed – Manhattan. I'd called Sally that morning to say I'd be bringing a guest. Sally thrilled. 'Do tell.'

He seemed anxious about meeting my friends – I joked with him in the car. 'Don't be so paranoid . . . They won't be interrogating you . . . Just this monthly get-together with all of my female friends.' I had to restrain myself once we were inside, through the handshakes and so this is Tom. This need to protect him. This other need, to let him be, to see how he dealt with it. (Maybe it was a test I'd, on some level, decided to put him through.) At the dinner table, with six women, one man (Josh), to not hold his hand or put my arm round his shoulder. To not do that thing I'd done before with the sisterhood, maybe three times, Tony, Steve, bringing a man for interview, interrupting his jokes which were taking too long, to tell them the punchline, trying to prove how funny he was. We sat and I gave his inner thigh a little squeeze to tell him it was all just a game.

Becky was half asleep bottle-feeding her baby whose name I've been told so many times. That I can't blame myself for forgetting because it was Chinese, the name and the baby – adopted after failed *in vitro*.

Drunkenness. And I'd glimpsed, as I left Tom to himself,

that he'd been filling his wine glass up more frequently than
the others. Hard to tell really because I'd been deep in discussion with Josh.

I did what I always try to do. Leave my dinner partner alone
to network. Tom was, after all, a professional male in a
respectable job, this is what people do at parties, they talk about
their careers and network. But then he was a stranger here and
had nothing to gain from endearing himself to anyone. He was
heading off in just a few days. I should maybe not have left him
alone for so long as I habitually do with New York men who
are only too glad to leave my grasp to flirt with successful
Manhattan women, so many of us single, so many of my female
friends asking me to bring a man over.

Tom did not flirt.

This moment I recall, half heard. Tom had started talking
to Becky. We all fear Becky because she has that baby and when
she is not there with it she talks about nothing but it. It was
there in her arms. I heard him:

'How old is he now? Nine months?'

Josh had been going on about this HBO project, this adaptation of some epic best-selling historical novel. But I saw what
happened.

IMAGE: Tom took the baby into his arms. Rocking it back
and forward, shhhing and humming to himself, a little song,
giving it his finger to hold. Carmella's 'tut'. Tom shooting
Carmella a glance and actually asking her what the fucking
problem was. He'd said 'fucking' to my friend.

Of the six: one lesbian, two divorced – one with kid, one
without – two terminally single, one with an adoption. All of
them, all night talking about sperm donors. All of them designer-
label-wearing *Sex and the City* girls.

Becky's baby in Tom's arms. Some exchange between Tom
and Carmella then, very quiet, then Carmella bursting out with
her sorries. 'You're a father, I'm sorry. I thought you were just
... S'cuse me. So many men. These days, you know. These
new men. So you're a real father, for real?'

'Yes. My son is ten.'

Carmella shouting across to me.

'*Mia Meggina*, you never said he has *bambino*!'

Me then turning from Josh, trying, quietly, to explain that yes, Tom did have a son, Sean, as in Connery. Me reading Carmella's face. She was saying, sorry, s'cuse me, you tell us nothing. Her eyes saying, no wonder you kept this from us. Tom holding this nine-month-old child like it was his own. No doubt feeling this rage against all the faces questioning him. Me, wanting to protect him. These women without child or man. So scared of their talk, he must have been, the only person he could relate to was a baby. So stupid of me to take him here.

The music louder downstairs now. Just checked the mobile. No texts or calls.

He passed the baby back to Becky, asleep from his arms, and excused himself to go for a fag. He told the same joke he'd told me about the English pop star and the cop and the word 'fag'. I tried to catch his eye but he was gone. I wanted us to leave together, couldn't. I had agreed already that we would spend the night in his hotel. The dessert plates taken away by Carmella. Tom smoking in the garden. As soon as he shut the door they were upon me.

'So, you gonna move to Scotland?'

I reached for the grappa, filled a big one then downed it. Filled another.

'But it's so dark, I mean, not just the weather, cos you know they only have six hours of daylight in winter, but I mean the people. Like humour-wise, so dark.'

'They're just rude. So negative and unhealthy.'

'Well, I mean it's white, isn't it. You never see a coloured face is what Debra said. Like the whole country, that bread they eat. All that white bread.'

'And they drink, God, they drink. It's something to do with the lack of light. What's that called – seasonal . . . ?'

'SAD – seasonal affective disorder.'

'Yeah, but I heard they have good skin there, cos of the lack of sunlight. Women look ten years younger.'

'Jeez, we should all move there. Oh Meggie, can you find me a Tom?'

'But seriously, how often you going to go back and forward?'

Sally's hand crossing the table to touch mine with that slow calculated compassionate smile on her face.

'Well, but this is a pattern for you. You told me. Your therapist said the same.'

The silence, like I'd just screamed cunt, like I maybe wanted to (like he did later). Quickly it was filled by the chit-chat.

'God, I wish I had a long-distance lover. So sick of the sight of Don's hairy ass.'

'I mean, what's the secret, is Tom, as you say – well endowed?'

'Short guys are apparently, it's a myth about tall guys.'

'Well, he was quite ... Scottish guys generally aren't that tall.'

'You worked out his enneagram yet? I think he's a type-three personality ...'

'No, he's more fourish, definitely.'

'Fours aren't compatible with ones, you're a one, right, Meg?

FLASHBACK: 1992 when Michael dragged me round London to meet all his mates. To have me measured by their gazes and their silences and their eyes that desired me and would in a second betray.

It had been a mistake. I'd been weak or stupid or both. Had I needed validation? Was I just showing off? A mistake. When we made love we whispered. Incomprehensible non-words, like our song.

THE FAG. Back in after his fag. The way they pounced on him immediately. Him having to defend himself. So what's your job? How long have you known Meg? Their conclusions pre-drawn. Their eyes measuring his shoulders, jacket label, income, sense of humour which was too complex for them to grasp.

I was trying to end the career chat with Josh. Eavesdropping. I couldn't interject, apologise on his behalf, take him away. God, I am so sorry that I did this. Damn their self-fulfilling prophecy of singledom. They were asking him about his friends.

'Well, basically, we do email. Just one really, a good friend, he's in Helsinki now. Edinburgh is a pretty lonely place.'

The told-you-so look on Carmella's face. Men were solitary

predatory sharks, and it was her role to protect her friends. He was refilling his glass. I said, 'We're tired, really we have to go.'

Where are you, my love? How can I sleep like this? Something has happened to you. My cellphone has little life left in it.

Can't rest. 10.45 p.m. 4.45 a.m. his time. He screamed that night on the bridge. 'Your friends are fucking cunts!' So embarrassed at hearing that word. He might have actually really wanted to jump. More things coming back to me from that night. Before when Tom was outside.

Sally's hand, reaching over. That thing she whispered.

'Ted still asks after you.'

'I have nothing to say to Ted.'

'Oh come on, he's maybe not the most stimulating of conversationalists but he's fluid and well respected in the city.'

'I don't need respect or the city.'

'You broke off so suddenly. Don't you see, this is what you do? It's all grand passion then suddenly it goes cold. Like Ted? I worry about you.'

'Gee, thanks.'

'No, but really, Meg, relationships are about day-to-day, intimacy and sharing things, I know you think it's dull but you have to downsize your ambitions a bit.'

I can't go there. Where Tom has tempted me to go. To give up on this stupid world and the people in it.

'But seriously, if you're planning on doing this long-distance thing again, maybe you should, I dunno, it's just an idea. It would take the heat off.'

'What?'

'Well, have you considered that maybe . . . No, just listen, no big romance, just some regular guy once a week for cuddles and going out and –'

'Oh please.'

Carmella butting in, then the others.

'So you're going to be faithful to this guy you've known for just a week?'

'She's a type one, that's what they do.'

'And you're going to see him – what? Every three months?'

Carmella again. 'And you're so gorgeous. Look at your waist. My God, I would kill to have mine back. If I was you I'd be out there having fun.'

'Thanks, but really, it's not quite appropriate right now.'

'No, but you so sure he's not got someone else in Scotland? Really?'

That had done it. They made me cry, all round me like I was recently bereaved. (When Tom makes me cry it's different, he gives – they take.) I kept thinking of the things he said. 'You Americans only ever cry sentimental tears.' 'You invade the world then weep at pictures of all the suffering you've caused as you give charitable donations to kids you've orphaned.' All their hugs, all six of them, taking their turns and stroking my head and telling me it would all be fine. 'Bitches,' Tom had said. 'Coven of witches.' And now I feel for him on that night. 'They envy your creativity,' he'd said. 'Can't you see how they prey on you?'

Nearly eleven now. My phone has probably just enough power to make it through the night if I leave it on stand-by. Can't sleep – ten Barbies staring at me. Big smiles, multiple dress options. Everything is waste.

I hear them downstairs now. My friends. He has not called or texted in fourteen hours. I have to get his landline number, 5 a.m., 4, no matter what time it is with him.

Went through the humiliating process of going back downstairs in my T-shirt while they had moved on to Martinis and were dancing and trying to get me to join in. Standing there waiting for Sally to see me. Asking so quietly if I could please just take the landline into my room. Hearing through the retro nineties hits their whispers about me.

Just laid the phone by my pillow. Got his home number from directory. Called and got his answerphone. Left another long message. To just hear his voice and let me accept this thing I feel in my gut.

Know I shouldn't but I'm checking my enneagram.

Type one. Type name – *The Perfectionist*. Personality bias: single-mindedness, anger, resentment, self-survival. Spiritual perspective: the inner child is deeply distressed at being separated from the essence. Negative habitual behaviours: focusing on errors; rejecting things/situations/people if they are not perfect. Recurring thoughts. 'It is a risk to be dependent'; 'I must focus on self-survival.'

Strategies: avoid panic over projected failures; beware of 'one-way-only thinking'; focus on forgiveness; be attentive to your anger symptoms; give people a second chance; accept less. Try not to be angry.

They're playing that song again. The fifth time now. Feet pounding the floor, screeching, drunken, along to the tune, all out of tune, all trying to outdo each other. Fifteen years out of date. *Cyndi Lauper.* He is the only contact I have in the world. I have no friends now.

'Girls just wanna have fun.'

Die

Edinburgh, City of ... was the question and the answer was someone had to die. Thank you, Mr Hemingway, Mrs Dalloway, Mr Cobain. The bar had locked the doors after twelve and he'd stayed there drinking till two thirty or so, he didn't know or care. Edinburgh, City of illegal bar lock-ins and rounds on the house. Memory flashes – of being toasted by the barman, of Hemingway being helped to walk out. Of this back door to the nightclub upstairs that was open till four. Of ordering doubles for three people and downing them all – to hell with me. Of dancing to Boy George, of flirting with a forty-something with immense tits, of puking behind a seat, over someone's handbag. Of staggering out in search of food. Finding a kebab place shut.

Five or six. To hell with the time. Street. Laughing at the last coherent thing old Hemingway had said to him: he knew just the man for the job. Just say the word. Five hundred and a photo. Mum's the word. Someone had to die. Jesus, if Tom couldn't keep his feet on the pavement and off the road it might just be him, some passing car.

What's the last thing that goes through a fly's mind when it hits a windscreen? Its arse. Ha ha ha. Why was he telling himself stupid jokes?

Five hundred quid, an address and a photo. Mum's the word. The demonic pull of the half-thought like that of the pavement. His ex. Sean's mother. Easy. If she was gone then he'd be principal child carer. He'd move with Sean to New York. Marry Meg, get the passports. They'd be a family. A hundred quid commission on top of the five for Hemingway and another pint and a chaser. It would be a knife. Silent. Clean. This image of Hemingway's drunken fingers trying to draw a line across his own throat. This sound he made. Shhhhhh. God. GOD!

Or himself. WORTHLESS PIECE O' SHITE. Hemingway

had sized him up all right. Army man, knew a coward when he saw one. The signs of failed suicide in his eyes already. Too scared to go through with it himself, pay someone to do the job for him. No. Kill Meg. It was her fault, all of this. Die with Meg, take her with him. KILL ME.

Oh it was so funny, this inability to walk in a straight line. This incredible focus on the texture of the pavement, that had to be done to get home, that had to be done so as to push away these thoughts. Big meeting tomorrow at nine thirty. Fuck it all. He was shouting at the sky. FUCK IT ALL!

But what was keeping him alive really? Only Sean. Poor lovely Sean. This was no world for Sean. He was too delicate, too damaged already. It might be the best thing ... Sean and his stutter ... It might be the best ... God, God. SAY IT! ADMIT IT!

But you never left your son, you left your wife, not your son, you came back for your son. No matter what crap failing father you were for him in those early years of nappies and ABC and sleeplessness when you cursed her and the world for the lack of sleep and all you wanted was to escape. You left her, and you regret that too, but you came back for him. Just to play some part, if nothing else to see him grow, to try to safeguard him from repeating the many, many mistakes you made before. My God, he is your son. He is of you, you should never ask him to redeem all your failures. Your father tried that trick with you. You cannot let him grow up without you. He has a smile you saw in your grandfather. He has the long delicate fingers of your mother. You will never tell him that he is your only hope. And this man in this bar said he had the solution, he drew his finger across his neck and made that sound of choking, of slashing, and smiled and said it would cost five hundred, the end to your problems, anyone you want, just a photo.

Howling he was, falling about. Mouth agape, bellowing out sounds by the gasping lungful, sucking the shitty stench of the street back in only to have it puke its way back out of him. His head against the stone, a wall. This howl, terrifying, impossible to believe this sound was coming from him. Donald Sutherland in *Don't Look Now*, when he finds his daughter drowned. Footsteps passing him by. Muttering about him, some female in heels, some guy stopping, stooping to look.

'Y'aw rite, mate? Too much o' the bevvy the nite, eh?'

Staring at the ground, at his hand. Knuckles. Blood. Vomit. 'Ye want a taxi, mate?'

Mate? City of . . . City of mates. City of camaraderie between the downtrodden. City of strangers who bought you another drink when you were too drunk to stand.

The woman whispering something. He couldn't see them clearly.

'Help him up or sumfin'.'

'Gie me yer hand, mate.'

Wasn't it enough to be seen like this? No, no. They had to, didn't they, humiliate him further by making him look up. City of strangers who went out of their way to help you. City of endless pity. City of fuck off and leave me alone.

They were early twenties. Neds. His football shirt, his number-two military haircut, her white leather miniskirt and fuck-me heels. Meg could never live here. He would kill himself if he lost her. The guy's hand reaching out to him. The generosity of spirit in the eyes. City of generosity. Genero-city. Generic-city. Someone had to die.

He laughed. At the ground that spun, at the hand that reached. He laughed into the guy's eyes. Flecks of vomit and spit.

'Fuck aff, ya cunt!'

Which only made Tom laugh more.

'Fuckin' alky bastard.' The guy was on his heel. Shouting back at him. 'Waste o' fuckin' space.'

Tom got to his feet, worried suddenly at the offence he'd caused. Wanting to try to explain to the guy that he hadn't been laughing at him but at everything, every fucking thing. This city and love and its impossibility. But it only made him laugh more. 'But what do you think of the city of Edinburgh? I need one word.'

He must have said it aloud. The number two broke away from the skirt and was running back at him, fist in air. Tom could have said, I work for the Scottish Executive, but maybe all the common man wanted was to punch the Scottish Executive.

Very professional, very Raymond Chandler. Those lines, where the blow was so fast Chandler didn't even bother to write it down. Where the next line was – He picked himself off the floor and rubbed his jaw. Just like that, picking himself off the ground, laughing even more at what a fucking great punch it had been. No pain just this incredible appreciation of this art form which was hitting total strangers.

'Ye want another wan? Eh, eh? Ya junkie CUNT!'

Oh, and then the wonderful cliché of the woman taking her man by the arm and pulling him away, kisses on cheek, so proud of his power, asking him please to leave the sad bastard alone and the guy being led away, arms pumped up to his side, fists still clenched, still swearing, and her whispering to him as her heels clacked, of what a big man he was, and the promise of putting his energy to greater use when they got back home.

Aw, but no, it was perfect. Thank you! Spitting blood on to the street. You had to hand it to these neds – down to earth, they were. There he'd been thinking about getting a contract killer to finish him off and this ned had hit him with some sense. He was alive. Alive! All would be well. To just sleep and wake to Meg's voice. The pull of the pavement, his head spinning. Yes, just a wee sleep.

Journal

Twelve twenty-four a.m. Six twenty-four his time. Just set down
the phone for the last time. Still no reply. No doubt about it
now. Tom is with another woman. Fourteen texts and six phone
calls. No replies. My friends are right. My stupid friends and
their stupid bloody enneagrams. I will, in all humility, have to
learn to live like they do. Damn him for making me believe in
something more. At my laptop now, talking to myself, no one
else to talk to. I'm done. It's over.

Two twelve a.m. Can't sleep. So tired with all of this. Phone
battery low, still nothing from him. Just been back though all
the texts I'd sent him. Maybe one offended him. The last three.

*I'm seriously worried upset I don't know what to think. You haven't
answered my calls or texts. I really hope you're OK. XX*

*Don't think I can handle this. Living with uncertainty and disappear-
ances and you so far away. It's too much like what I did so many years
back. I don't have the stamina any more. You have to call me now.*

*Call me at Sally's in Manhattan. Please before we go to bed. Or on
my cell. Otherwise I won't sleep. X*

It's that second one. Mention of having done this before. He
gets so jealous. Can't bring myself to send the text I've been
working over in my head this last half-hour. *It is over – We are
– Don't call me ever.* Because if it is over then so am I. I told
myself I'd never do this again. Fall for a depressive, an addict,
an obsessive, a loser. I'm finished. With love and men and this
stupid desire to be creative and feel my life could be filled with
beauty and hope and all these things so impossible to find in

myself. From this day forth I will live my life quietly, without scrutiny, without a partner, with no one to see me. 'The unobserved life is not worth living.' Damn him and Socrates.

Three fourteen.

Woken by my cellphone beeping. From dreams of Tom falling from the Brooklyn Bridge, his mouth open in a scream, nothing but cellphone beeps coming from his mouth.

SENDER: TOM. Four new messages:

NU FOND. CANT YORK

NEW MESSAGE: *ERRED FOND IN TOIL. AMM ASSS. HOP U K*

NEW MESSAGE: *SOPH NUFONE. LEEPS SDDMGGGMMG*

It's final now. He is a drunk. He has already betrayed me.

I-Tap

He'd tried to send her another text. Typed: Baby I'm trying to text you. And it came out: *ABABY GIGO USRWWWGONGTOMM TEEYWU U*. Tried to type Help and it came out: *HIDELLIP*.

It was 9.05. The man in the Carphone Warehouse was of no help. It was maybe that Tom was in a panic, that he'd kept raising his voice just asking for any phone, any bloody phone so he could check if his SIM card still worked. America, he had to call America right now. And the little guy had installed his old SIM and it *did* work. It was maybe the image of himself that he caught in the mirrored walls of the shop, in the painful minutes of the process waiting to find out if he still had Meg's number on there, standing in last night's shirt with blood caked on his lip and shirt collar, his face flushed with rage, weeping alcohol.

Somehow, half an hour ago, he'd woken in his own bed. Woken to his responsibilities, which were that he had better fucking get in touch with her right now, that he had to give a presentation in an hour that would seal the economic fate of this city. He had run the mile to Princes Street to buy a new mobile phone. It had been silly of them both to depend on technology, for him not to have written down her landline number, a pen on paper, the old way would have been all it would have taken.

In the shop and this new phone and the fucking send button was where his old delete used to be. The result being that he had tried so many times to type just one single sentence, tried to delete the gobbledegook then had to watch in mute horror as the graphic display showed a little envelope flying across the globe to the accompaniment of a cheery electronic jingle. Sending your message: *HIDELLIP*.

If she was getting these messages she must have thought he'd had a stroke.

SIM working – and her number right there. He'd tried to type as he always did, pushing the number four button twice to get an 'H', the six button three times to get an 'O' – every button having three letters. He'd tried to type: I have a new phone. And it came out: *GIG HICUTTEE A MODEY RHINONNEE.*

'Just look at this!' He was shouting at the assistant. 'Fucking thing isn't English, every time I try to text it comes out –'

'It's I-Tap, sir,' the scared-looking young man said. 'I-Tap lets the phone predict each word as you press the keys. It's much faster than the old Tap method because your phone pre-interprets your key presses as commonly known words.'

'Gimme an old phone now, I want to do it the way I always do.'

'We only have the latest phones, sir.'

'Can I use this to call America now?'

'I'm sorry, sir, you have to purchase call credit first.'

'Can I use your landline then, on that desk? I have to call this number right now, it's an emergency.'

'I'm sorry, sir, but if you'd like to fill in the paperwork we can have the phone up and running for you in ten minutes.'

'I have to be in a meeting in twenty!'

He stood there staring at the logo. Carphone Warehouse. Crap-phone Whorehouse. He frantically typed 'I love you'. It came out: *GIG LLLOOMUTTE XXXMONT.*

His last phone didn't have I-Tap. His last phone was still lying there on the bedside table stinking vengefully of shit. His last phone knew how to talk sense and never tried to predict anything which was maybe why it ended up falling into the crapper in the first place. *LLLOOMUTTE.*

And this concept of predictive text. Like all you ever said was so predictable a microchip could do it for you. Hello, Moto, could you send a text to Meg please saying I'm having technical difficulties and that I love her so much and will speak soon? And could you make it sound, not predictable, maybe a little poetic? Perhaps there were menu functions – Shakespearean, dreamy, sexy, goofy, Kafkaesque.

'OK, OK, I'll buy the phone and give me fifty pounds' call credit. Here's my card.'

The little chap at his desk with his biro, the three-page contract. Still not swiping the card.

'No, you don't need my home address and phone number. No, no, I don't want to be contacted with updates on special offers. Take my credit card now.'

Please God. Staring at the screen. NO SIGNAL.

'What's this? My last phone had a signal. How can I get her messages if I don't have a signal! She's sent me six. Why can't I read them?'

'You server is Virgin, sir, we don't have coverage in this part of the street, but if you walk just round the corner . . .'

In fifteen minutes he had to do his pitch for Edinburgh, City of . . .

'Fine, fine.' Tom was heading for the door. Nu-Phone in hand.

'Sir, your PIN.'

Tom did the four numbers, grabbed his card.

'Sir, your contract.'

He was running out, looking at his screen like it was a Geiger counter, for those little dots that told him he had a signal. Beep. YOU HAVE TWELVE NEW MESSAGES. Then he saw.

I don't have your home number. Your mobile is dead. You're either not answering by accident or choices. I give up now.

Know that I go to bed confused + disappointed + angry. I will not let any man do this to me ever again.

Trying to dial her mobile. No credit, the bastard had promised him fifty pounds credit. He was running up the street into a newsagent's, shouting over the waiting line. 'Do you do phone top-ups?' 'You have to wait in line, sir.' Running then through the street again to find an ATM. Getting the twenty out. Running into a shop buying something, anything, a Mars bar, so he could get change. Running again to a payphone. Dialling her mobile.

Call

'Meg, my love. My God.'
'Tom?'

'Baby, you have to listen, OK. Just listen, OK. I dropped the phone down ... My love. I sent you six emails. I have been through shit and hell to try to get to you. My love, all night and today ... I've a new phone and I just got your messages now, I'm on Leith Walk and I have do the Edinburgh, City of ... and I love you, my You.'

'Tom, it's three fifteen. I don't know what's –'

'Some guy beat me up. I had to get it out of the toilet, it didn't work.'

'Wait, wait, one thing at a time.'

'OK, OK, just know how much I love you. I'll explain later, I have to go to this meeting now. This guy hit me, this other guy wanted me to kill everyone.'

'Tom, are you OK?'

'OK? I'm ecstatic! I've been through the bowels of hell. I've emerged triumphant. I'm hearing your voice. Your sweet voice. I'll call you when it's done. I have to go to my meeting now, my love. My You. Meg, I love you more than ever. I can't believe it. I've been to the edge, I swear. I almost lost you in the toilet. I have a new phone now, it speaks for me and I don't understand it. I have to go to my meeting now my love, for you. For you. I'll make a go of it. I have some new ideas. I have to go now, I'm late. Bye, my love. I love you. Bye.'

'Tom – Wait. [Silence.] Tom?'

City of . . .

The mute horror on Boss McGregor's face, eyes focusing on the blood on Tom's lip, his shirt. Tom joking it off. McGregor asking Tom to please go home now and clean up. They could do the meeting without him. Tom striding towards the room where he knew the two quasi-autonomous non-governmental organisation officials were waiting, not caring about the blood, because Meg saw beyond appearances, and in the last mile of running, he'd actually come up with the concept that would save this contract and sell Edinburgh to the world.

McGregor was behind him, hand on shoulder, restraining, but the clarity of the concept pushed Tom into the corporate suite. Yes, there were gasps and eyes lowered as he entered but his revelation was as clear as the vodkas he'd had last night, as immediate as the voice of Meg, as intense as the hangover hammering his skull.

The two clients, sitting uptight in their tight high-street-store suits, were the male and female of the species. Both early forties. They had name tags on but looked so generic that Tom could not bring himself to read them. They were part of the problem, of what was holding this country back. Client 1 and Client 2. Numbers not names, like the way they liked to run this country. Tom smiled at them anyway as he took his seat.

McGregor sat down and was no doubt doing his damage-limitation routine. To hell with McGregor and limits. All these years sucking up to the mediocre fucker. This concept would set Tom up in a company of his own. He was on fire. Hot sweat, dry mouth, guzzling the water from the jug in the centre of the table. Saying, 'Hi, howzit goin'?' With an American accent, because his big idea was all about Meg and American capitalism.

McGregor shooting him terrified glances. Tom just keeping

it inside, this answer to all of Edinburgh's problems. This stroke of Saatchi and Saatchi genius.

McGregor: 'So, Edinburgh, City of ... City of. Well, we haven't got the exact phrase yet, but we have a list of positive phrases and buzzwords from a month of market research with tourists and local inhabitants.'

Tom looked down at the page. 'Things We Love about Edinburgh.' And he was back there again, last night, with the tip-top team of brain-dead brainstormers who'd told it like it was. Laughing at that punch that woke him to the truth. The solution to everything.

McGregor read stoically from the list as Stephanie threw glances at Tom, tutting to herself.

'"Things We Love about Edinburgh: the Castle, quality housing for the underprivileged, the Royal Mile, the Bloody History of Kings, the art museums, Burke and Hare, the grave robbers, good back-to-work initiatives for the long-term unemployed, the Dungeons Tour, the new Progressive PEACE programme for intravenous drug users, Robert the Bruce and *Braveheart*."'

Oh, it was a work of genius, could they not read between the lines? Did they not see the truth as direct as a blow to the face?

Client 1: 'Well, how's about City of the Castle and quality affordable housing?'

Listen to them, poor souls, Tom thought. With their 'and'. Rule number one of branding was nobody had ever based an advertising campaign on an 'and'.

McGregor: 'Great, let's keep going with this.'

Tom knew where McGregor was going – nowhere. Petty bourgeois bastard would love for the meeting to end unresolved so he could invoice for another one next week.

Client 2: 'City of battles and of peace.'

No. No. It was just not possible. Couldn't they see the problem here? The 'and' was trying to fasten together two opposing ideologies. The tourists' desire for a queen beheaded and streets running with blood *and* the socialist dream of a quiet affordable future. Tom picked up a blank sheet of paper from the table.

He had to speak. His silence was speaking loud enough as
it was. Didn't they see? The only way. The American way.
Hollywood. He was now in a movie and the movie was called
*The Man Who Speaks the Truth. The Man in White. Twelve Angry
Men.*

Tom: 'Gentlemen. Ladies. We're not getting anywhere here
with this and I have a very expensive relationship to sustain
right now with an American and so believe you me I want this
to be a success and for us to forge links with American investors.
Damn right I do, because I want to live in a prosperous city
and make a lot of money. God Almighty, yes I do. I'm sold
on the deal. Let's sell Edinburgh to the world as a place for
investment.'

He knew McGregor, if he could have, would have kicked
him under the table. Tom was conscious of Client 2, the woman
squirming at the sight of the bloody scab on his lip. McGregor
was interrupting.

McGregor: 'Yes, as Tom says, selling Edinburgh is the key.'

Tom: 'No, no. But let's admit here what a tough job it is.
And this was what I learned in New York at Caledonian Experience week. I learned . . . let me tell you how the rest of the
world sees Edinburgh. It sees castles and hills and history. It's
the past and the past is a nice place to come on holiday, but
not to invest a future in. Jesus, no, why invest in a place that's
going to tax you at 40 per cent and then give all the money to
socialist housing and back-to-work projects.'

Client 1: 'Well, hold on there. The councils are doing a lot
of good work.'

Tom: 'But would you want the council to run an ad campaign?
You know how many millionaires there are in New York? With
a population the size of Scotland?'

Shakes of the head. Clearing the throat. Eyes on the blood
now wet again on his lip. McGregor shuffling papers, coughing.

Tom: 'Fourteen thousand. You know how many millionaires
there are in Scotland?'

McGregor: 'Tom, if we could just get back to the list.'
McGregor eating his biro.

Tom: 'Fifty-one. Many have made millions here but don't live

here, don't invest back. Just give me a minute here, Monsignor
McGregor. So you see. We're back to our original problem again
and again. It's at the head of the notepaper. Item one – "How
to sell Edinburgh to the world." If we could just read the heading
again.'

The eyes all turned back to the page. He had thirty seconds
to do this, McGregor twitching, ready to interrupt. Tom sucked
his lip and tasted blood. The searing head pain was giving him
visions.

Tom: 'Well, I strongly believe that every problem can be turned
into an opportunity. You see, the answer is in the original question.'

The clients, confused, fidgeting. The eyes straining.
Rereading the same line. McGregor clicking his pen open shut
open shut. Shaking his head at Tom. Stephanie waiting for the
nod so she could call the police, or the men in white coats.

Tom: 'You see. We sell Edinburgh to the world. No, seriously. I don't mean hype and promotional material.'

Tom ran his hand over his face, feeling the wetness, seeing
the red. The thing I love about you, Meg said, is that you are
so honest, like Dostoevsky's idiot. This was it. Had been coming
for years. It was almost there – just needed the words already
in his head.

Tom: 'I mean, actually sell the city.'

McGregor: 'Tom, it's a fine joke and I always welcome
humour in our brainstorming sessions but we should really
move on.'

Tom: 'No, no. I'm not joking.'

It needed more. Some change of posture to silence McGregor.
He stood up and held his blank page in front of him, pretending
there was something written on it. His good sense told him to
shut up and sit down. But that other sense, the one Meg loved,
told him to keep going, to clear his throat and raise his voice.

Tom: 'So here's the plan. We set Edinburgh up as a company
and float it on the international market. Edinburgh Inc. Everything in it, the Castle, the streets and everyone in them becomes
an asset. Set up a solid border, razor wire, surveillance, the lot,
charge people for admission. Privatise every blade of grass. Turn

every irreversible social problem into an asset. Seriously, picture it. Like we do here already with the tours of the Castle and the Dungeons. Picture it. Leith land – junkie capital of Europe. There's already a *Trainspotting* tour, and one for the Dungeons. Update it. Get the recently rehabilitated jobs as tour guides round the sites of their own squalor. Give them the chance to be enterprising. Re-enact real clan battles with real weapons using the long-term unemployed as actors.'

Their faces. Like explaining Reaganomics to Stalin. It was not a sentence or a paragraph, it was a speech, and the strangest thing was every word was there already waiting. Fuck, he must have actually been saying it.

Tom: 'And why stop at Edinburgh? Why not all of Scotland? The English would be more than happy to be rid of all our tax-hungry mouths. Privatise the whole country. One share gifted to each citizen. Each individual would have an interest in making the best of their nation. I see a kind of utopia not unlike Butlins or Nike World or Disneyland but bigger, better. ScotLAND we could call it. Not even change the name, just the logo. And the slogan – I've got it – "ScotLAND, this place is history".'

In the mute terrified silence it flashed before him as empty as the blank page that fell from his hand – his future. He stooped to pick the paper up and realised he'd better keep on stooping if he was going to keep his job and have any kind of future at all. How could he afford to visit Meg if he was unemployed? How long would she stay with an unemployed Scot in this country with the second highest unemployment rate in Western Europe? The highest rate of alcohol-related death.

Save it. Save yourself.

'Sorry, my little joke,' Tom said. Cold sweat dripping down his sides. 'You see, actually what I'm trying to do here is just . . . to, eh . . . to get all the negatives out here in the open . . . on the table . . . so we can . . . be completely, totally . . . positive!'

The suits were shifting on their farty leather seats. McGregor staring at the ceiling as if waiting for a horde of angels to descend and save the day.

'Edinburgh, City Of . . .'

Another flash, cocktails with Meg, sushi dinner, champagne in Soho.

'There it is.' And he drew his hands through the air in that way McGregor usually did as if to demonstrate a huge bill-board filling the sky.

'A truly excellent idea.'

This one word that had been used in about fifty other campaigns for everything from men's electric razors to tampons.

'Edinburgh, City of Excellence.'

Silence then. The suits looked at each other, still in shock from his rant.

McGregor's palms upturned, thanking the angels. Then talking.

'Fantastic, so simple,' turning to the clients. 'What do you think, Henry? Julie?'

'Aye, well, they're both about the same number of letters.'

'Excellence, Edinburgh.'

'And they both start with an E.'

'Yes, yes,' McGregor was saying. 'Great idea. The whole campaign can be words that start with an E – Excellence – Engineering – the Enlightenment – European!'

Embolism. Epidural. Ecstasy. This flash through Tom's shat-tered mind. A billboard promoting drug use. A kid with a tab on his tongue. Edinburgh starts with an – E. Tom sat back in silent awe. Could have wept as he witnessed the clients sign the £100,000 contract that would keep the company, nay the country afloat for another year.

There he was, this man who had placed a noose round his neck readying himself to jump from the highest building in the city, only to discover on leaping that the rope was in fact elastic and he'd just invented bungee-jumping.

Hands were shaken and he even got a pat on the back from the male client, and the female was laughing about how he really had them scared back there for a while, but what a concept. Eh?

Then Tom and McGregor were alone after the door was shut and Tom had to apologise. Beg McGregor to keep him on. Promise he'd never pull a stunt like that again.

But McGregor was all Es – ebullient, enormously ecstatic.
Laughing and telling Tom that he'd run the ragged edge there,
but my God he'd pulled it off. Edgy, that's what you are. Edgy
begins with an E. McGregor thought it was maybe their good-
cop bad-cop routine that had worked. What a team we are, eh!
What a team.

On the bus on the way home sitting on the top deck
surrounded by pensioners. The grand irony that no matter how
much he aimed for self-destruction, the world still found him
funny. He had come so close.

Tom looked out at the skyline, the church spires reaching
into the grey sky. Yes, he was a funny man as Meg had said.
The world was laughable but liveable. Ten minutes and he
would be home to the phone and explain everything to Meg.

Call

'Tom?'

'Meg, sorry. What time is it with you?'

'Five thirty a.m here.'

'Oh You! You have no idea.'

'Tell me, please. I need to know what last night, what yesterday was about.'

'Meg. Please, just listen. I just got a contract for a hundred thousand, I dropped my phone down the fucking bog.'

'The bog?'

'The john, the fucking loo. I'm pathetic I know ... and –'

'What, wait I –'

'– I had to buy a new phone.'

'But I called your landline. I got it from directory enquiries ... I ...'

'I was drunk, in the shit, literally. I always told you the world is shit, well, I had my first encounter with how bad it could be.'

'You actually, seriously dropped your phone down the toilet?'

'Yeah, it was *Trainspotting*, I was Ewan McGregor and ... the worst toilet in the world, searching for his anal pessaries.'

[Laughter.]

'Why do you make me laugh, why can't I just hate you?'

'It'd be a lot easier. Really, I am hateful and to be honest I haven't scrubbed up as much as I should have.'

[Laughter.]

'Stop!'

'No, seriously, my sweet. How many men would go elbow-deep in their own crap to find the number of the one they loved?'

'You should have written my number on a piece of paper.'

'I emailed you five times.'

'My email's out of whack at Sally's.'

'But you didn't call me either.'

'I did! I did international directory enquiries to get your number.'

'OK, so we have to make some rules, methinks.'

'Carry our numbers in our purses.'

'Yes, exactly. God, I have to buy a purse, would a wallet be acceptable?'

[Laughter.]

'Tom, I'm so sorry, I thought you were . . .'

'Out drunk and fucking?'

'Well . . . actually.'

'And I did too. Thought you'd given up on me and were with your agent.'

'Josh, God, no way! Oh my love. I keep getting this picture of you . . .'

'My hand down the toilet . . .'

[Laughter.]

'Yes, my God, I'm so sorry.'

'Well, maybe we're too mobile . . . too cellphone dependent.'

'We are.'

'So from now on we call twice a day. Landline to landline.'

'God, sorry. I keep seeing you . . .'

[Laughter.]

'I know, it would make a good scene in a movie. Even though it's been done before, but I mean we could go for a close-up this time. Get the special-effects people to make up some totally authentic-looking Scottish crap.'

[Laughter.]

'My You, you have no idea, the hell I've been through.'

'Yeah, well, actually, I could do with a good wash, a sauna maybe then, a manicure to get rid of the . . .'

[Laughter.]

'Jesus, Tom . . .'

'We came close, huh? You were going to dump me. You know, dump is Scots for a shit. Like "taking a dump".'

[Laughter.]

'Stop it. We say that here too.'

'Baby, what's wrong?'

'I'm OK. I'm heading home in the next hour or so. I'm just. My God, I thought you were dead or, because of that night on the bridge.'

'Shh, it's OK. I'm alive but fragrant.'

[Laughter.]

'You were on the bridge and –'

'I was just joking, my love, just fooling around. Hey, it's only just over three weeks and you'll be here.'

'I know, my God, me in Edinburgh.'

'City of Meg.'

'Hey, what's this about a million?'

'No, it's a tenth of that, just under. Well, to be honest, I think I might make assistant CEO in a year. I mean, there's only three of us there but –'

'Really? That's amazing. OK, I've calmed down now.'

'No, but I'm thinking of going freelance. I could do this job better than my boss. You know ol' Freddie's line – "If it doesn't kill me it'll make me stronger."'

'But that's so great.'

'I know, we'll both be doing our own thing.'

'But you know you'd be a great director. You have to get back to that again. The way you talk. Seriously, if you could tell an actor half the things you tell me.'

'Well, we'll see. Small steps. One day at a time.'

'My God, it would be fantastic. I'll write the scripts and you'll direct the films. We'll do maybe five then retire. An Oscar or two.'

'We'll see. My love, I have to go back to work right now.'

'OK, call me, before bed. I don't care what time. God, I'm so sorry about –'

'I love you.'

'Damn you, I wanted to say it first.'

'Goodnight, my love.'

'My day's only just starting! When will you get that right?'

'Good day then, my love.'

'I believe in you, my You.'

'Meg?'

'Yeah?'

'I love you.'

'Love you too . . . Tom.'

'What is it, my You?'

'I'm sorry. I've been very bad in all this. If everything isn't perfect I get into a panic. I get tunnel vision about how it's going to fail cos everything has for me in the past. I've been blind to your feelings Tom, will you . . .'

'It's OK, my love.'

'. . . make me listen . . . ? I talk too much, I don't listen . . . Will you make me listen . . . stop me going tunnel vision? Will you blindfold me again?'

'OK. If you teach me how to use my new phone.'

'Of course.'

'It's maybe too hi-tech even for you.'

'My love, I promise I won't freak out again if you're away for a few hours. I'll trust and listen.'

'My You. It's OK.'

'Will you tie me down so I can't run? Make me quiet and listen. Will you?'

'It's OK, Meg . . . Wait, I want to see if it works . . . can we do a test? A quickie.'

'How you mean?'

'I'm going to text you now, we'll see how long it takes. Count the seconds. Wait. It's just a hi.'

'OK.'

'I'm sending it now. OK, it says sent.'

'Nothing yet.'

'Five, six, seven.'

[Beep.]

'I got it.'

'Eight seconds. Wow, can you believe that?'

'Nine thousand miles. [Silence.] I'm sorry, Tom.'

'Shhh, everything's going to be OK. I'm going to be rich. I'm going to work out. Everything's going to work out.'

3
WAITING

Email

Oh my You. How you make me laugh. I can rest now. Just back home. The traffic on the I 95 was terrible. All the way back – car and ferry – plagued with guilt over what I've put you through. The cars rushing at me like some kind of metaphor. The cottage – such a mess too. I've been living in chaos this past month. Files and papers scattered everywhere – pathways through piles of socks and knickers. Have to do some cleaning to set my mind straight.

Done now. Feeling a bit more calm. Was a bit confused by my cell though when I checked it. The screen said photo folder full. Maybe it was to blame for our breakdown. But seventy-two pictures! I'd no idea you'd taken so many! I do remember you were fascinated with my phone because it took pictures and you did carry it for me most of the time cos my bag was full. But seventy-two! Have to delete some texts or photos to free up some memory, so this won't happen again. But they're all so beautiful my You. Will you talk me through them? I'm going to download them all and send them to you. Feel so guilty you asked me so many times to send them and I didn't even know they were here. Hope you have a good day. How you make me laugh, my genius man. Will you leave me when you get rich? Love you even more.

Your You xxx
P.S. Included that link to personality-type site again. You are a four, methinks – me a one – a good match!

August 6
Reread my email to him. He's right – my email voice is different, and I hadn't managed to articulate any of the questions I needed to ask him. Have to face it – I almost left him yesterday, had

my speech prepared. I tell myself over and over – just two days without contact, but that scares me even more. Will this kind of crisis happen every time we're out of touch? A broken phone, a night on the town, a phonecard out of credit? He's explained it all, but still it scares me. Seems very much like a replay of our night on the bridge. Night five and he is a type-four personality – prone to violent mood swings.

Memory full. He'd said the photos I tried to send had maybe jammed his memory. But I hadn't even tried, forgot to do it. All those photos. I started to download them and the first was of me in the hotel bathroom on our last morning, taken from behind. Another – me at the hotel sink. Another – my garden, the rosemary bushes. Another – my face asleep. Too many to scroll through so I went back to the start. The very first – his hotel room. The sheets tangled. The morning after our first night? I checked one from the middle of the folder and sure enough it was from the middle of our week. Me on the beach, walking ahead – he'd recorded our whole week together and I hadn't even noticed. Like a movie in reverse, starting with our last day. As if he left them for me deliberately, clues to be decoded.

The night of the bridge. I scrolled through the file and there were maybe fifteen photos from that day and night.

One of me on the street, Lower East Side, wearing the sun hat he'd bought for me from the second-hand boutique. One of the mannequins in the window. I wasn't in shot. One he'd taken from the back garden of Jemma's pad. About midday it must have been, I'd been dying to introduce Tom to Jemma – for him to meet her beautiful kid, Zak (I babysit for him now and then). Seven or eight photos of the faces at the dinner party – Sally's – Brooklyn Heights. All the faces. Eva and Joan, Carmella, Tammy and Becky and Josh.

Another photo – late at night. My back (again) framed by the wires of the Brooklyn Bridge. The lights of downtown. And why my back? Why not ask me to turn and pose for a snap? Did he feel I was already walking away from him? Our horrific fight that night.

Just finished downloading – made some camomile tea and

sat down to go through them properly in hi-res. He has an eye for composition but there is something disturbing about them all. The answer is in there, staring back at me from the screen. Can sense it. But what is the question? Oh my Tom, I'm afraid to ask it. The night on the bridge terrified me as did last night. Two traumas in a month. Do I trust you enough to go to your country in three weeks?

Sending him an email now to ask about our fifth day. I know he doesn't like talking about it, but I've got to have some answers. Hope it doesn't freak him out again.

Detox – Day One

He'd been awoken by a sense of suffocating. The heaters had come on maybe. Seconds later he was running to the bathroom, retching up green bile.

The face he couldn't face in the mirror. The kitchen and the kettle on to have that cup of coffee that would kill the taste of the sick and give him the energy to face the day. The empty bottle of vodka on the Formica staring at him accusatorily. The calendar above the kettle. The picture of Edinburgh Castle at sunset. The days he'd marked. The word 'Dry' on the little squares for the 6th, the 9th, the 13th, the 21st of July. Over one month now since he got back and only four days sober.

His eyes drifting again to the empty Smirnoff bottle. The kettle clicked off.

Yes, it had to stop now. He sat in the living room with his cup of coffee. What a fucking mess. Whole place stank of cigarettes, soiled laundry and booze spilled on the floor and left there to dry. His fingers were shaking as he held the cup to his mouth. The thing rattling against his teeth. Jesus, not the shakes already. He'd really overdone it this time. The stink of the milk turned his stomach. He set the thing down and his fingers found the phone. Trembling, he called work.

'Food poisoning,' he said. Words abrupt, shivering.

Of course McGregor didn't buy it, but he reassured Tom that since the contract had been signed it would be OK for him to take a day or two off to get himself back in shape before they got down to work. Tomorrow was the weekend anyway, so he'd have the necessary three days straight to detox.

The cold sweats. The insomnia. The aimless pacing. The stomach cramps and aching muscles. The racing mind. The phantom smell of alcohol haunting him as it wept from his pores. The weeping for no reason. The having to force down the food. The terrifying dreams that might be delirium tremens. The migraine on day two that lasted till the morning of day three. He knew them all well. Had been dry for a whole six months that year after the divorce. He had to do it again.

Everything was pointing to it. Time to face facts. If he was still drunk when Meg arrived he'd lose her. Take yer pick, mate! – the lady or the bottle? Choose life, choose refrigerators and DVD players and life insurance, choose walks in the country. Choose the *Trainspotting* detox. Cliché or not he had to do it. Draw up the list, like Renton did. He'd already put his hand down the shitter, like Renton did, why not go all the way? Become the cliché.

– Ibuprofen – 24 tablets 400 mg for the shaking and the muscle pain and hangover when it finally kicks in.
– Rennies – 48 tabs to counter the stomach pain caused by the ibuprofen.
– 6 DVDs to kill the time till it was done.
– Copy of *Men Only* or *Hustler.*
– 3 days and nights uninterrupted – no work, no Sean, no contact with anyone that could encourage me to drink or drive me to drink. Not even Meg, possibly. (Although I'll have to tell her a wee fib to keep her away.) 3 days and nights to force the alcohol out of my system.
– Kalms sleeping tablets. Valerian.
– Six easy-cook ready meals.
– Detox powders.
– Milk thistle tablets for the liver.
– One litre of Robinsons diluting juice to make the 60 pints of water I'll have to drink taste of something.
– A bunch of flowers – just for me.

The living room, the clothes on the floor, on the sofa, from those nights he hadn't even made it to bed. The bedroom the same mess. The empty bottle of Smirnoff he hadn't noticed before under the bedside table that he must have hidden from himself. Flashback of mouthfuls before work, before sleep. The bathroom and the scum line round the tub. Memory of taking a piss in the thing a few days ago while on the phone to Meg. The kitchen again and now the daylight too bright, everything thrown into sharp relief. The stack of plates and pans in the sink. Day one was keeping busy, tidying up. But where to start and with what? OK, so he had maybe an hour till the cold sweat would start. Get dressed, no clean clothes, dirty ones then. Get it done. The supermarket. Walk, don't drive, too much alcohol still in the system. Food, pills, fags, porn. And some Fairy Liquid, bleach. A new mop, some scrubber things. The whole damn shebang.

He had to resist the urge – the day-one urge to go back to bed and sleep till two or three. But if you slept all day, then the night of day one would be without sleep, and you'd find yourself at 2 a.m. bone-dry parched, in panic, pulling on your clothes again, getting a taxi to any nightclub you could get into and as many doubles down you till they closed the bar. Then day two would be day one again. But the guilt would claw at you and make you hate yourself for starting again and so you would find yourself again at the off-licence to get that one bottled to give you the courage to start again the next day.

The supermarket and the mop and the scrubbing brushes and the bleach. Practically the entire home-maintenance aisle in his trolley. Then food. Day one was work on the food front. Day one you had to eat even though you puked it back up again. Think positive. The diluting juice. The flowers by the vegetable aisle. No choice, grab the biggest bunch. Good for self-esteem. Done. Now food. Face the food. Yes, he was shivering.

A philosophical treatise on chicken and the question of free will. That was where Tom was at mentally. Spatially he was in the poultry aisle meditating on the price of pre-boned chicken breasts versus pre-diced chicken thighs versus drumsticks. Working himself rather quickly to the verge of a revelation or perhaps a panic attack. Why was this choice of chicken no choice at all? Was he free to choose his own fate or was his life predetermined?

How about turkey drumsticks? Huge, could last a week. Cheap too. But probably stuffed full of hormones.

It was all because Meg had been talking about stages of love for weeks and sent him that attachment on the nine essential personality types; she thought he was a four and she included a link to a site, which he had read with increasing anxiety.

Type four. *The Tragic Romantic*. World view: Something is missing. Others have it. I have been abandoned. Type fours have impulsive, compulsive personalities, prone to addiction.

Free range then. What was the difference between corn-fed and free range? About a pound twenty. Too bloody expensive either way. He'd have to settle for steroid flavour.

An elderly woman reached past him, grabbed some chicken breasts and was away. Jesus, how could they do that? Be so content with all this crap. Oblivious to their own existential condition and to his. Something is missing. I have been abandoned in the poultry aisle.

Now, if he got the bag of eight pre-frozen breasts in individually sealed sachets he could take one out in the morning and it would be defrosted by teatime. Plus he'd always have something in the freezer for when Sean came round. But then he'd have to defrost the entire bloody freezer and break through all that ice to even force that big bag in there.

Type-four romantics want the unattainable (professionally) and the unavailable (in relationships). OK, point taken. He'd always been overambitious, then blamed the world when everything failed, and yes, Meg was more than slightly unavailable.

Pre-cooked might be an option, but probably flavourless and the skin was wrinkled and dried-out-looking. Jesus, who bought this shit?

Fours live in a state of denying the present and focusing on a distant hope. Yes, yes, OK. They become desperately disappointed when the thing they seek comes into reach. Bullshit, when he was with Meg everything would be hunky-dory. He'd cook meals for her, eat regularly and stop drinking entirely and his problems would no longer be problems. He was just about to give up on the chicken choices and start looking through the red meat when that other line came back to him. Fours have a tendency to walk away. Abandon lovers, careers and friendships.

OK, so now he was telling himself to stick with chicken just so he could for once in his life see something through. He grabbed the first chicken packet to hand and was thinking of that French poulet recipe thing with the mushrooms and the entire bottle of wine for the sauce – the possibility of having an excuse to buy wine.

Jesus, so if he was a four, wasn't that terrifying? Some bloody website she'd found had his entire life mapped out. He would break off his fourish behaviour this day, day one, in this very supermarket. Buy the wine and boil off the alcohol. It would be a stab against fatalism and a pretty good meal even if just for one. Coq au vin, yes, that was what it was called. Cock with wine. Chardonnay or Pinot Grigio or Sémillon Blanc. Now this was looking more like freedom of choice.

Of course, drinking to excess was very fourish, but on the other hand he would have his lovely French meal and throw back just one glass to celebrate his positive belief in his ability to shape his own destiny. Call Meg tonight and explain that he was not a four or any other damned number. Get her laughing about the whole shebang.

But the line at the checkout. All these bloody people. The obese woman in front of him stacking the conveyor belt high – the forty-pack of sugared doughnuts and the five litres of Diet Coke and that pile, eight high, of identical objects in styrofoam and cellophane. For crying out loud, was it even possible as an object in the world? Microwave fish and chips. Ready in two minutes. The fish and chips were actually lying side by side, pre-cooked, then frozen. Edinburgh, the global capital of fish and chips and here was this woman buying . . .

That was it. He was seeing himself running out into the car park, nothing bought, ranting to himself. These fucking people, uncultured, uneducated, lost, all of them – little minds shrink-wrapped and pre-frozen.

He forced himself to put the wine bottle back, to stay in line to wait and pay. Twitching at the checkout. Loyalty card, no. Cashback, no. Out.

As he made it back up the street with his huge bulging bags and his new mop he was running over the very last bits of info on Meg's website.

Fours often surround themselves with people they consider inferior and this creates an elevated sense of ego. 'No one understands me.' 'I am surrounded by idiots.' Fours often self-sabotage the foundations of their own security (careers, etc.) so that they can wallow in self-pity and have a sense that the world is against them. Romantically, fours often look for someone to save them from themselves. Fours in the final stages of personality deterioration are often suicidal.

Two for the price of one. Liebfraumilch, the advert in the off-licence said. Fucking horrible wine, which you could only find in a shit place like this, but it was only four pounds and there was no such thing as freedom of choice and he was, fucking was, a four. Four pounds it was. This had all been too traumatic. He would start day one tomorrow.

But as he stepped inside there was a man in front of him, fifty, drunk already, sorting through his coppers to pay for a bottle. Flash of himself after Meg had given up on him. Age fifty, counting out his dole money to fund his cirrhosis.

He was out, the mop bashing his gut as he pushed through the door. Day one. Up the hill, get home. It couldn't be starting already, it was just after eleven, usually it started around three – the cold sweats. No, it was just the hill, the heavy bags making him sweat. Or the image of himself that anyone who had ever tried to detox would recognise. A sweating man struggling up a hill looking like a professional house cleaner.

OK, so his six months, a year before, of going dry were preceded by six months of trying and failing to stay dry for more than three days at a time.

Front door. His fingers shaking so much. The keys a living thing in his hand trying to escape. That was the way it worked, the body, you had to fight the body, it threw obstacles in your way to make you fail, it had you bashing your shins, banging your head, swearing at yourself that if you just had that one drink you could make a start. In and up the stairs and inside he told himself that the pain in the arms and shoulders and ribs was just from all the shopping bags, that the ache in his lower abdomen was where he'd bashed himself with the mop at the off-licence door and then again on the stairs.

He set the bags down and sat himself in the kitchen, fingers fumbling for a fag. Acrid, dry, it needed a drink to douse the fire in his throat. He'd have to give up on the cancer sticks too. Hold on. One addiction at a time, one day at a time sweet Jesus. Don't go cold turkey on the whole world. Don't stack the odds too high because if you fail it'll only make you drink more.

OK – the flowers in the pint glass. His vodka pint glass, now filled with lilies, lovely, take three days to open. They would flower when he was clean.

Turning off the freezer, placing a tea towel on the floor to catch the drips. Then all the little packages opened. The yellow plastic gloves on. Worst things first. The goddamn toxic sink. Look at it. An experiment in DNA, it was. Whole new organisms breeding in there. A cure for cancer among the mould perhaps. One by one he lifted out the slimy plates, pots, cups, cutlery and set them on the table. A quick glimpse of what was left at the bottom. Horror show, particles, organic bits and weeping juices. Head turned away, nose on shutdown, he rinsed the sink with gallons of hot water, forcing his finger into the plughole to pull out and swirl about and squash down the hole all the unspeakables. Then the Domestos with the new scrubber, then Fairy Liquid because he didn't want his dinner tonight to be eaten from a plate that smelt of Domestos

But wow! With all the soap and suds and hot water it was actually rather fun. Kid in a paddling pool. He should do this more often. Like maybe once a day. Oh boy! What a stack of shiny clean plates and pots and pans. God, he was good at this. And this joyous need he felt pounding in his chest to stick on a CD really fucking loud and confront the horrors of the gas hob.

Laughing to himself as he tried to get Lou Reed's *Transformer* out of the CD cover with the big yellow washing-up gloves still on. The muscle-bound gay man on the back cover and him now with his new spray bottle of Mr Muscle. And my God, just look at it. One spray and fizzing its way through the grease. Leave for thirty seconds. And it was becoming a perfect day, all shiny and new. And he was in Central Park now with Lou Reed and Meg feeding animals in the zoo and then going to a movie too and then home. 'Glad to spend it with you too, Lou!' he shouted out. And to hell that this song was a cleverly veiled tale of a day in the life of a junkie in NYC. This surface he'd feared for years that stank of every meal ever cooked on it for a decade before he'd even moved in, sparkling now before 'Perfect Day' had even finished.

He just had to hear it again. Stuck it on repeat and was singing along while sweeping up and making piles of dust and fluff and crusts and timeless pasta shells and cigarette ash and receipts.

Something about reaping what you sow. Why the hell was that the last line?

Day one. Everything in the world was up for interrogation. The next track then and the new mop and the bucket and the bleach. God, he loved this album. New York and Meg. All this for you, my sparkling new love.

As the album ended he realised he'd mopped himself out of the kitchen and hence access to the other cleaning fluids, the diluting juice, the glasses and his cigarettes. He stopped dancing with his mop and stood there in the kitchen doorway, alarmed to find that the pounding in his chest was not slowing but accelerating. He sat himself down gently in the living room. Thought maybe if he could stop his mind from itemising all the things left to do then the pounding would stop. Hoover the rugs and the corners, sort out the mail, change the bed sheets, do a laundry. Stop. It couldn't be that stage yet. That was usually a night one. The withdrawal palpitations that felt like a heart attack that could turn into a panic attack the more you worried. No, it was OK, he told himself, he'd just got a bit overexcited with the mop and the dancing.

The phone rang and it was Meg. He didn't know what to say, had prepared nothing. She'd called three hours early. No way he could tell her what was really going on. About his anxiety that the pain in his lower abdomen was in fact not a mop injury but liver damage.

No, no. He had to keep it up. Be all joyous and excited. Telling her about how he was making the place nice for her arrival. Joking about the growth in the sink, his terror at

defrosting the freezer for fear of what he might find in there
– a woolly mammoth in the ice, some preserved remnant of
peat-bog man. He had her in hysterics, her telling him that he
shouldn't put himself down so much. Him telling her that he was
done with Scottish cynicism and his kitchen cleaning was an
embracing of American positivity and the glorious joy of all-
American cleaning products. Stop, she was saying, I can't talk,
you're giving me hiccups. Oh, but he was on a roll now and
her laughter pushed him further. He was on about his yellow
rubber gloves and how he felt like a fifties American housewife
and how maybe they should try a little slap and tickle with
domestic rubber. How he was going to buy himself a plastic
apron when she got here and walk round in it and nothing else,
being her *femme de ménage*. Silence then.

'My You. Did you get my email? Did you see our photos?'

'Sorry, not yet.'

'You OK, my You?'

'Yeah, yeah, I feel like Mr Muscle incarnate, this superhero
of domesticity.'

'You seem a bit . . . I dunno? Now it's me being the down-
beat Scot. You just seem . . . well . . . manic. You sure you're
OK?'

Now he had to face it. The little white lie. Three days he
needed alone.

'Well, yeah, I guess I am, it's just . . . you see . . .'

'What, my love?'

'Well . . . Sean. I have to take him to the Highlands this
weekend . . . his grandparents and well . . . I won't really be
able to talk, the mobile won't work up there.'

'You didn't warn me about this.'

'No, no, it was very sudden. His nana. She –'

'So, can I call you at their number?'

'Well, yeah, but, it'll be weird though. We could try and talk
but . . . they're like seventy now and I have to share a room
with Sean and –'

'So, what are you saying?'

'Well. It's best really if we don't talk for a few days. I can
email you, if they have a connection – I don't know if they do.'

'Two days? I'm not going to get to talk to you for two days?'

'Well, maybe three, with the travel.'

'God!'

'I'm sorry, Meg.'

'But . . . You know you let her control you too much. I can't. We can't just have these things come out of nowhere like this.'

'It wasn't the ex, it was my parents, they . . .'

She said her goodbyes, but he could tell she was angry at him. He'd been a fool for inventing this story on impulse about the Highlands. When he called her on Monday she'd be all positive again, asking him to tell her everything about the mountains and his parents and what they did with Sean, hillwalking or fishing or flying kites. And he'd have to make it all up. The lie would run for days and days.

Staring at the phone now back in its plastic cradle. He ran to the bathroom, catching the vomit in his hands, before finally finishing off in the bath.

Then these awful minutes rinsing it out. No food bits there to squash down the plughole. No food eaten in days. He had lied to her.

The shakes. Teeth chattering. The glimpse of his face, grey-skinned, eyes red, bulging wet. This wasn't supposed to happen on day one. Vomit on his jeans. He took them off and rinsed them in the bath. Confused then as to what to do with them. Dry them out on a heater? Do the laundry?

His trembling legs took him to bed. He couldn't even recall having taken the sheet and duvet cover off. He stared at the pile of bedclothes awaiting washing. A pile as big as a sleeping man, a bum in his pile of clothes. Corner of Twenty-Third and Eighth. Like they'd seen and walked past on their second day.

Journal

August 7

Crushed with guilt now. I know this is my fault. Two days of crisis and now he's disappearing again for three more. It's like the photos: he gets too needy; I get scared and pull back. He goes off by himself; I see it as rejection and go into terminal panic. Was I too cold with him before he lost the phone? Did he do it deliberately – subconsciously? All he's left me with now are the photos. Truth is in there somewhere.

The pic of the sixties sun hat. The one he'd bought for me that day. Fifth day together. Day of the bridge. In it I am half turning back to him, while walking ahead. Street of boutiques and trendy restaurants. Studenty, upwardly mobile, ultra hip. Ludlow or maybe Rimington. We'd decided to do our last two nights in Manhattan. He'd caught me mid-step. I was smiling back at him. The photo smile I can do with less than a second's warning. Dumb American smile.

I recall I'd been talking all morning on the drive about my friends, my many friends, how I wanted him to meet them all today – to show him off.

Yes, I had felt too needy the day before and had told myself to put on a brave face. He was leaving in just less than two days. The ironic shopping spree had been his idea. He wanted to buy me something, he said as his fingers stroked my neck, as a souvenir. Yes, that word had upset me.

But once we'd parked in the Lower East Side he'd been trudging along behind and I'd hoped the plan wouldn't falter. 'Don't worry,' I'd said, 'they're good friends, my safety net – it's not a test.' He'd tried to joke – Couldn't I bring my friends to Scotland instead? I look at the picture now and there is this distance. He was maybe as much as ten paces behind when he shot it. LOOK AT THE HAT NOW.

Yes, his reluctance to see the shopping through. (More than the usual male retail phobia.) And the melancholy we'd had the night before, after his long-distance call to Sean and my crying. Shopping would cheer us and it would be great to go public as a couple. (Ludlow Street, definitely.) I pointed out some fashionistas in a mix of sci-fi silver lamé and flares. Told him the seventies were coming back for the third time. He'd joked that Edinburgh was still looking forward to experiencing it for the first. Laughter, but still I had to take his hand and drag him along.

He wanted to buy me something. 'Chic and sexy – but still useful.' I'd insisted I buy him something comparable.

The retro boutique. Patchouli and musk scent, multicolours from many decades. A voice calling out to me.

'Meg, long time no see, babe!'

Belle and Carlotta. I'd tried to introduce him. 'This is my friend Tom.' I'd said. 'Friend . . . from Scotland.' Maybe their eyes scanned to check him out. Maybe that or the word 'friend' was why he'd excused himself to go out for a cigarette. I'd been chatting away with the girls and they'd been teasing me about my new beau. The photo he shot was of mannequins. Through the window, while we chatted. Mannequins, not me.

I must have sensed his awkwardness. (Did I really or am I imposing it now to make myself sound better?) I was out the door then and pulling him inside and putting on the hat and trying to get him to laugh about how it was the kind of thing my granny might have worn. So camp. Carlotta had asked if I'd seen Ted recently. Maybe that had been it. He didn't know Ted was gay. Tom seemed in a hurry to get the shopping over and done with. His awkwardness with my old friends was more than a little embarrassing. He'd buy me the hat, he said, if I got him some sunglasses. I'd tried different ones on his face – one pair was too yuppie, another too rock star, another too Trotsky. (He looks like Trotsky.) We settled for a big Californian-looking pair that almost covered half his face. What was that he'd said? 'I look like a blind man' or 'Love is blind' – something like that. I'd felt reassured – his sense of humour was returning.

In his photo I am walking ahead and turn back to him with a smile. The smile is anxious. Trying too hard. (Am I reading too much into everything again?)

'What's wrong, my You?' I'd said, putting on a face like a sulking kid trying to show him what he looked like. 'C'mere,' I'd said, 'I can't see your eyes.' I laughed as I lifted his glasses. What was it he'd said then?

'Oh, you know me, I'm just a little . . . I'm going to miss you, that's all.'

Not the first time he'd said that in the previous twenty-four hours. Then he'd gone off on one of his rants. About how it was the Scot in him and he couldn't have an innocent moment of happiness without already imagining its end.

I tried to joke, pulled him along by the hand. This happens to me. I can't help it. My tears the day before had left me feeling weak. My fear that if he broke down I would too again. Trying to be all positive – telling him about Sally and Josh and Jemma and little Zak who we were just going to meet, who was so cute I could just kidnap him and take him home and eat him all up.

Yes, I was insensitive. His son is ten. I hadn't realised how much being in a family home would upset him. That's the only explanation I have now for what happened next.

My You, I want to tell you these things, but you have gone again. It is my fault, isn't it? I have pushed you away. Feel silly now, analysing a sun hat. It's here beside me. How can I endure these days apart? Am I so weak – morbid, humourless? You make me laugh. I think of you in the Highlands with your son and am jealous. I can't laugh without you. Our song makes me feel like crying. If you knew how pathetic I am you would not love me. I'm so deeply flawed. I love you. I'm sorry for loving you. Must make myself stronger. Must sleep now.

Detox – Day Two

It had been a mistake to sleep in the day, because as he woke it was dark and the first thing he thought as he reached his shivering hand for the mobile to check the time was, Can I make the off-licence before it shuts?

Eleven fifty-five. So nine hours five minutes without the possibility of a drink.

The pile of bedclothes now seemed more animal. He was sure something had moved under there. No, it wasn't the DTs, he hadn't pushed the boat out that far. What boat? He had to get up, his mind was doing that thing that was usually day two. The manic counter-criticism of every thought with footnotes. The many voices.

Look at him, what a mess, he'll never pull this off.

Leave him alone, he's sick.

He's trying.

Try better, fail better.

SHUT UP!

He needed to get out of bed. To eat. He hadn't eaten prop-erly in five days. It was 11.56 p.m. He was glad to know that the off-licence had closed. There was no way he was going to hit the town in search of a nightclub.

The shit splashed the toilet bowl, a minestrone of many things that should have long since been digested. He needed to eat – to shit something solid tomorrow.

This was OK. Part of the process. The pints of water he'd drunk. He wiped his arse again and cleaned the wet seat, washed his hands, taking care not to look at the mirror face that would now be yellow, not from terminal liver disease but from the bare tungsten light bulb.

He sat there – living room – T-shirt, underpants, and turned on the TV. His panic at the supermarket had been a mistake. He hadn't made it to Blockbuster to get those six DVDs that would get him through these days, hours, minutes in which focusing on a book was impossible, focusing on himself, terrifying, which now had to be wasted watching all the latest mind-numbing TV. Yes, it was a bad idea to confront the world on night one of detox but at least he could swear at the TV.

He thinks love will save him.

Look at him shivering. He's sick – when she gets here she'll see it.

He lied to her yesterday and last week and will keep lying to her.

He thinks he's detoxing but all he has achieved is lying.

Type-four personality.

He's not been taking care of himself at all well since the divorce.

Come on, that was years ago. He loves this, this wallowing in self-pity.

Smirnoff is five times filtered. It's the cheap vodka that does the liver damage.

Alcoholic just like his father was – grandfather – stuttering his way through life. It's in his blood, genetic.

He should call Morna. She could get him help, like before.

So sad though. It's what he does. Setting everything in life on someone else. If he tells Meg she'll run. Americans are afraid of addiction. She works out every day. C'mon.

This is all her fault. The pressure she's put him under. Can't you see. He's just waiting now for her. He's lonely. It's understandable.

He's going to die like this.

She gets here in a month. He has to get dry before she arrives.

Go on, get dressed. Get a taxi. Victoria's – open till four – thirty-something crowd. Vodka and a mixer only a pound. Just one drink to take the edge off.

SHUT THE FUCK UP!

The five channels were football highlights, *The X Factor*; some reality TV show, some sci-fi B-movie with faces that looked like famous faces but weren't, and this serious documentary about Russia post-fall of the Berlin Wall. He picked that one.

A girl of maybe eleven in a suburban housing estate on her hands and knees barking like a dog. Growling at the camera. Surreal, maybe it really was the DTs. He changed channel and it was just adverts, then again and just more, so then back.

A shot of a boy in a psychiatric unit, whimpering like a lost puppy in the corner by the door, snarling whenever caring fingers came close, he was maybe ten.

Adverts. Cars and cellphones and semi-pornographic party lines. Yes, it was Friday night. In the gap between the ads he refilled his glass of water, added the Robinsons diluting juice.

Then back waiting, C4, the title on the screen: *Feral Children.*

It was perfect, the need to know what the fuck this was focused him away from the shivering – the pain in the gut that wanted food. A single oatcake with butter was all that he had managed to keep down. Face stuck to the screen as he tried to find out what feral children were. A psychologist. A shot of a deserted Moscow street. Litter blowing in wind, a pack of dogs running wild.

Voice-over: '*Kolya's mother was an alcoholic and drug user and took to prostitution to pay for her addictions.*' The image of this ten-year-old boy on hands and knees at the edge of a school play park, sniffing the air, lifting his leg, wet stain through his jeans, the puddle growing on the ground around him.

Voice-over: '*His mother was arrested in 2005. The social services couldn't find the father. He became officially a lost child.*'

Something was happening now. Sounds separating from sight. The room expanding – heat diminishing. The sound of shivering. Trying to focus on the screen.

Packs of abandoned dogs tearing open bin bags, fighting, roaming through deserted housing schemes. Dobermanns, poodles, schnauzers, mongrels. In packs like wolves. A big grey dog eating garbage, fighting the other dogs away.

Tom had to eat. The chicken drumsticks were a pack of twelve. It was too complicated. Eat two, freeze ten. The freezer was defrosting anyway. The drip drip drip from the kitchen that would measure the days he had left.

What are feral children?

An image of a kid, maybe nine, fighting with a dog on a street, wrestling the beast to the ground. Biting the thing's neck.

Voice-over: '*Incomprehensible as it seems, in the absence of parents or a competent social services network, these children have been brought up by packs of feral dogs. Modern-day Tarzans.*'

Then the tears came.

'*They quickly become pack leaders because they can find food. They have little grasp of spoken language.*'

My poor child.

'*Of the twelve discovered, only three have been reunited with their parents.*'

'Da . . . dah . . . duh . . . daa . . . ahh . . . ahd . . .'

'*And only one was found early enough to make the transition to human language and society. Maya was found when she was seven. Seven is the crucial turning point in child mind development.*' He'd walked out on Sean when he was seven.

Journal

Calm down. He's out of cell range, his folks don't have email – we've planned 'to grow old together' so a few days now should make no difference. I know, but feel so alone without his voice. Can't call my friends. Hate them now for how they made him feel. It's all in his photos. Can't write.

Fool and nostalgist, listening to our song again. Nonsense words. It won't make him call. Weeping at my laptop screen. Maybe it's true what Sally says – I'm built for longing, not for love. All day in my pyjamas. Can't face food. The cycle is repeating again. Have to tell myself not to hate him for doing this to me. Tell myself over and over it's good that he's with his family now, but then I go into these spasms of envy – that I will never have a child, don't even speak to my parents. I am withering like the lettuce. Damn fool. (He hates nature metaphors.) If I could just speak to him it would save me from what I know is going to overwhelm me.

Can't stop myself. His photo of the huge bay windows from the garden. Jemma's place. To the right of shot the neatly trimmed rose garden. Zak's toys; tricycle; sand pit; Zak's free-standing easel; paintings lying on the grass. The Japanese-style table, benches. The postmodern architecture. Jemma's husband is Ted Gruenberg, I recall telling Tom before we got there. 'God,' he said, 'the architect?'

It looks almost like a realtor's photograph. No people in sight. The reflections from the garden in the glass obscuring what's going on inside. A glimpse of an elbow maybe, the leg of Zak's play table. Nothing more. Tom standing there camera-phone to his eye in the reflection, shadowy, obscure, out of focus.

MEMORIES – all of being inside, so happy because Jemma

had taken to Tom so quickly. 'He's the real deal,' Jemma said and hugged me. 'At last.' A relief. Jemma had studied art history at St Andrews University and so knew Scotland well. Her and Tom had been chatting so effortlessly and what I'd overheard while I played with Zak had all been so positive. Jemma saying she sometimes missed the landscape. The history. I couldn't hear much because Zak was talking and talking about his friends at Montessori. (Beautiful Zak, how can I ever forgive him for not being a baby?) We were playing with Lego. No, Play-Doh. I was showing him how to make tyrannosauruses out of Play-Doh because he was going through his second dinosaur phase. The moment I'd found myself roaring dinosaur-like with Zak then felt silence around us and turned. Tom and Jemma standing there together at the breakfast bar just watching and I'd returned to the making of terrifying Play-Doh claws, happy in the knowledge that my best friend and Tom had what seemed like a real connection. And we, me and Zak, held our dinosaurs up to them, growling and shrieking with laughter. And Jemma had said we should open some bubbly to celebrate even though it was only three, but I was so happy for them both and us all and Tom had asked if it was OK to smoke in the garden.

No trace of it in the photo, what he'd felt. Unless he was maybe intimidated by the apartment. (The backyard alone is worth four million – they've turned down many offers from developers who want to build condos there.) I'd been moved almost to tears as Zak gave me a little hug when the dinosaurs were set down – that it was OK that Tom had a kid already. That I had reconfirmed for myself, just in our last week, after so many aborted decisions and recapitulations, that I would not be having a child. That the world really could be beautiful, with Jemma and Zak and Tom and Sean. I'd looked up at Jemma and her eyes too were wet. 'Look at you,' she said. 'So happy.' Then she opened the Veuve and there were three glasses but Tom was still outside. His photograph is of the facade. It captures none of what I'd felt. (Must try harder to put myself in the garden with him.)

He is looking back to us, cigarette long finished, stopping in his tracks. I see him watching through the glass, me laughing uncontrollably with a four-year-old and a millionaire mother. Him trying to fight the many pictures from his past – of days of beaches and birthday parties and so much innocent laughter. I see him staring through the bulletproof glass of a home more expensive than anything he has seen before. Trying not to cry in the back garden. Lifting my camera-phone to his eye to hide his face. And shooting us.

My love, the dinosaurs were for you and your son. You wanted to cry in my arms but I was on the other side of the glass. I know this now. I left you alone for two minutes and you shot me through the glass and I am an elbow and you are a faint reflection and that is all we are. My love, I am so sorry.

Waking

He was a Dobermann ripping someone's throat. He was Pongo saving his hundred Dalmatians. He was a film director with agents and producers and PR people, a whole auditorium-full waiting to see his first feature film. The same old dream. All waiting and the title credits finished and the music rose and then the screen was white, nothing there – minute after minute. The audience snarling at the screen.

Tom woke late on day two of detox after maybe ten minor awakenings and forced sleepings. It had been the drip drip drip of the defrosting freezer. The noises too loud, waiting for the next impact of a drop of water. This heightened sense was usually day three not two. Day three when the simplest of things became an ordeal. The coordination between hand and eye. The why of why make a cup of tea? The surreal impossibility of a tea bag and the addition of milk and sugar. Questions of how tea bags came to exist. The colonisation of India. Those little perforated holes.

The fearful first steps out of bed, expecting the muscle pain, finding it but not the slippers. Day two was the day of body as stranger. Of knocking things over like a gangly teenager who'd grown an inch in the night. Was facing your flat like a stranger. Was pulsing head pain that interpreted each encounter with an object in terms of the agony it might cause. Day two. Day of confrontation with a world that is not drunk.

Nine per cent of the population of Edinburgh were alcohol-dependent. Thirty per cent of the population of working-age adults in the Gorbals in Glasgow were on invalidity or incapacity benefits. One thousand three hundred manufacturing job losses in the last three months.

The facts didn't help as the Rice Krispies were poured. Fourteen painful steps with the bowl into the living room as the

noise of cereal was too much. The Twelve Steps. Step ten, you
must ask the higher power into your life, whether God, Buddha,
Vishnu or Muhammad, ask the higher power for help. Eat the
Rice fucking Krispies. Place your faith in the deities Snap,
Crackle and Pop.

Funny, isn't it, how humour gets you through a bowl of
cereal. Ye non-believer. Ye man who once went to an AA meeting
and had to leave because you couldn't withhold the laughter.
Ye who went on a three-day bender afterwards. And ye may
delude yourself, little man, false prophet, ye who believes only
in yourself and that only on a good day. Wash the breakfast
dish, ye of little faith.

Fuck YOU! He was shouting at the Fairy Liquid bottle.

It is day two, remind yourself of that. Day in the desert when
Satan comes to tempt you with an empire of slaves, whores,
horses, for the sands to burst forth in flower, for the world to
be made in your likeness if you would just take that sup from
his cup.

'Begone, foul fiend!' Tom shouted at the kitchen units. 'I did
ye with Domestos – did ye not know it kills 99 per cent of all
known germs? Away with ye!'

He was anxious then that the neighbours might have heard.
My God, but ye had to be wary of day two. The day two years
ago at the AA meeting when that fifty-year-old man at the
lectern had started ranting and groping at his own crotch.

'This is where Satan lives. Five years and I have not given
into his many temptations.'

And Tom had noticed that the guy had a very impressive
bulge where he was grabbing, increasingly impressive with all
the grabbing, it might have been the guy's wallet, but my God,
thought Tom, if Satan could give you a dick like that then all
hail Satan. He'd sat there at the back reading the signs on the
walls. The Twelve Steps. All Christian dogma with petty
disclaimers. There was no subclause there for men burdened
with great endowment. He had thought it his moral responsibility as an atheist to go up to the guy when it was tea-and-
biscuits time and explain the basic tenets of Nietzschean
philosophy. The coming of the Overman. But the talk was

interminable and the promise of stewed tea and soggy tuna sandwiches and equally limp handshakes had been too much.

Funny then but not now. This was what Meg loved about him. The man at the bottom whose laughter rose to the very top, who could quote from all the Western philosophers on his seventh glass of Chardonnay, that she had thought his third.

He was still in the kitchen. His perfectly clean kitchen awaiting her appraisal. Day two, he told himself, and Meg was always going on about days. If she could be so devoted to those seven days they had, then, for her, he would see day two through dry. The aching joints, like it was alcohol that had kept them lubricated. Drink water, force it down. One glass. Go on, get it down you. Two.

The freezer was not quite so terrifying now. In fact, a metaphor for the detox process. It would be defrosted when he was dry. Both dry together. Drip drip drip. The tea towel on the floor was soaked and there was a large puddle on the floor around it in every direction, but the snowy impenetrable waste-lands within had much diminished and the things in there seemed to be assuming normal proportions. He removed the frozen prawns and the oven-ready chips that must have been in there from before he bought the thing second-hand. Put them all in the bin. The noise of chips in bin seemed not quite right. A delay, like a long-distance call.

Day two – when everything went out of sync.

But he was doing fine. The muscle pain, yes, but not the migraine. The sweats would come back again but he'd left most of them on the sheets last night. No, he was feeling remark-ably good for day two. And the walls could do with a coat of paint. Take your time, he told himself. He lit a fag to try to work out the plan for the day.

Suddenly it was the bathroom, and just making it to the sink this time. The sickness could come at any time, he knew this, as he washed it away. The pain throbbing in his temples now. A second retch. Nothing. It was only 11 a.m. on Saturday. He wouldn't be clear till 9 a.m Monday and then the hardest part would start. The body not so sick but the mind still dependent. These little lies you told yourself minute after minute in the dry wasteland of the future that was one day at a time. Just one drink to celebrate how you'd been dry.

Great idea. He was dressing now. Fuck, why not? A day dry. Well done, Tom. Meg wouldn't know. And it was an old family trait, the drinking, nothing to be ashamed of, like the stuttering, three generations. Drip drip drip. So dry.

The keys in the lock. The future projected sound of the keys he'd have cut for her. *Mia casa sua casa.*

But he'd lied to her, told her he was in the Highlands with Sean. If he got drunk the first thing he'd do would be call her and confess. Or have to make up a counter-lie. Trip cancelled. No, he must remain true to her, or at least to that first lie.

Back inside. Pacing. The dust in the living room. Brushing then hoovering. He'd finish off painting the kitchen alcove, write her an email.

Day two – day of things started and not finished. Of sudden pauses midway through an action. Of silence descending. Of sounds of a man weeping in the distance, that came closer and closer until you realised it was you.

The echinacea tablets, milk thistle, the two ibuprofen and the two Rennies. Sleep now, sleep. Sleep, baby, sleep, as he used to sing to Sean. *The little lamb is on the green, with woolly fleece so soft and clean.* This song his mother had sung to him. It sounded now like some advert from the fifties. A lullaby selling biological washing powder. Maybe he had got the words wrong.

Just more reasons why you can't go outside. Day two and every little thing will set you off. You should have hired those DVDs from Blockbuster to kill the time. You can't watch the feral TV. Just sleep, dear Tom. Sleep, my You. Concentrate on the shivering and its rhythm will bring you sleep. So soft and clean.

Journal

Email

My You, I know you don't have email access and I should be able to deal with this. Can't sleep. I need to speak to you NOW. I am heading into the tunnel again – compulsivley thinking, washing, cleaning, planning, unplanning, becoming fixated. Come back to me, please. I feel I have done something wrong. I'm self-attacking. Seeing nothing but flaws. Where are you, my You? XXX

Email

Sorry for last email. I just worry that you have been in an accident. Worry also that if you don't call I shall take it as rejection. Please find a way to call me. Please.

Send or delete?
Delete.

August 9

- Because he makes me laugh uncontrollably and I lack spontaneity.
- Because for once in my life I have found an equal.
- Because I need to be not so self-obsessed and survivalist.
- Because he lives so far away and I fear intimacy.
- Because of his accent.
- Because he has shown me how lonely I am.
- Because I was just about to give up on men for ever.
- Because he is so intense and I am so dull.
- Because together we are perverse, unpredictable, terrifying, unknown.
- Because he makes me forget my severe inner standards.
- Because we sleep late.
- Because he cries so much and no man has cried with me before.

– Because I have cried in front of him and felt stronger for it.
– Because of the blindfold.
– Because he says love is impossible but still loves me.
– Because he has not called and will not for over forty-four
 hours more.
– Because I have a sense of constant déjà vu with him.
– Because when I think of him my belly, gut, ovaries ache.
– Because he stops me analysing myself to death.
– Because if he was here he would stop me writing stupid lists
 about why it is I love him.

New File

Face what you fear, Meg. NO MORE LISTS. Write about the
bridge. A walk first. Just to see some other people. I can hear
them outside. Laughter on the beach.

Back. A family. Spoke to the mother for a bit. She talked
only about her kids. They were flying a kite with their dad.
Depressing.

OK. RIGHT. WRITE. Keep busy. Check the photos.

Sally's dinner party, our second-last night. Yes, he'd been
freaked out all day, yes, I had been testing him with my friends.
But he hadn't even looked at me that last hour and had been
drinking to excess, refilling his glass out of defiance. Chatting to
Becky about babies and diapers and sleep routines and to Carmella
about how wonderful it was she was an actress and all the Scottish actors he knew. And he had them roaring with laughter, all
of his anecdotes about his shit job in corporate communications.
Re-telling the same jokes he'd used on me that second night.
Making me feel like a fool.

His boorish booming laughter. All this I have written before.
Have to stop mulling!

OK. Awkwardness of being thrust together at the door with
coats and handshakes and air kisses and whispers in my ear that
Tom was great, fab, but a bit drunk maybe – 'Let's call you a
cab.' Sally's face at the door. 'You OK, sweetie?'

I'd decided the walk would do us both good. Wanted just
to quieten him. Walk the Brooklyn Bridge together and have
a moment looking at the view before deciding our fate. But

he was ranting by my side as we walked the up-ramp. Not even looking at anything. Shouting, drunk, obnoxious.

NOTE: When men shout at me I walk away. He'd asked then if he could use my phone again. Must have been when he took the last photo.

Angry at his silence. At having to wait for his drunken steps behind. Questioning whether I'd go back to his hotel or get a room by myself. (I guess I'd been drunker than I admitted and I despise drunkenness in myself.)

Things he said about bridges and Scotland – I sense only the feeling of being shouted at (he was shouting facts at me). Something like – 'Did you know the Scots invented the suspension bridge? The Forth Rail Bridge, 1890 or so – the Golden Gate – no Golden Gate without the Forth – we did it first. OK, yours is bigger, I'll grant you that, but still. The Golden Gate.'

Caricature of a Scottish drunk. Maybe doing it deliberately to provoke me. If that was the case he achieved the opposite effect. NB That feeling I get just before I leave someone. The list of his failings – that he was just a passing fling. That shouting, even if joking, was an act of violence. The unspoken questions of my friends in my ears. 'What you doing with this guy anyway, sweetie?' 'Are you OK?'

Was he trying to hurt me?

We were three-quarters of the way across the Brooklyn Bridge. He was shouting about how it was the Fourth of July, and didn't we know how to celebrate? There should be fireworks. Independence Day, alcoholic co-dependence day. It would have taken too much to tell him how it had all been downsized since 9/11. No fireworks, but still hundreds of people were there, couples mostly, arm in arm, holiday snaps, flashes going off. The rants in the past – Fredo, Jacob, Michael – had all been behind closed doors. But we were in full public view. I was assessing the distance left, another hundred yards, as the joggers ran past. Thinking of the strangers his shouting was embarrassing. No way out, only onward. Focusing on the number of steps to the other side, where I'd get a taxi and call it a night.

He made no attempt to catch up. Like I should stop and wait for him. 'The miracle of suspension bridges,' he shouted. 'Genius, it is – the weight pulling them down is what holds them up! Can you fucking believe that?' Laughing to himself.

I had to stop, ask him firmly to lower his voice – he couldn't behave like this in my city – rules of etiquette – he was being a white British boor, what if every race here thought they had the right to shout above everyone else? This I said.

So many drunken sorries of his, pawing at my hand. I pushed onward.

He jumped topic, shouting about my friends. Putting on their voices. This high-pitched caricature of an American woman.

'Ohmigod, you're a real father. Ohmigod, Meg, you didn't tell us he had a kid.'

Then shifting again – 'You know the only way to live is from death backwards. That was wotsisname, German philosopher. Fuck that.' Shifting back again. 'You know, they're smart, they're smarter than us. Your friends really have a knack. Oh boy, did they do the business on me tonight!'

I think now about my dad. His bourbon-stinking wet kisses that woke me from sleep.

Hating him then. A hundred feet from the end. That the last four days had been something I'd wanted so badly I'd imagined it with this anybody. This drunken nobody. Hating myself – for being a fool for love again, for planning on ending it again. GO BACK TO THE PHOTOS.

No more photos of that night. Just flashes now. Unrecorded. One when he caught up and tried to kiss me. One of the view of Manhattan when I turned away to give him my cheek as his drunken lips smeared my face. One then almost as if he'd seen what I'd seen. A thing imagined. Like I wanted it to happen. Him climbing up on to the railings that faced the river.

'Wey-hey!' he'd shouted. 'Fuckin' *Saturday Night Fever*.'

'Come down. It's not funny.'

'Come on down! For your million-dollar prize. S'OK. I'm a

tourist, we have to do this.' Him singing – '*Night fever, night fever.*'

His drunken feet on the ledge. Me moving closer – didn't want to make any sudden movements. The thought of him falling freezing me to the spot. Him shouting – not at me, at the sky.

'If I'd just met you ten years ago. Eh? Fuck. No kid in Scotland. I'd be an American by now, eh? Native New Yorker.'

'Not funny.'

The joggers passing not batting an eye.

'You know, all my life I wanted to do this. John Travolta. Wey-hey!'

'Don't look down, OK. Just look at me, OK.'

His eyes shooting at me then.

'Oh my You, look at you. I've been trying to look at you all night. You know, the thing is – Whoops.'

He almost slipped. Clung to a suspension wire.

'Tom, you're scaring me. Please! Climb down.'

'Did this once before, didn't have the guts.' (Some bridge in Scotland, he'd said.) 'Couldn't go through with it. Scared me shitless. Week of the divorce. No one around, night. Felt like an arse. No one to see me go. That's the thing though, eh? If there had only been an audience I'd have done it! New York City, eh?'

Me standing there. Embarrassed by how much embarrassment he was causing me. Ashamed that that was maybe all I really felt. 'Shhh, it's OK.'

'My God, this is a great bridge, must have been built by a Scot. It's a bit breezy. Travolta must have had a stuntman, eh!' He was singing 'Night Fever' again. Me scared he'd lose his balance.

HOW DID IT ACTUALLY HAPPEN?

I had to do something. People were staring. Him gripping the wires. He'd started crying. His head down. I took that as my cue to move another step closer.

'Fucking fuck!' he was shouting.

Me edging closer and trying to talk him down, but then it

came to me that this was not my first time, or second. Threats of self-harm. Michael. Arturo. Jobe. I can't live without yous. Something told me that moving closer would make him fall or jump. Never accept love as a threat. I can't save you. A love based on that is abuse.

His howling, drunken tears – his hands on the cable. Some tourists stopped and took a flash photograph. That set him off.

'Thank you, New York City!' Shouting. 'Someone cares at last, someone! Thank you. Line up, line up, only five bucks a shot.'

Staring at me, eyes red, saliva dripping from lips. Saying, 'It's impossible. You and me and all this.' His hand sweeping out, him almost stumbling. 'We are IMPOSSIBLE! You hate me already. We're over already. I should just jump. Now! PUSH ME. GIMME YOUR HAND. COME WITH ME!'

And I walked away. Couldn't face him then, can't face this now. EXCUSE: It was maybe the sound of a taxi horn honking below, reminding me of the architectural layout.

'You're on the wrong bridge,' I shouted back at him. 'Look down!' What he saw then I see now. Not the imagined three-hundred-foot fall to the East River, but the fifteen-foot drop into the log-jammed traffic. The layout is all wrong for suicide.

The joggers passed. I waited for him to climb down and come to me like an obedient dog. A cyclist whizzed between us, another heading towards him. 'Watch out,' I shouted, 'you're on the goddamn bike track.'

'You're right,' he said, wiping tears on his jacket sleeve. 'It isn't the Travolta bridge, is it?'

'No, it's about a half-hour south. The Verrazano. Brooklyn to Staten Island. You could take the A train there tomorrow.'

His laughter then. His arms around me, his many kisses on my face, ear, neck. People passing us by. Me feeling resistance in my body to his tight hold. 'No, no,' he was whispering. 'I hear you, I hear what you're thinking. Don't go there. Be here with me. Meg, be here with me again, my You.'

This image of myself now – walking away, breaking into a

run, crying, shouting back over my shoulder to leave me alone. Somehow, I didn't do that. He didn't say sorry.

He was holding me at arm's length. 'God, look at us. Tragic lovers on the Brooklyn Bridge. Honestly, I'm sure we're in a movie. *Kramer vs Kramer*? *Hannah and her Sisters*?'

I hid my face in his shoulder.

'You can't even kill yourself in this city without turning into a cliché,' he said.

Damn him for being funny. That was it. His face so serious when he said it. I couldn't stop myself. Angry at him for asking me to laugh it all away. But he wouldn't stop, kept on going.

'God, I'm such an ass. Here's me thinking of the dark water. Bang! My torso ripped apart by the impact . . . If I was lucky I might have hit a taxi. Jesus. A broken knee, at most, a dent in a fender, a lifetime of litigation against a millionaire who lost a day's earnings on Wall Street because of the trauma.'

Telling him to stop, stop it. Telling myself the same.

'This is just so me. Wanting to go out in epic style and not even making the local news. I keep telling you, I reach for the stars, De Niro, Travolta, but always end up Woody Allen!'

I forced myself not to laugh.

'We oughta get da hell out of dis movie,' he whispered.

There is another image, not taken, that I see now.

They hold each other there at the taxi rank, after the bridge, while hundreds pass them by. Heads resting on each other's shoulders, eyes closed. We move tighter over his shoulder, to her face – then her eyes open. She looks out at the cityscape and shivers. He thinks she is trembling because of his touch, and so whispers in her ear. The camera moves in for the close-up on her eyes. The out-of-focus reflection of the city lights in her dark wet irises. The actress's performance is award-winning. The music rises. No dialogue but we can read in her face that she has already made up her mind – she has to leave him. The music builds, the angels descend and the audience weeps. Fade to black. Roll the titles.

He does scare me. How do I know he hasn't killed himself already? Maybe the Highlands is a lie. This sense now that his love for me is addictive, obsessive, unhealthy. Can't go on like this. Have to call him now.

Detox – Day Three

The mobile had rung. 2.30 a.m., it said. So he was on day three now. It must have been her. He was not ready yet. Hard, but let it ring on. Still night. He drank his water from the bedside table. Leaning over was painful. Shoulder, arm, wrist, spine. Every muscle competing. The bare duvet was soaked with sweat, he shivered as he pulled it off. Still wearing jeans and T-shirt. Fuck, it was day three but night two and there was no way now he could sleep.

It was her that had rung. 8.30 p.m. her time. Should he just call her now? No, remind yourself. You are supposed to be in the Highlands. One more day and you will be clean. This is for her. If you speak there'll be that one thing that touches you, that upsets you or is left unresolved, that will have you going out searching for that drink.

Day three – the day when the liver starts to repair itself and the mind quietens. When the body is free enough from alcohol to attempt a drive, to the country maybe, in full confidence that if stopped the breathalyser will be below the mark.

He located his slippers, the shivering was back. Day three after the twenty pints of water and the fifteen tablets of milk thistle. Day three, when you had to get out of your flat to let your thoughts fly up to the sky, not bounce back off the walls.

Tom dresses. He will walk, outside. Night and he walks the backstreets, coat wrapped tight round himself. Away from people and pubs and clubs. Away from the street, just a left and a right and a left again where Morna lives. He needs architecture not people. 3 a.m. He walks south to the Meadows. Past the squalor to the villas and town houses. In his mind he is preparing a tour of the city for Meg, all the best parts of the city. The highlights of the Edinburgh Festival. He walks faster and the shivering stops. Exhilarated just by the rhythm of walking, he is singing to himself.

'*One day at a time*,' putting on his country and western drawl. Sweet Jesus. Not a soul around. Empty streets. Victorian tenements. Window boxes, SUVs. A ghost walking through a world where the rich live. Homes – two million pounds, not dollars. The huge bay windows. The tiny manicured gardens, the Victorian wrought-iron fences. If he had two million he would give one to Sean and spend the other on Meg. He would live on Fire Island. Come back here three times a year to see Sean. Or even better – take Sean away every school holiday. Hand in hand with Meg he'd show Sean Paris – La Grande Arche de La Défense, the *Mona Lisa* of course; Rome – the Colosseum; Athens – the Parthenon, then things no longer there. To stand at Mandraki and tell Sean of the Colossus, taller than the Statue of Liberty, that once stood astride the harbour. And the Hanging Gardens of Babylon, now just ruins in Iraq.

Walking through the streets and the sight of the window boxes made him shiver now. '*If I were a rich man . . .*' He was not a rich man or a fiddler on the roof. Day three – the most dangerous day. When all of life was revealed to you with a lucidity even the sober did not possess. Entire societies laid bare. It was happening as he stared at nineteenth-century merchants' mansions and the streets beyond built to house the workers. Histories of slavery and the wealth of nations carved in stone whispering their secrets to him. 3.40 a.m. and Tom is only half a mile from home but he has come a different way. It is always like this: these solitary walks filled at first with so many ideas and the hope of catching that next revelatory thought. The moment always somehow lost . Laughing at yourself for thinking a walk could teach you anything.

Ftuuh ftuuh ftuuuh.

Tom turns to find the source of the noise. Like someone running from muggers. Trainers on wet ground. His eyes find an abandoned school playground. Here as long as he could recall. Never a kid playing football on it. At night the junkies huddled in dark corners with flash of fire under tinfoil. Biro pens to suck up the fumes.

Ftuuh ftuuh ftuuh.

Tom has stopped now and is staring, eyes adjusting to the dark. The noise, the playground. Pitch black. Sound of feet running over wet gravel. He sees him now. Maybe forty, head shaven, wearing a T-shirt, shorts, trainers. Sprinting is the word. A shadow sprinting at 3.47 a.m. Private ritual for the man, it must be. Tom stops beneath a tree, so he can't be seen watching.

The man's T-shirt is grey, his trainers worn. He sprints the playground in nine seconds like all hell was chasing him, then stops, breathes. Tom, transfixed, will not light a cigarette now because it might alert the running man to his presence.

Four, five times. Each the same, the man in the dark, no one knows he's there. Sprinting across the abandoned playground, fighting himself to go faster. Something scary about it. What's the story? The man has been at the pub all night and felt guilty so went for a run to work the alcohol away. The man lives alone and needs to be alone all the time. The man cannot jog with other joggers, he needs to sprint late at night with no one around. The only man to use this park in many years. Enters here at night, through the hole in the fence the junkies made. He does this alone every night.

Look at him. My God. Sprinting from one end to another. No wristwatch Tom can see. Measuring his own time with his breath. The sounds from the street beyond of drunken clubbers heading home and the man has started on his next length. Tom focuses on his face now, what little he can see – a face so concentrated it could be anger. The feet pumping. A man racing himself.

It has to mean something. Things don't just happen. The feet pounding the abandoned gravel where children were once meant to play. At 3.50 a.m. It must mean something, otherwise it is terrifying.

Things going out of sync. The man stopped and Tom hears screaming in the distance. The man is running again – a plane overhead.

It does not stop when he gets home. He cannot sleep. Watching his feet as he paces, and from a flat down the road – rave music. Boiling the kettle to make breakfast, but it is only 4 a.m., and outside a man is shouting, 'Johnnie, JOHNNIE!'

In sleep all will come back into sync. But there can be no sleep. All the world is splitting in two. Like a student film. Like an editing machine. Audio on one track, picture on the other. So easy to flick the wrong switch and everything goes awry. Picture of people talking and you hear a stream rushing. You see the stream and hear traffic. Day three – God, to just have that drink, and make it all synchronise again.

Sleep impossible, but possible with pills. Twice the dosage of valerian, one drowsy-making antihistamine, a sniff of lavender and a difficult book. To just sleep. He grabs a pillow and puts it between his knees and one behind his back, goes into foetal posture, feeling the soft pressure all around him, tucking the duvet round his feet, making his 'parcel' as Meg calls it. Twenty-five days till she comes. One day at a time.

Sweet Jesus.

How strange time felt now. Not like the month before when they'd been learning how to cope with the distance. Now that it was closing there was something new. He turned off the bedside lamp as if it would help him stop the thoughts, but they only became more clear in the darkness. He and Meg had not really connected recently. Were moving in different directions. Him to their future, making plans for her tour of his city. And she – drifting into their past. He hadn't noticed the exact point of the transition. He closed his eyes to try to sleep.

Maybe twenty minutes trying to calm the thousand thoughts. Maybe a couple of pages of Bertrand Russell's *History of Western Philosophy* might bore him to sleep. He'd been rereading the same two pages on Heidegger for the past four months. This one line – '*Live your life backwards as if from the point of death.*' Running the line over in his head, it gradually slowing. To sleep now. To live your life backwards.

The sound of high heels on the floor of the flat above.

His mobile said it was 4.42 a.m. The noise that sounded like furniture being moved that he knew was the bashing of a bed headboard against the wall. The rhythm would get faster and soon there would be the moans. Four forty-four on a Sunday morning and the neighbours always fucked at this time. Sure enough she started moaning, or maybe it was the sound of her baby crying. It would last no more than six minutes. He'd timed them before with the clock on his mobile. Sometimes she shouted when she came. Usually Tom had a wank listening to them, and tried to time his rhythm with their thrusts and moans. He had once, about a year ago, managed to come just as his neighbours did. And he'd lain there laughing to himself, trying to picture the scene – a cross section of the building. This couple in post-coital cuddle above and him twelve feet below staring up at the ceiling as his dick spasmed soft against his gut.

Tom stared up at the white ceiling and the sex sounds didn't match what he saw. The swirly Artex plaster painted white. The round white paper Ikea lampshade that never quite sat right. The plastic thing that the wires were tucked into. The little hole between it and the ceiling, where the noises came from.

The rhythm accelerating. The moaning almost pornographic, a good night by the usual standards, but he did not feel like wanking. Not at all. The whole scene struck him now as rather pathetic. They always fucked once a week at exactly the same time. Just after the clubs shut on a Saturday night. She worked in Tesco and he was a brickie. He'd met them a dozen or so times on the stairs as they carried the baby buggy up. Not just moans. There were words tonight.

'Oh God, it's good, God-God-GOD!'

Tom was willing it to end. When it was done there would be a minute or so then he would hear her heels again. She must fuck with heels on. Probably suspenders and stockings too. They must have stripped-pine flooring, not carpet.

She came. A loud long guttural groan. Then the silence.

Loneliness was just one word among thousands that flew through his head in the next minute. And there were sixty minutes in an hour and twenty-four hours in a day. The pillow between his knees, the one behind his back, the one he hugged with his arms. The water by the bed, the basin just in case he was sick again.

The shout from the street. 'JOHNNIE! Wake up, ya cunt!'

And loneliness was not the minute after minute as it happened. Loneliness seemed to call to him from his future, '*Live your life backwards as if from the point of death.*' He was seventy now, clutching pillows to approximate a human presence.

Loneliness was a long-distance call. A man living alone without a phone would not feel the same. He would see the same people each day. Would talk to the grocer, the butcher, the checkout girl at Tesco, the guy at Blockbuster. But the people around Tom were passing shadows while he waited for that call. To be truly alone was to be waiting.

It had been something to do with Morna. Days and hours now without her. Four streets away. A phone call, a text, walk round the block in time of need. A cup of tea, a fag, a spliff, a hug. Just over two weeks since he'd ended it with her. Could he really be so lonely after such a short time without a woman's voice in his flat, her hand on his chest as he slept? He made himself get up, telling himself that he was being melodramatic. People lived alone for years and they didn't sink into this kind of self-pity. The neighbours had been fucking and he hadn't fucked in over a month. Maybe that was all it was. He needed to call Morna now. Just on the pillow by the phone was Bertrand Russell's *History of Western Philosophy*. Page 175. Earmarked.

Apparently, the Greek Stoics lived naked in the wilderness for thirty years without seeing a soul, not even each other.

Journal

August 9

Midnight. Buzzing. A mosquito in my room. Want to kill it. Can't find it. A migraine maybe. My entire eating/sleeping routine is shot. Nauseous. Can't face food. Was weak to call him earlier. He promised he'd call tomorrow which is now today. The longer I wait the colder I'm becoming. The ice is nearly over my head now. Soon he will not be able to touch me. When he calls I may not even pick up.

Or perhaps I will talk only of past lovers – punish him. Show him he can't leave me alone for this long. Am regressing rapidly. It is all his fault.

They were in the box in the closet where I thought they might be. Photocopies of the letters I'd sent Michael – summer of 1992. (How narcissistic to photocopy my own letters.)

August 14, 1992. I wrote:

> I love the way your letters go up at the end like the curl of a smile, the way you cross out words, again and again, like you're angry for getting one wrong. (I spend hours trying to interpret the words you tried to hide.) I love the details, the things you write about your apartment, your dog, that make me feel closer to you than ever. (Say woof woof to Spike for me.) I miss you so much, but there are hours in the day when I'm alone waiting for your call or letters, when I'm overcome with the most profound happiness. Flooded with all the words I have yet to write to you.

That time after our two weeks when I'd come back to the US, two months before my promised return to London. So many pages written about longing and waiting. I would spend days composing a letter to him. So immature. The evidence piles up against me. The pretentious tone, that I'd written three letters for every one of his – not even waiting for a response, that I never seemed to really reply to what he was saying. Running out, excited, to the photocopy shop. Mailed the original and filed the copy.

Clear to me now – I was in love with the idea of love, and not the lover. Poor Michael. Another photocopy – my diary – date August 18, 1992. The end of the second month together after the first failed separation.

We slept all day again. Clinging as if daylight itself would hurt us. I tried to get up but he pulled me back into bed and we made love, sleepily, then slept. It was almost three when I got up and I was grumpy with him. We fought. One minute we are full of joy, jumping around naked, locked in a sweaty embrace, then we are just bodies and this terrible sadness overwhelms me. I start to hate myself for being lazy. How can I ever do anything if I am like this with him? His breath sends me to sleep, I wake covered in his sweat, we eat, fuck, laugh, dance, fuck, sleep, dress, eat. Like infants feeding on each other, we are breasts, beasts, heart-beats, dumb, able only to mutter baby talk. How can he find work like this? He keeps putting it off. We are running out of money. I am drained by this love. I am useless. Lazy. I want more from life. I will never be a writer. How can I get any perspective on anything if I remain stuck in this dreamy waking that never wakes? I must force some kind of break – need my own time – away from him.

Next page. Paragraph underlined. August 21, 1992.

I am hiding this journal from him, writing so small he won't be able to read it. I dreamed of making up a secret language like da Vinci, in a mirror, so he won't understand if he finds it. All of this is making me ill. So many secrets. I wish he would go away so that I could write again. Long beautiful letters like I used to, from thousands of miles away, but he is in the next room.

Another diary entry. Two weeks later.

The wind in the trees. The sky is streaked with wisps of white.
I can breathe again. We are on another month's trial separation.
Feel guilty for not being able to tell him why. A week apart,
and he was in tears last night on the phone, but today there are
clouds and skies and I have hope because at last, again, I can
write.

I had thought our separation would bring out the best in my
writing, but it is clear to me now – I had created pain so I could
write about it. A post-mortem for a death I'd brought about.
The only honest line is maybe this: '*I have to escape from this
terrible clinging weakness that wakes inside me when he is inside
me.*'
I need air. After midnight now. Tom, where are you?
I tried to walk but it was so dark outside – crescent moon –
couldn't see the sea. The waves sounded too near, terrifyingly
so. Told myself, calm down, just high tide. But the crashing
waves and nothing but blackness. This tiny island will vanish
one day when the waters rise. How many years till my home
is swept away?
Just had a lie-down. Couldn't rest, couldn't let it rest. A
migraine it is now. Shivering. Pulled on Tom's jeans. Can't speak
to Tom till this is all worked out. Love is a psychological addiction. Have to get back to the root of my first research. My
Stages of Love is no help now.
Just googled 'love, stages of'. 1,865,083 sites. The seven
stages of divine love on sufi.com. The five stages of love by
Meher Baba. The nine stages of ecstasy on femininejoy.com.
The eight stages of love – a collection of songs from Bangra
movies. The four stages of love in ancient Greece: Epithemia,
Phileo, Eros, Agape. The four-step penis-enlargement
programme. The twelve-step rehabilitation programme for sex
addicts. Six books on love addiction checked out on Amazon.
The final stage in each – Suicide, Commitment, Resentment,
Repetition – all contradictory. Laughable really. The fifth
stage according to Swami Yahru is called Tazurro or

Tamaloq or Humility. The final stage is Disillusionment – is Commitment.

Relief on finding there's no truth to any of this. Perhaps I've been overly melodramatic, leaving so many men just because of some book I'd read.

Trying to recall now what that first book said. I'd tried so hard to explain it to Michael, showed him the passage – telling him I was anxious he was approaching the final stages, that something terrible was about to happen. Sixteen years ago. That love addiction is like a disease – passes from one person to another – I was so worried I'd become addicted myself. Evidence: after Michael I'd started again, so quickly with Arturo. Image now of him holding me, telling me that I was probably just afraid of commitment – and as far as he knew that was the final stage of love, not any of this psychobabble. After I left him I promised to learn from past mistakes. The island is part of that. My studies, my routines, beach walks, diet.

But the men have all been the same.

LIST: Toby drank to excess. Saul had OCD. Arturo – borderline personality disorder. Jed threatening to move to New York if I didn't visit him in LA. Toby, the stalker. And Michael, of course. How many times have I told myself? – no more addicts or obsessives, no more long-distance longing.

That night when I flew back to be with Michael. 1992. His student flat in London. The hollow sound of him weeping on his knees, terrifying. He confessed, he'd been with another woman while I was away, a one-night thing. Said I'd driven him to it, with my many leavings, my hot then cold. How disgusted he was at himself. He wanted only me, begged me to forgive him, if I went back to the US he'd kill himself, many such threats. Telling me over and over that it was me that had driven him to it.

Never again.

Looking round my room now. At 'our' bed. Too late to think straight. Too late in the day for us. So tired now. Yes, it is true, Tom is the same as all the others. His love is too intense. He's addicted to me. Feel so foolish now, for my thoughts of a few days ago. Move to Scotland – make a new start together. I am not in love with Tom, I have merely been drawn in by his addiction to me.

I can't do this again – I'll let our relationship die slowly through lack of contact. Move back to Soho, the tenants are out in a month. He doesn't know the address. No, too cruel. Email him, tell him it's over. No, I owe him an explanation at least. I'll call him and explain all of this. Ask his opinion.

Another day to get through before I can call. Can I even bear to hear his voice?

Am sick to my soul.

New You

The waking not so bad. Jolly bloody promising, in fact. Morning, day three. Today she will call. He's six hours ahead. Middle of her night. Big plans. To get fit for her, join a gym. OK to drive now. Gyms are, as always, miles from anywhere – a secret policy to exclude those who can't afford cars no doubt. Fifteen miles after checking the location on a website – an enterprise park. It looking just like he'd imagined as he parked the car. Concrete object that had not an architect but an accountant with a slide rule. How many bodies can we squeeze into a given space? A logo as big as the building. THE NEW YOU – pictures of tight arses, bleached blondes grinning as they did weights and dives. Above the front door, a window of cyclists, pedalling like hell. American-style hard bodies going nowhere. Trying to fight his scepticism. Walking through the doors that opened for him as if they had been waiting. THE NEW YOU the poster said again at the reception. The girl behind the desk like the one in the ad. Do this for Meg. Make yourself well.

'I'd like to sign up for the new me.'

'The New You,' she corrected.

'The new . . . you? Sorry, but I'm me,' and he had to stop himself saying, 'and you are you. Surely this makes sense. I have no idea who you are, let alone want to be you.'

'Yes, sir. It called the New You.'

He took a beat as the confusion circled him and the rage started. He ran the required words over in his head. 'I'd like to be a New You.' Yes, he would love to have been her for a day, to lie back and fondle those pert breasts and run his hands over those taut trimmed abs. But grammatically, existentially, it seemed wrong. The usual diatribe against the stupidity of marketing words brewing. Stay, he told himself, get a membership, whoever the who you are. She was asking for his credit-card details without even facing him.

'I'll just page Terry to show you round the New You's facilities.'

See – even the girl was getting confused now. No matter how many people were trying to be a New You, there was no such word as Yous. The communal plural of you was us or them, not yous. Unless you came from Glasgow – 'So youz comin' oot furra pint?' Or was it that all the little sub-yous were aspiring towards the condition of becoming a unique and singular You, that in their unified conformity to solitary perfection they would become a new transcendant universal? An as yet unuttered neologism. The Yous. Each alone fighting who they'd been to become a collective possessive noun, a monument to grammatical and philosophical absurdity. And at the end of this process, they would welcome the new members, all voices as one – 'Hi, we're the New Yous, who are you?'

Waiting for Terry and his introductory tour. A hip-hop song playing, the lyrics all about sex and money and bitches, and the sight of the sixty people sweating their obese, un-sexy, old selves out on the bikes and rowing machines and abdominators to his left, and the ultra-chic ultra-expensive fitness gear on the rack to his right with a picture of a perfect smiling twenty-year-old blonde wearing the branded name of the gym across her perfect tits.

That was it. He shouted, 'Cancel the transaction.' Got his card back and stormed out past the hundred or so fat, old, ugly, struggling singular yous.

Meg loved the old you. Fuck the new one!

He parked the car in a lay-by. Had to breathe for a second. Swearing at himself for his lack of guts, at his gut. To be afraid of fitness. Day three. Craving that one drink that would drown the stupidity of the world. Noah's flood. He would never have the courage to try to improve himself. He'd find any excuse. The aggressive hard-sell American music in the gym. The sweatshirts made in sweatshops in Malaysia. Better to sit alone and sulk and think. And drink.

One more try. Arthur's Seat was on the way home. Great big lump of mountain-like granite at the foot of the city. Nature would cure him. Another mile, then he parked. Locked the car door and started up the gravel path and there were trees and the air was clean and as he climbed Edinburgh became a shadow in the fog. He would take Meg here, it wasn't the epic Scottish Highlands but it was at least a high bit in the middle of the Lowlands.

Progressing along the path, mud and stones and ferns. She would love this. The Scots pines he was passing – a hundred years older than her country. The thistles that looked like product placement for Scottishness, that had made her laugh when he'd mentioned them to her.

'Trust the Scots to find a national flower that's got thorns,' she'd said.

To have her voice beside him as he joked about the indigenous fauna, the thick-woolled orange-dreadlocked Highland cows, which were not like the usual industrial milk machines, not beef for the slaughter, but were put in places such as this so tourists could take photos. Scottish-celebrity cows. Oh, it made him laugh thinking of her by his side, as they trudged the hills, deconstructing Scotland.

'And the kilt too. Another fallacy – invented by the Victorian English gentry, so they could go in fancy dress when touring Scotland. This cute little miniskirt version of the plaid.'

'The plaid?'

'Two metres of raw tartan the Scots wore as their only garment – wrapped it round themselves to sleep in the hills and glens as they tended their livestock. Banned in 1748 by the English.'

'Stop, stop, you're destroying my dreams!'

Granite and bracken. A family approaching on the path. A kid in a pushchair screaming for sweeties. Behind them, another family with a five-year-old, shouting, 'Bored – bored!' Tom left the path and headed into the long grass. Had to be alone with Meg in his mind. But still the sounds and sight of them a hundred yards away. The Nike sportswear. The Next chinos. The baby dressed in Baby Gap. Then a man with his dog running from him, a schnauzer. Shouting, 'C'mon. C'mere,

Arnie. Arnie, come the fuck here!' To name your dog after Schwarzenegger.

When he took Meg here he'd have to make sure it was on a weekday when the Nike Schwarzenegger scum weren't here to defile nature with their pathetic Scottish attempts at being American.

Over a fence and off the path. Through the ferns. Alone at last. A field of real cows and sheep. Eating grass. Lives lived head down in the same field. Just like the local humans. God, fuck. He'd come here to get away and it was just the same. The cows, the thistles, caricatures of themselves. Living, eating, munching clichés. If she wanted to see the real Scotland then it would be a five-, six-hour drive north through the silent Highlands to meet his now silent father in the nursing home. Nine hours to get to her in New York if he flew direct. Shit! He'd lied to her about the Highlands. He'd have to make up some stories before they spoke.

His every pore sweating now, weeping, wanting Meg, the touch of a woman, Morna's massages. Sick with need for a drink. Meg and her days. Day three dry.

God, he had to get the hell out of nature. A mile to the car. The Twelve Steps. Step four. Make an honest inventory of the problems/habits that you need to change. The first thing that needed changing was the whole fucking Twelve Steps. The belief that belief in a higher power could save you.

Why this now? The joggers. Why this hatred now? Another withdrawal symptom? Look at them, so fucking happy to be in nature. These so-called Scots with their weekend hills and glens and their American trainers, and 'Lovely day's and 'Hello's. Didn't they know he was on day three? Fuck their passing smiles. The skies had to weep right now and drown this world in blood and sweat and cum and Smirnoff with a slice of lemon in a pre-chilled hi-ball glass with crushed ice.

Keep walking. Get back to the car. Meg'll want to come here with you. Feet on the path. One, two, three. God in fucking hell he needed a drink. The salt on the edge of a margarita glass. The perfection of a pint of Guinness. The clean cut of a shot of tequila.

Fuck, another one jogging by. What's with the smile? Like you're one of them now, even though you are shivering in an old raincoat. He'd come here tomorrow just to show them, half a bottle in the car park, then stagger, Smirnoff in hand, along their jogging path, making lewd suggestions and crashing into them. The fuckers that shopped in Marks and Spencer's and bought nothing but organic produce and paid their monthly direct debit to Amnesty International and subsidised an African orphan, who believed the world would be a better place if everyone jogged on a Sunday and was just like them.

'FUCK YOU!' he'd shout. 'All of youz,' in his best proletarian accent. 'The folk in the housing schemes – think aboot them!'

And they'd make a detour around him, worrying about what had come to their lovely country park. Such riffraff.

'Naw, naw,' he would shout, swinging his vodka bottle, 'it kills me, so it does. Did ye know, serious, why folks in the schemes are so sick and alkies the lot o' them? Ah'll fucking tell ye!'

Joggers waiting to get past him now. The voice screaming in his head.

'Ah'll fucking tell ye. There's schemes on the outskirts whir it's a three-mile walk to the nearest vegetable. No, for real, and you jog around and say these people would have a better attitude towards life if they had better nutrition – their poor children are deprived of vitamins and essential omegas. But did ye know? Did ye fuckin' know? The seventies. The socialist social planner that stuck them on the edge of everything, beside a motorway, going fucking nowhere!'

Three fat bourgeois in their two-hundred-pound hiking boots accelerating past him. Looking over their shoulders as if they could hear his inner mind.

'No, listen! It's true. I work for the government, I've got the facts.'

The rest of his diatribe pouring out as he walked the silent path ranting secretly to himself. 'Right ... so if they want to buy a fucking tomato, a fucking carrot, I'm serious, the only thing within a mile is McDonald's. If they need to buy the essential ingredient to make – let's say – a fucking Caesar salad. It's a two-mile drive and well, hey, they don't have a car, so it's a walk along the motorway. I've seen them, I have – an anorexic junkie mum walking her kid by the side of the motorway in search of sustenance. This is town planning, right? I'm talking Sighthill and East Pilton and on the fucking motorway, right, there's these big fucking posters from the Scottish Parliament telling these people they should eat more fucking vegetables . . . IT MAKES ME WEEP. IT MAKES ME FUCKING . . .'

He was actually shouting now.

Stop! It's just day three, just the alcohol screaming.

Day three was the day you stopped in your tracks in the middle of some field. The day you remembered that you still cared for all of the suffering masses who you couldn't save and the reason why you first started drinking was because you cared. Day three – the day when you realised you'd wasted ten years and the future would be the same if you didn't do something radical to save yourself. Now.

It started with running the last mile to the car. A detour through the bracken, just to get away from people. No one around. Lungs, heart, these things somehow still functioning. Keeping on. And somehow it had become funny. This hilarious image of himself. A solitary silhouette in an empty landscape in an old raincoat and trainers. Running like someone chased – an escapee from Saughton prison. Laughing at how good it felt to be actually running. No one around. Breath and feet on gravel. Ten, eleven, twelve. No earphones, no iPod. No solitary pursuit of a better body. Just running. Twenty-one, twenty-two, twenty-three. Something the lungs did, some ridiculous long-forgotten pleasure in just being a body. Thirty, thirty-one, two, three. Something about bracken and ferns and heather and wee birds in trees twittering. Not a soul around. Laughing at himself, shouting out.

'A fuckin' tree.'

'Fuckin' clump of grass.'

And he recalled that day with Meg, when they'd put 'fucking' in the middle of every word.

Black-fucking-bird, land-fucking-scape.

Yes, he would have to get some proper trainers if he was to do this again. He'd have to find places more remote so there would be no possibility of encountering other people. This is what a body is for. Yes. Forty-nine, fifty. 'Fuckin' thistles!'

A whole new kind of jogging it could be. A new anti-jogging movement. Bit of wild-man weekend – bit of New Age rebirthing – bit of drunken ned. Screaming like this, at the fucking flowers, cursing the earth. Great marketing concept. 'The cursed earth.' Very eco but yet anti-eco. Fuckin' shrubs. Fuckin' ferns. Fuckin' mud. See them now, like some Monty Python sketch, in their thousands on the horizon. Screaming their solitary hatred at the indigenous flora. Meg would laugh.

Back at his car, out of breath and this nature thing wasn't so bad. Yes, there was hope for a yes in the world. The run had pushed the last of the alcohol out of his system and this kind of high was new. Tonight was the night. The first communication in three endless days and nights. He'd ring Meg at the agreed time and tell her of this ridiculous new-found joy. He'd buy trainers tomorrow. Jogging suit. The whole shebang. He'd drive here every day before work and do a mile or more. Less than three weeks till she arrived, he'd work off the gut, stay dry for her. She'd find him fresh-faced and rosy-cheeked. Yes, yes, yes, I can change. Telling the weeds by the side of the car – yes, I am the new fucking You.

Call

'Hello.'

'Hey, Meg baby, I've been calling and calling, why didn't you pick up? God, your sweet voice . . . I've had this incredible . . . No, wait, let me hear you first.'

[Silence.]

'You OK, Meg?'

[Silence.]

'What's wrong, my You?'

'You called me "your You".'

'You are my You.'

'I'm sorry, Tom, it's just . . . So how was the Highlands?'

'My God, so beautiful! So many incredible things! You sure you're OK?'

'And your parents?'

'They . . . well . . . they're still there. Hey, I've taken up jogging. Can you believe that?'

'Great. [Silence.] Tom. It's been too long, we have to talk . . . there's things we have to talk about.'

'We *are* talking.'

'We're not connecting.'

'We are, my love.'

'No, but you seem . . . maybe it's me . . . three days is too long . . . [Silence.] I thought you were dead I . . . I've been really . . . angry at you . . .'

'Really?'

'Been so weak.'

'It's OK to be weak.'

[Silence.]

'Meg?'

[Silence.]

'I'm sorry. I've been very bad, can you just talk? Tell me a story . . . one of your naughty stories?'

'You sure?'

'We have to try and connect.'

'We *are* connecting . . .'

'Maybe it's a bad idea. We should maybe talk first.'

'I can give it a try . . . You've caught me a little off guard here.'

'We have to do this, so I can know how to talk to you.'

'What? This some kind of test? Meg?'

'I'm going next door. [Silence. Footsteps.] I'm lying here, waiting. I'm putting your blindfold on.'

'Are you sure? Jesus, you sure you're OK?'

'Yes, it's on now. Waiting for you now.'

'God, I don't know where to start. I missed you. I guess that's not very horny. OK.'

'We need to do this before talking. OK, Tom?'

'OK, so you're on my bed, my love.'

'Go on.'

'You're here, you're on my bed.'

'I'm with you in Edinburgh. I'm tied down. Go on.'

'I'm standing over you, whispering, teasing your pussy with my fingers, stroking your ass. Making you beg. Making you wait.'

'Good, go on.'

'You can hear me talking to you.'

'Maybe you're talking to someone else? I can't see. I'm blind-folded.'

'Uh . . . OK, you think it's me, talking to myself. You can't see.'

'I can't see.'

'I'm talking to . . . this guy. Uh . . . he's at the door. I'm letting him in now. He's in the room . . . you sure?'

'Yes, go on.'

'OK, he's getting his cock out. He smells different from me, you're getting scared. You can't see. He speaks to you. I'm going to fuck your tight cunt, he says, and you're panicking – this wasn't part of the deal. He's pawing your ass. I'm just watching. Standing back. This guy . . . he stinks of alcohol. Just any guy.

A guy I met in a bar. Big guy. Asian, maybe black. I told him all about my naughty girl. How she liked to be blindfolded. This guy with a big cock ... He's biting your neck now, flipping you over, forcing his cock into your mouth, you're screaming, gagging. I ...'

[Silence.]

'Meg. You OK?'

[Tears.]

'God, I'm sorry, babe.'

[Tears.]

'Meg, my love, did I ... ?'

'I'm just a little ...'

'Oh, sweet, sweet love. Don't cry. I'm sorry.'

'No ... It wasn't you. I'm just. At myself. I made you do ... I'm just angry with myself. [Silence.] Tom, we have to stop this.'

'Of course.'

'No, not this, I mean ...'

'What's wrong, my love? Was it the guy ... when I said ... ?'

'No, I dunno. I just ... us ... I mean ...'

'Tell me.'

[Tears.]

'It's OK, I'm sorry. I love you. I've missed you so much.'

'No, no, listen.'

'I'm listening.'

'I worry that this is turning ... I don't know.'

'I'm sorry, Meg, I just, I didn't know what you wanted me to say, I ...'

'Let me say it. OK. I worry that ... I started this. Right? I only get off on bad stories. That I ... I want things to be bad. Maybe because of past things or ... I worry ... I just want to be loved, but when it comes I can't accept it. I push people away. I hurt them. Maybe I want you to scare me so I can have an excuse to leave. I dunno.'

'I would never hurt you.'

'I know.'

'Not even if you asked me to.'

[Silence.]

'Sorry. Meg – you there?'

'Still here.'

'I thought you wanted me to . . .'

'Do you think I'm cold?'

'No, no way, my love, you're so . . .'

'It's just. Sometimes all I want is to . . . I just hate the way couples get and I love that we're so pervy and then other times . . . you still there?'

'I'm here, Meg.'

'Other times, well, I worry that maybe I can't do intimacy like normal people . . .'

'Meg.'

'. . . that . . . I have to fantasise just to feel anything.'

'I didn't mean to upset you, my love.'

'No, no, it's not you. I'm crying about me.'

'OK.'

'I just. I know it's my fault. Doesn't it freak you out? Wouldn't you rather we had normal, healthy . . .'

'Normal, healthy . . . phone sex?'

[Laughter.] 'I guess you're right.'

'Meg, you there? Maybe we should stop it, though, if it freaks you out.'

'It just worries me that . . . I get angry sometimes and so destructive . . . and maybe the scary sex is . . . You don't think I'm sick?'

'No, no – it's just the phone. Like we need something a bit more extreme to, you know, bridge the gap.'

'Maybe.'

'I'm sure that's all it is, nothing to worry about, you're fine, Meg. You'll be here so soon.'

'I hear you. It's not that I want to stop all this, it's just . . .'

'If it freaks you out we should stop.'

'No, no. You know, in fact I think it's really healthy, people have all these hang-ups. It's straight people who really hurt each other. When we do it it's like cathartic or something. It's naughty. I dunno.'

'We shouldn't do it again. OK?'

'OK. My You. You're such a sweet man.'

'Deal?'

'OK, deal. Tell me something funny.'

[Silence.]

'Well. OK. Shit.'

'What is it, my love?'

'God, I can't make you come, I can't make you laugh. It's like I don't know what's happened to me. I've lost my sense of humour, my . . . my mojo ain't working.'

'That was funny.'

'That's me, Mr Funny.'

'You are.'

'OK, so when you come here we'll just be like normal and we'll be fine. OK. Just two weeks five days. Can you believe it?'

'Five days two weeks.'

'We'll play at something else.'

'Mr and Mrs Straight.'

'Yeah, right, we could have really candy sex and that would kind of be kinky in a whole different way. Like . . .'

'Like being married.'

[Silence.]

'What's wrong, You?'

'I'm sorry, Meg. I guess I'm just tired and . . .'

'I shouldn't have said married, right?'

'No, not at all. We're already married in our own special way. You still got my ring?'

'Of course. I shouldn't have said married. When people get married – they tie each other down, I don't ever want that.'

'Funny.'

'What?'

'You want me to tie you to the bed but you never want to be tied down.'

[Laughter.]

'Yeah, I guess. Maybe the two things are connected.'

[Silence.]

'Tom . . .'

'What, my love?'

'Can I tell you a secret?'

'Sure. What?'

[Silence.]

'No, I'm being silly. It's OK, never mind, another time. OK? I have to go now.'

'Already?'

'Yeah. Sorry. I have to wash my face.'

'Well, OK.'

'Have a good evening, my Tom cat.'

'Have a good morning, my puss.'

Journal

August 11

I can rest now. Feel so foolish. I learn, yet again, that pre-drawn
conclusions don't work with us. As soon as we talk every thought
I had seems melodramatic, redundant, laughable. These three
days of madness. DELETE. They are deleted.

You will not do this to yourself again. Say 'I'.

I WILL NOT DO THIS TO MYSELF AGAIN.

He will call at 11 p.m. his time. My day is mine. Today I
will not write about him or me. He has his Highlands and I
have my island. Today I will spend having a life.

Groceries. Fresh air.

Just back from Sal's store. Just shopping for veg, no desire
to chat, but Sal, in her sandals, was all smiles and hugs – 'Where
the hell you been? Thought you'd upped an' gone.' And gossip.
'They say Old Pete's leavin', yup, be worried if I was you. Need
a good neighbour.' And the veg. 'You want some that asparagus?
Fresh today, from upstate, organic – throw you in a bunch.
Some oranges too, for free.' And Sal's grandchildren, climbing
up the walls outside, barefoot, long hair in tangles, big smiles
and talk. Amber and Sam.

'I got a new kite. Big one. Poppa says it's the best.'

'I'm sure it is.'

'Does loop-the-loops, goin' to the beach later, you comin'?'

I said maybe – might be by there later.

And old Nebby, the dog sleeping at the front door, and
Augie buying his tofu, talking about the drought. And Dee
Dee in his long skirt and mascara handing out flyers for the
Mardi Gras.

'You comin', sexy? We could do with some competition.'

Me and my lists – black-eyed peas, arugula, spinach, pine
nuts, Brazils, dried mango, honey, and none of them letting me

get it done, interrupting me, hugging me, asking me so many questions. Grateful for that.

'Yer lookin' skinny. Gotta get some protein in ya, sweetheart.' Jenny in her tie-dyed T-shirt (no bra) passing round the lentil lasagne, for free.

Yes, they made me laugh. Looked at me with kind eyes. My nosy neighbours who make it their business to know mine. A half-hour outside talking to Augie about the campaign to preserve old Fire Island – keeping the big real-estate money out. (They want to build a road and bring on cars.) I signed his petition. Then watched the kids climbing on to the roof and jumping off, their dirty feet, animal energy, it took me back to why I first moved here. Call them hippies if you like. I don't care what people call them. Or me.

Back home. The burden that is waiting for his calls. This process of trying to prepare myself for him. Trying to be sensitive to his moods. To be positive for him.

I have fresh asparagus and lentil lasagne and have felt a mile of sand, warm under my bare feet, happy in the knowledge that I am not alone here – no matter how much I hide away – there are people who care. Jenny and Sal and her wild grandchildren doing handstands for me, asking me to judge who's best. So many friends. From what I can gather he seems to have none. This is what men do, make you feel your friendships are superficial. Lock you up in your prison of two then you fight till one is the victor. Old patterns. To hell with that. I'm going to call Sally now and chat about anything other than me and Tom. Then call Carmella, then Becky. Yes, my life is here and I've been weak this week. Today I know – I can be happy within myself. I shall eat and repair and take stock. Today I am having a day off from us.

Write it.

TODAY – HE CAN GO TO HELL.

And my journal and these script pages too!

NOTE: Must be wary of these fluctuations in myself. (Should have bought some St John's wort at Sal's.)

Script

EXT. FORTH ROAD BRIDGE + FORTH RAILWAY BRIDGE. DAY
Shot of the two bridges taken from Fife. Overlooking the Firth of Forth. Edinburgh in the distance. The new bridge in the foreground, old one in the background.

[VOICE-OVER]
Edinburgh, City of Engineering.

Cut to:

EXT. SCOTT MONUMENT. DAY
Close-up – a man abseiling. Pull out to wide shot to reveal him at top of monument. Princes Street far below him.

[VOICE-OVER]
Edinburgh, City of Excitement.

Cut to:

EXT. ROYAL MILE. DAY
Close-up on the face of the statue of the philosopher David Hume. Pull out to wide shot to reveal university students in graduation robes walking past.

[VOICE-OVER]
City of Enlightenment, of Education.

God, Tom could write this stuff with his eyes closed. But that was the old Tom. He was the New You now. Ten days dry. Lunch without a drink. Stephanie had remarked that he looked healthier. But he also sensed they were all wondering what had happened to his sense of humour. No more ironic ripostes to the inane ideas that McGregor was always throwing round the room.

McGregor: 'Dougie Donnelly. How's about we get Dougie to do the voice-over?'

And Tom didn't object. Didn't say what he thought, that getting a local football presenter whom no one outside this tiny insular town had ever heard of would not sell Edinburgh's excellence to the world.

Tom: 'Great. Sounds great.'

McGregor: 'Oh, and by the way, they want us to put in some shots of the call centres and their new enterprise park on the outskirts. I know, I know, it's not exactly excellent or Edinburgh, but hey, it's what the client wants.'

Tom had filmed thirty different call centres in the last three years and they all looked identical. Same grey partitions, same monitors, same ruthless turnover of anonymous staff. Last year he'd suggested, look, why don't we just use the same shot in every video, no one would know. But today, Tom said, 'Great.' Not 'fab', or 'awesome' or any of his cache of ironic refrains which usually would have had the rest of the office giggling. No. Everything had to be 'great'. He had to buy into the dream of self-improvement. Do that impossible American thing which was to believe in yourself, even though you knew the self to be not a thing but all that was left when there was nothing left. He had to believe in himself. Make himself a character in a story. With a goal and obstacles and a happy ending with Meg.

The company logo in the ready-made Woolworths frame. The plastic flower on McGregor's monitor with its smiley face and Californian shades. Tom at his PC, trying not to judge, to just get the work done.

McGregor: 'Hey, just got this great copyright-free CD. *Authentic Sounds of Scotland.* Track three. Just stick it on now, see what you think, Tommo.'

He'd started calling him Tommo. Some attempt at buddiness. The music started up from McGregor's PC. Tinny and electronic. Soaring synthesisers then bagpipes.

McGregor: 'Yeah? It's kind of ... Moby. You know – "The old and the new." Like we're looking to the future but celebrating our city's past. Yeah?'

McGregor's plastic flower gyrating its stem obscenely.

Tom: 'Yeah. Great. Really great.'

And it was the same, later that day, filming on the banks of the River Forth. He'd seen this happen to others before. The corporate men who no longer cared. Who tried to get the job done so they could be away early to go back to their hobbies, their wives and kids. The cameramen who locked off the camera on the tripod and stood back. The sound recordists who turned off their headphones and just watched the levels instead. Yes, it was the way to survive. He too had hardened himself. His leg muscles were taut now after the two-mile jog before work every day. His gut was diminishing. Work washed over him with a certain melancholic detachment. Two weeks till she came.

He called out to the camera:

'I-Com project seventy-five. Edinburgh, City of Excellence. Tape one. Take seven. And action.'

A fifty-year-old bald sweating man in an off-the-peg Asda suit that his wife had no doubt bought for his on-camera premiere, the bottom button of which wouldn't fasten over his gut. This man was standing in front of an empty field which may once have been something and was now little more than remnants of concrete and rubble, the occasional weed. About half a mile square. The man was the Chief Executive Officer of Caledonian Enterprise Ltd. The area of rubble behind him was, as the sign, left of frame, declared, the HOPE PARK ENTERPRISE ZONE. Even McGregor had been doubtful that it would sell Edinburgh to the world, but it was what the client wanted.

How Meg and her friends had laughed at his stories of corporate video in this country without corporations.

A secret shot of vodka from his hip flask in the ten minutes it took the camera crew to set up on the tripod and plug in the mike would have helped. He'd have faced the client, made him laugh, put him at ease, would have turned the one-hour interview with a monosyllabic quango clone into one glimmering confident sound bite with state-of-the-art digital surround-sound funky synthesised copyright-free music that would sound a lot like Moby and would sell an area of quality Edinburgh rubble to the world's leading multinational corporations. If only he had that hip flask.

No. Not now, not ever.

Tom's voice behind the camera. 'Take eight. We're running
– and action.'

'Hello and welcome to Edinburgh, City of Excellence.'

The man did actually move one of his hands at that point,
gesturing behind to the rubble or perhaps the sky. And he did
actually say 'City of Excellence', even though the city was twelve
miles away and they were filming an empty field.

The woman from Scottish Exec PR was standing behind him
throughout with her checklist of buzzwords that had to be
squeezed in and which were making the sweating quango man's
delivery even more wooden, if that was possible.

Take eight. And action.

'We are entering a time of global change and promise. In this
time of transformation Edinburgh is centrally placed to –'

'And cut,' muttered cameraman Frank. 'He looked at the
lens again.' Frank was ex-BBC. His claim to fame was he once
spent three weeks in an igloo waiting for that BAFTA-winning
slo-mo shot of a killer whale catching a seal in its mouth. That
was ten years ago.

'OK, OK.' Tom walked into shot and was talking quietly in
that confidence-instilling way he'd learned working with avant-
garde actresses in his twenties. Carefully explaining to the suit
again that he had to look at *him*, the interviewer, not the camera,
and certainly not both. Then bounced back to the side of the
camera in that enthusiastic way he'd learned that made the
camera-shy feel it was fun.

Take nine. Camera running. The suit gave Tom the thumbs
up.

'And action.'

'In this time of global transformation Edinburgh is centrally
placed to become a global leader.'

Of course, the guy had said global twice in the same sentence,
but to hell with it. He was still talking and if they were lucky it
would be a take. Tom lowered his eyes, which was a mistake
because the suit was supposed to be looking into them. Realising
this, he looked back up, weary of this thing he did when he could
no longer contain his frustration. Yes, it was just about to happen.
The suit had faltered. Yes, he was raising his voice.

'Let's go again, right away. Take ten – and action!'

'We are standing here before the Hope Park Enterprise Zone. Our excellent new centre of innovation and excellence.'

'God in hell!' He really had to stop muttering so close to the camera mike.

Call me naive, Tom thought, but it would be nice for once for words actually to describe real things and for all those things to come together into something resembling meaning.

And the camera had kept on rolling because he'd forgotten to say cut and the PR girl was in and leafing through the script. He couldn't help himself.

'OK, we can't say, "excellent centre of excellence".'

'Excellent new centre of innovation and excellence.' PR girl correcting him. Great tits. Double E at least. But just like all the interviewees in this fucking video, like Edinburgh itself, she would never learn how to capitalise on her assets.

'Centre of excellence,' she read again from her sheet.

And it was all his fault for having come up with this fucking buzzword. Fuck, this was what they thought branding was: say the buzzword as many times as you could in one sentence.

'No, no, I mean, that's like saying "our pizza place in which we make the most pizzaesque pizzas".'

'It's been signed off. We have to say what it says here.'

'But you're using the same word as adverb and adjective in the same sentence.'

'It took four meetings to sign off on the text.'

'OK, OK, fine. Great.'

Take eleven. The guy even added another excellence where none should be. To just have a fucking autocue. Take twelve – the suit had looked back at the lens again. Tom's swearing had become audible on the main mike. Then he started doing that thing he did when he lost it. Putting on that falsely excited high-pitched encouraging voice. He'd just heard himself saying, 'Great, we're really making progress, you were great. Let's just go again. Tape at speed. Speed. OK, take thirteen. Action.' The suit had introduced a robotic hand movement to indicate the park behind. Cut. Cut.

Jesus, can't we just get an animation to do this, dub the voice on afterwards? This thought but not said. Jesus, try to feel for the poor bastard, this sweating bureaucrat that legitimately elected representatives of the devolved Scottish Parliament had picked to be the voice of the city. The Scots had once been great thinkers and had practically written the American and French revolutionary constitutions. Use your brain, Tom.

'OK, OK. Verisimilitude, the camera never lies, right? Look, I know this, OK ... anyway, what I'm trying to say is, it's the words. I mean, we're standing here – you say "centre of excellence", but all the audience sees is the field.'

'Zone of excellence,' Double E repeated.

'Yes, exactly. But we can't film this ... this ... field and say this is a zone of excellence. We can't fix this with post-production graphics, OK? Prospective perhaps. Prospective zone of excellence. Or potentially excellent zone. Because, I mean, look at it, there's no excellence here. Not yet. But think about it, if we say "potential", then it's not a lie. I mean, this field has so much, wouldn't you agree, potential? In fact, nothing more than that ... this almost infinite potential.'

'Zone of excellence,' said Double E again.

'Zone of potential excellence! C'mon, just one more word. Please? We agree?'

Frank turned off the camera. Motioned for Tom to come closer. Whispering.

'Man, ah dunno, but Jesus. I canna keep the camera steady if you're makin' me laugh like this.'

So he still had a sense of humour. The jogging and the detox hadn't killed it. Or perhaps he'd just become laughable.

'Right, right, sorry.'

'No, it's funny, but we huv tae get this done soon or we're on overtime, eh?'

'Yes, yes, right, sorry, OK. Let's just get this done.'

Each take, each second, each frame would be hell. But they'd get it done and back in the editing suite they'd cut some sense into the suit's words, covering the edits with all of the twenty-five shots of the rubble from different angles. Of the sign by the motorway turn-off. Of the close-up of the Caledonian Enterprise logo. Taking great care not to use any of the shots that established the exact locale as only a half-mile from one of the worst high-rise housing schemes in Europe. Stick on McGregor's *Authentic Sounds of Scotland* CD, which built to a rousing synthesised bagpipe climax, and top and tail it with more logos and everyone would be happy.

Half an hour more and take nineteen. Cut again. Cut. Repeat. And action.

'In this time of global transformation Edinburgh is centrally placed to become a global leader. We are standing here before the Hope Park Enterprise Zone. Our excellent new centre of innovation and excellence.'

Call

'Hi, You. How was your day? I want to hear all about it.'

'Aw, Meg. I really can't. Hey, I uh . . . jogged another mile today.'

'Really? Great. I went for a walk too. I'm feeling really much more positive. I was looking at the Edinburgh Fringe on the Net. It looks so cool.'

[Silence.]

'Look, babe, this isn't the right –'

'It's my fault, isn't it? You're withdrawing from me. This always happens. I was too intense last time and now you're withdrawing.'

'No, not at all, it's . . . Sean's here, he's staying tonight.'

'Oh, OK. What are you guys up to?'

'He's logged on to his Second Life thing. He's building a house with some friend from California apparently.'

'But we can talk? Can we? Just for ten or so. We still have to catch up'

'Well, yeah, but I can't really relax when he's here. You know, it's not like we can do our usual.'

[Laughter.] 'We don't have to do our "usual", silly!'

'Yeah, but I can't even . . . don't think I can even start a conversation. He might come through and –'

'Aw. I thought you told him all about me.'

'I did, of course I did, he knows all about –'

[Sean from next door. 'Dah . . . daaah!']

'Just a minute, Sean!'

'Go on. Can I speak to him?'

'Not such a great idea.'

'I'm going to meet him in two weeks anyway. Can you believe it?'

'Yeah, he's looking forward to meeting you too. It's just –'

[Sean from next door. 'Dah . . . dahhh!']

'All right, goddamnit, I'll be through in a minute.'

'Talk to me here. What's up, my man?'

'He wants me to help him build this virtual house. Jesus!'

'Just a few words, pretty please?'

'Well . . . you know, he's . . .'

'I don't care about his stutter. I just want to say Hi, that's all.'

'No, but when I say a stutter, I mean –'

'I'm sure we can both manage a hi.'

'Dah . . . da . . . DAH!'

'All right, all right, for Christsake!'

'You, you OK? You have to tell me what's happening here.'

'Look. I'm sorry. I can't do this right now. OK. I'll call you when he's asleep in an hour or so.'

'You OK, Tom? You sound . . .'

'I have to go. I'll call your landline in two hours' time. When he's asleep. OK, I have to go now. OK?'

'Tom? Hello?'

He had given neither Meg nor Sean the attention they needed. Had been caught in the middle. But damn it, to be honest, he resented her because her call had made him short-tempered with his son. Because he'd felt guilty for letting Sean stay in Second Life for another hour past his bedtime, yet again, while he waited for her call. Because he had hidden himself away in the bedroom and told Sean not to disturb him. Because throughout all the rituals of Sean's bath and pyjamas and teeth-brushing and folding out the sofa bed he had been impatient with his son. Snapping at him.

'No, you get the pillow. You're big enough now. Do I have to do everything for you? Jesus!'

Not listening, not even trying to work out what Sean was trying to tell him. He resented her for asking to speak to Sean, for not knowing. It was his fault. For not telling her more than the little he had. She couldn't have known. He resented her making him raise his voice to Sean when he asked if he could stay online for a few more minutes.

'Puh . . . pluh . . . eee . . . puh . . . puh . . . Dad –'

For not letting Sean finish the word for himself.

'C'mon, kiddo, no way, it's after ten If your mother finds out I let you stay up this late she'll kill me.'

He resented her making him do that thing the psychology books said you should never do which is polarise the divorced parents and their separate parenting techniques, putting the child into the zone of conflict – making the kid blame himself. He resented her for this thought that flashed through his head as he tucked Sean in and turned off the top light and put on the night light that Sean couldn't sleep without, for having turned him into this father who paced the flat trying to kill the hour after his son had fallen asleep waiting for the minutes to tick down to when he could call her again. For making him think the unthinkable, which was that a drink would help. That if he nipped out to the off-licence, it wouldn't be wilful abandonment and a child left at home alone. Resenting not having done that, minutes and tens of minutes fighting that impulse.

He resented her having made him sit in his home, at his kitchen table, dry and shivering, for turning him into this man who had to perfect himself for her arrival. For making him fear the day, days after she would arrive when she would meet Sean. For the things he hadn't discussed with her yet and was fearful of discussing. This image that he couldn't face. Of Sean, waking as he did at six or seven, and climbing into his father's bed for his little cuddle only to a find an adult woman there. And this had to be confronted at some point, three years of hiding his women from Sean, hiding the truth about Morna from Sean, and Meg was the first woman he could ever really introduce to his son as his 'girlfriend'. The phrase, 'This is my girlfriend.' Imagining now – Sean after a night with Meg here – struggling to explain to his mother later that Dah had been in bed with in bed with Meh . . . uhgan . . . me meh . . .

'You were in bed with your father?'

'Na . . . noh . . . non.'

Sitting there in his God-awful kitchen now, not drinking tea or coffee but water, running over the details: when Meg came it was better that she got a hotel room on Sean nights. He would have to break this to her before she arrived.

He'd book the hotel room. A good hotel, on his credit card. The night of the sleepover would have to be like this. She could help him put Sean to bed. They would sit up and talk but when it came to bedtime, he would order her a taxi. Kiss her goodbye at the door and reassure her that it was just one night per week and that he loved her so much but she had to do this for him. Put it in the most sensitive of terms. That she would check into her room, get a good night's sleep, a break from his pawing, his snoring, she might even benefit from it. And then she could wake early, as early as six, and get a taxi back and join him and Sean for breakfast. Really, the taxi, both ways, he'd pay. Given that she'd be asleep for the whole thing it was only really like they'd been apart for an hour.

Not resentment now. Just the exhaustion of its aftermath, the question of the logistics and compromises, the phone call he'd have to make to the ex to explain this procedure. And guilt, for having resented Meg at all, for even a moment.

He would apologise to her for his brusque tone when he called her back in forty.

To kill time Tom had washed the dinner dishes, emptied the bin, remade his bed, checked his email, run a bath, quietly so as not to wake Sean. Had a bath, considered a wank, but couldn't face it.

Fifteen minutes till the call. Her voice would sound wounded. He would not tell her of how, tonight, she had seemed like a great burden to him, and how he was tired from second guessing her moods.

'Dah . . . dah!'

Sean had woken after only fifty minutes. Poor Sean. A nightmare maybe caused by Second Life. Tom went through to his son in the sofa bed and held him. This half-awake state Sean got into, which he wouldn't remember tomorrow. In which Tom kissed his head and told him over and over that he loved him and everything was OK. There was no need to be afraid of falling because no one could fly. There was really no such thing as special powers, or virtual houses, no need to start making the world all over again. No, no such thing as Second Life.

Journal

He just called me back. Are these many trials sent to test me? He talked of Sean. Said children exhaust your creativity. That I am lucky to be free of child-rearing, that my writing is a greater gift to the world. (He doesn't know of my two hundred pages about him, maybe twenty on Sean.) I tried to be cheery but I sensed a blockage in him. He was reticent at first but, after half an hour of gentle encouragement, I got him to confess.

When I'm staying, he said, there will be this awkwardness over Friday nights. (Sean sleeps over every second week.). I said I might go to London that night. He said, no way could I make London and back in a day – he'd get me a B&B for the night. Or I could stay with a friend. He'd call a taxi to take me over there, an hour before bed, kiss me goodnight, a taxi to get me again in the morning. That way nobody would be upset. I reminded him that I was planning four weeks or more – did we have to do this how many times? He apologised. I said it was OK, I was cool with it. Lying.

He doesn't want me to meet his child. This much is clear. Men with children. No matter how much they strive for independence the child comes first. He has no idea how much this hurts me. He sees only his child and sees him above me. Why did I know this would happen? Six weeks ago he wanted me to be a second mother for Sean. Has he forgotten so soon? He said he wanted to have a second child with me. It was me that was scared, that said no. Now he uses his child as an excuse to pull away from me.

I will not be upset again. I have learned from last week. Must keep learning. The patterns, the stages.

Thinking about *The Stages of Love* and Michael.

NOTES. STAGE SEVEN.
Love betrayed by the beloved. This period near the end of love
is marked by volatility. The lover's projected ideal has grown so
all-encompassing that the beloved herself often fails to live up
to it. The tiniest event can trigger doubt and anxiety. The things
she says, a little slip here or there, a thoughtless banality or
careless turn of phrase can threaten to shatter the image he has
of her. He prefers to hold her at a distance. 'The thought of a
distant town where he once saw the beloved, throws him into
a sweeter reverie than does her actual presence.'

Is this the way he sees me now?
If I had only finished my *Stages of Love*, then I might know
how to act now.

The volatile cycle of hope and despair leads ultimately to a
violent need to resolve all doubt.

Tried to rest but couldn't. Again, I sense he doesn't want
me. Again, I tell myself I will not repeat past mistakes. But
then this thought itself I have had many times before. The
final stage – amnesia. Psychology book on addiction. A whole
paragraph came rushing back. Eight stages not twelve. Note-
book five.

Because the pain is so great, the addict swears never to repeat
the deviant behaviour again. He will be different and think differ-
ently. He will live a new life and never go to those places that
arouse such need, he will avoid all mental associations, images,
sounds that trigger memories. But the prospect of keeping these
promises – the same ones he has made and promptly broken so
many times before – only heightens the sense of frustration and
adds to the addict's despair. He knows it is only a matter of time
until the obsessive thoughts start to crowd again and he will be
caught in the addictive cycle once more.

This researched after Michael. Have I forced myself to forget what I did to Michael? Is Tom my fated repetition?

August 13

Weeping over a pair of Coco Chanel black patent-leather stilettos from the eighties. A storm last night. My window ledge piled high with sand. I'm looking out at the edge of Old Pete's shack. Something flapping in the wind over by the dune grass. A thread, a string, a flash of red. A T-shirt? A child's kite maybe. Left when the tourists left.

START AGAIN – the stilettos. Take it slowly.

I went for my walk, past Old Pete's hut when – a voice – 'I see ya.'

The sun-beaten wood of his fence, his grey hair and eyes peeking out above. I was sure I'd heard him say this to me before, last week – his way of saying hello maybe. I'd waved back, that was all, and kept on going. We're neighbours but apart from storm forecasts and the septic tanks we've nothing really to say.

'I see ya,' he called out again. Funny thing to say. I stopped and shaded my eyes to see better. He was round at the gate.

'Hey, neighbour, how ya doin?'

He'd caught me off guard. He just stood there, silhouetted against the sun, the dark glow of his bare red chest, his head haloed by the white shock of hair.

'I see ya too,' I replied.

His shadow hand motioned for me to come inside.

'Got sumthin for ya,' he said, his back to me as he led the way indoors.

Only neighbourly to accept, but as everyone knows, Old Pete lives alone now, this past three months or so, and hasn't talked to anyone since Charlie died. (Maybe those few hundred yards of beach are the necessary distance between those who are in bereavement and those that aren't. A distance that might be respect or maybe just a fear of loss, as if grief was something you could catch – this American paranoia I hate in myself.) It was maybe desire to defy that or the thought that if Tom had been here he'd have walked right up and shaken Old Pete's hand, hugged him, patted his back. Or maybe the need, burning into me, as the sun hit my back, to resist introspection and really make an effort to relate.

I took my time following, watching his tall arched body from behind, the thin strong legs which could have been those of a man twenty years younger if not for the sun-browned skin, the liver spots. A little guilty, as I stepped in, that I had been so self-obsessed over the years that I had never taken up his many offers to come over sometime. But that is the way round here. Pioneer mentality – you only talk to your neighbours in times of crisis. Maybe I was in crisis. SLOW DOWN. Describe.

Inside and the place was nothing like I'd imagined from the rustic exterior. Not the usual temporary furnishings – fish boxes for seats, futons and throw rugs. No – not a place but a palace, a boudoir. I had to duck my head as I came in to avoid being hit by a plastic seagull, dangling upside down from a wire. The *Mona Lisa* with a holographic grin. The first word was pink. (Not the word he said, because he said very little.) He was pulling on a shirt, Hawaiian palm trees, rummaging around in an ashtray. The place smelt of patchouli and hashish. But pink. Yes. The walls were, the sheepskin rug by the fire was too, the cover on the sofa was Tibetan-looking but impossibly pink. A fifties ladies' hand mirror, face down on a copy of *Vogue* from the seventies on this camp little deco table.

I may have apologised. (Had to say something.) Maybe that or the fact that my eyes had come to rest on the board on the kitchen door that was covered in photographs from the annual Fire Island Mardi Gras. All of them of drag queens. Maybe twenty years' worth?

'I see ya.' He looked directly into my eyes – lowered them just as quickly to the relit reefer between his fingers. 'Yeah?'

'Well, sometimes, not in a while. Feel free.'

And I such an idiot because 'feel free' sounded like some kind of trying-too-hard hippie phrase, and he was one of the original Fire Islanders from the sixties. A hippie and a drag queen. Old Pete and Charlie. I'd heard from Sal at the store that Charlie had died of 'the illness'. Eva, too, had said something similar. 'The sickness.' The land of free speech and we're all still scared to say that one four-letter word: Aids.

'I'd love to,' I said and took it from him, it seemed the thing to do. Was rabbiting on. 'Give it a try anyway, usually it only makes me morbid. I guess I was more of an uppers person, you know, when I did these things, sorry, you had something for me. God, listen to me, I should chill out, huh. I dunno, I'm having a sort of moody day today and –'

'I see ya,' he said again with a smile. 'I see ya.' I kept thinking. Maybe it was his accent. It sounded Queens. If Tom had been there he'd have joked about drag queens from Queens and done the accents – both of them. I put the thing to my mouth and drew on it. It tasted of my twenties (the sixties had come back for their first time in my twenties). I told myself to stop analysing, to inhale and hold.

He had his back to me again, he was in the wardrobe.

'Yeah, somethin' for you. S'OK. Take a look around, take anythin' you want, I'm movin' out, week or so.'

'Really?' I was coughing on the thing. No, it was no good, my attempts at chilling out – give me dope and I freak, talk for hours about the history of hashish and what effect it was supposed to have.

I remember thinking that if Tom had been here he'd smoke it all and get Pete to open a bottle and I'd have chilled and stayed. Tom's little hand squeezes, giving me confidence. He'd have made Old Pete laugh, asked him about the seventies, then the repouring and Tom laughing and giving this man in so much pain permission to talk of his grief, asking him to go on. The eighties, the nineties. And the day would have gone on and on into night at the end of it the old man and Tom would be holding each other at the door in tears of laughter, and Tom would reach out for me and bring me into the circle. Holding me tight in the big family hug, bringing me so close to hold my neighbour. Tom drunk and kissing both our faces. The Scots, the most cynical nation on God's earth, till they get drunk. I recall thinking if Tom had been there I could have dealt better with Pete's silences.

I didn't inhale. Was looking for his ashtray.

'So much stuff, you know,' Old Pete said from the closet. 'Jeez, she has so much stuff! Where are they?'

He called him 'she'. Memory that Charlie called himself Charlotte. She. 'She has,' he said, present tense.

Too many things to ask. The place looked like the sixties in LA, like the roaring twenties in Berlin. The couple of puffs must have been taking effect because I asked, 'OK, to look at your photos?'

An affirmative grunt. Him still in the closet. Me peering closer. The many pictures of the many drag queens. The seventies, the eighties – the bodies fuller, the drag more extreme. The sickness must have started. Feather boas, Chanel and Victorian corsets. The same face in every photo, arms round others. Shaved off eyebrows and a very square jaw. Gradually growing older, sicker.

No one had told me this. It just came to me.

Charlie made up for Old Pete even when he was too tired to lift an arm. Charlie insisted on being a woman every day. Charlie didn't see his sickness, only his need for an ever more perfected femininity. The photos. Old Pete's always on the edge of frame, the straight guy in love with the fabulous drag queen. The first person he had loved, the last. The word unnatural came into my head, not the drag queens but surviving beyond the death of your lover.

'Yup, movin out,' he called through. 'Nothin' here for me now.' Maybe the weed talking – he kept on as he went through the closet. The waves scared him now, he said. The rhythm. Used to soothe him but now he kept waking up thinking they'd stopped.

He came through, handed me the stilettos. 1960s, beautiful, but too big. Patent leather, five-inch heels.

'Thought they might fit ya.'

A size forty-two and I am a thirty-eight, aged thirty-eight. Close to tears, because Pete had helped Charlie dress as a woman every day. Because the shoes were too big. Because they'd been so expensive. Because he was my neighbour but a stranger and he had let me into his life. Because he'd just asked me if I'd like to buy his house, real cheap, or take care of it till it was sold, and again how I could take anything I wanted and he had given me the spare keys. I couldn't meet his eye. His non-judgemental voice again. 'I see ya.'

And I saw their last day. Things in the place conjuring images. On that day he put her make-up on for her and held the mirror to her face, her arms too weak. And had watched her smile at herself and couldn't see the face she saw. And put her wig on for her because the hair had gone and shaved her chin so the skin was smooth for the application of the foundation even though he knew nothing of make-up. And cleaned up the incontinence pads without discussing the matter as he had done for two years or more. And long after Charlie had ceased to be Charlie, on that last day, he saw her again as she wanted to be seen. And that hand mirror finally as Charlie's hand dropped, he waited and waited, then took it from her clenched fingers, then held it close to her face, to her mouth, to look for the moisture stain of breath.

The pink seagull dangling above, the stilettos on the floor beside me. Trying not to cry. He didn't reach out or even touch, just sat cross-legged, Zen-like, on the floor, feet away from me, nodding to himself.

'I see ya, I see ya.'

I see Michael now. His weeping declarations of love more and more passionate then desperate then the threats to himself. I tried to walk out but he grabbed me, threw me back inside, the broken mirror, the slash in my lip. An accident, I accept this now. My blood on his hands and him crying sorry sorry, over and over and how he'd take care of me, never let me go. And I ran. People said he'd gone crazy; he'd left the country; that he was in hospital; he was with a new woman; that he'd turned gay; that he'd started drinking. I disconnected the phone. I packed and ran to a quiet place, to write about love, the story of love, to learn from it, to make sure nothing like that would ever happen again. I ran from him to write.

And Old Pete, he reached to hold me but I ran. I was out on the sand and crying over plastic seagulls and drag queens and this pair of stilettos in my hand. Because I had just thought the most cynical thought ever in my life – 'I have to write this

as a movie.' It starts at the end, with Old Pete clearing out his
shack. Flashbacks as he goes through their many things from
the last thirty years. Years pass in minutes, summed up by a
dress, a lipstick, a novel left by a bedside. The Victorian hand
mirror on the table.

What kind of monster am I? Running from the living who
need. The dead so much easier to romanticise. I'm so sick, so
alone now.

I can't help myself. Just been through *The Stages of Love* again.
Notes – Abnormal Psychology. This, terrifying:

> Addicts will go to great lengths to deny their condition, starting
> again and again in different places. They may spend many years
> in relative quiet before a major relapse. The intensity of relapse
> can be intensified by the duration of the period of retreat. One
> subject spent almost fifteen years alone before finally repeating
> and re-enacting the original trauma. The result was fatal.

Four valerian. Six years since my last panic attack. I promised I would call him at noon. Three forty a.m. now. Have I
sought out Tom just so I can put Michael's story to rest? It's
me. Has been all along. Me that's sick. The addict.

Call

'Old Pete, such a sad story, Meg, beautiful.'
    'No, no! But don't you think, there's things maybe too precious to tell anyone? Like how could I ever turn Pete and Charlie into a movie?'
'Well – it would move people.'
'No! No, just . . . look at all these great male writers, Pulitzer winners and they document their lives and write about their lovers, and ex-wives, children, people get hurt, court cases, humiliation, don't you think that appalling?
'So people get divorced, it happens, if that's what you mean . . . ?'
'God, you make me mad, can't you see what I'm asking?'
'Not really.'
'You must agree that this is wrong. They hurt people to write about the hurt. Like they feed on it . . .'
'I'm still struggling here to find your question.'
'You see! You've got double standards is what! Fine to write about other people but what if someone wrote about you?'
[Silence.]
'Put it this way . . . I'd have to kill them.' [Laughter.]
'If I wrote about you you'd kill me?'
'No, of course not. [Silence.] . . . People are shit, it's fine. It's OK, Meg, I just don't get why you're so upset.'
[Silence.]
'But the way we talk sometimes. It's like we're both watching this movie about these people in love, and we're just, like, in the audience.'
'*Hiroshima Mon Amour.*'
'Exactly and *Before Sunrise* and –'
'Meg, why are you so manic?'
'I just want to believe it's real. Sometimes I worry we're not

in love at all – just this story we tell each other so we can believe. You don't think I push you away do you?'

'I love you, you know that.'

'I just . . . I scare myself, Tom . . . and the one thing I forget in all this debating with myself is you. Really, you. My You, I'd never want to hurt you.'

'How's your writing? You still haven't told me what it's about.'

[Silence.]

'I'm trying to tell you if you would just listen!'

'I mean, is it a sci-fi, a thriller, a book, a script, a poem?'

'I'd rather have you than some stupid pile of pages . . . I don't want to hurt you.'

'There you go again. You're not making any sense, my Meg.'

[Silence.]

'Actually, I'm thinking of giving up the writing. No, in fact. I'm convinced of it. It's got to stop'

'Why the hell?'

'I . . . just feel it's evil or wrong . . . or . . .'

'My You, you are so crazy.'

'You call me your You. That worries me too.'

[Laughter.]

'You are my You'

'But don't you think . . . ? You and You . . . like we're the same. Like you're all the the yous in the world. The one you. Like the biggest story in the world, like we're setting ourselves up for disaster.'

[Silence.]

'OK, so I'll call you Megan from now on.'

'God, listen to me. I'm self-sabotaging again. I don't know what's wrong with me.'

'So – OK, we use our real names. I'd like to hear you call me Tom.'

'No, no, I love our You . . . it's just . . .'

'My little Meg.'

[Silence.]

'My Tom.'

[Laughter.]

'Are you OK now, my Meg?'

'Yes, I'm OK, my Tom . . . Tom, listen to you. I'm sorry. We have our little fights, then somehow I never notice the transition, you have me laughing or something, then I can never remember what the problem was.'

'There's no problem, Meg.'

'You're so sweet, I don't deserve you. Just tell me one thing. Like, remember our fight night?'

'I don't think you'll ever let me forget!'

'No, but I mean, the next day, so many arguments, but then we were making love by the end of it. How could that even be possible?'

'You are impossible. You want me to talk about our last day?'

'If that's OK, my You. God, listen to me, we gave up on our names for like –'

'– a minute, max.'

'And the way you finish my sentences for me.'

'And you me. My You.'

[Laughter.]

'OK, so our last day.'

'Actually, Tom, no. I take it back – I don't want to hear about our days any more. It's not right. I'll just remember it all by myself.'

'I can tell you if you want, easy.'

'No, it's not right. We should talk about something else.'

'My You, you are deeply insane.'

'In-fucking-sane.'

'Yes, im-fucking–'

'-possible.'

[Laughter.]

Bridge

The regimen of daily calls to Meg, of jogging. At first one mile then two. Then setting the clock for six thirty to push for that third mile. Then calling her at 3 p.m. Ten days till she got here.

Tom had just finished filming the bridges for the *City of Excellence* DVD. Finished early because he wanted to get it done as simply as possible. No running around trying to capture the vitality of the very first days of the Edinburgh Festival. No messing around trying out new things, arty angles, slow pans, tracking, time lapse. None of the things he'd usually have attempted to make it feel like he was really shooting a real film. No. Just one simple locked-off shot for twenty seconds, framed as per his instructions. The vista from the Firth of Forth. The newer bridge in the foreground, the older behind, behind that the city of Edinburgh.

He'd sent the video crew home early. Made up some excuse – had to do a recce of other possible views. He'd be a few hours, they should go on ahead. He wanted to be alone, that was all. Ten days till she arrived. Something told him he had to face the bridge again.

Some change had taken place since he'd stopped drinking. Three weeks dry now and he felt not just dry but like he was hardening. Not just his muscles from the jogging. No, something interior. So brittle he could crack. This inability to feel. His humour had dried up. He wanted to stand in the middle of the bridge and stare at the waters of the Firth of Forth and make the tears break.

The suspension wires in his hand. No cars around. It was just after four. No rush-hour traffic yet, no police to ask if he was OK and could he move his car from the ramp.

The water three hundred feet below. Grey like the sky.

Overcast, so few days of blue in a Scottish year. The clouds clouded everything, every thought. The sky above New York was infinite. It opened the mind. Like the top of your skull had been removed. Brain exposed to the sky, vulnerable. Ambition, dreams, everything tentative, yet possible.

He was most certainly not going to jump. This wasn't that day after the divorce, this wasn't that night with Meg on the Brooklyn Bridge. The purpose of this exercise was the absolute opposite.

A certain thing had to be done. It required solitude. Checking over his shoulders to see if the roads were clear. The words whispering in his head. Just listen to them. Talking to a landscape, as ridiculous as that seemed. Move your mouth. Say them, get them out.

'Please make it all OK when she comes. Please make her still love me. Keep me dry. Make it all OK. Make her want to stay with me. Live here with me. Please, make it all OK.'

The one word he'd not said was God. Was Our Father. A solitary seagull passed overhead. A single plane circling before landing at the tiny airport that called itself International. And God had died even in the time of his father but still he himself was a father. The clouds so low above his head, pushing down with all the weight of history. He should show his son more love.

Staring out at his city through the suspension wires. Feet on the edge. What would it take to make him weep? To mark this day as one of revelation and hope. A car slowed down as it passed him, and he felt embarrassed. He climbed down from the edge thinking nothing more profound than what a fool he would have looked if Meg had seen him.

Journal

August 15

To write or not to write. This ethical choice I've set myself. If I had just told him at the start that I was writing about him. How has this snowballed into such a huge lie? If I give up on our story now then it feels I've wasted this time apart. Like I give up on men before the end. So close to the end now. But will it hurt him?

It's made more confusing by his manner. He was sweet today but something has changed. He talks without his old sarcasm about jogging, keeping fit and diet. He's been doing sit-ups and got his abs back. (I shall miss holding his beer belly!) This detachment is maybe part of a process. The decompression before I arrive. We are calmer at least. Calm before the next storm?

In the attempt to decide I have reread everything written before and compared it to the new journal. I am fond of these pages. They make me laugh. No one would ever buy our story. 'Too much talk,' the producers would say; 'The story goes backwards.' But we're funny in that way – starting out from cynicism and ending up with naive hope.

What if I was to finish it then gift it to him?

Or am I being seduced by words? Words that will cause him pain?

Do I fear what is hidden in that last day?

New File. List 7

REASONS AGAINST:

1. Every portrayal is a betrayal. Admit it. When you were with him you thought: If I could just write down what you said. If I could just capture that moment we just had. The moment moves on. It is morbid to record.

2. To write of love is to write of death. To live on in memory. Easier to write of love lost. The fear maybe of love dying even as the beloved continues to live. The secret desire for the love to end, so you would be forgiven for writing of it without guilt. You can't write and love at the same time.

3. To write of love is to betray someone you know to an unknown audience. A universal one. To write of love is a Christian throwback. To ask God for acceptance.

4. The more you write about love the less you can feel. Writing is distance. You step away to write about what was close.

5. If you achieve perfection in words about love the more the reality disappoints.

6. Love is spontaneity in the moment. So many voices, all lost to time. Gems, thrown away. Abundance. Joyous waste of words and voices discarded and then the next and the next. To record them is like killing a butterfly so as to keep it.

REASONS FOR:
1. Love stories inspire – e.g . . .

He's calling now. Finish this tomorrow.

August 16
Breakfast of oranges. Old Pete dropped off some things from his freezer. Red meat – they were carnivores. Won't touch any of it but was glad to see his face. No jokes with Tom today but we are so gentle. Phone silences have started now and they approximate our old same-room ones. Josh on the phone four thirty – bullying and teasing me into sending him something. Josh said that what I'd told him before sounded very indie – a finale at the start then the lovers part. He said it'd make a great movie – dual and multiple protagonists were in now, after *Crash* and *The Hours*. So silly! He wanted to know the end. These movie people – they love it more when you keep them hanging. I told him in my best Edinburgh accent to 'get to fuck'.

Josh made me feel extremely anxious about writing – ever

writing again in fact. Another day wasted worrying over this choice.

Still cannot decide.

August 17

The decision is made for me. Tom's calming voice on the phone today. He wants me to bring hiking boots so we can climb his new-found hill. He makes choices without fear of repercussions and things happen. He jumps straight in. (If it had not been for his boldness we may not have made it past a one-night stand.) I worry myself in circles and do nothing. All this gnashing of teeth. I fear and fuss and work out all the possible outcomes then it all becomes a crisis and I'm too scared to do anything.

He just *does* things.

I must be more like him, that's the answer. So I will keep on writing. Finish it before my arrival. Will somehow find the guts to show it to him. If it's a private story just for us both, then so be it. (Don't want him to kill me!) If he hates it we shall burn it. Together.

New File.

Nine days till I head to Edinburgh. Our last day – Chelsea, downtown. How did I go from this fear that Tom was a madman – to the next when we made our love bond? I have promised myself I shall not upset our new state of peace by asking him for any more details.

Morning. Day after the bridge. His hotel room. I didn't want to wake. Hung-over. Fear of facing him. No memory of how we got back to his hotel room, of how I ended up again in his bed. (It had been late and the plan to sleep at Sally's shot. Already in Manhattan and no cabs back to Brooklyn?) Definitely recall attempts at hailing cabs. Fifteen blocks' walk to sober us up. Silent. The cab finally and I had taken it to his hotel just to make sure he'd make it back safely. Him too drunk to walk. For sure, I felt deeply disillusioned and had no intention of spending any more time with him. (Did I ask the receptionist for another room? No rooms available?) No memory. And I had not slept at all well. He is a boor when drunk and snores. The whole ending of our fight night – appalling. I lay awake. We'd forgotten to shut the blinds. Staring out at the lights of Manhattan, feeling as far from any man as I ever have. The smell of his body, the weight of his arms, that he so carelessly threw over me – as if in sleep he could reclaim me. The room spinning. This possessiveness of his. This exposure of his total weakness and dependence.

The bridge. I was still in shock, I think. A sense of his potential for violence, to himself, possibly even to me. Hadn't wanted to wake on that morning. Couldn't face the averted eyes I would have to give him, to hide my tear-bloated face that would tell him, if he saw, that after many sleepless hours staring at the skyscrapers I had decided, there could be no more lovers. No more love.

He was up and retching in the sink. His smoker's cough and the alcohol. I pretended to be asleep and was running through my escape plans – I'd say, 'Could you get me a coffee, from the restaurant, a real one, not the sachets?' – when he was out of the room I'd leave swiftly – later in the day, text him a goodbye. Or – dress quickly while he was in the bathroom, then kiss him on the cheek at the door, muttering something about a meeting – a text I'd just got – I'd text myself so he would hear the beep. A quick peck, then a see-you-later, then I'd turn off my phone for the rest of the day, head back to Fire Island. Sit and wait till he'd gone. But I had this sense that if I ran, he would follow me all the way back home, miss his flight. Needing and pleading on my doorstep. Visions of endless hours crying, of sorries and accusations and exhausted reconciliations. Of days spent building up his strength enough to get him on his plane. The mental planning had kept me there too long in bed. He'd done his vomiting, washed out the sink, was humming to himself. God, that scared me. This way he moved from despair to joviality. Like a kid who beat you up one day then came round the next to ask if you wanted to come out and play. He'd told me this had happened to him. Aged ten. The abusive alcoholic parents. Mentioned in passing that his dad used to hit him when sober then kiss him when drunk. (Or was it the other way round?)

No touch. Minutes of frigid silence. He was naked before me.

'Sorry about last night,' he said, 'I do this.'

Not a pleading voice. A sincere, tired sorry.

'I seem to have a fear of everything being OK. I go, as you say, into self-sabotage mode.'

Pretending to still be sleeping, waiting, fearing the touch that did not come.

'It's OK if you've already decided to leave me. I was a pig. If you want I'll go now and you can get dressed by yourself. Sorry I blew it.'

It was anger then that got me up. At how, every fucking time, it was like this with him. Pre-empting me, forgiving me in advance. Saying what I felt and didn't have the guts to say. I was up and staring at him. Fuck, I could have screamed. 'Fuck you.' 'Fuck off.' 'Leave me alone.' His playful face, eyes still red from the puking.

'We have one day left to undo everything. We could have another fight, a big one if you like. That would be ideal. I could go back home really hating you.'

'Not funny.'

'Come on then, give it a go. How shall we start?'

Moments, me just sitting there, sheet wrapped round me, covering my breasts. Eyes, tired, last night's wept mascara.

'Tell me about me. Dare you. Gimme the worst and I will too. About me – you. You're not talking. I can see how angry you are.'

Too many things to say.

'OK, so me,' he said. 'You think I'm an alcoholic, a violent drunk. Yes?'

'Yes.'

'And you would be justified in that assessment, but you should know that I fear alcohol as much as you maybe feared me last night. Told you already my dad was an alkie. I was twenty-three before I had my first sip. And yes, I know what you're thinking – it's no apology and you would be right.'

'Right.'

'Point two, right now, you're thinking this has been a mistake. Be better not to risk contact at all. You should know I've never

hurt anyone in my life, not physically. My dad once fell over in the street. I was probably eleven or so. I helped him up, he said, Hit me, I know you hate me. Hit me and we'll be mates. Get it done, son. Just fucking hit me. I raised my fist and fell into him weeping. We both did.'

A sad story from childhood, but abusive men always do that. I had nothing to say.

'OK, so you're not talking.'

I looked up at him.

'So you want me to tell you about you?'

I shrugged, I may have laughed. At that moment I found him contemptuous.

'OK, so the way I see you. Point one – and I'm not making apologies for saying this, but you have a fear of conflict. Point two – your closest relationship ever has been with your therapist. A New York cliché by the way. Which is point three – your fear of cliché. Point four – this world you've set up to protect yourself from contact. Point five is that, really, I sense that you have a need for affection but your understating of it is confused. And this is not just you, it's very American. You are in grave danger of becoming one of those women who prefer a book to a lover. Right? Point six – you were lying there pretending to sleep but I know you were working out ways of letting me go. Like when people get fired. Yeah?'

I could have punched him. Kissed him. Told him so.

'God, I hate you.'

'Say it louder, I can't quite hear you,' he shouted.

I had to kiss him. My melancholy Scottish man.

The kissing and fighting and laughter – no end to it all day. Day of impossible reconciliation. Of Ground Zero. WRITE OF THAT.

I had forgiven him somehow, partially, given him another hour at least. I'd been in the hotel bathroom, moisturising. Through the gap in the door, him naked, still on the bed, leafing through *Time Out*.

'A day in Manhattan!' he shouted through. 'So let's be tourists.'

'Been there, done that.'

'I know, but you ever done the Empire State? Like Kong, ya know, da King. S'a primal need. I gotta be dat monkey.'

I'd been up the Empire State five times before, with Tony, Jed, Arturo. I knew most of what was in his *Time Out*. I had long since exhausted the diversions of New York. I wanted just to lie down, to calm down. He proposed the Beckett.

'Saw it last month.'

'Dey gotta Broadway version of *Billy Elliot*, can you believe dat? Da guy dat wrote it was a Marxist. How's about da dancers from Bali? OK, so, yeah, been dere, seen dat, done dat.'

His phoney Bronx accent again turning into Woody Allen.

Beside him then and fastening my bra as he flicked through the pages. He wouldn't stop.

'Jeez, but, y'know, all my life, I never seen Central Park. Shame on me, *oy vey*. We godda do it.'

'I don't want to do anything.'

'Ground Zero den. Dere's a museum. For real.'

I'd hoped he'd pass over it. Move to the next page. The Bruegel and Broadway and the Berlin performance artists who bled on to canvases. But he was well past B.

I tried to tell him Ground Zero was a place those of us that lived here didn't need to visit. We'd smelt it in the air. Its ashes had covered our window ledges. Our curtains and clothes stank of it – of concrete and melted steel and unspeakable things. You took your clothes to the dry-cleaner, took yourself to your shrink.

I didn't want to go. Almost seven years since. It was his last day.

Maybe he insisted to torment me. These final stages. A sense of it as I accepted – him taking me there to become objectionable, to flaunt our very real difference in my face. I owed it to him – to let it end with a fight. In spite of myself, I accepted.

The A train. Eight stops and then we were there at the viewing platform. Three middle-aged Midwestern women, posing at the barrier, all smiles for a photo. Ashamed. I wanted to go. His voice was Ewan McGregor then. Ironic. *Trainspotting*.

'But s'a great real-estate opportunity, don't ye think?'

Not funny.

'Ah mean, subterranean car-park possibilities, eight floors o' malls. Been dyin' for this in Edimbra. Wur castle, as yee ken, is weel past its best. Bomb it tae fuck's what the cooncil wants, set up a museum, build a mall, in homage of course.'

Really, not funny.

I remember it well (everything I feared confronting here). Him saying how amazing it was, impossible to picture an absence. To be standing before it and not see the bent steel, the ashes, the heroic firemen. This space like any other, he said, a hundred workers with helmets, this floor of unified concrete.

A cliché to ask, he'd said: 'But where were you when it happened?' I said: yes, it was cliché. His story was a good one, one he'd been holding back from me, he confessed. He was in his marital home in Edinburgh, packing boxes, preparing to move to New York – a job directing TV, Channel 13; the family were going to move, a visa and everything.

The ex-then-wife took him through to the TV. The same loop of the second plane hitting. The first thing he thought – ashamed of it now – wasn't 'The poor souls', no, was 'Just my luck.' And sure enough the job contract was cancelled three days later and the move was off, and that was the end of his career and his marriage.

Inappropriate to talk in such a way. Couldn't work out if he'd intended it as a joke. Then he went one worse. Held his two fingers to the sky. The victory sign. Then spun them round – the fuck-you sign.

'Tom, what the hell are you doing?'

'Just tryin' to see what they might have been like. Two big things in the sky.'

I told him to put them down. People would see. Sick.

'So are we going to have our fight, right now?'

'I'm going.'

Yes, I headed away. He was telling me about Chomsky – the other 9/11. The assassination of this or that South American leader by the Americans. Some documentary by Ken Loach.

Yes, picking a fight, to end it. (Easier to call it an ideological battle.) But I'd walked the wrong way. Couldn't turn back, he was there behind me. Then on my arm. The tiny streets of the Financial District, the deco towers built on older alleys. Exchange Place, William Street, Beaver, the same on either side, street stalls everywhere, no space to move among the masses. Smells of hotdogs and pretzels. For sale: fake FDNY caps and T-shirts; sweatshirts with an angel floating between the two vertical shadows. Others with a girl naked but for a fireman's helmet. Two-for-one Twin Tower Popsicles.

'Just like the Vatican,' he said.

A cartoon poster of Uncle Sam holding up two victorious fingers just as he'd done. A calendar with a now-you-see-them now you don't hologram of the skyline. 'Wanted Dead or Alive' Osama T-shirts. The faces selling all these things – Greek, Asian, Jamaican, Cuban, Puerto Rican. Americans all of them.

He was nudging me, pointing it all out. 'God Bless America' T-shirts – his and hers twin coffee cups, one tower on each. A smirk on his face. How did I feel? His wit in poor taste. Ashamed of my country, more at myself. To just tell him this was no place to play the scathing European social critic. In America we didn't laugh at those with less education, different tastes. No ivory tower to laugh down from. We're all struggling to make a buck, pick ourselves up. Selling our history is as American as the Constitution.

Something he'd spotted got him excited. He had no cash, I had only my card. He ran off to find an ATM and left me standing among the stalls. Twin Towers snow globes, kitchen towels. The same words everywhere – HEROES, ANGELS. I was pacing around, anger mounting. Started wandering in the direction I thought he'd gone in, but the next block was just more of the same. Tourists. Shoulders and heads and elbows. Loud music blasting. 'Born in the USA'. The hangover and the claustrophobia. How would he find me? I turned and bumped into a kid with a burger, the kid crying as it fell to the dirt. 'Sorry, sorry.' Pushing past. In hell. He'd left me here. 'Hey, lady, hey!' Some thickset Latino street vendor holding up a thong with FDNY written on the crotch and motioning for me to come and buy. Hating him then, for making me hate all these poor ignorant immigrants . . .

A hand on my shoulder. Tom.

'Don't you ever do that to me again! You hear!'

A smile on his face. 'Ever?' he asked. 'But I'm going tomorrow.'

A pause – break for breath.

Him saying he'd bought me this T-shirt as a going-away present. I walked. Any direction, just to get away. No idea where. South Street, William. Broad. Pearl. Toward Battery Park, the FDR. Leave me alone. Go away – not said. Him half a block behind, a block. Me not turning to look. Going nowhere, just away. Only two blocks to the river.

'Hiroshima,' he shouted after me. That was it, something snapped. I turned.

'What?'

Him beside me in a few steps. Broadway and Battery. Taxis accelerating toward the Expressway. Could hardly hear him, his voice raised.

'We're doing that scene from *Hiroshima Mon Amour*. She walks away, he follows. All day and night.'

'So your point is what, exactly? Jesus, everything with you is just movies. Let go of my fucking arm.'

'I just thought, maybe you had something to tell me.'

'No,' I shouted. I had nothing to tell of. No great love in a world war. No close encounter with death. No separation from a lover across the ideological divide. No initiating childhood trauma. No child I would betray. All I'd ever had was the fear of intensities such as this. I had nothing.

'You going to keep on running away?'

'I don't know! Leave me alone.'

Battery Park. I sat on a bench by the ferry terminal to the Statue of Liberty. He sat beside me. I thought I'd seen his point, apologised, asked him to explain. He started, then stopped short. Another argument. Me walking away. Him not following. Me stopping. Coming back to him. The next silent bench, him reaching for my hand gently as we watched the foreign families with flags and baseball caps and candies lining up for the

ferry to Ellis Island. He suggested we forget all this and go and
do the Statue of Liberty. Get it done, do something dumb. The
sickness in my gut. Nothing I could do. Sentences started then
left unfinished. Silences filled with tourist laughter. Actions
stopped before the end. I wanted to kiss him – pulled away –
to slap him – stopped myself. Pacing away again just to get
myself together. Going nowhere. Staring at the black kids
playing Frisbee on the grass. Mother with twin-stroller. His
hand on my shoulder.

'We're going in circles,' he said. 'Remember, like that couple
on the beach.'

(Maybe it was me that said that?) A sense of déjà vu. Knowing
that no matter what we tried to do with these last twenty or
so hours it would be the same. If we tried to eat we'd push our
plates away after a mouthful. A tour of the statue and we'd
break off and head back on the ferry we'd just left. Maybe it
was me.

One of us suggested a cab. Two cabs. One each. Away. Apart.
Another decision attempted. A cab hailed. Me inside alone. But
something about his face through the window, no kiss goodbye.
I was out, in his arms again. The taxi driver swearing as he
sped away.

Walking block after block up Broadway, heading back toward
where we started. No talk then. Fingers intermeshed. Silent
squeezes, circling of thumbs. The growing hot wet between us.

Try to remember – making love again on the last night. No,
it was not anything he did. We did nothing all day. Couldn't
see a single thing through. Every conversation aborted. Our
differing views – architecture, aesthetics, reality TV. What does
it matter what you or I think of the Bush administration if I
will never see you again?

I'm back again with *Hiroshima Mon Amour*. And it is true,
apart from those first tortured loves, I have suffered no great
tragedy – my life itself is maybe the tragedy. A very minor one,
something undocumented. The life of a film extra. Someone
starting with infinite hope then stopping and endlessly restarting,
each time the hope diminishing as I grow older. The increasing
caution taken with human contact. My fear of change. Can I

really live in his country? Do I want to make his sadness mine? The temptation of succumbing to the pre-written tragic ending?

No, he is more. He knows me better. Better than I know myself.

That final night. Our roles reversed. I blindfolded him.

I call him in an hour.

Speech

'LOSER, I DID IT!'
     Tom could have wept with joy. Sean racing past him, to the top of Arthur's Seat, shouting down at him. Four clear perfect words.

'LOSER, I . . . DID . . . IT.'

As Tom hiked the path, he stared up at his son. His son who had just spoken properly for the first time in two years.

Rewinding in his head as he stepped up. He'd told himself he had to explore Edinburgh with his son, to make an effort. To draw up the Edinburgh tour for Meg, only five days till she came. Something to do with being dry and taking his son to the hill he jogged every day. Thirty minutes after school, no tourists around.

Sean was shouting again.

'LOSER, LOSER.'

Those footsteps up and these feelings he was trying to fight – Morna had said singing was the answer, the lungs at full capacity, overriding the feared words. Fearful then of facing Sean at the top. Of being physically close as they looked down at the city. Of him not knowing what to say, of his son stuttering again. Don't mention that he hadn't.

'OK, so you win. I'm just an old man.'

Sean saying nothing. Tom out of breath. Sean standing there at the top. Eight hundred feet above Edinburgh. No talking. Tom standing silent beside his son and turning to look at the view. Seeing something that might have moved him fifteen years ago. The clouds casting shadows over the aged city, the church spires and council tower blocks piercing the clouds, the gradations, every mile becoming increasingly blue, out of focus, something as a film-maker he would once have tried to capture. In time lapse.

'Duh . . . da . . . dahh . . .'

The stutter again; he was standing too close.

'What is it, kiddo?'

'Ah . . . chooos, I jus . . . I . . .'

'You just what, kiddo?'

'Maaa . . . mumum, mah, muh . . . s . . . ssss. Muh saaaa . . .'

Mum says – wait, let him say it.

'Sssays . . . yuh . . . yoo, you . . .'

Let him speak. Don't look at his eyes. Wait for him to speak first.

'Yooo . . . yuh . . . gonna . . .'

I'm going to. Sean more confident with Americanisms, just like himself, so gonna was fine.

'Gonna, gonna, guh, gu . . . gonna guh, guh oh, gonna go . . .'

I'm going to go.

'Aga, aggag, gonna, agag, goh . . . a wah, a wah, way, way, gonna guh awah aga . . .'

Mum says you're going to go away again. Let him say it for himself. Wait for him to speak. You're on a hill overlooking the city. You've been here jogging every morning for the last three weeks. And have learned how to wait for that last breath that will give the power to make that last step.

'Nuhh . . . nu . . . nh nuh nun u, New York.'

The sentence he knew already. Mum says you're going to leave again and go to New York and never come back.

'Muh, mamuh, sss, mu, sss, suh, sss, sez . . .'

He should not interrupt his son when he was about to finish a sentence. This distance – shouting distance. Screaming at Meg on the bridge. She'd walked away. Walk away, thirty feet, shout at him. Do everything all the psychologists say you shouldn't. Run away from the problem. It was crazy, but if there was one thing he'd learned from Meg and from this time apart it was that every crazy thing had the possibility of the impossible breakthrough within it. Part theatrics, part experiment. He walked away from his son. Shouting STAY THERE. Finding his place on a heathery hillock. Sean thirty feet behind him. Something telling him this was right. To have to shout.

'I'M GOING NOWHERE. TELL ME I'M GOING NOWHERE.'

It might backfire at any second. Sean going home weeping to his mother and an hour before she put together the words that said his father had shouted at him.

Shout again.

'OK, KIDDO. SHOUT "FUCK" AT ME! Your mother doesn't like you swearing. SHOUT, FUCK OFF, DAD!'

Sean laughed, nervous.

'GO ON. SHOUT, FUCK OFF, DAD!'

'FUCK OFF, DAD!'

'I'M A LOSER, TELL ME I'M A LOSER, SAY FUCK, A FUCKING LOSER, YOU'RE GOING NOWHERE!'

'YOU'RE GOING NOWHERE, DAD!'

Yes!

'SHOUT, FUUUUUCK!'

'FUUUCK!'

Thirty feet of heather and grass and wind between them. Shouting obscenities. This was the only way to talk to his son.

'SHOUT, EDINBURGH SUCKS TO FUCK!'

'EDINBURGH SUCKS TO FUCK!'

'SHOUT, COCK ANUS SPUNK CUNT LOSER ARSEHOLE!'

Sean laughing now, doubled over, then getting himself together.

'DAD, YOU'RE COOL!'

Thirty feet away. Oh, he could have run then and kissed that head that no longer wanted to be kissed. Screaming 'Thank you' to the sky. But if he went too close, the stutter would return. He kept it inside, yes, that was what these weeks apart from Meg had taught him. Keep your love inside, let it grow.

A moment then as they climbed back down, through the dirt and grass and heather. Witnessing his son ahead of him, against the city beyond. Sixties high-rises, the burned-out and boarded-up windows. The castle, the city, the grass in the wind, the wind in his ears. Staying dry had cured him, and he could cure his son. He would be patient not pushy. Spending more quality time, not desperate to get away. Finding that correct distance, gradually working closer. No thoughts of leaving his son and his country now. No more escapes. A project, a long-term one. Thirty feet apart. Next week it would be twenty-nine. Then after ten more weeks, nineteen, then the shouting would be quieter. Just tell me, he would call to Sean, and Sean would semi-shout without a stutter. Fuck the therapists, this was his responsibility and his goal. A year and they would be talking on the same patch of earth.

Thoughts that became feelings as they descended the stony path together. As something swelled in his chest and made him the one without speech, unable to speak for fear of the tears he could not show his son. That swelled even more for the hiding.

That this child needed a father and that was his true role. That this child was as much of this landscape as he was of his own genes. The fight not between Edinburgh and himself but against the Scot inside. The subconscious Scot who wanted to fail and blame the world for it. The landscape, the skyscrapers, all parts of his body. Lungs and liver telling him that even if it pissed with rain and there were no jobs and no future he still had to learn to accept. My God, this was his home, and let no one put it down. Proud. He was actually thinking these things. The joy on his son's face. The joy of shouting. To no longer be screaming at the world alone. To hear that voice coming back, the ten-year-old mirror of his own, screaming to the sky.

'My love, my love,' he was murmuring incantation-like on each step as they descended to the car park, all the three hundred yards watching Sean's back. Sean wanted to head back to his place so he could have an hour on Second Life, before the drop-off at his mother's. Yes, that was fine. This phrase over and over in his head as he drove. 'Yes I do.' Checking Sean's face in the rear-view mirror. 'I do. I want to grow old with you.'

Journal

August 21

Tom talking today of picking me up from the airport, of sight-seeing and the Edinburgh Festival (almost like a tourist guide). Me so focused on finishing writing up our last day. I apologised for being distant. Working so hard to get the journal done so I can decide whether it is a book or a script or . . . When I arrive I have to know why. I will not be a tourist. There is something in our last day, I sense, that might make me stay with him. Longer. I cannot find it. Something so small, something he said.

Our conversation rests on pinpoints – he senses that. Too many phone silences today. Something about him now – organisational. Him apologising again for his lack of humour. Sweet man.

Just in case, I have travel insurance. (Ashamed to even think this.) I lose two hundred on the cancellation. Just have to get this done before I can decide, for sure. No, I am being silly. Can't expect him to be my comedian all the time. He's just anxious about my arrival. He worries about keeping me entertained. I can't even tell him that he will be enough. If we can just get back to that point before he left. When I decided we had to be together again.

Last day. (Before the hotel.) We were on Canal after Ground Zero, after the failed cab. A thousand Chinese street stalls – toys, cellphones. My hand in his. Weak. He'd maybe sensed that. That, maybe, why he held my knuckles to his mouth. Kissed.

'You should know,' he said. 'I'll hate myself for this for ever.' No. Too genre. START AGAIN.

'You and me, we are . . .'

No. It moved me.

'Can we drop this and just get some chips?'

Something like that – banal but beautiful – some cultural misunderstanding over a word, something to do with food. I can't get there. Can't recall. Something inappropriate, it had me holding him.

Am seeing us now – arms wrapped tight. Letting go to the feeling that this would only happen once. Giving in to the fear, bred into me, of being seen as one of two who hold each other on a street corner. Emotion in public. I closed my eyes, surrendered to his arms tight and warm. Then as if seeing us from above. Picture of lovers, stuck in their own time, as thousands fought past. No one noticing. The camera ascends from the lovers' faces to capture the others. Chinese, Puerto Ricans, Afghans, street stalls, haggling, upping the price, yellow cabs, trucks offloading – hazard lights flashing. Up and up, the architecture, the chaos of the city, the flow and trade, homes, temporary, negotiable. Then Chinatown, Little Italy, Tribeca, Soho, Union Square, then this tiny island, this country, ocean's edge.

Bullshit cinema language.

What had he said? I agreed to go back to his hotel.

Nothing more said but all understood. We needed to be alone, to talk if we could work things out. The taxi – day of no endings – I was changing again. He had tried to make a joke – stopped before the punchline. Words hanging, on Fifth. View of the Empire State, Herald Square. I had not made up my mind yet – if I forgave him for last night, if I could go back to his hotel.

The door opening. His room. The chambermaids had been in. The bed stripped down and made afresh. Marriott-branded mint on the duvet. Like we'd never been there. Something he was trying to say as he sat there on the edge of the bed.

'They even –'

I knew it before he said it so I did.

'They even packed your bag. Didn't they?'

His shoulders shaking. Low sound, terrible, shaking the room.

'Tom?'

Couldn't help myself, stop the need. All my life maybe running from this. A full-grown man, howling in my childhood ear. My hand on his shoulder.

'It's OK. I'm here. I'm still here.'

The kisses so gentle at first. Then frantic. Lips, neck, eyes, our clothes a thing in the way of skin, closer, the need. Our movement, breath.

He was inside me. Moving together. He stopped short. Cried. Held me.

Day of things started not completed. Final night without finality. That makes me seek a conclusion. I must finish this before I come to you, my love. My tears are happy ones now. The miracle of your weakness teaching me to accept my own. Yes, we are stronger for it. My love, these pages are sixteen years – for you. I blindfolded you that night, my love. Tried to tie you to the bed. Didn't want you to go.

August 22

Today Tom talked of beauty. I was trying to catch up. Things he said – belonging, home. So happy, he said, finally, everything resolved now. I had not understood clearly. He'd wished me goodnight before it was my night. He says he has changed. He has changed for me. I only know him as he was.

Been packing. Arranged for Sal to come and water my plants.

Am rushing this now. Afraid I will spoil it with haste.

I must try to write of beauty. The beauty that makes me want more. The one moment that has convinced me to go to him. That thing he said.

TRY AGAIN.

Our last night. His hotel room. Waking after our nap – maybe 10 p.m – to find him touching my face, staring.

'Look at you.' His fingers on my cheek, my lips. Suddenly aware of how I was. Half undressed, skirt tucked up around my waist.

AGAIN.

I had blindfolded him before. Just a game. He said it was fine to reverse roles. I'd put it over his eyes, stood back then, watching him, prone and vulnerable. Only one minute then he said it was too much. He had to see me – couldn't let our last night pass without seeing me. Enough of playing games. I'd been hurt by that, like he was saying the blindfold for me had been just a game. In those few minutes when he'd lain there naked on the bed this mad thought had flashed before me. I could tie him up, could leave him there all night. Make him miss his flight. He pulled the eye mask off, apologising – maybe he would never understand what I'd felt, he said. He was maybe the opposite, had to see to believe.

How had I felt then? Like a whore – all I'd wanted to show him was how much more it felt to touch and not see.

Start again.

He lay there stroking my face. Calming me. Touching my lips.

'That little scar. So beautiful. I'll never be able to forget your lips,' he said and pulled away.

'I'm sorry. I shouldn't have. I've ruined it now.'

'What?' I was asking, feeling it was my fault. 'What about my lip?' Covering my imperfection with my fingers. Afraid to tell him the story of how it had come about. That night when Michael pushed me.

He leaned on his elbow, smiled to himself, kissed my chin, reached to kiss my lip, my scar. I pulled back.

'What? Tell me.'

'No.'

'Please.'

'You sure?'

'Yes, for chrissake!'

'OK, OK.'

He rolled on to his back then, staring at the ceiling.

'Something I've learned. I don't know if it applies to men the same way it does to women.'

I had to know. His portentous gravitas. 'C'mon, what film are we in now? Tell me!'

'No film.'

He took the blindfold again and placed it over his eyes, not fastening it.

'OK – you must never tell a woman what's most beautiful about her.'

'What? This some theory of yours? God, you're such a sexist old fogey.' I tickled him. Had to know.

'Never tell,' he repeated.

I know the jist of it. But as I try to recall it the language seems foreign. Not mine. Or his. Maybe he read it somewhere.

'That one thing you find so beautiful. That tiny thing she does, all the time, that she seems totally unaware of, which only proves to you how innate her beauty is, that is a secret even to herself. The way she raises her shoulder to her cheek when you stroke her there. The way she plays with her hair. The way she looks down when you are talking then slowly raises her head, her eyes looking up at you through her hair with that smile that grows as she comes full face to you. She doesn't know that she does that. "You do, you do, it drives me crazy!" you want to say, to make her laugh. But you can never tell her.'

And I wanted to know. Had he done all those things as he'd told me, as if by way of illustration, over the past few days? Stroked my cheek and turned his fingers through my hair. Even as he was saying these things I found myself blushing and lowering my head, then after a breath, raising my eyes to look at him through my hair. At first flattered then feeling betrayed. That he had done this with so many women before. Some male routine. My reactions so similar to so many other women. Seeing him with other women in the future. Then angered that he could take me apart like this. Reduce me to some effect. Then touched by the melancholy tone of his voice. I had to know. Where? From something he'd read. It sounded like Stendhal or Kierkegaard's *Diary of a Seducer*. The Marquis de Sade even. I had to know what men knew even if it would undo everything I had thought was secret to myself.

'Tell me.'

'If you tell her of that one thing, she will try to find it in herself, become conscious of it. Self-conscious.'

He was talking of her not me. I needed to grasp the 'me' from the 'she'.

'Tell me.'

'She will either try not to do it again or become curious and try to feel what it feels like when she does it. She'll be so amazed at first that you found this thing in her. This turn of her head, this bite of her lip. Will want to see herself as you do, through your eyes. She'll practise it in the mirror for you. Go through all the moves, raise her shoulder, look up at herself through her hair, and that thing, once so innocent, will become a performance of its former self.'

Our last night and he apologised for spending it in this abstract manner. I asked him to go on, get to the end. Calmed him with touch, wanting to know.

'And one day when she has done it for you deliberately, perfected her thing to make you happy and you do not respond, she will think that you no longer find her beautiful. So you must never tell her of the way she plays with a wine glass, of the way she closes her eyes when music touches her, of the way she walks on her tiptoes even when not wearing heels, of the way she sings to herself when dressing, of the way her hips brush against yours when you walk hand in hand.'

'No, stop stop. You got this from somewhere. What's the book?'

'Shhh. Ma bonnie lass. Let me finish.' Some old Scots accent, some device to throw me off the scent.

'Rimbaud, right?'

His eyes still closed, his voice relentless then.

'Never tell her of this one special thing she does. Keep it inside and when she catches you with that hidden smile on your face and says, "What? What is it?" you must simply say, "Nothing, oh, nothing." Teach her how to appreciate your nothings and to know that they are full of so much. Never tell her of the way she blows the hair from her face every few minutes. Of how she makes these "mmmm" noises when she eats, of how when she paints her toenails her face is filled with some unspeakable sadness, of how laughter starts inside her, rising from her crotch to her belly, her chest, then flushing through her face. You must, most of all, never tell her of how her laughter makes you weep for all of the days ahead when you will not be the one that has made her laugh.'

I have to stop again. Had he even said these things? This nineteenth-century voice. Am I trying to reach a conclusion? Falling back on other texts?

Our problem: perhaps we are both so well versed in texts on love, wanting it but quoting at each other. And that is maybe what made me weep as he spoke, eyes closed, facing the ceiling. My poet, my drunk plagiarist. Us both stealing texts and me wanting them to be authentic on our last day. I had said I was living in the wrong century, that he looked like Lord Byron.

'Go on,' I said.

'Tell her of her beauty and you will have destroyed another part of her that was once spontaneous. You will be helping her on her way to exhausting what she has left of herself that is unknown. With her next lover she will consciously make an effort not to do that thing that she does. Or do it deliberately to see if he finds it beautiful, and if he does she will be touched by the melancholy of yet another subtle loss. Another part of herself sacrificed to self-consciousness. And since the last gesture has become artifice she will push you, as time passes together, to find that thing she does not yet know about herself. So you must tell a little lie to protect her from the knowledge that will destroy – tell her when she asks, 'What, what is it?' that you were thinking of something else. A song, the way the light hits the curtains. And as you lie, you should know that, somewhere inside, she knows it too. That lie is saving you both, because, like you, she too has her things about you. You asks her, "What, what is it?" And she will raise her head slowly, and look up at you through her hair, and play with her wine glass, and in that silence you will both know that there must always be secrets. Secrets . . .'

He was whispering. His last words hard to make out.

'Tell me.'

'Secrets you must always keep from each other.'

His tears on my hand.

'My love. So beautiful, who wrote that?'

He buried his face in my breast.

'My love, where did you get this from?'

He started stuttering, stammering, fragments of words, gasping breaths.

'Eight years of . . .'

'My love. Shh, shhh. My melancholy Scottish man. Just tell me.'

'I'm no writer,' he said. 'You write better than me. I'm sorry.

If I could just write like you, my love. Such things, no one has heard, not in so long . . . I'm . . . I'm so sorry . . . I . . .'

'Just tell me, shh. Eight years . . . Working in TV, you wrote your own scripts and nobody wanted them, is that it?

'No, no, Jesus. Eight years . . .'

'Tell me.'

His breath finally calming in my arms.

'. . . Of marriage.'

He wept. I held him then and we slept. To love someone and not tell them why. The eyes that would tell me of my beauty, closed.

The scar on my lip. That I sometimes covered with my hand when laughing because I knew the skin stretched. A defect. I touched it.

The thought then that if a scar from violence could be a thing of beauty, then all could be redeemed.

Then stroking his face. Letting myself explore his defects. His weak chin. Balding head. Greying eyebrows, the single strands that stuck out silver. Nostril hair. The sheet I pulled back, to see, to hold, to look. His sagging belly. His shrunken dick. Looking at him. Sleeping man, vulnerable, drinker, weeper, man with none of the things I have desired then feared in men. Man sleeping, childlike.

To tell him it all now. He is asleep in Edinburgh. But what if?

What if all the problems in the past were to do with saying too much? This destructive need for total disclosure. What if, finally, with Tom, we can live without the need to own each other, the hatred that ensues from that? What if we could live, secretly not talking of our love, keeping it alive through denial, acknowledging the need for distance?

We had talked of this before. Day two. How lovers make themselves believe that every time it is new. The willed amnesia. How every lover subtracts from what is left. How I loved grunge because of Michael and Hemingway because of Jed and miso soup because of Arturo and Bob Marley because of Tony. But what if it was the other way round? If every lover had not been failure and waste? If each had been subtly building to the point where all these things would come together in summation? What if all those failures had been necessary to take me to the point where I would meet another in whom all of my other lovers were forgiven? For whom all my failings were a thing of beauty that I can only ever learn from eyes staring back into my own? And you will see something in me that I cannot know. And that shall be our secret. Shhh. Don't tell me. My You, we are both you, and in that we lose our selves.

Yes, must put an end to love stories. You will write the ending with me. That is the only way.

To live with a secret. Like this journal. Maybe I shall write it of all our days and years, and when you come to me at the end of a day in Edinburgh and put your hands on my shoulders and ask what I am writing I shall say, 'Oh, nothing.'

Not the crushing need to possess, not this tortured fluctuation between suffocation and escape but finally this need for distance, acknowledged, between us, every day.

Just confirmed my flight. I arrive in Scotland in four days. (My little secret – I may never come back – Shhhh. Remember – don't even tell him.) Must play it cool on the phone today. Shhh.

Call

'. . . to the Highlands and live in a caravan with hippies.'

'Wait, Tom, great, stop. I'm just worried about excess baggage.'

'We'll drive north and find an abandoned hotel and have our pick of a hundred empty rooms.'

'But they've been clamping down. Don't you read the papers? New security measures – they can pull you in and ask about your relationship to the person you're staying with. I'm worried about passport control.'

'I want to show you it all, my love.'

'OK, OK, but it's nine here. The flight's tonight from Newark – 9.25 p.m. That's, wait a minute, 3.25 a.m. your time. The I 215. I get in to Edinburgh at 9.05 a.m.'

'Wait, hold on, you get in when, today?'

'Tomorrow, silly, I have to pack now.'

'But how many hours till I see you?'

'OK, I drive to Manhattan, I hang out with Sally, I just wanna say goodbye, a half a day, then I get my flight at . . . I have to head off now.'

'My love, how many hours?'

'Time zones, I can't do the math.'

'You get in at?'

'Tomorrow, your tomorrow – 9.05 in the morning.

'It's 3 p.m. here.'

'OK, so eighteen hours. I dunno. You're so sweet, but you want me to miss my flight?'

'Yes, no, of course not. Sorry . . . I love you.'

[Silence.]

'Jesus, I hate that.'

'What?'

'Every time – it's like this contest and you always say it first and then all I've got is saying it again, then we just keep on going, like saying it more would make it, I dunno, mean more or . . . Why can't I just say "I love you" first?'

'My Meg. You're doing your inverted commas thing again.'

'Well, I am in analysis after all.'

'You're so . . . New York.'

'Now you're doing it.'

'What?'

'Don't tell me you're not, like it's just so New York to be in analysis. That's what you just did, Tom.'

'You could hear me using inverted commas down the phone?'

'You said it smiling.'

'You heard me smiling?'

'Yes, yes! And I'm smiling too now cos you just won't let me go! I really have to. You can tell me tomorrow. You're being a pig.'

'Oink-oink. Baby [laughter], you're over-analysing now.'

'Typical thing –'

'– for a man to say. [Laughter.] You are my love, my only love. My Meg.'

'I guess I am. So how do I get to say it?'

'Simple. I love you.'

'If you beat me to it, maybe I should just say nothing in reply.'

'I could get paranoid.'

'I thought silences were supposed to speak louder than words.'

'Not down the phone.'

'There are some people out there who just say I love you and I love you too. No problem. Daily. Jeez! Tom, I have to pack.'

'How's about you pretend I didn't say it first?'

'The thing is, it can't be a reply. Saying I love you is not a reply. It's got to burst out of you. Don't you think?'

'So, I get to say it first on Mondays, Wednesdays and Fridays, and you get to say it at the weekends.'

[Laughter.]

'I'm serious, Tom. I do . . . I hate saying it second, not because I don't mean it, just that it sounds so . . . Why do you always have to jump in first?'

'I'm a needy man.'

'I just need a few seconds and then I could say it.'

'So just say it.'

'I can't now.'

'I'll be quiet, you say it first.'

[Laughter. Silence.]

'I'm waiting. C'mon, hit me with your best shot!'

'You are so not being funny.'

[Laughter.]

'Go on, just for me. My little Meggie moo.'

'I'm trying. [Silence.] This is silly.'

'OK, so we do it with lines from movies, we do the "as Lauren Bacall once said to Humphrey Bogart".'

'As Lauren Bacall once said to Humphrey Bogart.'

'I love you madly.'

'I . . . did they say that? I can't . . .'

'You don't have to do the Bogart voice. OK. How about songs?'

'Like . . . ?'

'I love you till the day I die.'

'I don't know. Sorry. I'd like to say something different that means the same. Without analysing.'

'*Chex kir la blue.*'

'That's what, Czech?'

'Serbo-Croat. How's your French?'

'*Mon Tom. Je t'aime.*'

'*Nazdrovia.*'

'No, I know that – cheers in Russian!'

'OK, expletives then. I'm running out of languages here. I fucking love you, as they say in Edinburgh.'

'I fucking love you too.'

'*Vrat teen sl boon.*'

'German?'

'No. Just made it up, give it a go. *Scomusc talor. Togal sbumety.*'

'The Cocteau Twins.'

'Yeah, yeah yeah.'

[Laughter.]

'*Vros duble muff.*'

'You know there's no such thing as a private language.'

'I know, I know – *Oy squelcha licky lick.*'

'*Oy vey, Tom-ushka*, what was that?'

'A nationality that does not exist, yet. We could live there.'

'Stop, mine Tomascino! I gotta pack, sleep, the appalling habits of humans.'

'*Istob deem deem dunky dunky . . .*'

'. . . What is that, doughnuts? Are you on acid, Tom?'

[Laughter.]

'I love you.'

'You said it first again, see!'

'I did.'

'You fucking did.'

'I love you.'

'Stop it, you're getting –'

'I fucking love you, You.'

'See you tomorrow.'

'Whose tomorrow? Yours or mine? The earth spins, spin the wheel, take a chance.'

'My You, you are so funny but I really, really have to pack now.'

'OK.'

'And Manhattan – you promise you won't freak out this time. I'll be spending most of today with Sally – I know you hate her. Will we be OK this time?'

'Yes, my love. No more freaking out. Night-night, my Meg.'

'I'm in full sunlight here, Tom. Do I have to explain all this again?'

'Sunlight, right, daytime. What day are we on?'

[Laughter.] 'Night-night, my man.'

'God, I hate our real names. It's light here too.'

'Night-night, even though it's your day. See you in mine.'

'See you in yours. Yeah and I love you.'

'Wow – See – you said it first.'

'Did I really?'

'Shh, our little secret. Have a safe trip, see you so soon, my You.'

Waiting

Trying to be his old humorous self, the call had left him exhausted. It was just after 3 p.m. with him now and she would not arrive till tomorrow, and in that time there would be no phone contact. She'd be driving to Manhattan, and it would be difficult to chat in transit, she'd said. She would be stopping over at Sally's, and the situation was awkward at Sally's; so no possibility of an intimate exchange. Then booking a cab, to make sure to catch the 21.25, with two-hour obligatory check-in time. Calling from airports always made her fraught, she'd said, too much human confusion interrupting. So she would text, not call, when she got to Sally's, to the plane, to say she was on schedule. Then the nine hours of silent flight.

These details told in a text message. A long one, with many Xs. And he'd cancelled, after much negotiation with the ex, Sean's usual negotiable Friday-night stay so he could meet Meg, alone, at the airport. A sense now that these next eighteen hours might be the most difficult of his life.

An hour since her text and so much to be happy about, but he was waiting. Little left of him that was not waiting. His pulse counting the seconds, he caught himself holding his breath. In the attempt to laugh it off, he told himself he was becoming some cinema cliché of a man waiting. Montage of shots. De Niro alone. Pacing, trying to watch TV, smoking out the window, staring at passing strangers, pacing, staring the face down in the mirror. 'You looking at me? You looking at me?' He was walking from room to room, fidgeting, picking up things. A taxi receipt from the hall floor, a book from the bedroom, he'd emptied the bin in the kitchen and put in a new bin liner and tied the old one even though it was only half full. Still only midday but he'd run himself a bath with some of the anti-stress oils Morna had given him. Then decided against. Didn't want to have to rush out of the wet, feet slipping on the lino, if she changed her mind and called.

Yes, he was pacing. And it was stupid to check the email again. She wouldn't even be at Sally's yet. Trying not to think of Sally's coven counselling Meg in her eleventh hour.

'I mean, is it, like, marriage or what?'

He sat in front of the TV trying to calm himself. Think. Think of something, she'd said, something beautiful, so beautifully her. The last week when he'd woken her early through impatience and need and she had been so graceful, so sleepily poetic.

'The sun's rising,' she'd said and he was laughing, telling her it was impossible because it was still morning with him so it had to be her night. 'Maybe there's two suns,' she said. So her.

He would take a nap to kill a few hours. She was leaving at 21.25. Minus six time zones. Tomorrow minus six. Impossible arithmetic. Pathetic, he knew, but he'd brought the landline to his bedside and placed it beside his pillow. Just in case she rang him in the middle of her night or flight if that was even possible. He closed his eyes.

Waiting was just one word but there were so many nuances within it. He spent maybe a half-hour trying to work out all the thesaurus variations. Gave up. Pulled out one of his favourite printout pictures of her. Shopping together in Soho. It would always be like this with her. Her walking ahead. Her six hours behind, ten years ahead. If only he'd met her ten years from now. Impossible arithmetic.

Her face on the bedspread. His cock in his hand. A wank to get him to sleep.

Look at you. My pretty, naughty girl. Your cocky sexy cleverness.

Five futile minutes killed struggling to come. How many more attempts over the next day and night? He put her pictures away. The phone beside his pillow. Perhaps it'd be better on the bedside table, less chance of fumbling, dropping it if she rang. He didn't want to freak her out by picking it up after just one ring. Make her wait, better, two, three rings, so that she wouldn't know he'd been doing nothing else but waiting.

This is not panic. I do not need a drink. Breathe. Breathe.

Only two minutes since he last checked. Numbers – three weeks dry, seven without a woman's touch. Well, not quite, he'd wanked in Morna's presence. No touch. Thank God for that. No good at lying. If he'd fucked Morna Meg would see it on his face. Thank God nothing had happened.

Damn mattress. Shoulder's aching from holding the phone to his ear for so many hours in the last week. Still light outside. Hours of it to get through. Up on his feet. Pacing again. A video then. One from his art-house collection. Tarkovsky, Godard, Pasolini, Wenders, Herzog. Three hundred, all on VHS. His DVD collection was pitifully small, mostly just sci-fi for Sean to watch. Right, why not arrange them alphabetically? That would kill an hour or more. Fifteen minutes in and he was distracted again, reading the blurbs on the back. Eight Godard movies. *Le Mépris* with Brigitte Bardot, story of a scriptwriter whose wife grows to detest him for selling out. English translation – *Contempt*. No, he couldn't.

Staring into the fridge. Organic broccoli, rocket, spinach, beetroot, Little Gem lettuce, wild salmon, chorizo, spanako-pita, taramasalata. This all for her. Couldn't face eating. Don't disturb one thing in there. They were arranged like an artwork.

Almost two hours killed. He could walk. That's it. No point sitting here just waiting, old misery guts, get your new trainers on. Not just a walk. Go for a jog.

Moments of enthusiasm as he got dressed in his new sports gear. Not the countryside, not the car, he'd jog round the city centre and work out all the places he'd show her when she got here. Great plan. Four hours more of daylight.

Out the door and jogging on the spot trying to decide which way to go. Not south to the villas of Marchmont. No, up Leith Walk to the centre. The National Portrait Gallery. Yes. The Royal Mile, pick up a programme from the festival people on the way. Spend hours later working out things for her to see.

He was off. Not looking at the street. Breathing her in with each step. Rhythm of feet on ground, of lungs, in out, mind finally coming into sync with body. Not even seeing the charity shops and pubs and off-licences and pawnbrokers and massage parlours. In out. Heading to the centre.

And he was not killing time, because he was getting fit for her and she would redeem it all. So many people, look at them, bustling round never having a moment of communion with themselves. These normal people. These norms. Hating everyone else as they queued in line at the supermarket. Like everyone was in your way. Like life would start as soon as you got out of the store.

The top of Leith Walk and his lungs were raw from the incline. Then it started, the quiet, growing euphoria. He turned the corner past the obscene concrete shopping mall and then, the slow cinematic reveal, there was the Castle, Princes Street, the George IV Bridge. So many years taking it all for granted but now he was seeing it with her eyes. Hearing her voice.

'My God, but the buildings are from when? I mean century-wise?'

'Seventeenth.'

'No way!'

'Yes way. The first floor, then each century or so they built upwards.'

Breathing in his city, and yes, it was more beautiful than New York. Edinburgh, the Athens of the North. Yes, it would move her so much she would stay. They would walk hand in hand through heritage sites and see re-creations of life in other centuries. Hand-woven cloths. Tartans dyed with natural plant colours. These things he had long since viewed as kitsch which she would renew for him.

Jogging the Royal Mile now, past St Giles Cathedral. He would walk her inside and show her the statue of John Knox, explain as she hugged his arm that Knox held the key to his self-loathing. That there were still to this day followers of Knox in the islands of Harris and Lewis, hardliners who believed laughter was a sin, that singing was permissible only in homage to the Lord, who sang hymns in Gaelic, and each followed the other and they were all out of sync, but their voices sounded like waves breaking. Terrifying and beautiful. He would tell her these things.

Running too fast, he had to stop and pause for breath.

Hundreds of young people around him. So many cultures. His makeshift jogging gear was no doubt embarrassing to the fashionable eye, but the young people were dressed as goblins and ghouls and queens and kings. Of course, the festival. She would be here just at its end. They would watch the fireworks together. No need to tell her that Edinburgh made all of its money in one month from the tourists. That after the festival it sank back down into poverty, the only lines queuing not those for the Japanese Noh theatre but those at the jobcentre.

Negative thoughts descending. Keep on running, but he couldn't. Thousands of tourists. No space. The queue for the Castle covering the cobblestones.

The statue of David Hume just feet away. And he'd tell her it was the Scottish Enlightenment philosophers that paved the way for the revolution that founded her country. That Scotland's own revolution had failed. Our own. He would say 'our', he would be proud to be Scottish for once as he told her. His sense of humour which she thought so dark, so ironic, was really just a national trait. Negative wit of a downtrodden people with no real nation status.

He struggled to get through the tourists. No progress. A man dressed as William Wallace posing for photographs with tourists just ten feet from him, five pounds a photograph. Dressed in the plaid. They looked Japanese but had American voices. Four of them in their twenties, standing beside Wallace, giggling, as their friend set the shot. The Wallace raising his plastic broadsword to the sky, striking a pose, silently screaming at the heavens, his face painted blue, his white teeth gritted.

And he'd tell her that there was a statue in a car park in Stirling, near the site where Wallace defeated the forces of Long Shanks, the English King, in 1312. And the statue was made by a local man in 2001, and in its naive style, recreated the exact visage of Mel Gibson in *Braveheart*. That every six months or so the locals knocked the head off, seeing it as an insult to their heritage. That three years ago he'd had to film the statue for a promo video for the local council and they'd had to add the head digitally in the edit suite.

That was it. Breath and wit wasted. A girl dressed as Mary Queen of Scots handed him a flyer for something called *Mary Gives Head*.

This country. This fucking country. You had to laugh.

Five thirty now, two hours spent and the jog home was listless and the shop signs were now messages to him. Poundstretcher. Save the Children. Fingertips Massage Salon. The Kerry-Oot. Two for one. Buy two get one free. Bubbly.

She would want to toast her arrival.

It wasn't for him, he wouldn't touch it. But the Scots were aye thrifty and the deal in the off-licence was exemplary. Two for one, so good in fact that he doubled it. Quantity at a certain point becomes quality. He was walking home, not jogging now, because the jogging might break the four bottles. Many excuses like that over the two hundred yards. The reality was within five minutes he was home and she would not be here for another – mental arithmetic – what sixteen hours or so. She would arrive with Veuve Clicquot anyway and he'd have to face that. So why not?

Champagne. So much to celebrate. She loves you. Loves you so much that she's coming to you. Seven weeks apart. And you've been faithful to her. Jesus, that was something to drink to. A year with Morna and he'd shagged how many behind her back? All of that over now, drink to that. That night with Morna, he'd proved his integrity. No penetration. Till death do us part.

The cork popped. Home and sitting there with celebratory bottle and pen and paper and a festival brochure. Yes, the plan was working out. Circling events, checking times, drawing up a shortlist, cutting it back, planning the time required to travel from place to place.

Her first day in Edinburgh.

10 a.m. Gerhard Richter retrospective at the Museum of Modern Art.

12 p.m. Bali dancers street theatre. The Grassmarket.

1 p.m. Lunch at the new sushi place. Ichi-ban.

3 p.m. *The Idiot*. Theatrical adaptation of the book by Dostoevsky in the original Russian at the Gilded Balloon.

5.30 p.m. Tequila cocktails in Cuba Libre with authentic flamenco dancing. A bite of indigenous Cuban food.

7 p.m. The Traverse Theatre. New version of the Hindu mystery play *The Mahabharata*.

A bottle done, another opened. Cheers to that. So much to celebrate. She was coming so soon. God, she howled when she came. To be inside her, feeling her muscles tighten round him.

To just lie down. He wasn't drunk. Just a wee snooze. My love. My Meg.

Still daylight outside. He would tell her about daylight.

He was walking along a beach. The sun was setting. There were palm trees above. Textures beneath his feet. The sound of an ocean. Waves breaking every three seconds or so. The horizon was infinite, the waves infinitely the same. He turned and saw the others there. Neo Sinatra, Bo De Niro, Deedee DiCaprio. They walked through him, past him. He was not yet fully formed. Something was wrong. His face and skin and clothes were missing, his movements slow. He was a shadow of a person, in negative against the beach and the palm trees. An absence of information. He walked to the sea and found he could step in and submerge and still breathe underwater. He walked miles and miles beneath the waves looking for another island. There were no fish, whales, seaweed, rocks. Endless graphic grey blue. The drop-down menu said he could fly. He clicked on it and rose through the water to look beyond. The same grey blue on every horizon. The menu said home in Second Life island was 300,000 miles from where he'd started. More by the second. He wanted to know, as he flew, how far he could go before he would return, the world was a globe, it must be sometime soon, a million miles over the same featureless sea. It must soon be the island again.

Tom woke with a start. Dark outside somehow. As the shapes of his bedroom formed, it came to him. Two bottles of bubbly. His fingers searched for his mobile. 9.32 p.m. The mental arithmetic. She was six hours behind. Another how many to go? God, if he could have just slept through the whole night, the whole of the next day. He was up and in that space-time only drinkers know. Waking before night. Dry, brittle, shivering.

The dread as he got to his feet. This thing felt before, in his days of detox, was back. The total silence around him. There were only two things to do to make the silence go away. To go for a jog or have another drink. He had jogged already today and that had been what led him to drink. To drink then. Two bottles of bubbly in the fridge. She'd only expect one when she got here. No, he wasn't back on the booze, this was just a momentary regression. Just a glass to calm the nerves. The pop and the pint glass filled to the brim, swearing as the bubbles spilled over. Gulping down the first mouthful through the bubbles, waiting for them to settle, refilling, half a bottle in a glass. Better, better. Taking a seat. The shivering stopping. Another mouthful. He'd have time tomorrow to freshen up. He'd go for a jog, then wash and shave, eat something, then wait.

Fuck. What now? This tightening in his chest – beginning of a hot rush from chest to face. The voice telling him. Fucking stupid, all this. Teenage fantasy of a long-distance romance. Parody of passion. She would not move to Scotland. Not become a second mother for his child. No second life.

Calm yourself. Another mouthful. See, that's better.

He must not be impatient. His impatience was what had destroyed everything before. He picked up the mobile and checked the time again. His hands, look at the skin, the wrinkles. Meg had placed her hand to his, compared finger length. She had said that his long index finger was an indication of assertiveness. How he must like to get his own way.

She had not texted. Had said she would. She'd been in a car crash, been caught up with a friend, she was out, drinking with other people, men, flirting. Worse, she'd forgotten her promise that she'd text from Manhattan. Worse still – she'd been indifferent to the pain this waiting would cause him.

Anger then. He couldn't sit there second after second in this room she had never shared with him. Damn her and her social life and her friends. He got to his feet. He could not wait like this. Weeks now of waiting for her. How many hours, days, just waiting. He was no longer a man but one who waits. To have a day by himself like before. She had destroyed all that. Ironic that this woman, this dream of escape, had imprisoned him all the more. Made him stare at walls. To hell with their stupid adolescent love. Another drink. Fill it up again. Second-last bottle empty, the last bottle then. No worries, he'd buy another one for her tomorrow, a better bottle.

He couldn't watch a video, he couldn't watch TV because of the celebrities and the adverts and the adverts endorsed by celebrities, he couldn't jog or walk the streets because they would be filled with drunks, he couldn't eat because even the thought of it made him sick. All he could do was sit before the computer. Yes, lose himself in another world. Take the bottle through. Log on to Second Life.

The waves were crashing. He was back on the beach and surrounded by people. Zed Reeves and Tama De Niro and Devil Houston. The animation was better tonight. When he hit the forward button he moved without delay. When he hit fly he flew, when he hit stop-fly he descended. It was the usual place, the place marked haven. Where people started before they journeyed forth. He hit turn and looked at what was before him. Tony Schwarzenegger and Tina Bardot were sitting on a bench together. He walked towards them. The icon said they were chatting. He wanted to sit and chat. He went through the menu to find the sit command. A bubble appeared.

'You do not have enough credits to sit here. Do you want to buy credits?'

No. He walked back and approached a svelte woman in a silver jumpsuit.

Kiki Kidman. The drop-down menu gave him options: chat, shout. A box opened. Speak: 'Hi, Kiki, wanna chat?'

No reply. Kiki turned black. A box opened. 'Kiki is shape-shifting right now.'

Whoever Kiki was. Some woman in Taiwan, or Hong Kong, some man in New Jersey or Suffolk. He walked away.

The speech bubble opened. Message from Ziggy Cruise.

'Hi, Dad,' it said. 'What you doing online?'

Tom hit the turn button. Ziggy was in front of him. His son had changed. Ziggy was a fully grown man now, had a beard and a black suit. Tom wanted to type: 'You should be in your bed.' He hesitated. Drank another mouthful.

'*Thought I'd find you here sometime soon,*' his son said.

He needed to log off, right now. This was no place to meet his son. He typed: '*Nice to meet you too.*'

'*Did you check out the disco? It's total cheese but they play no so bad tunes this time of night. Mum's asleep, by the way. Total fluke meeting you. S'cool though.*'

Ziggy was a man now.

'*Sean, can't do this, I'm new here. Can I call you?*'

'*Follow me – show you some good shit. Be cool. By the way, you got to do something about your avatar – it's not fully formed. Go to appearance on the drop-down menu, and click on change.*'

Sean was talking to him. With attitude. Tom could almost hear his voice.

He followed his son through the park over the beach to this place called Center. Pictures of landscapes floating in the sky, drop-down menus that said 'Go here' – a desert, a snowy waste-land, an infinite city.

'*Cool huh, Dad? You wanna fly to the city with me? Watch a movie together?*'

Tom was in tears.

'*Gotta go.*'

No escaping anything. When was the last time he'd taken Sean to a movie?

'*Gotta go, kiddo.*'

'*Say hi to your girlfriend for me. Mum says I can meet her Weds. That cool?*'

'*Yes. OK. Nite nite.*'

Tom logged off. Minutes staring at the screen, crying. OK, I'm crying I'm fucking crying. Let me be. The glass to the mouth. The trip to the kitchen to refill. OK, he was a drunk, OK, he'd tell Meg about that. Meg, Megan Hunt, Meg hunt, my cunt. He couldn't escape the computer screen.

Email. New.

Meg, my love.

I am in the last hours before you arrive and now everything is clear. I don't think I can bear this. I sleep alone every night.

I am an intimate person. You know that. I need touch, I want to feel you beside me. I hug a pillow and look at your pictures. I wank with porn. Seven weeks now. I am tired and sick. I want to eat your ass, sleep in your sweat, my hand on your waist.

No idea where he was going with this. She would be at Sally's now or on the Brooklyn overpass. She hadn't texted.

Sorry. Sorry. I'm a whore. The last three years I've barely gone four nights without a woman in my bed. I take what I need and it has been loveless. I am so confused. Can't touch another woman after you. Have never cried or laughed like we did. But I need contact. Can't live waiting. It is killing me. I am drinking again. Can't bear this.

An ultimatum. It's weak – I am the man who gave you an ultimatum, a story you'll tell your friends. In time you will forget and get involved with one of your many admirers. I am not an answer. I am someone who worships you and everything you have done and are yet to do and in time you will thank me for releasing you.

It felt better to say these things. He would never show it to her. Get it done. Say the worst, exorcise it. Then tear it up. Meet her at the airport. Another mouthful just to get it done.

You are a perfectionist and I am far from perfect. I am here. I cannot move from here. My ultimatum is a threat now that I write it. My country will thwart and ignore you. There is no place for your passion for life here. I've already answered the question I've been too afraid to ask you. Live with me here. Emigrate to the UK. Stay with me with or without some stupid fucking vow. Promise me you will. I hate this place. I must bring this to a head now. We had this idea I'd meet you at Cannes, at the Venice Biennale – in Seattle, Rome, Hong Kong. I told you I was a success but I live on a tiny salary. I'm sorry if I painted this picture of a glamorous jet-set life for us – believe me, I wanted to believe it. I thought believing it could bring it into being. These are the facts.

After you leave I can't visit you as I said I would. Not in October or December. I have no money. The pressure I have been putting myself under to make more is killing me. I can't live with you for four months in New York. Even two would be a push. One is realistic. Like a holiday. I can't leave my son for any longer than a month. Can't take him with me to be with you.

You can't stay here. New York was an accident. You would become depressed here. I would turn resentful and destroy all that is vital in you. When you arrive you will see I drink to excess. I may be an alcoholic. I don't eat well or exercise enough. I can't take care of myself. I enter into relationships just because I can't face eating alone. I suffer from depression and anger. The anger, like the depression, is abstract, not aimed at anything or anyone. The anger makes me depressed. I have thought often of suicide.

I make women love me then crush them with need. Strong women. I need them to save me. I have done this all my life. No one who has ever loved me will speak to me. I abandon them when I've made them as weak as myself. I search for others and use them up. Emma, Mandy, Liz, Fiona, June, Morna.

I had a strange foresight that something in New York would change me. I told you this. That I sensed something was coming. I thought you were strong, so strong, strong enough to make me change, to help me escape this. But I am so weak.

I want us to stop communication immediately. All of it. Texts, phone calls, letters. I need time. A year even would not be long enough.

I am not asking for you to wait for me. Go and find love and use your energy and your talent. So many people love you, will fall in love with you. Everywhere I went with you their eyes lit up when they saw you. I have felt such jealousy and anger at seeing you with others. It was selfish of me to try to keep you for myself. I would lock you in a cell. Punish you for how free you are. I don't want to discuss this. It has taken me seven weeks to get to this point and I have no energy left. I don't even want your pity. I am not trying to be melodramatic to bully you into staying with me through guilt.

Go, please. Live your life. Go now. I couldn't bear for you slowly to come to these same conclusions about me. You would leave then and it would be harder still. I need to be alone now.

Tom printed it out. All the worst said, the intended exercise – in catharsis – done. But on rereading, all of it was true. He was, really, terrified of meeting her tomorrow. The last of the bottle and still only midnight. The email, unsent, said it all. Fear of messing up in smaller ways – Better to fuck up on his own terms. He knew this pattern. This was his fate, his drunken fate. As solid and welcoming as the phone now in his hand. A relief, a release, like a sigh, an ejaculation. It is ringing, and she will understand. He hears himself sigh before she picks up. He is weeping and that too is a release. He says her name.

'Morna, I'm sorry it's late.'

Journal

August 25

Just woken from a little siesta at Sally's (she insisted we have some celebratory wine with lunch). Since my call to Tom, so playful, this strange inner calm has not left. I said goodbye to the house, sensing that it need not be goodbye – that all the crises of these past weeks were necessary, leading me to something better. The same feeling on the ferry and the drive. The island was quite beautiful this morning (a line of white in the blue) and the roads remarkably clear. Even Sally was calm, did not pry or question. She is happy for me and held my hand over lunch. It's 4 p.m. Five hours twenty-five till my plane leaves the ground. I'm in Charlie's bedroom now (she's at her dad's today), feeling so different from the last time we were here. This urgent panicky need to tie down everything has left now that I'm on my way. Texted him – just simple things – my schedule. No reply of course, he must be sleeping. There may be many trips like this to get through. I may make something of this script or not. Maybe it's a book? Maybe nothing at all. Will see what happens. Strange sense of quiet.

Charlie's Barbie dolls line the walls. She's cut their hair short and given them tattoos. They look punk. Funny, I was a punk. Just laid out my dress and eye mask for the flight. Have put the Cocteau Twins on. Sally's pottering about downstairs.

One thing has come back to me. Maybe the music, maybe the room. Charlie's dad left a year ago. She is eight. My dad left when I was eight. Tom left Sean when he was seven.

A vow to myself now. No more leavings. He has Sean. I will not make him leave his child again. Somehow we will find a way to be together. I will not run away this time. I shall see this through to the end. We will finish our story together.

Heading now to my flight. The end of all my flights. If I could just tell you this, my Love.

Morning

Tom woke in her warmth, her hand over his chest, knees spooned behind his. The smell of her. Rosemary. Morna moaned as he sat upright in bed. An empty bottle of Liebfraumilch on the bedside table. The mobile in his hand, searching through the messages to see if there were any from Meg. 5 a.m. Meg would be here in four hours. One message.

Heading to airport now. Love you so much. xxx

Morna pulled the duvet back over them both. God, it was coming back to him now. He had cried in her arms, it had been the kitchen, he had told her how sorry and scared he was and she'd stroked his head and said, Shh, it's OK. He'd told her that maybe this love for this foreign woman was something he needed because it was his last gasp, and she'd said, Shh, as they drank her wine. The bedroom and still crying, telling her he was so glad she was there, as a friend, because he had no friends, and she had been stroking his back and saying, Shh. Shh, it's OK, just sleep. And how he couldn't sleep because her body was so warm and her touch was too much and couldn't they sleep more apart because he couldn't and maybe he should take the sofa. And she whispered, Shh, just sleep, it's OK. And how he had woken in the middle of the night, half asleep in some dream of Meg, his hand on her hips, the soft curves, the wet between her legs. The rhythm like breathing and her breath quickening and her waking and holding his face and telling him, 'Naw, we're havin' a wee cuddle, that's all, it's OK, you're wae her now, just go tae sleep.' And him then hard and sinking between her legs, just to taste, not a betrayal, he told himself, just a kiss. His mouth wet with her. 'Naw,' she kept saying, sleepy, Naw, not a word but a breath, a rhythm. 'Yuv got tae see her the morrow.' 'Naw, s'not rite. Naw.'

Looking at her now, sleeping. Nothing had happened. His

feet then, on the floor. Slipping on the wet, used condom under-
foot. The images flashing back. His head in his hands then, the
shaking. Her hand on his shoulder.

'S'OK, lie down, gies a hug.'

The weeping. Her arms around his shoulders, her breast
against his back.

'S'awright, Ah'll no tell anyone. S'OK. No like ahm gonnae
stalk ye and come banging on yer door and tell her. It's wur
wee secret. OK?'

The silence of the room.

'I'm sorry. I'm sorry. I'm sorry,' he whispered to the walls,
the door, the woman's face he could not face. 'I'm sorry.'

4
ARRIVALS

Estranged

It wasn't exactly the right word to express what Meg felt as she took her seat on the plane. 'Estranged' was the wrong word. 'Alienated' – too strong, too political. And this had been the problem in the last hour as she'd sat there at the departures gate rereading again all she'd written of their love story. Trying to think of the best possible ending, but failing to find the words. The calm slowly turning into this other feeling. One very much like the one felt in the months before, when an emotion could change in an instant, in a text message or phone call, into its opposite.

'Distanced' was probably closer but was an awkward word. Now that the plane was about to take off, the distance between them had become real, was no longer a fiction they lived daily. She would not be able to speak to him on the flight. There could be no gradual talking through of all the stages – I'm taking off now – I'm over the ocean now – still over the ocean – I'm landing now. This time would be a silent one and when she arrived in Scotland after the lost night of flight, he would be before her, sound and picture in sync. Then she would know if this estrangement, this alienation, this lost word could make the months apart finally bring her back to the state where she could find the right words again. What would be their first words to each other at the arrivals gate? 'Hi.' 'Wow.' 'Darling.' 'Meg.' 'Fuck.' 'Let me take your bag.' 'I brought the car.' 'How was your flight?' 'My love, look at you.'

It wasn't estrangement or distance – the closest word was 'anxiety'. But, as she knew, being aware of the role of narratives in life, before the final act there is always a moment of silent anxiety and doubt. The second narrative peak, the crisis, before the descent into the happy denouement. It was partly the thought of that that'd made her be so decisive on the last day. Calling the airline to ask for a window seat because he said he always took the window seat. And an hour yesterday emailing everyone – she would be in Scotland for a month or maybe more – that she could be contacted by email or cell. The hour she'd spent, mostly on hold, to the server to ensure her cell would work abroad, the extra eighty bucks paid to have the international roaming facility added to her account. The final hours spent online researching Scottish history and Edinburgh, and the Castle, and the seven hundred years of kings. This portrait she'd found from the eighteenth century of one of the Stuarts that looked so much like him. The long nose, the goatee, the world-weary face. The words underneath that read 'The Old Pretender'. That she just had to print out and was going to gift to him on her arrival, with a handwritten inscription beneath that read '*We are not pretending. Meg xxxx*'.

This was fate and fated. It had to be. Act Three was always the inversion of Act One. It started with an airport; it would end with one. And once the story was done, the end reached, then finally she could start to live.

She had to fly with his eye mask. Every detail had to be exact. On arrival, she had to be wearing exactly what she'd worn on their last day together, seven weeks ago. It made her smile as she dressed in the mirror, ten minutes ahead of the schedule she'd set herself – the Vivienne Westwood tartan skirt, the hold-ups and heels he'd asked her to wear for his departure. It made her smile, thinking of his face at the arrivals gate. The ring too. She hadn't worn his wedding ring since that last day. It had been sitting there by the edge of her laptop. A reminder, an idea, but not a thing in itself. She went through this silent ritual of slipping it on her finger again, feeling its weight, its width, the difference in their finger sizes. It might slip off. She wound her hairband round her finger twice to hold it in place. Then, bag in hand, thirty-two minutes ahead of schedule, she said her goodbyes to Sally and was on her way.

The rituals at the airport, now changed because of the latest terrorist scare. The hand baggage had to be no bigger than a certain size. The list of questions about aerosols and soft drinks and vacuum-packed things.

'Did you pack the bag yourself?' 'Has anyone asked you to carry something for them on to the plane, miss?' Did she look like a miss? Wearing a wedding ring.

She stared out of the window as the plane accelerated. Trying to put herself in his seat, on his day of departure. The lift in her gut, this sense of the impossibility of flight. Of putting your life in the hands of others. Fate, fated, she told herself. Give in, let go, surrender. It's OK to be weak, he said. The heights of New York seen so many times before, but from five hundred feet above they seemed seemed like a drawing, a sketch. Child-like. A spoiled child's drawing. Filling every inch of the paper. Insubstantial and foolishly arrogant. Looking through his window, touching his wedding ring. Yes, feeling as he must have felt. The impossibility of everything. Like an airplane, at once heavy and light. Hanging in the sky, like his suspension bridges. She might never be coming back.

The woman beside her had put on her headphones. It was OK to do the same. Meg popped the three valerian into her mouth, swallowed with the complimentary water. Did not take the eye mask from the complimentary travel pack but went into her pocket, as ritual required, and found his. She pulled it over her eyes and in self-imposed dark measured and assessed each thing she had done to try to duplicate his departure. Maybe an hour or so of trying to, but she couldn't sleep. Pulled the mask off and suddenly felt very alone on this flight with three hundred people. Sleeping faces so prone and vulnerable. The old Hasidic man stretched out on the three empty seats, his toe pushing through the hole in his sock. The young Asian woman sucking her thumb with her headphones still on, her movie long finished. The old woman snoring beside her. Wide awake, staring. Extras, they were extras in her romantic drama. Imagining them in other scenarios she would write for them. Yes, she was cold, alienated, estranged. A scriptwriter surrounded by extras. The plane dipped to the right. Right was east. Suddenly she was seized by anxiety again. She was not travelling to Scotland to be reunited with her lover, but so she could find the ending to her script. Tom was not a story. She had been faithful to him in these seven weeks but still she had betrayed him with this other man, this man he had been for just a week.

The first thing she would do on arrival, once they'd settled, maybe in his car, maybe once they were inside his home, once they'd had the duty-free champagne – she would confess. I have written this story about us, my love.

I-Map told her that they were travelling at 630 mph. That the Atlantic Ocean was 21,000 feet below, that it was 3.32 hours till arrival. None of this computed. There was just her and a window. And the window was black, a mirror of her waiting face. She pulled on his eye mask again. Yes, this must have been how he had felt.

Arrivals

Just one drink to kill the fear. But he had to drive. Pick her up from the airport. Meg coming through the gate. Smiling. What would he say?

The turn-off to Glasgow, a mile before the turn-off to the airport. The M8. This shorthand Morna had in her texts, not calling him My love, My you. M8 her secret code for everything they were. Mate. M8. He could still smell her on his skin.

The sign then. Forth Road Bridge – Airport. The choice. Fifty miles an hour and just over a minute to the turn-off to the airport. More than an hour ahead of schedule.

He would lie to her. Nothing happened with Morna. Tell himself that. Bury it. These thoughts stuck in the logjam before the turn-off.

Meg's insistence all last month that meeting Sean was so important to her. That they could in some way bring Sean up together.

Meg, please. I don't want you to come. Please, let your flight be delayed. The plane diverted. A freak weather storm forces you to land in Finland. You are snowbound there for a week, it is only another week till you have to go home – you have to make the decision to see me or to fly home. Fly home, go. Leave me alone. Please. Those first seconds, when you see me. When you see me against the other bodies in the airport.

Go please, get back on your plane. Let me not have to face you. A storm, ice on the runway or oil – you can't land. Leave me alone. Let me drink cheap vodka and fuck women who I'll impress with how well travelled I am. You go. Let me stay here and tell them where I've been till I'm done.

If you knew about Morna. If you knew Morna.

'Shh, it's our wee secret. Ah'll no tell her.'

The smell of her.

The turn-off just there, and he'd been so anxious to get there quicker. Pissing other drivers off. Indicator jumping from left to right every few hundred yards. He was in the wrong fucking lane for the airport and the turn-off was getting closer and the fucker in the SUV wasn't letting him back into the correct lane. OK, he would drive across the bridge then head back, take the B-road and get there even faster. The bridge turn-off was empty. He felt the pull of it. He was a paranoid hour ahead of schedule. Nothing behind him.

The bridge wasn't a symbol for Meg now – just a bridge, he told himself that.

To park at the edge and laugh at it all. To have done with this romantic Scottish crap about standing on the edge. Once and for all, to laugh at himself and still be laughing when he saw her walk through the arrivals gate.

She was your only hope of change and you drowned it. You want it to be like this. You want to be miserable, useless Eustace. You.

He parked in the pre-ramp car park. Got out. The wires of the suspension bridge familiar in his hand again. The grey waters of the Firth of Forth, the waves whipped by wind not reflecting the sky at all. Not mirroring the bridge or the planes passing overhead. Just shadows, these things were, in the waters that hypnotised, that pulled you down into their cold grey indifference.

Waking

The jolt of landing had woken her. Had she slept through the whole flight? This woozy sense of being hung-over. The elbow in her shoulder.

'Sorry?'

'S'awright, hen.'

So the woman was Scottish. And talking to her, her nodding at the in-flight TV, all Meg got were fragments – movie, Tom Cruise and a word that sounded like poof.

'I'm sorry, I have my earplugs in. What was that?'

'Nae worries. Nae probs. S'awright.'

'Are we in Edinburgh already?'

'Aye.'

'Aw. Did we fly over the Castle?'

'Aye, probly. Ye fay the States then, eh?'

'Am I from the States?'

'Aye, like a said, yer whit, New York?'

'Yes, I live in New York State.'

'Aye, it's no bad. No ma cup o' tea bit whit can ye do, eh? So whit yea daein here?'

'What am I doing here?'

'Boyfriend, is it?'

'Well, actually . . .'

'Oh aye, lots of Yanks daein that now. Wimin. A bit sad tho, don't ye think, thut ye havtae come aw this way tae fine a man. I seen a thing on the telly. Aw these 'merican wimin flyin over tae find a man, cos o' the water. Christ, it's the what-you-call-it. The pill in the water. Fuckin' whatsit called. Estro. No fuckin' oestrogen, aye, in the water system in New York. S'a fact, serious, like. Turns men intae poofs.'

My God, it was a different planet.

'No that ahm prejudiced or nothin', keep masel tae maself,

ah mean it's a fine place, bit Ireland's the place fur you – the sooth, aw these wee villages an that, five men tae every woman. I'd dae it masel if uh hud the dosh.'

Laughing to herself as they disembarked. Tom didn't have an accent this strong. And all the things he'd said about Scotland, all the clichés, seemed to be lining up in front of her to get through the passport check. Fascinating, to come from a city so full of cultural difference and still be dumbfounded by such otherness.

Just five or so minutes and she would be on the other side. His face waiting for her. That smile that broke on his face that in turn broke something inside her. She would let him speak first just so as to hear his first words. She texted him. *Am here. C u in 2 minutes. xxx.* Holding her breath as she walked to the sliding door of the arrivals gate, then stopping and closing her eyes for a second, waiting for all this to become real. A second, telling herself this is Edinburgh. I'm in Edinburgh. She stepped towards the sliding doors and they opened. Deep breath. Stepping over the threshold.

A face rather like Tom's, the long nose, the weak chin, waiting. A little boy running past her into the man's arms, the mother stooping behind her to pick up the child's dropped bag. A white teenage girl with streaked blonde hair in the arms of her lover, his hands fondling her ass as he lifted her from the ground. A large Italian woman, struggling with an overloaded trolley, bags of duty-free alcohol jangling past her as her steps slowed. She searched but couldn't find him. The faces instead of two middle-aged men in worn suits, like Russian gangsters, the one on the left also like Tom but with red hair and shorter. A taxi driver with a handwritten sign that read MCIVOR. A young man in a shiny nightclubbing shirt standing beside him laughing to himself, with a sign in his hand that read I LUV YOU. Tom was not there. She was sure now that her eyes had scanned the whole area. There was no barrier for people to wait behind, just elasticised security tape stretched between two temporary stands. Every face searched in the place and the place was tiny. He'd joked with her just two days ago that it was more like a bus station than an international airport. He wasn't there. Maybe because of the delay in customs. He hadn't replied to the text she sent him when waiting in line, and then during those awful ten minutes or so when the pasty-faced man in the ill-fitting official suit asked her the same four questions twice. Length of your stay? How much money do you have on your person? Are you here to work? Relationship to person accommodating you? She'd hesitated about saying lover, she'd been sure he wouldn't have that on his list. Friend. Good friend, she'd said. We are. The delay with the queue and then the questions had maybe been as long as forty-five minutes. She'd possibly made it worse by becoming frustrated with the guy, almost shouting at him – 'Do I look like a terrorist?' Tom had maybe gone for a cup of coffee or a cigarette. But the Starbucks was right there to her left and from where she'd stopped she could see the arrow sign for the smokers' zone pointing to outside. She scanned the bodies beyond the glass, huddled by the door, hoping he would walk into her field of vision. Minutes and he wasn't there. He wasn't here.

Grey linoleum, grey walls, yellow-grey strip lights. Newark in miniature.

She had planned to step past this point into his arms. Instead she spent minutes just standing there, looking up every time the sliding doors to the outside opened, hope rising in her chest. Her one shoulder bag was getting heavy. Her two wheelie bags, one in each hand, resting now against her hips. People pushing past with 'excuse me's and one who had said, 'Fur fuk sake.' She freed her hands and got her phone out, texting him again. *Where ru, my love?* Another minute and another fifteen or so hopeful entrants through the sliding doors and she was texting again. *Am here – where ru?* Another minute, another text. She was hoping as her eyes were on the screen that she would suddenly feel a hand on her shoulder. *AM GETTING WORRIED xxx.*

Fifteen minutes and she felt people were staring at her. She dragged her bags towards Starbucks. Getting more than worried because he was never late, was always the one to call or text minutes before they'd scheduled. The last of her fellow passengers filed past her, hugging and kissing and weeping in the arms of the waiting. He was not here. From Starbucks a tall man in a suit kept staring. The place was emptying, unlike any airport she'd been in before. There were maybe ten or eleven people left, some sipping coffee, some at the bureau de change, others in the newsagent's. He was not here and she had to fight the feeling of humiliation as the Starbucks man leered at her again, eyes over her body, the short tartan skirt she'd put on specially for Tom. Another minute and another text sent. MY LOVE I'M WAITING AT ARRIVALS WHERE THE HELL ARE YOU? xxx. Maybe the signal was weak, maybe Verizon had lied when they said her phone now did international roaming. Maybe he had been trying to text her to tell her he was waiting in the car park. Another minute and an announcement came over the PA: 'KLM 105 – now arriving from Amsterdam.' The surge of people then from behind her. The repeat of all the emotional reunited-at-last scenarios she'd witnessed twenty minutes ago. And he was not here. She fought the thoughts that swarmed around her with the new arrivals. A wheelie bag hit her ankles, nearly knocking her to the ground, her hands grabbing for her falling phone, as the woman muttered, 'Sorry, luv.' The thoughts now fears. He was still in bed. He had forgotten. He had freaked out last night and got drunk and was lying late in bed with another woman. He was not here.

Another two steps into his country and setting down her heavy bags yet again. She craned her neck to the left and saw past the shops to the rest of the terminal. Go and look for him. No, best if she stayed where she was. Why wasn't his phone turned on? No doubt her fault. Damn Verizon. He was running late, she hadn't got his messages, best to stay where she was. No point in two people roaming around searching for and missing each other. But such a tiny airport. If she went looking for him they would be sure to bump into each other, literally.

She heaved her shoulder bag back in place and freed her hands to take the two wheelie bags, moved herself towards the two security guards.

'Excuse me, are there two arrivals gates here?'

'Aye, there's wan domestic wan tae.'

'Sorry? A domestic one? Where is that exactly?'

He pointed it out. 'Just tae huner yards and up tae the left.'

She got him to repeat it. (Jesus, the accent.) Then repeated it back to him.

'Two hundred yards then up to the left?'

'Aye, domestic.'

Well, that was it then. Tom had probably assumed she'd changed at Heathrow and got a domestic to Edinburgh. He'd be waiting for her at domestic arrivals. She was trying to run but the wheelie bags kept overturning and bashing against her ankles. Damn and fuck.

The faces at domestic. Domestic faces – fewer ethnics, all the males variations of Tom but he wasn't here. She was trying to call long distance to Verizon to find out what the fuck was wrong with her phone. She was put on hold with fucking Mozart. Five dollars a minute on hold. And fuck Tom. Was this some kind of sick Scottish joke? Was he going to burst out from behind a postcard display with a bunch of roses and shout, 'Hey, gotcha!'

Dragging the damn wheelie bags back to where she started. They kept flipping over. And every time she stooped to turn them the right way round she sensed the male eyes on her in such a short skirt. And he wasn't here.

Back to where she started, but on the other side of the line now. She caught herself, stupid, staring at the arrivals gate people, as if he could possibly come from there. She checked the time on her cell. Forty-five minutes since she'd arrived and she'd arrived half an hour late. Fuck him, fuck and damn him. Starbucks man was still leering. Moving towards her.

''S there a problem, love? You need a lift?'

'A lift? What the fuck is a lift?'

'Yer American then. How d'ya say it? A ride. Ye fancy a ride?'

And Tom had already explained this to her and it was a sexual innuendo.

'I'm OK. Really.'

His eyes on her legs. His smile. Fuck him and fuck Tom. This was no joke. She could just turn round now and get on the next plane home. He wasn't here.

The man was lingering.

'Please, just fuck off and leave me alone.'

She stood there humiliated as he sauntered away, waiting no doubt for the next lost woman on the next flight.

The PA announced that American Airlines Flight 212 from Chicago was now arriving. They pushed past her, laughing and shouting names, all warm and intimate, and then she knew. Something horrible had happened. He'd been running late and been driving too fast on the freeway. He'd had a few drinks last night to calm his nerves. He'd woken hung-over. His hand–eye coordination had not been what it should have been for the traffic. He'd been impatient to get to her, he'd taken risks. She felt it in her bones. He'd tried to overtake in the logjam. He wasn't here. The oncoming traffic bearing down on him. He was. She couldn't face the word as the tears broke on to her face. He was injured. It wasn't possible, she'd come all this way. He wasn't. He couldn't possibly be. She wasn't going to think the word, it was something from a movie, life wasn't tragic but banal. He was caught up in traffic, he was in an ambulance, but there was no way he was dead.

Watching

Tom sits in his car in row E, car park 2 at Edinburgh International Airport. His mobile phone ringing. It is her again. The last hour she has rung him every three minutes, texted him twenty-two times.

What he learned today on the bridge.

He sits in his car, no will or power available to him to make him exit. He sits in his car not crying like he thought he would, like he wanted to. The distance has fallen between him and the things of the world again. He pictures her crying at the gate, in the taxi rank, on her cell.

What he learned about himself today on the bridge. Staring at the water below.

She will appear through the doors soon. Beside him on the passenger seat is the unopened bottle of Smirnoff he bought at the Sainsbury's in the shopping mall after the turn-off from the bridge.

It had been cold on the bridge. Its coldness was still with him.

Tourists passing by with wheelie bags. When she exits she will not see him there in his car parked two hundred yards away. She does not know the make or colour of his car. He must just watch her from here. She does not know what he felt there on the bridge. He can never explain these things to her.

And the waters below said . . .

The future with Meg would always be like this. Him struggling to perfect himself, to impress. Four weeks together and then she would be gone again. And then the waiting again, for the finances to come in so he could afford to fly, afford the childcare for Sean in his absence. Three months, four. The waiting, the slow accumulation of pound after pound. The postponements. All the time living in this perpetual state of detachment from where it was he actually lived. Unfeeling, uncaring, living only for that love that lived once a day at the end of a phone line. And in that absence there would be Morna. And Morna would make love to him and never tell. And he would be living a lie and Morna would accept that. He would try to end it with Morna again and be weak and call her late at night again.

On the bridge he'd asked the waters to grant him pardon, and they had passed beneath, not even laughing at his predicament, not responding. Some day three hundred years from now those very same particles of water would cross the ocean to arrive in America, with the same indifference.

Staring down at the waves, he had decided he must finally face where and who he was. That throwing himself into those waves would be a joke, with no audience. Morna was not a compromise, but the reality. Morna was there in the water waiting to catch him.

Meg had come all this way, waited all this time to see him and now he was going to end it. The eleventh hour. He had told himself that it was best this way.

But still, always a but still. But still.

He'd parked the car an hour ago. Had put on their CD. Those lyrics that were non-words – a woman singing of the ecstasy of just singing. He undid the top of the Smirnoff. The Cocteau Twins. The first mouthful.

This was the plan. To sit in his car and just watch her as she came through the doors. As she waited, as she dialled his mobile again, as she dialled directory enquiries to get the number for his office, his home. Her standing there. Waiting an hour, crying. He would watch it all from this distance. Car park 2.

The second mouthful and the tension in his muscles slackened.

How could he do this to her? How could he explain what the waves had said? And they had said nothing.

If he was going to go to her and try to explain, then their next weeks would be one constant argument with the waves.

A million apologies for petty lies.

'I got the times wrong,' he would say.

Wait and watch her pass. No melodramatic confrontation, just minutes and hours of dissipation.

Send her a text. *Sorry you came this far. It's over between us.*

Then turn off his phone so she couldn't ring back. She would maybe check into a hotel for a few nights, do a tour of the city before she left for good. Then knowing as she left, nothing said, everything understood, that it was over. Back to where she belonged. In a dream.

No sight of her at the sliding doors.

Another beep. By way of ritual he went into his mobile address book and started deleting her messages. She'd sent twenty-three in the last hour. He couldn't bring himself to open and read them. Saw only the first few words on the menu before he hit delete.

My You, where ar
Are you in traffi
Am worried si
Baby, please wh
Am terrified someth
My God, where ar

Staring at the sliding doors. The remaining text messages were the old ones. The special ones among all the passing ones that said *Call you in 20. R u up? Have to shower then will call.*

Sleep well in my love my dark muse. Xx

Our love is so strong. After you called I couldn't sleep. I reread all your texts. You are a poet my You xxx

I am you too. And you are me. We are not two Is. Not an us. I thank you for making me twice myself. Meg is not me is me and you. Your name for me is better than all the mergings which only deplete. You double not half me. Meg xxx

There she was. Coming through the sliding doors, her two wheelie bags, look at her face, her long beautiful legs, her tartan skirt. Just look at her. Meg, my love. Staring round, scared.

Her mobile in her hand. His rang beside him. Even from here, he could tell her face was red from tears. He screwed the top back on the vodka. She was talking now, his voicemail must have clicked on. She was talking and he couldn't hear. He would never hear her voice again. The last time he would see her was now, through a windscreen.

She was standing there phone to ear. He had to turn on his phone. As soon as his fingers found the button it started ringing in his hand. The thing hit the car floor. He was reaching for it, for the door handle. The door fell open, he was falling out, screaming across the car park. It couldn't end like this. Waving his arms in the air. MEG. MEG! I'M HERE.

5
RETURN

Film

L ong shot. Exterior. Airport terminal. Passing people in fore-
ground, out of focus. He runs to her, she drops her bags.
Their arms around each other, we cannot hear what they say.
The music starts – their song. They kiss, mouths, necks, faces.
No dialogue. She holds his face, looks into his eyes, he lowers
his.

Close-up. He starts to weep. She holds him tight. Her face
over his shoulder. His mouth moves but we cannot hear what
he says. She holds him tight. We sense that she already knows.
No dialogue. She stares over his shoulder into the beyond. The
song rises. A female vocal singing words in no known language.
Cut to:

The ride home in his car. Silence. No dialogue. His finger
on the CD button. Their song again. It comes into sync. They
are listening to the soundtrack. She is close to tears. No dialogue.
She looks out and sees the Castle, the church spires. The historic
city of Edinburgh.

Montage. The music rises. Keys in door. His flat. His
bedroom, her bags. He sits on the edge of the bed, weeping
head in hand, not meeting her gaze. She holds him. Zoom in
on her face as she looks over his shoulder out the window.

Extreme close-up. She takes the ring from her finger. She
gives it back to him. She kisses his forehead. His lips move. He
talks and talks and pleads. We cannot hear a word he says. The
chorus begins. The female vocal rising. She steps away. Her
fingers linger for a moment above his head.

Montage: She wanders through ancient cobblestone streets,
alone. The Edwardian, the Georgian, the medieval. All around
her people dressed in costumes from many ages. Repeat of
chorus. A man, grey face paint with a noose round his neck. A
young couple arm in arm laughing dressed as a medieval king

and queen, handing out flyers to everyone they pass. She stops, takes a photograph of the king and queen before the Castle. The female vocal rises, sounds not words. Cut to:

Clouds. Pull back to reveal her face, staring out of a plane window. The note goes on for ever. She sits back. Takes out her eye mask. The vocal ends, there is a sound then, so quiet, almost unheard, of the singer taking an in-breath. She pulls the eye mask on. The song ends. Fade to black.

Opening

The credits roll. A cinema filled with a thousand. Her eyes closed. The hands from behind on her shoulder. Squeezing deep into the tense muscles. The hand beside her squeezing hers so hard. Film agent. Josh. The lead actress weeping beside her reaching for her other hand. The screen obscured now as the many rise from their seats to applaud. Frenzy of hands clapping. The director, Frank, leaning back from his seat in front, trying to find her hand to hold, her hands already full, whispering, 'We've done it. Just listen to them. They love you.' People in the rows behind, the air pushed across the back of her neck as they applaud. The lesser credits rolling in diminishing font size as the song reaches its end. Second Grip, Best Boy, Third Assistant Director, Assistant to Ms Douthwaight, Lighting care of. This film was shot with Panavision lenses. Processed by Kodak. A woman three rows behind her shouting, 'Speech, Speech.' Frank's hand clasping the hand of the lead actress still clasping hers.

The Tribeca Film Festival organiser walking on to the stage with a mike stand in her hand.

Frank: 'It's your story, not mine.' Tears in his eyes as he pulls her hand closer, kissing.

'Speech!' The voices now joining the handclaps, an insistent rhythm.

Frank rising to his feet with the dignified grace of the old man he is. The applause breaking into an hysteria of randomness, each handclap trying to outdo the others in speed and intensity.

Meg sat back. Her two hands taken by agent and lead actress. The tears they were shedding, their fingers digging deeper, their eyes, as hers, focused on Frank walking down the incline of the rows and rows of cinema seats.

Frank climbed the stage. The tech guy readjusted the mike stand for him then scurried. Flashes then. A hundred cameras recording this night.

'OK,' Frank said. 'Quieten down. My God, you people. What's got into you?' Frank knew how to do this, had been nominated for three Golden Globes. An Oscar. Never won one.

'OK. *Distance*.' he said. Waiting for the crowd to settle. '*Distance*,' he said again. 'I'm not branding the film here. And believe you me, my life in Hollywood has not been easy. Once in a lifetime a script lands on your desk, and the note from the agent says "A love story", right? And we all know there's no future, no money in love stories. But you get this script that has you crying from page ten.'

The crowd silent. Waiting.

'Five years it's taken us to get this to the screen. Five hard years. And every day I reread the script and it gave me faith. *Distance*. I've never felt closer to a script in my life.'

A cough in the auditorium, nothing more.

'All I did was point the camera in the direction that was written there in the script. All I did was try to encourage the actors to have the guts to do what was on the page already. I've said enough. All credit where it is due. *Distance*. I can't ...' Readjusting his mike. 'I really can't ... I'm sorry. I have no right to be here. Back there in row M is the writer. When I read her script – God, I'm sorry. In row M. She should be here now, not me. Megan Foster Hunt. Meg, come down here. Come down.'

The faces all turned to row M, searching for her. Meg took a breath and rose to her feet as around her hundreds did the same. Standing ovation. Applauding the air.

Cinema

'It so sucks, Dad,' moaned Sean.

'Will you be quiet for once and stop blabbering? Jesus! We're trying to watch the film.'

Not only had Sean's stutter gone this last year but now, with a vengeance, he had to criticise everything his father did. With all the latest Americanisms.

Morna's hand in Tom's. 'Let him go, he's fine.'

'OK, so why don't you just head to Morna's, hang out with Ian tonight?'

'Sure, outta here,' Sean said as he got up from his seat. Pubescently stumbling over the rows of bodies on his way.

It wasn't so much the film. He didn't like the actors. They were too young. The version of him too witty. Every line the guy said – too clever by half. Had that really been the way she'd seen him? Not so much the film as the music that had him fighting back the tears as the titles rolled. The Cocteau Twins.

He had to remind himself. Everything was OK now. He had his own corporate media company, number 5 in the UK, and a salary of 75K. He spent six months of the year shooting ads and corporates in Milan, Athens, Paris, and there were contracts in the next year that would take him to LA and New York. His ex had remarried. Sean thought of him now as a friend, and it'd only be another year till Sean was off to music college. It was a thing too subtle to explain that had him hiding his face from Morna as he stared at the credits.

It had come to him, that, right now, he could have had the life he and Meg talked about. Meeting each other in other countries, spending six months of the year together. They'd met at the wrong time. That was all. Five years later and everything could have been OK. If only he, at the time, had given himself more time, not brought it all to a crisis in one single moment.

If only he had had the patience then, that he had learned to live with now.

Morna squeezed his hand in the dark.

'You OK?'

'It wasn't really like that . . . We never did those things.'

'It was fab, and you wir Ewan McGregor. C'moan, he's no as hansom as you but you should still be proud.'

The seats around them emptying.

'C'moan, buy ya a drink. Pint of soda and lime, eh?'

Four and a half years dry and it had been her that had coached him through every day. One day at a time. Her that said that the therapy for Sean was a pile o' shite and all it needed was a wee bit paternal luv'n'care and a wee bit o' time, and encourage him wi his computer stuff and his music an just tae no be such a fuckin' fuck-up and wait an' see.

Outside the cinema and it was just another film to everyone at the Edinburgh International Film Festival. The couples walking past. 'Like Bertolucci,' said some guy. 'Naw, totally flawed,' said some retro-punk chick. 'Pretty fucking sexy though, eh?' said a student. 'Aye, but McGregor's past his best now.' 'Contrived,' said another voice. 'The woman was a typical victim,' said another.

Morna's hand pulling him along.

'C'moan, you, let's get the hell outta here,' she said, quoting the film. Laughing.

Five years ago he had told Meg of that night when he and Morna had wept at a film but couldn't look into each other's eyes. And it was like that still, even though Morna now stayed three nights a week. Her to her morning rituals and him to his willed-for extra half-hour of sleep. The smiles over her shoulder thrown to his pretend sleeping face. Him sensing that she loved those moments he stole from her. A schoolboy caught peeking. Her dressing, her noises, her singing to herself in the bathroom. These things of sad beauty he could never tell her – how she reminded him, in those moments, of Meg.

'Ye comin' back tae mine then? Ian and Sean'll huv the sofa bed an' the futon.'

'Actually . . . I . . .'

'Nae probs.' Her lips on his cheek. 'See you the morrow.' Watching her then, swaying down the street. What a woman. To have sat with him through this love story that was his not hers. She'd thought the female lead immature. 'Mibbe I'll write 'bout you one day too,' she'd said. 'Your heid must be bloated. Don't think ah'll ever get it through ma door,' she'd said.

She turned back to wave.

The morrow. Yes, he would see her tomorrow. This woman, whom he'd come crawling back to after Meg. This mother of his son's best friend, who believed that friendship was greater than love. This woman who signed on and worked voluntarily with kids with learning difficulties. This woman who'd held him and helped him through the breakdown. Whose eyes he still could not face. Whom he could not make come, who stroked his head after and told him that it was fine. That they'd work on it through time. This woman who told him it would only be a year or so till the kids were up and gone and then they would move to the country. This woman who had saved his life. Whom he now called You.

Opening

The many hands agent Josh thrust into hers, with the names and who they were whispered into her ear – the guy from Columbia who was so pissed they hadn't got the international rights and they just had to work together on her next project and what was it going to be, and the guy from HBO who wanted her – 'I want you,' he'd said – for his new cop series that wasn't really a cop series at all but needed a woman's touch, and the anorexic version of Scarlett Johansson who came up to her and was too moved to speak because the film had touched on so many things her therapist had brought up and in a month, after the next shoot, they should definitely, totally, get together to talk about obsessive compulsive disorder.

The party at the Marriott was nearing its end and he'd been staring at her all night. This night in which, even after she'd been on the stage and given her brief speech, she'd still remained relatively anonymous. Witnessing all the handshakes and cards exchanged and 'What an incredible movie', and the many 'Oh my God I nearly cried', all addressed to the director and the film stars, as she stood there by the doors, at first smiling to herself, then feeling as alienated from it all as she had been before the film had been made.

He'd been standing on the edge of the crowd. Was not her usual type but then Tom hadn't been either. Tall, broad shoulders, strong chin, his back a little stooped. His tux obviously hired for the occasion, too short around the wrists. His shoes unpolished.

The masses moved to the centre when the female lead arrived, fashionably late. He had been still standing there alone by the bar as Tom had been. She'd waved – Hi.

'Hi,' he mouthed back.

She took the twelve steps towards him.

'So, what you doing here?'

'Well, actually I shouldn't really . . . I did the website. But really, well, hell, I know everyone says this here, but really, I'm an actor.'

He didn't know who she was.

'What did you think of the film?'

'Yeah, great. I mean, from an actor's perspective, it was a hell of a role. I trained at RADA, sorry, it's in –'

'In England, I know . . . Shh,' she said as she reached beneath the table, her fingers finding one of the bottles of Veuve in the crate. 'You have to hide this in your jacket, OK?'

He laughed, embarrassed. 'OK,' was all he said as he did as she asked. So then she said:

'Let's get the hell outta here.'

She was not entirely convinced that he had the guts or talent to see this through. An outsider, definitely. And a failed actor. It might take that to get it done.

She took his hand in the corridor to the elevator. He laughed a little on entering.

The last five years she'd booked rooms on the fifth floor. She couldn't recall the exact room number it had been that first time with Tom and had never found the same window view.

The actor stood there rather self-consciousness in the elevator as they ascended. Not speaking. Not kissing her neck, not groping at her crotch, not like the others. One floor to go and she leaned over and put her lips to his, her tongue in his mouth. His hands then a frenzy. His fingers finding her nipples though the blouse.

'I want you to say something, OK?'

'OK.'

'That you're too drunk to fuck, that you just want a hug.'

The door, the floor, the elevator pinging.

'OK, that's cool.'

'Say it.'

'I'm too drunk to fuck, I just want a hug.'

The card that unlocked her room door. She had to stop there and set things out. The champagne from the minibar. She didn't want to freak him out. He had to drink like Tom had drunk.

She flicked on the TV, put it on mute and threw him the remote. He sat on the edge of the bed, bottle in one hand, remote in other. His accent was not entirely American, a hint of that RADA English. She took her travel bag into the bathroom and changed into her Vivienne Westwood tartan skirt. Pulled out the flight mask. Stepped back out, paraded herself in front of him in the gap between the bed and the TV. She raised a leg to reveal the tops of the stockings, the clasps of the suspenders, just as Tom liked it.

'Wow, just like the movie!' Then he was laughing. He was maybe too young to grasp the importance of this, the reverence required. She would pay him if she had to. She had long since given up on finding a man to do this with who was in any way her equal. As if sensing the judgement in her silence, he threw himself across the bed and was clutching her thighs.

'No!' In the five years in which she'd tried to perfect this scenario she'd learned that it only worked with rules. He'd have to agree to it all in advance or she would cut it short. These were the ways. Everything had to be done exactly as she said. The lights had to be off. The eye mask, fastened. He had to whisper things she couldn't hear, and make love to her slowly. She had to have the eye mask on so she could feel.

Long Distance

The old dream waking him again. His art-school graduation film. Everyone seated in the cinema. Waiting. The
lights went down. The pre-title credits rolled and then there
was nothing. Just white on the screen. This dream he knew so
well. Sean's psychologist said it represented his fear of failure.
The same dream but not the same. There were pictures this
time. The sprockets not quite in sync, the images sliding across
the screen. No audio. The footage hand-held, like a home movie.
Her face as she tried on a hat, turning to him to ask what he
thought. Her back as she walked over the Brooklyn Bridge.
Her face sleeping, not waking, as fingers entered the frame to
stroke her face. A flash of her eyes, the rhythm in her body,
her breasts in her hands, that moment just before she threw
her head back. Her walking on the beach. Her face in the bathroom mirror flossing her teeth, then turning to the camera,
laughing, asking. Her mouth moving and no words. The words
he knew. 'What are you doing, my silly You? Put down the
camera.' The last shot, her face going out of focus as she leaned
to kiss. This blur of hair. This thing not seen. Skin to skin. No
sound.

Awake, he ran though the now daily list of positives again.
Everything was OK. His son sleeping at Morna's house. No
meetings for two days. The daily dose of Prozac. Everything
to be happy about. But the daily checklist was failing him. It
was not yet day. Five years and he hadn't tried to contact her.
Her many texts and emails, long since deleted. But her mobile
number still in his memory. It probably wouldn't work any
more. She'd moved on. 0019177831797.

Phone in hand, moving to his bedroom. He wanted to tell
her how he'd just seen her film. How very romantic it had
seemed. How he was glad that their ending had made a new

beginning for her, but something about her film was bothering him. The images, like the dream, would not leave him alone. It was that last sequence, their last moments after the airport, at his flat, after he'd confessed. The footage had been mute, framed by a window, people passing in the foreground, the soundtrack rising, a wide shot, so it was impossible for the audience to see the actors' faces. He could recall clearly what had happened on that day. Such a thing would be too nuanced for audiences to understand. After his confession, after his many tears, after she pulled her hand away, she nodded. She nodded gently, without saying a word, like ... almost like she'd always known this would happen. And he too, had nodded back, felt a great sense of relief, of release. That in truth was how they left it. Their great love had been cancelled and they could both return to their image of themselves as fated, alone, tragic. No soaring of orchestral strings, no finale. Just two people scared of the great love they'd come close to sharing, backing away and stepping back into their own lives again.

He dialled. He wanted to thank her for having walked away then, for having forced him to face up to who and where he really was. To apologise for his years of silence. It kept ringing. Fear starting, of her picking up, of hearing her voice. He'd given no thought to what time it was with her. The old half-remembered routine of subtracting six hours. He checked his mobile. It was 6 a.m. Midnight her time. A click and then it was her voice.

'Hi, this is Meg, I'm not available right now, please leave your number and I'll get back to you.'

Messages

She had twelve voicemails and fifteen texts on her cell. She went through the texts first as she applied her anti-ageing cream in the hotel-room mirror, then hit speakerphone. Eleven of the usual, then one. No words. The sound of a phone changing hands. Of breath. Of static, crackling. She was about to delete it, but then a whisper, a breath. Barely audible. The click of the phone as the call ended.

She listened to it again and again. Unlike the others. All these messages with so many words, too many, and this one of breath. Second after second. A minute of it. A man's breath. Then the click. Again. Just in the second before it was ended, one word whispered on a sigh, inaudible but familiar. The screen said unknown. One of the many deleted.

She called her service provider for the last caller's number. The woman said it was international. Asked for her password. Told her she'd had it barred before, asked if she wanted it put back on. Said she could put her through, but Meg wanted the number. She made her repeat it, twice, so she could write it down.

It was ringing in her ear. And as she waited the thing that she grasped, the flaw in her love story, was that it had to have an ending, but endings in life are always false. It just keeps rolling on long after the credits have finished, a mess of un-resolved conflicts and moments and memories of warmth, then its lack and the need that makes it all start again and that was in so many ways harder to accept. She would never make another film.

A click then a breath.

'Hello?'

His voice still strong.

'Who is this?'

So like him, not to have caller ID, so like him to doubt that she would ever call him back. Who is this? She waited as the many words rushed at her. She could hang up. She should. So many words over so many years but only one left to say. Who is this? he asked. And 'me' had become an empty word. Who is this? The old impossible dream that they could lose themselves in each other. His old name for her. She took a breath then said it.

'You.'

Acknowledgements

The author would like to thank the Scottish Arts Council, UNESCO, Edinburgh City of Literature and Varuna: The Writers' House, NSW, Australia.